Looking at her had become an exercise in torture. Send her in.

He wanted her. Plain and simple. Whether that want would go away after a few hours of fun—as usually happened—he couldn't be sure. This wanting, the one keeping him up at night, felt different. Rooted. Like it wouldn't die with fast, primal sex.

What he didn't need was a woman getting inside his head and staying there. His adult existence had consisted of the hunt to find his mother's killer. It was, in fact, all he knew—emotionally speaking. He had no room for anything else. No room. Zero.

When he found the killer, maybe then. Now? No way. He'd blow off his own head trying to juggle a relationship with his mom's case.

But Jenna was looking at him with those amazing blue eyes and that punch to the chest ripped his air away.

Hell with it.

D1079637

BT 187 8887 4

THE MARSHAL

BY
ADRIENNE GIORDANO

Published in Great Britain 2015
by Mills & Boon, an imprint of Harlequin (UK) Limited,
Eton House, 18-24 Paradise Road, Richmond, Surrey, TW9 1SR

© 2015 Adrienne Giordano

ISBN: 978-0-263-25292-7

46-0115

Harlequin (UK) Limited's policy is to use papers that are natural, renewable and recyclable products and made from wood grown in sustainable forests. The logging and manufacturing processes conform to the legal environmental regulations of the country of origin.

Printed and bound in Spain
by CPI, Barcelona

Adrienne Giordano, a *USA TODAY* bestselling author, writes romantic suspense and mystery. She is a Jersey girl at heart, but now lives in the Midwest with her workaholic husband, sports obsessed son and Buddy the wheaten terrorist (terrier). For more information on Adrienne's books please visit adriennegiordano.com or download the Adrienne Giordano app. For information on Adrienne's street team, go to www.facebook.com/groups/DangerousDarlings.

For those who've known personal tragedy
and understand that the heart never forgets.

Chapter One

This was a switch.

Deputy US marshal Brent Thompson stood in a Chicago hotel ballroom among a throng of impeccably dressed political big shots that, for once, he didn't have to protect.

Tonight he was a guest.

Whether that made him happy or not was anyone's guess. But he'd stay another hour for Judge Kline, a woman he'd spent two years watching over after her husband and children were murdered by some nut who'd been on the losing end of a ruling. Judge Kline had ordered him to pay a $1,200 fine and somehow he was mad enough to wipe out her entire family, leaving her to deal with guilt and rage and heartache.

Crazy.

Sometimes—*sometimes? Really?*—Brent didn't understand people. Or maybe it was their motivations he didn't understand, but the human race baffled him.

Tonight Judge Kline, who'd refused to allow her life to collapse under grief, was smiling. A welcome sight since her eighty-five-year-old mother had decided to throw one hell of a shindig for the judge's sixtieth birthday.

"Brent?"

Brent turned and found the ever-polished Gerald Hennings, Chicago's highest-profile defense attorney, weaving through the crowd. Accompanying him was a petite blonde in a floor-length bright blue gown. She had to be over fifty, but may have had a little work done to preserve her extraordinary looks. Her perfect cheekbones, the big blue eyes and sculpted nose were duplicates of the ones Brent recognized from Hennings's daughter, Penny. Didn't take a genius to figure out this woman was Mrs. Hennings. Brent held his hand out. "Mr. Hennings. Nice to see you."

Five months earlier, Brent had been assigned to protect Penny Hennings after yet another nut—plenty of nuts in his world—had attempted to kill her on the steps of a federal courthouse. Penny had nearly put Brent into a psych ward with her relentless mouthiness and aggressive attitude, but he'd formed a bond with her. A kinship. And, much like Judge Kline, they'd remained friends after his assignment had ended. For whatever reason, emotionally speaking, he couldn't let either one of them go. The fact that they'd all experienced tragedy might be the common denominator, but he chose not to think too hard about it. What was the point? None of them would ever fully recover from their individual experiences. All they could do was move on.

Hennings turned to the woman at his side. "I don't think you've met my wife, Pamela. Pam, this is Marshal Brent Thompson. He was *the* marshal."

She smiled and—yep—he was looking at Penny in twenty-five years.

"I know," Mrs. Hennings said. She stepped forward and gripped both of his arms. "Thank you."

The gesture, so direct and heartfelt, caught him sideways and he stiffened. Freak that he was, he'd never gotten comfortable with strange women touching him. Most guys would love it. Brent? He liked his space being his.

But he stood there, allowing Penny's mother to thank him in probably the only way she knew how. He could go on about how he'd just been doing his job, which was all true, but even he understood that he'd worked a little harder for Penny. She reminded him too much of his younger sister, Camille, and he hadn't been able to help himself. "You're welcome. Your daughter has become a good friend. And if I ever need legal advice, I know who to call."

Mrs. Hennings laughed.

Mr. Hennings swooped his finger in the air. "You're not working tonight?"

"No, sir. Judge Kline is a friend."

"How nice," Mrs. Hennings said.

"Yes, ma'am. I worked with her for two years. She would always tell me if my tie didn't match. That happened a *lot*."

"As the mother of two sons, I'm sure your mother appreciates that."

Mother.

Mr. Hennings cleared his throat and, in Brent's mind, the room fell silent. He glanced around, looking for…what? Confirmation that the room at large wasn't listening to his conversation?

Maybe.

All around people gabbed and mingled and pretty much ignored Brent. *Imagined it.* He exhaled and once again the orchestra music—something classical—replaced the fog in his brain.

He'd fielded comments about his mother almost his entire life. It should have been easier by now.

Except for the nagging.

Twenty-three years of gut-twisting, anger-fueled obsession that kept him prisoner. "My mother died when I was five, ma'am."

Social pro that she must have been, considering her husband's wizardry with the press, Mrs. Hennings barely reacted. "I'm so sorry." She turned to Gerald, shooting him the stink-eye. "I didn't know."

Moments like these, a guy had to step up and help his

brother-in-arms. "No need to apologize. I think about her every day." And knowing how this conversation would go, the curiosity that came with why and how such a young woman had died, Brent let it fly. "She was murdered."

Social pro or not, Mrs. Hennings gasped. "How horrible."

Brent sipped his club soda, gave the room another glance and came back to Mrs. Hennings. "My sister and I adjusted. We have a supportive family."

"I hope they caught the person who did this."

"No, ma'am. It's still an open case."

A case that lived and breathed with him and had driven him into law enforcement. If the Carlisle sheriff's office couldn't find his mother's killer, he'd do it himself.

"Are the police still looking into it?"

Brent shrugged. "If they get a tip or some new information. I work it on my downtime, but downtime is short."

Mrs. Hennings, obviously still embarrassed by bringing up the subject of his dead mother, turned to her husband. "Can't one of your investigators help? You do all sorts of pro bono work for clients. Why not this?"

"Pam, those are cases where we're defending people. This is different."

Brent held up his hand As much as he'd like help, he didn't want a domestic war started over it. "Mrs. Hennings, it's okay. But thank you."

Still, down deep, Brent wanted to find the person who'd wrecked his family and had saddled him with a level of responsibility—and guilt—no five-year-old should have known. Every day, the questions haunted him. Could he have helped her? Should he have done something when he first heard a noise? Was he a crummy investigator because all these years later he still couldn't give his mother justice?

At this point, if he couldn't find this monster on his own,

he'd take whatever help available. Ego aside, justice for his mother was what mattered.

Mrs. Hennings kept her gaze on her husband. "You were just complaining that Jenna is bored with her current assignments. After what Brent did for Penny, give Jenna his mother's case to investigate. It'll challenge her and keep her out of your hair. Where's the problem?"

Mr. Hennings pressed his lips together and a minuscule, seriously minuscule, part of Brent pitied the man. If he didn't agree with his wife, his life would be a pile of manure.

Mrs. Hennings shot her husband a meat cleaver of a look, then turned back to Brent. "My husband will call you about this tomorrow. How's that?"

With limited options, and being more than a little afraid to argue because, hey, he was no dummy either, he grinned at Mr. Hennings. "That'd be great. Thank you."

JENNA SLID ONTO one of the worn black vinyl bar stools at Freddie's Tap House, a mostly empty shot-and-a-beer joint on the North Side of Chicago.

How the place stayed in business, she had no idea. On this Wednesday night the sports bar down the block was packed, while the only people patronizing Freddie's were an elderly man sitting at the bar and a couple huddled at a table in the back.

The bartender glanced down the bar at her and wandered over. "Evening. Get you something?"

You sure can.

"Whatever's on tap. Thanks."

He nodded and scooped a glass from behind the bar, pouring a draft as he eyed her black blazer and the plunging neckline on her cashmere sweater. "Haven't seen you in here before. New in town?"

As much as she'd tried to dress down with jeans, she

hadn't been able to resist the sweater. When dealing with men, a little help from her feminine wiles—also known as her boobs—never hurt. "Nope. New in here, though."

"You look more Tiffany's than Freddie's."

Already Jenna liked him. "Are you Freddie?"

"Junior."

"Sorry?"

"Freddie Junior. My dad is Freddie. I took over when he retired."

He slid the beer in front of Jenna. Once more she looked around, took in the polished, worn wood of the bar, the six tables along the wall and the line of empty bar stools.

"Slow night," Freddie said.

Lucky me. She opened her purse, pulled out a fifty and set it on the bar. Next came the photo taken the week prior by a patron in this very bar. He glanced down at the fifty, then at the photo.

"I'm not a cop," Jenna said. "I'm an investigator working for a law firm."

"Okay."

She pointed at the photo of two men with a woman in the background. Jenna needed to find that woman. "Have you seen her in here?"

He picked up the photo and studied it. "Yeah. Couple of times. When a woman like that walks into a beer joint, there's generally a reason. Kinda like you."

Figuring it was time to put her cleavage to work, Jenna inched forward, gave him a view of the girls beneath that V-neck and smiled. Most women would love the idea that a fifteen-pound weight gain had gone straight to their chest. Jenna supposed it hadn't hurt her ability to claw information from men—and maybe she used it to her advantage. But she also wanted to be recognized for extracting the information and not for the way she'd done it.

Did that even make sense? She wasn't sure anymore.

All she knew was her need for positive reinforcement had led her to using her looks to achieve her goals. That meant wearing clingy, revealing clothing. Such a cliché. But the thing about clichés was they worked.

"Any idea what her reason for being here was?"

Freddie took the boob-bait and leaned in. "No. Both times she met someone. Why?"

All Jenna could hope was he'd gotten the woman's name. "My client is being held on a robbery charge. He says he was in here the night of the robbery and he met this woman. Her name is Robin."

"Where'd you get the picture?"

"Friends of my client."

He dropped the picture on the bar and tapped it. "Birthday party, right?"

"Yes. My client and six of his friends. Any idea where I can find her?"

"Nah."

"Did she pay by credit card?"

If she paid by credit card, there would be a record of the transaction, and Jenna would dig into the Hennings & Solomon coffers and pay Freddie a high, negotiated sum for a look at his credit card receipts. From there, she'd get a name and two calls later would have an address for Robin-the-mystery-woman.

"Cash."

Shoot.

Freddie may have been lying. Jenna studied him, took in his direct gaze. Not lying. At least she didn't think so. Again with the wavering? Didn't she have a good sense about these things? Yes, she did. For that reason she'd go with the theory that Freddie seemed to be a small-business owner who wanted to stay out of trouble while trying to make a living. She dug her card and a pen out of her purse, wrote her cell number on the card and placed it next to the fifty on the bar.

"How about I leave you my card? If she comes in again and you call me, there's a hundred bucks in it for you."

Freddie glanced at the card. After a moment, he half shrugged. "Sure. If I see her."

Jenna took one last sip of her beer, slid off the stool and hitched her purse onto her shoulder. "Thanks." She nodded toward the fifty. "Keep the change."

Chapter Two

At 9:00 a.m. the following morning, Jenna stepped into the Hennings & Solomon boardroom and found her boss, the man known around Chicago as the Dapper Defense Lawyer—Dapper DL for short—sitting at the end of the table. Not a surprise since he'd called this impromptu meeting by sending her a text at 7:00 a.m.

Not that she minded the text. When that happened, it meant he needed help, and that little boost—that feeling of being the one that Gerald Hennings, defense lawyer of all defense lawyers, called on—never got old. From the beginning, he'd had faith in her. Even when her application to the FBI had been denied and she'd taken a job at a PI firm as their quasi receptionist-turned-investigator, he'd seen potential and had hired her as one of his two full-time investigators. She'd always be grateful for the opportunity to prove herself.

She'd also be grateful that he'd never—not once—hit on her. Most men did. Simple fact. As a former Miss Illinois runner-up, part of her success came from men wanting to sleep with her. And, let's face it, some men were idiots. When those idiots wanted to seduce a woman, they started talking.

A lot.

"Sorry for the sudden meeting," Mr. Hennings said.

"No problem, sir."

Given his choice of the conference room rather than his office, she assumed others would be joining them and took a seat two chairs down.

Penny Hennings, Gerald's daughter and a crack defense attorney herself, swung in, her petite body moving fast as usual. "Sorry I'm late."

She hustled around the table and took the seat next to her father. The guys around the office secretly joked about the killer combo of Penny's sweet looks and caustic mouth. A viper wrapped in a doll's body.

"You're not late," Mr. Hennings said. "Relax."

"Hi, Jenna." Penny high-fived her across the table. "I love these unscheduled meetings. It's always something juicy."

Mr. Hennings smirked. "Don't get ahead of yourself. It's not a client."

Penny made a pouty face. "Boo-hiss, Dad."

The boss laughed and shook his head at his daughter. "I ran into Brent Thompson at a function last night."

Now that got Jenna's attention. She'd worked with Brent briefly. He'd been assigned to protect Penny from a psycho who'd tried to blackmail her into throwing a case. Each time Jenna had locked eyes with the studly marshal, her blood had gone more than a little warm. He had a way about him. Tough, in charge and majorly hot.

"Really?" Penny said as if the idea of her father and Brent running in the same social circles was ridiculous. "*You* ran into Brent? Was he working?"

"No. He was a guest at Judge Kline's birthday party. Apparently he was one of the marshals assigned to her after her family was murdered."

"Huh. I had no idea. That man is full of surprises."

"We got to talking about his mother."

For whatever reason, Penny's eyebrows hitched. *"Really."*

Jenna cocked her head. "That's the second time you've said 'really.' What about his mother?"

Still focused on her father, Penny ignored the question. "He doesn't usually talk about her. I don't know the whole story. He mentioned it to Russ, and Russ told me."

Russ—Penny's FBI agent boyfriend-soon-to-be-fiancé, if Penny had anything to do with it—was a great source of information, and Jenna had learned to use him sparingly, but thoroughly. "What about Brent's mother?"

Mr. Hennings turned to Jenna. "She was murdered twenty-three years ago."

Frigid stabs shot up Jenna's neck. If her boss wanted shock factor, he'd succeeded. "Wow."

Penny glanced across the table. Momentarily stymied, Jenna gave her the *help-me* look. "The case is still open," Penny said.

Her father turned back to Jenna. "You've indicated you'd like more challenging work."

Despite her temporary paralysis, Jenna sensed an opportunity coming her way. "Yes, sir."

"You know what they say about being careful what you wish for."

"Sir?"

"Brent's mother's case, it's cold. My wife has gotten it into her head that we should have our investigators work it."

Jenna sucked in air. A cold case. Simply amazing. For months she'd been craving something more than paper trails and fraud cases. Something she could tear apart and hone her skills on. But this? Could she handle a murder? If it were here in the city, she might be able to pull it off. Her list of contacts was growing, and her retired detective father still had people who owed him favors.

"Hang on," Penny said.

Yes, hang on. "Did the murder happen here?"

Penny threw up her hand. "Hang. *On.* Dad, I'll do anything for Brent, but we're attorneys. This case has no defendant. Therefore, no client. How do we do this if there's no client?"

"It's pro bono."

Penny dropped her head an inch. "I'm... Wait... I'm confused. Again, no client. How are we working pro bono if there's no client?"

"We're helping a friend. I'm not sure how we'll do the paperwork. There may not *be* any paperwork. I really don't know. All I know is that your mother had that look about her."

Penny sat back and sighed. "I know that look."

Jenna raised her hand. "Where did the murder happen?"

"Carlisle, Illinois," Mr. Hennings said. "About sixty miles south of here."

Oh, no. She had zero contacts that far away. Even Russ probably wouldn't be able to help her. Although, maybe he knew someone who knew someone. Heck, maybe *she* knew someone who knew someone.

"You're hesitating. I assumed you'd be interested."

"I am. Interested."

I think. Breaking a cold case would send her value on the professional front soaring. A cold case would prove she had skills beyond her looks.

Still with her hands folded, Jenna took a minute to absorb it all. Twenty-three-year-old murder. Sixty miles away. No contacts. Juggling it with other cases. *Piece of cake.* Hysteria cramped her throat. *I can do this.* She inhaled, straightened her shoulders and channeled Jenna-the-lioness, the Jenna everyone around the office knew.

"I can handle it, sir. Thank you."

"Good. Penny is your point person on this." He turned to Penny. "You're the logical choice. I can't give it to one of the associates. Technically, this case doesn't exist. Plus, he's your friend."

Jenna flipped her thumbs up. This was a chance to have a profound impact on someone's life. "Works for me. Let's solve a cold case."

"GOOD MORNING, MARSHAL THOMPSON," Penny Hennings said in the snarky voice that had earned her the Killer Cupcake moniker from law enforcement guys who'd been on the rough end of one of her cross-examinations.

Brent stepped into the Hennings & Solomon conference room—a place he'd been countless times before—and smiled. "Good morning, *Ms.* Hennings," he shot back in a damned good imitation.

Penny popped out of her chair, cornered the huge table and charged him.

He held his arms out and folded her into them. "You're like a teeny-tiny bird," he cracked.

She gave him a squeeze, then shoved him back. "Well, I was going to be nice, but now I'm not." He unleashed a teasing smile and she rolled her eyes. "Don't think that smile will work on me," she said with sisterly affection. "I'm a lawyer. I'm *immune.*"

"Yes," came a female voice from the end of the table. "But I may not be."

He'd know that voice anywhere. Jenna. Five months ago he'd been standing in the hallway right outside this room and spotted her amazing body gliding toward him in a way that would make any red-blooded male drop to his knees. He'd seen her dozens of times since then, and she'd invaded his mind on a regular basis. She was one of those women lucky enough to have her weight evenly distributed, but with a little extra magically landing in all the right places. With her long legs—perfect for a guy who clocked in just shy of six-four—and a body that was more lush than slim, Jenna Hayward gave him an itch he seriously wanted to scratch.

Right now, though, he needed fresh eyes on his mother's case, and his mother always took precedence.

He held his breath, readying himself for the sight of Jenna to knock him daffy. By now he knew to prepare for it. That first day? He'd been toast. He released his breath, turned and there she was, sitting with her shoulders back and one hand resting on the tabletop. Her long dark hair fell over her shoulders and draped over her red blouse. The blouse with one more button undone than was technically appropriate. He studied that extra button and imagined…

Don't.

He brought up his eyes and found her staring at him, head tilted. Their gazes held for a long second, the blue of her eyes sparking at him and—*yeah, baby*—he started to sweat. Slowly, knowing exactly where his mind had gone, her lips eased into a smile that should have dropped him like a solid right hook. *Bam!*

"Nice to see you, Jenna," he said.

Very nice.

She stood and he moved to the end of the table, holding out his hand. She took it, gave it a firm but brief shake. "Hello, Brent. Always a pleasure."

"It's like a reunion in here," Penny said.

Penny. Right. They had company. He unbuttoned his suit jacket and took the seat across from Jenna, leaving the head of the table open for Penny. Her meeting, her power spot.

He waited for Penny to get settled and then angled toward her. "Thank you for doing this."

"It's the least we can do. You know I hate to get mushy, but you mean a lot to us. If we can help you get some kind of closure, we'll do it."

Brent slid his gaze to Jenna. Talking details about his

mom in front of people he barely knew never came easy. The basic stuff about her murder and the case still being open, he'd gotten used to. Now he'd have to get comfortable with Jenna real quick. And not in the way he wanted.

He swiveled his chair to face her. "Are you sure you want to do this? It's been twenty-three years. The case is as cold as they get."

"I don't mind a challenge, and if we can figure this out, well, I suppose we'd all be…satisfied."

"I'd be more than satisfied. But listen, there's no pressure here. If you can dig up some leads, it'll help. A fresh look might crack it."

"Maybe," Jenna said.

"Where do we start?" Penny asked.

"I can tell you what I know, take you to the crime scene, go over whatever notes I have. The sheriff is a good guy. I can't see him being subversive. Right now, he's got an unsolved murder messing with his violent crime statistics."

Jenna's eyebrows hit her hairline. Yeah, that statistics line sounded harsh. *He* sounded harsh. After spending eighty percent of his life wondering what happened to his mother, he'd forced himself to detach. Emotional survival meant burying the pain. Stuffing it away.

Coping 101. Brent style.

The phone at his waist buzzed. "Excuse me, I need to check this."

Text from his boss. They had a tip on a federal fugitive. He shot a text back, stood and buttoned his flapping suit jacket. "Ladies, I'm sorry. I need to go. Jenna, call me with your schedule. Outside of work, I'm at your disposal."

She gave him that slow smile again—simply wicked— and his chest pinged. Son of a gun. In a matter of minutes, she'd figured out how to distract him from thoughts of his mother.

Whether that was good or bad, they'd soon find out.

THAT EVENING JENNA rode shotgun in Brent's SUV while they drove the sixty miles south to Carlisle, Illinois, a place so foreign to city girl Jenna that she wasn't sure she'd even speak the same language.

Maybe that was a tad extreme, but Brent had exited the tollway and immediately engulfed them in miles and miles of farmland. Could she get a Starbucks? A Mickey D's? Anything commercial?

Not even six o'clock and the late October sky suddenly had gone black. She smacked her legal pad against her lap. Marshal Hottie had taken off his suit jacket and rolled his shirtsleeves a few times. The slightly messy look fit him. The suit look fit him, too. He was one of those men who could wear anything and still look good. Not fussy, pulled-together good, but rugged good.

She smacked her pad against her leg again and he glanced down at the offending noise before going back to the road. The man had an amazing profile. Strong. Angled. Determined. Even the bump in his nose added to his I'm-in-charge persona. She'd like to see his hair—those fabulous honey-brown strands—a little longer, but he was working the short, lawman look nicely.

"I'm not great with sitting," she said.

"Not the worst thing. We're only five minutes out."

"Can you give me a quick overview? Are you okay with that? I don't want to upset you while you're driving."

"Jenna, it's been twenty-three years. If I need to, I can recite the facts of my mom's case in my sleep."

"I guess after a while it becomes…what? Rote?" *Ugh. What a thing to say.* "Wait. No. Bad word choice. I'm so sorry."

Brent shifted in his seat, switched hands on the wheel. "First thing, you've got to get over that."

"What?"

"Worrying about offending me. I'm fairly unoffendable.

And when it comes to my mom, if finding her killer means dealing with you speaking freely, I'm on board. Do your thing, Jenna. Don't get hung up on my emotions. If it's too much, I'll remove myself and let you work. I need you focused on my mom, not me. Got it?"

Well, hello, big boy. "I sure do."

"Good. I called the sheriff this morning and let him know we were coming. He'll meet us at the house—the crime scene—so you can take a look."

Jenna jotted notes. "This is the house you grew up in?"

"Yes. My father still owns it."

"Does he live there?"

"No. He's off the grid. Haven't seen or heard from him in nine years."

She stopped jotting. "What's that about?"

"Wish I knew. When I was in college, he paid off the house and left me in charge of Camille, my then seventeen-year-old sister. I was on a football scholarship and had to figure out how to stay in school, play ball and get my sister through high school. My aunt and uncle lived next door so they helped until Camille graduated and went to college. Now she lives in the city with her newly acquired husband."

And, wow, Marshal Brent was a machine with the way he recited his life history. "Who lives in the house?"

Brent cleared his throat. "We lived in it until Camille left for college and I could afford to move to the city. Now it's empty. It'll stay that way until we figure out who killed my mother. I pay all the bills and the house needs major work, but I don't want anything painted or repaired. There might still be evidence somewhere."

In an odd way, it made sense. Who knew the secrets buried in the floors and walls? Any major construction would wash away potential evidence. "I understand. It's smart. And amazing that you've maintained the house on your own."

Not to mention the fact that at nineteen, an age when most young men were focused solely on the number of women they could sleep with, he'd managed to help raise his younger sister. "Your dad, is he a…um…"

"Suspect? Yes. The husband always gets a look. They haven't been able to clear him." She tapped her pen and Brent glanced at her. "Get over this hesitation, Jenna. I need you unfiltered and open-minded."

Sideways in her seat, she focused on him. She couldn't quite grasp his he-man attitude. Sure, he had the physical size of a tough guy, but even the most hardened men had to feel something when their mother had been murdered.

But he wanted unfiltered. She'd give it to him. "Tell me what happened."

A corner of his mouth lifted and hello again, Marshal Hottie.

"Atta, girl. It was just after midnight and we were sleeping in our rooms. I woke up to a noise in the living room—I'd later find out it was my mother hitting the floor after someone blasted her on the skull. We never found a weapon."

Jenna jotted notes in her quasi shorthand, but paused to look at him. His features were relaxed, as if he was deep in thought, but other than that, she sensed no anxiety. They might as well have been out for a Sunday drive given his body language.

"I heard the back door shut. I figured it was my dad coming home. He worked second shift at a manufacturing plant. Farming equipment. But the house got quiet. Usually, when my dad came home, he walked straight back to their bedroom and the floorboards squeaked. That night? No squeak. I stayed in bed for a few minutes thinking about it, and then got up to look."

"Were you scared?"

"No. I don't know why. I should have been."

Jenna took notes, letting him focus on the road and on the facts of his mother's murder. Facts she was stunned he remembered with such clarity and, again, recited rather… dispassionately. He hooked a left onto another rural road and pressed the gas. *What speed limit sign?* "You left your room?"

"I walked down the hall to the living room and found her on the floor." He tapped the top of his forehead. "Bleeding. Then I got scared. My mom's sister and her husband live next door and I ran there. My uncle went back to check on her. He called 9-1-1 from the kitchen phone, grabbed my sister and brought her to be with me. My aunt and uncle put us in their bed and told us to go back to sleep. By then, I was too scared to do anything so I stayed there." He glanced at Jenna and then back at the road. "I can't figure out if that's a blessing or a curse."

"Probably both."

"Finally," Brent said. "She's unfiltered. That's what we need. For twenty-three years the same man has had this case. He's done a decent job, but he only sees what he sees."

Just ahead, a crossing came into view. To the right, a few houses with lit windows dotted the two-lane road. Brent cruised past them and continued on for a quarter mile to a second set of twin, single-story homes with cute porches she'd bet were great for sitting on during summer. One house was dark, the other with only a porch light. He pulled into the driveway of the darkened one, parked and cut the engine.

"This is it," he said. "If my aunt and uncle are home, they'll be over in three minutes. Guaranteed."

Jenna sat forward, scrunched her nose at the darkness. "I'm assuming the electricity is on."

"It's on. We've got ten minutes before the sheriff arrives. You want to go in?"

She nodded.

He slid from the SUV and came around to open her door. A gentleman. *Love it.* The front porch light flashed on and she flinched.

"Sorry," Brent said. "Motion sensor. Should have warned you."

"No problem."

Side by side, they walked to the porch. Brent swung his keys on his index finger once, twice, three times, and then snatched them into his hand.

Jenna stopped at the base of the stairs. "What about other suspects?"

"The sheriff thinks it might have been a robbery gone bad. Back then the only one in town who locked their door was my dad. Every night after he came home he'd lock up. My mom would wait for him. The working theory is an intruder came through the unlocked back door and tried to rob the place."

"Do you believe that?"

"Maybe. Carlisle isn't that big. Eight hundred people. Everyone knows everyone. There was a junkie who lived across town. He's moved away since, but they looked at him hard thinking he needed cash to score drugs. Couldn't make a case."

Junkie. Jenna made a note on the pad she'd brought from the car. "Does the sheriff know where he is?"

"I keep tabs on him. I'll get you his address. Then there's my dad. He left work that night and said he came straight home. No one knows what time he left the plant, and there was no security video inside the plant back then. He punched out at midnight, but theoretically his buddies could have punched him out. Guys did that all the time."

"How does that feel?"

"What?"

Please. Did he even realize how repressed his emotions were? At some point, Brent would need to stop burying the agony of his mother's death and let himself grieve. Obviously, now was not the time because this boy was locked up tight. "Thinking about your dad killing your mother. How does that feel?"

He climbed the stairs, waving her forward. "I have no idea."

"Pardon?"

Facing her, he let out a long breath and scrubbed his hand over his face. "I can't go there. I've thought about it over the years, but I don't want to believe he could do that to her."

"Did they argue a lot?"

He shrugged. "He yelled. She yelled back. Beyond that, I don't know. I was too young to draw any conclusions about whether they were happy or not."

And somehow, with all this trapped inside, he'd managed to stay sane.

"Anyway," he said. "The sheriff's name is Barnes. He's on board with you poking around, but don't irritate him. He needs to be involved."

She wrote the sheriff's name down so she could check him out. Maybe ask her dad's contacts about him. "Involved to what extent?"

If she had to check in before every move, they'd be sunk. She didn't and wouldn't work that way. Part of being good at her job—at least she hoped—meant shifting on the fly. She had no interest in checking in every ten minutes.

"To the extent where you don't aggravate or blindside him. If you're coming here, give him a heads-up. If you get a solid lead, give him a heads-up. If you want to question one of his citizens, give him a heads-up. Beyond that, I've got your back. You need a battle fought with him, I'm your guy. I know his buttons, and that makes me good at not pushing them."

And, oh, her heart went pitter-patter. This man, screwed-up emotions and all, might be her dream come true. He knew how to work people without them turning on him. "Brent Thompson, I think we'll make a great team." She faced the house, took in the peeling paint on the front door and breathed in. "Take me inside. We've got work to do."

Chapter Three

Brent shoved his key in the lock on the front door, stared down at the weathered handle and held his breath. Beside him, Jenna moved, ratcheting up his already spring-loaded tension. Straightening his shoulders, he released the breath he'd been holding.

"Are you okay?" Jenna asked, her voice mixing with the whistling wind.

With all the open space out here, he'd grown immune to the wind noise. Except tonight. Tonight that wind could have been a brass band in his head. Why tonight should be any different from the thousands of other times he'd stepped into this house, he wasn't clear on, but it definitely had something to do with Jenna-the-investigator, a near stranger wearing that red blouse with the extra unfastened button still taunting him, entering his space. The place where his life had been decimated.

"Brent?"

One, two, three. Go.

He turned the lock and shoved open the door. "I'm good. Just thinking." Flipping the inside light switch, he stepped over the threshold. "Come in."

When Jenna stepped in, he closed the door, shut out that damned wind and pointed to the living room floor. "Crime scene."

Jenna glanced around, taking in the sofa and the end tables all covered with sheets. Her gaze traveled to the front windows and the dusty drapes. Last time he'd been here, he'd forgotten to close them. Not a huge deal since his aunt and uncle watched over the place. Even if someone wanted to break in, what would they get? Thirty-year-old furniture. That's all. Everything else had been tossed or cleared out, all their childhood memories and valuables split between Brent and Camille.

All that was left here was the place his mother had died.

"Wow," Jenna finally said.

"Yeah."

"This is the original furniture?"

"Yes. The floor, too." He gestured to the hardwood. "It's never been refinished. In case you were wondering."

"I was. Thank you."

"Everything is relatively the same."

She took a step, and then halted before turning back to him. "May I?"

"Can't investigate standing here."

She walked around the furniture, peeled back a corner of a sheet to inspect the sofa then backed up to study the floor. After a minute, she squatted and ran her hand over the area where he'd found his mother beaten and bloody. Suddenly, the way Jenna's black slacks stretched over her rear seemed a whole lot better to think about.

Yeah, think about the beautiful woman instead. For once, he'd let his baser needs take the lead.

"Your bedroom is down this hallway?"

At that, he blurted a laugh. What timing.

"What's funny?"

He shook his head. "Nothing. Yes, bedroom is down the hall."

She inched closer to the sofa and his palms tingled, the flicking shooting straight up his arms into his chest.

"Right there," he said.

Jenna stopped and looked back at him. Her eyes, her body, the way she moved, all of it left him...*affected*.

"What?" she asked.

"One step to your right. That's where she was when I came down the hallway."

Without moving, she stared at the floor, studying the details—the grain of the wood, the seams where blood had seeped, the scuff marks—he'd spent years obsessing over.

Outside, a car door slammed. Sheriff Barnes arriving. Brent turned away from Jenna to open the door. The cruiser was parked behind his SUV. Brent held up a hand. "Hey, Sheriff."

Barnes, in the drab beige uniform the Carlisle Sheriff's Department had used since Brent could remember, strode to the porch, hat in place, bat belt—otherwise known as his gun belt—snug on his hips. Over the years, Barnes had filled out, but at nearly fifty-eight, he could still chase down perps.

He shook Brent's hand. "Brent, good to see you."

Not really, but what else was the guy supposed to say? "Thanks for coming, Sheriff. Come in."

Barnes stepped into the house, spotted the gorgeous brunette in the killer blouse and did a double take. *Right there with ya.* Every damned time Brent looked at her he had that same feeling. A little helpless, a little stunned and a whole lot horny.

Jenna glanced up, smiled and strutted toward them. Brent cleared his throat. "Sheriff Barnes, this is Jenna Hayward, the investigator I was telling you about."

Barnes shot him a look, and then shook his head. "But damn, if I had an investigator that looked like her, my crime rate would skyrocket. Everyone would want to be investigated."

In Brent's office, if he'd made a comment like that, his

superiors would have sent him to sensitivity training. Out here in Carlisle? No one much cared because they knew Barnes was a good, honest man who'd sooner sever his own hand than use it to touch a woman other than his wife. Unsure how Jenna would feel about the remark, he turned to her, offered an apologetic nod.

"Now, Sheriff," Jenna said, "you'd better watch yourself. I tend to get bored easily and may come looking for a job."

Barnes shook Jenna's extended hand, locked eyes with her, and the way she smiled, all crooked and *come-get-me*, once again reminded Brent how she used her looks to play men.

Particularly ones foolish enough to get played.

Finally, the sheriff got a hold of himself, straightened up and turned to Brent. "I have the copies you wanted in the car."

"Thank you." Brent swirled his finger. "I was about to review the scene with Jenna."

"Want me to do that?"

Not a bad idea, but he wanted to give his version of what he knew from that night. "I'll handle the first part and you can summarize the investigation. That work?"

"Whatever you're comfortable with."

"Sheriff," Jenna said, "I appreciate you letting me look at your files. A lot of people wouldn't."

Barnes shifted his hat between his hands. "I was a deputy back then and this was my first murder case."

His gaze went to the floor, the spot where Brent's mother had died, and the damned flicking stabbed up Brent's arms again. Anymore, he couldn't be in this house without the failure tearing at him. He inched his shoulders back and focused on Jenna.

"Anyway," Barnes said, "this case has stayed with me. I've got patience, but I need someone with imagination who can see more than I'm seeing. All I know is I want it solved."

Didn't they all.

Brent gestured down the hallway to his childhood bedroom where the hell began. "Let's start there."

JENNA FOLLOWED BRENT down the corridor, tracking his footsteps on the threadbare rug as he demonstrated the path that led him to discovering his mother's body. She glanced up at the peeling wallpaper—white with roses—and wondered how long it had been there.

"I looked out the door, but didn't see anything," Brent said. "My parents' bedroom door was closed, so I went to the living room, where the television was still on."

Something in his tone, the flatness, the lack of emotion, the *detachment*, again struck Jenna as odd. This was his mother and he was reciting these facts as if reading from a script.

"The house was quiet," he continued. "I figured my mom had fallen asleep on the couch. She did that sometimes."

Jenna jotted notes as she walked. At least until Brent stopped short and—*smash!*—she collided with him. Her chin bounced off his back, her pad fell to the floor and her pen…well…that sucker plunged into him. She gasped, dropped it and instinctively rubbed the wounded spot. A spot that happened to be on Brent Thompson's extremely tight backside.

The shock of her hand in a place it seriously shouldn't have been must have registered because he spun toward her.

Holy cow! She'd just groped a US marshal.

And liked it.

What a nightmare. She smacked her hand against her chest. *Bad, hand, bad.* A horrified giggle blurted out. *And it gets worse.*

"Okay," she said. "I'm going to beg you to believe that

was a completely—*completely*—unintentional thing. It was a reaction. If I'd hit your arm, I'd have grabbed it. I swear to you. Total accident."

Defuse it. Yes. That's what she'd do. Before they both started stuttering. She leaned forward, went on tiptoe and, keeping her voice low, she added, "But seriously, your backside is a work of art. Pure heaven."

At that, Brent's lips spread slowly, like melting butter inching across his face, and Jenna's brain seized. The man had a smile—one he didn't show too often—that could spark a fire in a saturated forest.

"Heaven, huh?"

"Pure. I am sorry, though. Really."

Not really.

"You don't look sorry."

But the sinful grin told her he was enjoying the game as much as she was. Sure, she liked flirting. Did it often and with purpose. But with Brent, it was just plain fun. They both knew the spark was there. They'd just chosen not to do anything with it.

At least until she'd groped him and decided they definitely needed to do something with it.

The sheriff stepped into view at the end of the hallway. "It got quiet. You two okay?"

Brent's gaze traveled to the open buttons on her blouse and back up, giving her a heavy dose of eye contact. "Are we okay?"

"We are A-okay, Sheriff. Just having a little powwow here."

"Powwow," Brent said. "Is that what it's called?"

"It is now, big boy."

A squeak from the back of the house sounded and Brent winced, the move so small she'd almost missed it. In the second it took him to realize she'd witnessed his unguarded response, he threw his shoulders back and jerked a thumb toward the end of the hallway.

"Someone's at the back door. Probably my uncle. Let me check this."

Turning from her, he strode to the end of the hall, hung a right and headed to the kitchen.

If it was his uncle, she'd get an opportunity to put a face to a name. As she always did, she'd lay on the Miss Illinois-Runner-Up charm and let him get comfortable with her before interviewing him. She may have been rejected by the FBI, but they were clueless at how adept she was at handling men. Her four brothers could attest to that.

Regardless, everyone here the night of the murder needed to be interviewed. Any one of them could hold one small detail they deemed irrelevant, but might actually be important. Anything was possible.

Even twenty-three years later.

"Hey," Brent said. "Figured it was you."

"We just came from dinner." Male voice. A little gravelly. Older. "I saw your car outside. You didn't call."

Jenna and the sheriff stood in the living room giving Brent privacy with his uncle. At least she guessed it was his uncle.

"The day got away from me," Brent said. "Come into the living room. I want you to meet someone."

"Really?" The gravelly voice raised with that recognizable tone every unmarried, twenty-eight-year-old woman knew and sometimes, in her case, despised.

Did Brent's uncle think he was bringing a love interest home to meet his family? And what? Showing his girlfriend the place where his mother was murdered?

Twisted.

But, well, she'd seen plenty of *twisted* in this line of work. Simply put, people were weird. Brent just didn't strike her as one of the weird ones.

"Don't get ahead of yourself," Brent said.

"You're not getting any younger."

Finally, Brent laughed. "As you keep telling me."

He stepped into the room, his uncle on his heels. Given Brent's size it was no shocker that his uncle stood a good six inches shorter. He wore tattered jeans with an untucked flannel shirt over a T-shirt. His scuffed work boots clunked against the hardwood as he came into the room. Under the brim of his baseball cap, one which Jenna's mother would ask him to remove in the house, his gaze shot to Jenna and then to the sheriff.

He nodded. "Sheriff, everything all right?"

"Just fine, Herb. Brent asked me to meet him here."

"Uncle Herb, this is Jenna Hayward."

Herb removed his cap, came toward her and shook her hand. "Hello."

"Jenna is a private investigator."

That got his attention. He looked at Brent, and then swung back to Jenna.

"No fooling?"

"No fooling," she said. "I work for a law firm."

Brent waggled a hand. "Remember the lawyer from last spring?"

"The mouthy blonde?"

"Seriously," Brent said, "you did not just say that."

Oh, he sure had and Jenna couldn't help smiling at the spot-on description of her boss. "That's her. She's one of my bosses."

Brent glanced at her. "Sorry. They were asking me about Penny and I was trying to describe her. I didn't mean it the way it sounds." He went back to his uncle. "Jenna is helping on Mom's case. The sheriff came by with files."

"Good to hear. I'm glad you'll get some help on this." Brent's uncle addressed Jenna. "We need to get her justice. She was a good girl."

His uncle gripped Brent's arm, clearly a gesture of affection and support, and something kicked against Jenna's ribs. Brent's father may have abandoned his family, but his uncle sure hadn't. These poor people. All these years they'd been struggling with loss and heartbreak and injustice. "Brent, do you mind if I talk with your uncle a bit?"

He shrugged. "Sure."

But Brent didn't move.

"Alone?"

For a moment, he continued to stand there and then he blinked. *There we go.* Slowly, it all registered. "Gotcha. I'll walk outside with the sheriff. Get those files for you."

"And, hey," his uncle said, "head over and see your aunt. She misses you. Jamie is there. Catch her before she goes home."

Jamie. Brent's cousin. He'd mentioned her on the ride over.

On his way out, Brent waved in that yeah-yeah-yeah way people used when being nagged. The front door closed and Jenna moved next to Herb. He focused on her face, which she'd give him bonus points for. "Thanks again for helping," Brent's uncle said.

"No need to thank me. Brent is a good guy. I had no idea about his mom. It's…well…tragic."

"It is. But Brent, he turned out to be a damned fine man. Taking care of his sister the way he did. A lot of boys would run from that. Not him. He latches on."

He sure did. "So it seems. May I ask you some questions regarding the night his mom died?"

"Whatever you need. But the sheriff has it all in his notes."

Of course he did, but hearing it *and* reading it were necessities. "Yes, but since we're here, I was hoping you could walk me through what went on when you got here."

He took in the room, studying the now-uncovered furniture. His gaze landed on the floor in front of the sofa. Slowly, he ran his hand over his face, a gesture so similar to the one she'd seen Brent use it sent a chill up her arms. Like father like son, only this wasn't the father and Brent wasn't the son.

Finally, he looked back at Jenna. "She was a mess. Poor thing. I found her right here. Right where I'm standing."

The exact spot Brent had indicated. "When did you first see Brent?"

"He came to the house, ran inside—we never locked the doors back then—screaming and crying. Scared the hell out of me." He shook his head. "Long as I live, I'll never get the sound of that boy's screams out of my system."

It was hard to picture. Strong, solid Brent at five, terrified and begging for help. She hated the thought. Hated the idea that he'd dealt with that trauma. "What time was this?"

"Just after midnight. Maybe 12:10."

After checking her notes and confirming the time with what Brent told her, she pointed at the front door. "You came in this way?"

"Yes, ma'am. Usually we come in the back. Cheryl always kept that door unlocked. That night, Brent must have run out the front door because it was open when I got here."

"Brent was with you?"

That might have been a trick question—no might about it—because she knew where Brent had been. He'd told her. Still, it never hurt to let the witness give his own assessment.

"No. He was back at the house. Poor kid was howling something about his mom and blood. My wife called 9-1-1 and I came back to check on Cheryl and get the baby— Brent's sister. We always call her the baby."

Staying focused on the scene, Jenna moved to the entryway. "So you're on the porch and the door is open."

"Yeah." He walked over and opened the door, letting a

burst of cool air in as he pushed it back against the wall. "It was like this when I came in."

Jenna faced the living room, accessing the layout—sofa blocking her view of where the body would have been, the end table and side chair that could have hindered the murderer—all of it part of an investigation that had gone nowhere in twenty-three years.

Herb walked back to the sofa and pointed. "She was right there. Kind of curled up, but not really. Her hair was all bloody."

Head wounds bled more than others due to all the blood vessels. Jenna had learned that from her dad.

She drew a map of the room, marking an X where the body had been found. "Were these chairs here back then?"

"Yes. They may have moved them when they were living here, but Brent put everything back when he started working on the case."

"Then what happened?"

Herb scratched his cheek and then gestured to the floor. "I leaned over her, checked her pulse. I couldn't find one, but I'm no doctor. By then, Barnes—he was a deputy then—had pulled in. I ran back to get Camille before she woke up."

More notes. He'd left the body so he could get Camille. Parental instinct would be to protect the child. Made sense. "The sheriff arrived and you went back to your house with Camille? Did she see the body?"

"No. I covered her eyes when I carried her out. I took her next door and came back. My wife was trying to get hold of Mason."

"Brent's father?"

"Yes, ma'am. She wanted to warn him, but we didn't have cell phones back then, and he'd already left work. I waited for him to pull up while the paramedics were in here with Cheryl." He flipped his palms up, and then let them drop. "Helluva night, that one."

The heaviness in his voice, weight saddling his vocal chords, drew her gaze. For her, this was a job. For them, she couldn't imagine. "Do you need a break?"

"Maybe I do." He started for the door, but then stopped and gestured to the floor. "All these years I've been thinking about what my nephew saw. I don't know how a boy recovers from that."

Jenna's guess was the boy in question hadn't recovered. All he'd done was bury the pain deep enough that it would allow him to go forward, to keep searching, to get justice.

Only problem was, all the anger he'd stuffed inside him would eventually go boom. And that would cause an emotional landslide.

Obviously wanting to be done, Herb turned toward the still open door. "Do you need anything else?"

"Not right now. I'm sorry if I upset you."

"It's all right. I want to help. If we solve this, it'll give Brent and Camille peace. Maybe then he'll sell this damned house."

"It must be hard living right next door."

He shrugged. "If someone lived here, gave the house some life, it wouldn't be so bad. Now it's just an empty place where my sister-in-law died. It's a damned morgue."

OUTSIDE, THE GARAGE spotlight illuminated the driveway, and Brent spotted his aunt Sylvie marching across the patch of grass separating the two homes. She made a direct line for him, her face, as usual, passive. No pinched brows, no big smile, no tight cheeks. Nothing to indicate her mood. He'd always said she'd make a great spy. Bringing up the rear was his cousin, Jamie, who wore that slightly amused grin that meant she wasn't the only one in trouble.

He shifted his gaze back to his aunt and—yep—all that passive behavior meant one thing, she was about to yell at him for staying away so long.

Might as well take it like a man.

While the sheriff unloaded the copies of evidence files, Brent walked across the driveway, the heels of his dress shoes clapping against the pavement and the lack of traffic noise reminded him that he wasn't in Chicago anymore. Coming back here, with all the contrasts to the city, brought back all that bubbling agony he fought to control. And he didn't want that. He wanted it buried where he didn't have to deal with it. What he needed was to stay strong—for Camille, for his aunt and for his uncle.

They could turn into basket cases if they chose, but not him. His day would come, though. When they found his mother's killer, then he'd figure out how to deal with all the garbage he'd packed inside him.

"Hey, Aunt Sylvie." He held out his arms and his much smaller aunt stepped into them.

"Don't *Hey-Aunt-Sylvie* me, young man. You know you're in trouble. You didn't even call to tell us."

She backed away from the hug and stared up at him. Since his mother had died, his aunt had turned her fanatical focus on him and Camille. Whether it was her own grief or simply wanting to make sure they had a mother figure in their lives—maybe both—was still up for debate, but Brent never questioned it. Aunt Sylvie always made sure they were cared for and had hot food in their bellies.

For that reason alone, he always answered when she called. No matter what.

Even when she griped at him.

"I know. I'm sorry. I got caught up at work and didn't get a chance to call."

Jamie stepped around her mother, went on tiptoes and smacked a kiss on Brent's cheek. "Hey, cuz. Good to see you."

"Hi, James."

He'd started calling his cousin James when they were

kids and the nickname had stuck. She never seemed to mind.

Obviously done ranting, Aunt Sylvie waved at Barnes, who'd finished digging a file box from his car and had set it on the trunk. "Sheriff, how are you?"

"I'm good, Sylvie. You all right?"

"Oh, we're just fine." She shot Brent the stink-eye. "Wouldn't mind seeing my niece and nephew a little more."

Guilt, Brent had enough of. Hell, he had enough guilt to fill the Chicago River. "You know how to drive. And Chicago is only an hour."

As usual, her mouth dropped open and she gasped. "Look at you with that smart mouth."

"Merely an observation."

Jamie cleared her throat. "What's in the box, Sheriff?"

The sheriff glanced at Brent, unsure how much to reveal, so Brent took that one. "That's for me. Copies of Mom's files."

With that bright spotlight shining down on her, Aunt Sylvie whipped her gaze between Brent and the sheriff. Brent knew right where her mind had gone. "Has something happened? A lead?"

Dang. He'd been insensitive. He knew her. Knew how her mind worked and the slow-curling panic that fired every time the sheriff pulled into one of these driveways.

And Brent hadn't warned her.

Gave her zero notice about Jenna investigating. *Moron.*

Brent touched her arm. "No. But there's someone I'll introduce you to in a minute. She's inside talking with Uncle Herb. I think she can help us."

"Who is she?"

"An investigator. Remember the lawyer I helped last spring?"

"That adorable little blonde?"

Adorable. Penny would hate that. She'd like Uncle Herb's description better. "Yes. The investigator works for her law firm. They offered to help with Mom's case."

Aunt Sylvie cocked her head. "She's good, this investigator?"

"She is."

And she's got a body that drives me insane. Not that he'd say that, but he was a man, and men had needs. Needs that Brent had been sorely neglecting lately. Needs that maybe Jenna could help him with.

When they were done finding a killer.

Because as much as Brent fantasized about a long night with Jenna in his bed, his priority was catching his mother's killer. If he and Jenna got involved, something told him it would get ugly when he walked away. And walk away, he would. He liked coming and going as he pleased and not having to explain himself to anyone. He didn't see that changing anytime soon.

The snick of the front-door latch sounded and they all turned toward the house. Jenna came down the porch steps.

She walked toward them, her coat flying open to reveal her blouse and the slacks that fit her curvy body in all the right ways.

"Wow," Jamie said. "She's pretty."

Aunt Sylvie gave him a bored look. "*This* is your investigator?"

Brent grinned. "Yep!"

"Which body part made this decision?" she whispered.

"Well, look at you with that smart mouth," he said in his best Sylvie voice.

Without giving her an opportunity to respond, he waved Jenna over. "Come meet my aunt and cousin."

After doing the introductions, Brent turned to Aunt Sylvie. "Jenna will be poking around. Don't freak when you see a car in the driveway."

"Yes," Jenna said. "I'd like to chat with both of you, at your convenience, of course."

Aunt Sylvie pressed her lips together, and then shot a look at Uncle Herb who nodded. She didn't like talking about her sister. Ever. Growing up, Brent had craved stories about his mom, but the memories were too painful for his aunt and she typically ran from the room sobbing. Over the years, Brent had been conditioned not to talk about his mother. Which pretty much stunk.

"Of course," his aunt said. "If it'll help. I'm available anytime."

"Thank you. I'd like to read through the sheriff's files first. Would it be all right if I call you in a day or two?" She looked at Jamie. "Both of you?"

"Sure," Jamie said. "Anytime."

"Thank you."

"Well, have you eaten?" his aunt asked Brent. "I could fix you something."

A meal would serve him good right now, but the night had dragged on and, as hopeful as he was about the new energy Jenna brought, talking about his mother, reliving that night, had drained him. Time to get back to Chicago, where the sounds of the city would drown the noise in his head. Silence, he'd learned long ago, was his enemy. During high school and college, football helped smother it. With football, the energy it took to step to the line and get his head beat in was all the distraction he needed. When he became a marshal—nothing boring there—silence was no longer an issue. Pretty much, the US Marshal Service was involved in everything from judicial and witness security to asset forfeiture. If it involved federal laws, US marshals were there. One day he could chase down a fugitive, the next make sure a witness didn't get blown away by someone they'd just testified against.

Out here, in his childhood hometown where the streets were desolate after six o'clock and the only outside noise came from birds or cicadas or blowing leaves, the quiet created emotional chaos.

Gotta go.

He leaned down, kissed his aunt's cheek. "We need to get back to the city. Maybe on the weekend."

"Saturday," she said. "After church."

He laughed. By now he should know better than to throw out a maybe. His aunt took a maybe and turned it into a definitely.

"You could come early and go to church with us."

Now she wanted church too. Years since he'd done that. Which was a shame. He used to enjoy church, but now it gave him too much time to reflect on things he shouldn't reflect on. "Don't push it. Saturday for dinner. I'll be here. I'll see what Camille is doing. Don't worry. I'll channel the guilt from you."

She waved her hands. "Oh, with the sass."

He kissed her again. "I love you. Good night."

"I love you, too. Drive carefully. No speeding."

"Yes, ma'am."

He turned to Jenna. "All set?"

Please let her be all set.

She nodded. "You bet."

He shook hands with the sheriff. "Thank you. I'll call you with any updates."

"I'd appreciate that."

On the way to his SUV, he grabbed the file box off the back of the sheriff's cruiser, the weight of it, as always, easy to handle. Most of what was in that file he'd probably seen already. Except for the photos. Being a marshal, he'd learned to take emotion out of a case. Even when it came to his mother. He could read the forensics reports, investigator notes and the autopsy report. All of it, he could handle. Even some of the crime scene photos showing the exterior of the house or certain pieces of evidence were tolerable. But not the ones of his mom's body. Those were a different damned beast, and he couldn't find a compartment big enough to control the massive anger those pictures would unleash.

Balancing the box against the SUV, he opened the back door, shoved the box on the seat and walked around to get Jenna's door. By the time he'd gotten there, she already had her hand on the handle.

"I've got it," he said.

"Again with this?"

When he'd picked her up at her apartment, she'd teased him about the gesture. What she didn't know was his aunt would skin him if he abandoned his manners. Plus, he liked doing it. "Yeah. Again with this. Get used to it and don't argue."

He held open the door and waved her into the car. To that, she tilted her chin up and saluted. "Yes, sir."

And the look on her face, so serious with her cheeks sucked in and her gaze straight ahead, made him laugh. Really laugh.

In front of his mother's house no less. Helluva thing.

She slid into the car and the interior light illuminated her face and the grin that—*wait for it*—would cause the punch to his chest. Jenna Hayward was beautiful, but she wasn't one of those everyday beautiful women you could find anywhere you looked. On sight, she took a man's legs out from under him. *Bam!*

He leaned in to get a whiff of her perfume, something floral but light. Not allergy inducing. *Thank you*. Once again, his eyes went to that extra undone button on her blouse and the lush skin under it. He caught a glimpse of lace and swore under his breath. "Okay, Miss Illinois, cut the wisecracks."

She straightened up. "Miss Illinois?"

"You think I'm going to let you anywhere near my mother's case without checking you out?"

HE KNEW. Not that it was some big secret, but she didn't necessarily flaunt her beauty queen background. In her line of work, it didn't gain her anything. All she knew was that at the age of twenty-one, after years of working the pageant circuit, years of hearing her mother coo over how beautiful her daughter was, and the resulting pressure of it all, she'd had enough. Enough of the dieting, enough of having to look a certain way at all times, enough of the show. She simply wanted to be Jenna. A pretty girl who liked to eat cake and pester her detective father with questions about cases.

Playing along, she scissored Brent's silky tie between two fingers. Nice tie. Nice man. Nice everything. And she so adored the way he interacted with his family. Teasing, but firm and loving when they tried to give him any nonsense.

"My pageant days aren't classified information. All you have to do is check Google. And, by the way, you failed. I didn't win. I was the runner-up."

His lips lifted slightly as he watched her play with his tie. "I didn't fail. I knew that, but decided it wasn't worth mentioning. Those judges were either blind or stupid. I'm guessing beauty contest judges need eyesight, so that leaves stupid."

Did that just send a hot flash raging? This was their problem. That connection, that heat she couldn't ignore. "Marshal Thompson, are you flirting with me?"

"Nope. Calling it like I see it."

She flicked away the tie. "I was fifteen pounds lighter then."

Where did that come from? Sure, her brothers liked to taunt her about packing on a few pounds, but her pageant weight was impossible to maintain. And Jenna had a thing for food. In that she liked it.

"Yet another tragedy," Brent said.

"What?"

"That you were fifteen pounds lighter."

In the lit interior of the car, she studied his face. Looking for the tell that he was charming her into possibly removing her clothes. Which, if he kept talking like that, just might happen. Without a doubt, every one of her brain cells must have evaporated. Only explanation for this attack of flightiness.

"You don't like skinny women?"

"Brent?" his aunt called from the front of the house. "Everything okay?"

He backed away and straightened. "We're good! Seat belt jammed."

He shut the door, came around the driver's side, hopped in and fired the engine. "If we stay here, she'll be all over us."

Jenna waited. Would he answer her about the skinny women thing? Part of her wanted to know. The other part wanted to run. Although the extra fifteen pounds had only brought her to a size eight, it still bothered her. Made her wonder what men saw when they looked at the ex-beauty queen whose body had gone fluffy.

At the road, Brent hit the gas and the car tore through the blackness of the country road, the only sound being the radio on low volume. Tim McGraw maybe, but Jenna couldn't tell. She was more of a pop music girl.

"No," Brent said.

"No what?"

"I don't like skinny women. And it's a damned shame you think you looked better fifteen pounds lighter because, honey, you're wrong."

Oh, she might like where this conversation was heading. "I don't think I looked better."

"Liar."

"Hey!"

"Just admit it and be done with it. I saw your picture—nice gown by the way—and I can promise you, from a completely male perspective, you looked like a bean pole back then. A guy my size would break that girl in half."

"Did you somehow get drunk when you were outside with your family?"

He smiled at that and she liked the sight of it.

"Calling it like I see it," he said again.

"Well, thank you, I suppose. For the compliment."

"You're welcome."

"It never hurts to hear someone appreciates your looks."

For a quick second, he turned and the dashboard glow lit his face as he helped himself to a look at her body. "I definitely appreciate your looks. I'd imagine most men do. I think you know that."

The side of his mouth quirked again—all male and sexy and devilish—and my, oh, my, Jenna's stomach did a flip. "You're flirting with me."

"I might be."

"Is that wise?"

He laughed. "Probably not. But as I recall, you do your share of flirting."

She shifted sideways in her seat and the belt scraped the side of her neck. Darn it, that'd leave a mark. Forget it. She needed a snappy comeback, but the big ox was right. Her flirting wasn't personal, though. *What?* How insane would she sound if she said that? When she flirted, she did it to get somewhere, to make progress. Flirting for her had become a tactic. A strategic tool in her arsenal.

"We're adults," she said. "Let's just throw it out there that there's chemistry between us. Or am I totally wrong?"

Sounding a little desperate here, Jenna. What was it with her? Always needing the ego boost. Always needing approval. Blame it on her years of being judged in contests and her failure to get into the FBI, but she couldn't get through the day without wondering what people thought of her.

"You're not wrong."

"About the chemistry, or flirting not being wise?"

"Both."

She sighed, turned to the front again. "I need to do a good job on this, Brent. It's important to me."

"News flash, honey, it's important to me, too. If you don't want me flirting with you, I won't flirt, but you set that tone the second I met you in the hallway outside Penny's office last spring. Make up your mind what you want from me, Jenna. If you want this all business, it'll be all business. It can't be both ways. You decide."

This man could have grown up in her household. So direct and strong and honest. "I want to do a good job for you. For your mom. She deserves that."

"Yes, she does."

"I like flirting with you. For once, it's not a prop. It's fun and you have a great smile that I don't think you show enough. It makes me feel good that I can get you to smile."

And again, it all rolled around to what made her feel good. Pathetic. She waved her hands and looked out the window. "No flirting."

"Fine. No flirting. And yeah, you get me to smile, and that doesn't happen a lot."

So much for no flirting.

"There's one thing I want to know."

"What's that?"

He glanced at her. "I'm not being a jerk here, I'm seriously curious."

"I've been warned. Ask away."

"How does someone go from being the runner-up in the Miss Illinois pageant to being a private investigator? And, again, I'm not being a jerk."

"I don't mind. People have asked me this question a million times. My father is a career detective. I've always been fascinated by what he does. I'd sit and ask him questions. Two of my four brothers are also cops and will probably make detective. I guess you could say we played a lot of real-life *Clue* when I was little."

"So, how'd you get to being a PI? Why not join the PD?"

Leave it to him to pursue it. Most people were satisfied with the my-dad-is-a-detective line and dropped the subject. Not Brent. He had to know it all. She looked out the window where the tollway lights dimmed in the distance.

She turned back to him. "I was a psychology major in college."

"I could see that. You study people."

"I like to know what makes them tick. After I graduated, I couldn't see myself in an office all day counseling people. I needed to be out and moving, so I applied for the FBI."

He shot her a look, and then went back to the road. "You wanted to be an agent?"

"I did. And I wanted it bad."

"Did you go to the academy?"

"Nope. Never made it that far. They rejected me."

There, she'd said it. Not many people knew and she held her breath, waited for a crack about the beauty queen wanting to play G-man, or in her case, G-woman.

But Brent watched the road ahead as the tollway entrance drew closer. *Shouldn't have said anything.* The man was a US marshal. He'd succeeded where she'd failed. What did she expect him to say? *Dumb, Jenna.* Heat rose in her cheeks—thank goodness the car was dark—and she rested her head back.

"That's a shame," he said. "You'd have made a good agent. You wouldn't have needed your cleavage to do it, either. Don't sell yourself short, Jenna. You're beautiful, but you're smart, too. Don't ever forget that."

The air in her chest stalled and she squeezed her eyes closed. No one, not even her mother who often rolled her eyes at Jenna's clothing choices, had ever said that. *He knew.* But she couldn't get crazy here. He wasn't offering a glass slipper. All he offered was an opinion.

Still resting her head back, she eased out a breath. "You might be flirting with me, but I don't care. Thank you for saying that."

He shrugged. "That time I wasn't flirting. It's not complicated. I like you and you've got a brain. You don't need to be half-naked to be good at what you do."

Suddenly, Jenna wished he'd been flirting, because she might have just fallen a little in love with Brent Thompson.

Chapter Four

Two days later, on a sunlit Saturday morning that reminded Jenna that October could be a beautiful month, she pulled into the driveway of Brent's childhood home and absorbed her first daytime sight of it. What she'd missed the other night was the peeling paint on the porch poles, the rotting window frames and the roof that needed to be replaced. All of it added to the permeating sadness from a house that hadn't been truly lived in—or loved—for years.

And here she was, digging up—metaphorically—the body buried there. After sorting through the copies of reports, photos and witness statements the sheriff had provided, Jenna needed more time at the scene. Something bugged her. And the lack of a murder weapon was top on her list.

Blunt force trauma. That's all the report had said. Crime scene photos showed a wound with a right angle. Square weapon? Possibly, but that could be anything. A trophy, a kitchen appliance, a statue. Plenty of household items had square bottoms.

Across the yard, Brent's cousin exited her parents' home. Like the other night, Jamie wore her shoulder-length dark blond hair pushed back in a headband that Jenna assumed was her go-to look. Also her go-to look would be loose jeans and a navy sweatshirt on her average-sized frame, and

Jenna found herself a little envious of the comfort wear. The only place Jenna wore that look was inside her own home.

Jamie spotted the strange car in the driveway and paused. Finally, recognition dawned and Jamie waved.

Time to work.

Jenna gathered her purse and her briefcase and swung open the car door. A crisp breeze blew her hair sideways and she shoved it from her face. Next time, she'd do a pony-tail. With all this open space, her hair couldn't be counted on to cooperate. "Hi, Jamie. How are you?"

"Hi. It's Jenna, right?"

"Sure is."

"No Brent?"

"He had errands this morning. He said he'd catch up with me in a bit."

Jamie turned toward the house, her gaze focused as her shoulders drooped. "He thinks he can handle all this, but I worry about him. This house is an albatross."

Negative energy oozed around Jenna, sending prickles up her arms. How did Brent's family stand the constant reminder of tragedy? Jamie shifted back to her, the fine lines around the woman's eyes deepening as she squinted. Being a woman who could peg another woman's age fairly accurately—a gift really—Jenna put Jamie at thirty-nine.

"You were a teenager when his mom died, right?"

"Yes. Fifteen."

Ooh, so close. Only a year off. "It must have been rough on all of you."

"Not as rough as Brent and Camille had it. And even my useless uncle."

Jenna nodded. "Brent told me about that. He said his father has always been a suspect."

"As far as I know."

"What do you think?"

"I think he's spineless and doesn't have the stomach for

murder. But I've lived in this town all my life and wouldn't have believed it would happen here, so what do I know?"

That was about as direct of an answer as Jenna could ask for. "Do your parents hear from Brent's father?"

"If they do, they don't tell me." She shrugged. "We don't talk about him much."

In an odd way, Jenna understood. Nothing would change the man abandoning his family, so what was the point of stewing? Stewing wasted time and already battered emotional reserves.

"Do you remember anything from that night?"

Jamie sighed. "Sometimes it feels like it was yesterday. I woke up when I heard the sirens. I came out of my room and my mom told me Brent and Camille were sleeping and I should be quiet. Then she sent me back to my room." Jamie turned, pointed to one of the side windows on her parents' house. "I watched from that window. I wasn't sure what happened, but I got scared—really scared— when I saw the ambulance. It was…"

She stopped, put one hand over her mouth and the other over her eyes. Her shoulders hitched and instant guilt landed on Jenna. She touched Jamie's arm. "I'm so sorry to put you through this."

After a few seconds, Jamie dropped her hands and heaved a giant breath. "It's not your fault. I know we have to do this."

"Thank you."

"Anyway, I saw Brent's dad arrive, and he started yelling and going crazy. I knew it had to be Aunt Cheryl."

The window Jamie had pointed to was midway between the front and rear of Brent's house, so Jenna walked to it and surveyed the immediate area. Only a sliver of the back porch could be seen from that location. "Did you see anyone come out the back? Maybe walk through here?"

"No. I was asleep until I heard the sirens."

Nothing here. And Jenna was losing precious time to restage the murder scene before Brent arrived. Based on witness statements found in the sheriff's file, she'd prepared a timeline showing when each person came into play. Who knew if it would amount to anything, but that was part of the investigative allure. Sometimes the most obscure details broke open a case.

Jenna wanted to break open this case.

Without asking, as she'd often done, for her father's advice. If it came down to it, she'd ask. Her ego wasn't so giant that she wouldn't seek help when needed, but for now she'd do this alone.

She walked back to Jamie. "Thank you for talking with me. Every little bit helps. I'm going to head inside and look around."

"Sure. I only came by to drop the pies off for tonight. My parents are out. Will you be all right by yourself?"

Jenna waved her off. God knew she'd been in worse places than this. Three weeks ago she'd been traipsing the south side of Chicago at two in the morning looking for a drug dealer, but she hadn't exactly been alone then. Like today, her .38 had accompanied her.

"I'll be fine. Brent will be along soon."

Jamie took a pen and scrap of paper from her purse. "Here's my cell number. I only live five minutes away. Call if you need anything."

"Thank you. I appreciate that."

"Anything I can do, just let me know."

Jenna stuck the paper in her jacket pocket and waited for Jamie to drive off before digging out the house key Brent had given her.

For a few minutes, she'd been afraid Jamie would stay and, at this stage, Jenna needed time alone at the scene. Family members would distract her. They'd stand around, disrupting the energy and asking questions when she needed quiet. If they didn't ask questions, they'd be thinking them and she'd sense it.

Times like these, it was better for her to work solo.

Inside, she dumped her purse on the floor and, remembering her father's constant warnings, locked the door behind her. Could never be too cautious. A spear of light through the closed drapes illuminated the darkened room. Jenna assumed someone must have closed the drapes after they'd left the other night. She flipped the light switch and the overhead fixture came on. Not great lighting, but it would do. And she had a flashlight if necessary.

She glanced around at the covered furniture. *Need to see it.* Yes. She'd pull off all the coverings to see what was under them, and then pull the cushions to search for bloodstains. Crime scene reports indicated blood had only been found on the floor, but Brent wanted fresh eyes and she would provide them.

She worked her way around the room, gently lifting sheets off the furniture. Even with minimal movements, dust particles floated.

Prickles snaked up her arms again. Sad existence, this house.

Unlike the exterior of the home, the dark blue upholstered side chairs were in good shape. No tears and minimal fading. In the crime scene photos the sofa was a floral pattern. One way to check. She spun back to the sofa and peeled the sheet off one arm. Underneath she found white fabric layered with different shades of red flowers.

She uncovered the rest of the sofa, still positioned in the spot where Brent's mother had died. Jenna would outline where the body had been found, go through her timeline and see if anything struck her. From her briefcase, she grabbed the crime scene photos and set them on the floor. Rather than put tape on the floor, she opted for string. Plus, if Brent walked in she could yank the string up quickly. As much as he played tough guy, she didn't want him to face an outline of his mother's body.

After measuring the distance from the windows and finding the exact location where the body had been, Jenna used the photos as a guide and positioned the string on the floor. From there she went to the back door and unlocked it. *Sorry, Dad. Have to do it.* The door had been unlocked the night of the murder and, for timeline purposes, Jenna needed everything as close to that night as possible.

"Door set. Body there. Murder weapon?"

She breathed in and her temples throbbed. *What the heck?* She wrapped her fingers around her forehead and squeezed. The crazy headache had come from nowhere. Or perhaps she'd been distracted. Either way, she had ibuprofen in her purse.

Along with her flashlight.

Flashlight. With no murder weapon she'd have to improvise. She checked her watch. 12:30 p.m. *Darn it.* She'd been here forty-five minutes already and had spent too much time on the photos. *Dumb, Jenna.* Brent said he'd arrive by 1:00 p.m. and now she'd have to rush.

She hustled back to her purse and grabbed the flashlight-slash-improvised-murder weapon.

A snick sounded just on the other side of the door and she stood half frozen, flashlight in hand as the door came open. Brent's head snapped back and, all at once, his arms were in motion, reaching for his waist.

Gun. Blood barreled into her already aching head. *No, no, no.* "It's me!"

For three long seconds he stared at her, unblinking, his gaze hard and steady, but at least he wasn't reaching for his gun anymore.

"It's me," she repeated, her body losing some of the paralyzing tension.

Bending at the waist, he dropped his hands to his knees and shook his head. "You scared the hell out of me!"

"I…I…I'm sorry. I was getting something from my purse and heard the lock. You saw my car outside."

A gust of wind smacked the door against the interior wall and Brent stepped in, nudging her sideways so he could close it. "I know, but…" He scrubbed a hand over his face, shook his head.

"But what? You were about to draw on me."

He winced, then leaned back against the wall. "I'm sorry. Being here gets me crazy. All I saw was someone holding a weapon."

The flashlight. He'd thought it was a weapon. Ironic since she'd planned on using it as such for her reenactment. "Then I guess we scared each other."

"Hell, yeah. I'm not used to seeing someone on the other side of that door. Damned near gave me a heart attack."

He glanced around, spotted the sheets off and the photos scattered around. He turned his back to the room. "What are you doing?"

"I was, um, reviewing photos." She rushed to the photos and the body outline. "Hang there a second. Let me scoop this stuff up."

"It's okay. I'll…wait…what's that smell? Did you spray something?"

Did she *spray* something? "No."

He looked around, took in the room, the drapes, the furniture and then stared up at the ceiling. In a burst, he lunged back to the door quicker than a man his size should be able to move. He whipped open the door. "Out!"

What the heck? "Why?"

"Gas. Get out." He clamped on to her arm and dragged her to the door. "Didn't you smell the gas when you came in?"

"No. But I've been here awhile. I was distracted."

But the gas might be the reason for her sudden headache. Of course. What an idiot. Who doesn't smell gas?

Just as they got to the door, her foot wobbled on her skinny boot heel and her ankle gave way. Pain shot clear up to her knee, and she grabbed a fistful of Brent's jacket for balance. "Ow!"

"Are you passing out?"

Passing out? "No, dopey. I twisted my ankle."

"Don't call me dopey."

Suddenly, she went airborne and landed on Brent's shoulder in a *whoosh*. "What are you doing?"

"You just said you twisted your ankle. I'm getting us out. Or would you rather fry when the house blows from that gas leak? Your choice, Miss Illinois. I can take you back in."

Jenna gasped. What. A. Jerk. "Be nice."

"Hey, you called me dopey."

Brent marched down the stairs, moving quickly from the house. Apparently her weight wasn't an issue for this big boy. "I didn't mean it *that* way. I was teasing. Put me down."

"Which ankle hurts?"

"The left."

"When I put you down, don't put any pressure on it. Just lean back against your car."

With one hand on her back, he eased her to the ground. His hand slid over the side of her hip to her thigh where he held her leg. And, oh, the feel of his hand running down her body made that headache seem a whole lot less annoying. She lifted her foot, hung on to Brent's arm and levered onto the hood of her car.

"You good for a sec?" he asked. "I need to shut the gas off."

"I'm fine. Go."

He tore around the far side of the house, disappearing while she checked out her ankle. She set her foot down, didn't feel agonizing pain and considered it a bonus. So far, so good. She tried a little weight on it. Ew. A pang bolted up her calf, but nothing unbearable. "Junior ow."

If it were broken, she'd know. She hoped. Having never broken a foot or ankle, she wasn't sure. At the very least, she wouldn't be able to put weight on it, which she could do. If it was a sprain, she'd at least get around on it. Just not in high-heeled boots.

"What are you doing?" Brent shouted as he came around the side of the house, his face all hard and yummy angles.

Had to love a man on a mission. "I have sneakers in the car. I'm taking my boot off so I can put them on."

"Just stay in your sock. There's a doc in town. We can run over there and get it x-rayed." He squatted in front of her, pushed her hands away and lifted her foot. "I'll take the boot off. You ready?"

"It's not that bad. What's up with the gas?"

One hand braced around her calf, he guided the boot off and—wow—his touch was soft but with rough skin that caused friction. Friction and thoughts of Brent. Without clothes. All those solid muscles waiting for her to run her hands over. Jenna tilted her head up to the perfection of blue sky and prayed she didn't make a fool of herself in the next five seconds.

"I don't know," he said. "I turned the main off. I'll call the gas company and get them out here."

Needing to demolish the lust filling her body, she shooed him away. "Make the call. I'm fine."

"We're still getting it x-rayed after I make this call."

He dug into the front pocket of his jeans for his phone and dialed. While he waited for the operator to connect him, he scooted next to her, leaned against the car and patted his lap. "Slide that foot up here."

"Look at you being all Mr. Caretaker. I like it."

He shrugged. "Can't help it. I'm on hold. Let's hope the house doesn't blow."

"You left the front door open. It'll air out."

"True. Did you get anything done before I got here?"

Meaning, had she made any miraculous discoveries. Not yet. "I had everything set up and was about to run through my timeline when you showed up. I got waylaid by your cousin."

"She was here?"

Jenna nodded. "Dropping something off for your aunt. I got to talk to her a little bit about that night. She was watching from her window."

"I know. I read it in the file."

"Have the two of you ever talked about it?"

He waggled his free hand. "Some. I had questions related to the investigation and she answered them. That's about it."

Again with burying his emotions. How the hell did these people not discuss this? With her family, they talked about everything. Even her father. Maybe he wasn't free-wheeling with his emotions, but if something bothered him, he spoke up. Brent's family? Forget it? They were cinched so tight they'd never be free.

Jenna sighed. "That seems to be a habit with you."

BRENT'S BODY DAMNED near turned to stone. What the hell was Jenna muttering about? "What does *that* mean?"

Jenna eased her foot off his lap. Obviously the woman wasn't stupid and had a fine sense of when she'd irritated someone. Good for her because she'd just royally peeved him. He stood and shook out his legs while waiting for the gas company to take his *emergency* call.

"Brent, I don't think it's a shock to you that you hide your feelings about your mother. It's obviously a defense mechanism—self-preservation maybe. I don't blame you. I'm not sure I'd be able to do what you do without squashing all those feelings. Still, it's not healthy."

Unstable territory. And really, he didn't want to have

this conversation. Outside of discussing her case, he didn't talk about his mother. Or his feelings about her death. Why give rage room to drown him?

"I don't like to talk about her."

"I realize that."

Tired of the crummy hold music, he pulled the phone from his ear, put it on speaker and set it on the hood of her car. "Then why are you bugging me about it?"

"I'm not. I made an observation. It's what I do. I observe. And you, my friend, are an impending train wreck."

"I know I compartmentalize, but if I let loose, I'll tear this town apart."

She tilted her head, pursed those lush lips of hers and—no—not going there. Not letting Miss Illinois mess up his thinking. At least not any more than necessary.

"Maybe you *need* to tear this town apart. *Maybe* if you let some of it out, it'll clear your head."

"Ha!" All that festering anger with the lid blown off? He wouldn't know what to do with that hell on earth. She could take her psychological evaluation somewhere else. Finally, the hold music ended and he scooped up the phone, jabbing at the screen and taking it off speaker. "Hello? I need to report a gas leak."

He eyeballed Jenna who eyeballed him right back, then stuck her tongue out at him. Crazy woman. Still, he had to grin. When she returned the smile, he waved her off, but knew he'd have to be careful with her. She had a way of defusing him and he wasn't sure if he was losing his edge or he'd met his match.

After finishing with the operator, Jenna sat two feet in front of him, leaning on her sporty little BMW, her long dark hair pulled over one shoulder, looking like the vixen she was. Time to face facts. He liked her. A lot. And it wasn't just about her looks—although he couldn't complain about them.

He liked the challenge of her. How she questioned every damned thing. Annoying, sure, but fun, too. Call him a masochist.

"They're sending someone out," he said. "Let's head into town and get that ankle x-rayed. By the time we get back, the gas company will be here."

"So that's it? Conversation about your mom is over?"

"Yep." He smacked her on the hip. "Let's get you in the truck."

Ninety minutes and a mild sprain diagnosis later, Brent pulled back into the driveway. A utility truck was parked on the road, but he didn't see any workers. They were here somewhere. "We've got activity."

"All my notes are still in the house. The, uh, photos are on the floor. Just so you know. I didn't get a chance to pick them up. I'll do that now."

He wouldn't object. Having never viewed the photos, he wasn't about to start looking now. "I'll get the crutches for you."

"I don't need them. I can hobble."

"Humor me. Use the crutches for a few days. Your ankle will heal faster."

"Yes, dear," she cracked. "At least I can still drive."

Yeah, like he'd let her drive with a sprained ankle. He'd figure that one out later, but he might be carting her around until that ankle healed enough for her to ditch the crutches. He hopped out of the truck, grabbed the crutches from the backseat and brought them around to her side. Antsy pants already had her door open, ready to go.

He held the crutches up while she slid off the seat, balancing on one foot. "Do you feel comfortable on these?"

"They're fine. If it's clear of gas, I'll be in the house."

"How are you gonna get to the floor?"

She shrugged. "I'll sit on the couch and lean. You worry too much."

"Wha, wha," he said, hanging on to her as she moved across the walkway to the steps. "Hold up. Let me check inside."

The front door was still open—nothing to steal in there but old furniture—and he stuck his head in. No gas that he could detect. He hopped back down the steps. "It's good. Just don't stay in there too long. Get your stuff and get out."

He made sure she got inside then walked around the side of the house where he found a middle-aged guy wearing a neon orange vest with the gas company logo on the back.

"I'm Brent Thompson."

The guy checked a work order that he'd shoved in his back pocket. "You're the owner?"

"Yes."

Technically, his father owned it, but—yeah—not going there.

"I found your problem in the basement." He pointed to the rear of the house where the only entrance to the basement was an exterior door with a broken lock he hadn't gotten around to fixing yet. "It's the furnace. The flexible line leading from the furnace disintegrated. Must be pretty old."

At least twenty-three years. Brent had kept up with basic maintenance on the house, but the furnace? He couldn't remember the last time he'd checked that. Last year maybe, when he'd changed the filter. "Do I need an HVAC repair?"

"Nah. I took care of it. I'm checking a few other things while I'm here, but I think that's the only issue."

That would be welcome news considering his budget couldn't stretch for a repairman. Maintaining two households meant juggling funds. A lot. "Thanks. I'll be inside. Let me know if you need anything."

Inside, he found Jenna on the living room floor studying photos stacked on her lap. If he hadn't shown up earlier than expected, she could be dead right now. Or at least hospitalized.

And he'd have found her. In almost the exact spot where his mother's body had been.

His chest hitched and he rubbed it, digging his fingers in as he pictured shoving that ache down. Down, down, down.

Jenna covered the photos with another file and glanced up. "I'm fine. I couldn't bend with the crutches so I slid down the arm of the couch. It wasn't pretty, but I managed."

"I would have helped you."

"You were busy."

He smiled and then pointed to her lap, letting her know he knew she'd hidden the photos from him. "Thank you."

"You're welcome. How's everything with the gas company?"

He glanced around the room, imagined walking in here and finding yet another woman he cared about on the floor, and that damned hitch in his chest happened again. "How long were you in here before I arrived?"

"Forty-five minutes. Why?"

"Did you see anyone outside?"

"No. But the drapes were closed and I locked the front door. Safety first, you know."

Something wasn't right. He hires an investigator to help him and suddenly, with the investigator in the house, there's a gas leak. Didn't strike him as a coincidence.

"Brent?"

"From now on, I don't want you coming here alone."

She drew her eyebrows together. "Why?"

"Because you were out here alone and there was a gas leak."

"And?"

Miss Illinois was not this dense. Not by a long shot. "It doesn't seem off to you? Like someone doesn't want you in this house."

"Oh, come on. This was a freak thing."

"A freak thing that happened when you were here alone

trying to find a murderer. What are the chances of that? I'd say not good. I'm done talking about it."

She sat on the floor staring up at him, her jean clad legs flat in front of her. "First of all, can you squat down before I get whiplash? Either that or hand me those crutches so I can get up."

He squatted. "There's no discussion. You're not coming here alone."

She shook her head and gave him the you-foolish-boy look. "That'll slow things down, don't you think?"

"Call it collateral damage. I'll live with it."

She scooped up the items on her lap and smacked them against her leg. "I'll pay more attention next time. Even if someone cut that gas line—which I doubt— if I'd opened the drapes, I'd have seen someone outside and could have called for help. I was careless. That's all. Next time I'll open the drapes."

"I don't care."

"Brent! I have a job to do and not being allowed in here will impede that."

Now I'm done squatting. He stood, purposely looming over her because—yeah—he was about to lose this battle and any position of power would do right now. For added effect, he crossed his arms.

"If I showed up later, this could have ended differently."

Now they were getting to the nasty core and his throat burned clear down to his stomach. Dammit. He scratched his head with both hands, really digging in and feeling the pressure. Sexy Jenna Hayward had managed to crack open that long-locked door. He paced the floor, threw open the drapes and stared out. If she pursued this, he was toast. *Let it go.*

"Forget it," he said.

Please. Forget it.

"So, that's what this is about?"

"You're not coming here alone. End of it."

She smacked the photos on the floor. "This may shock you, but that doesn't work for me. You don't get to order me around and expect me to fall in line."

Forget letting it go. The woman never gave up. He spun back to her, jabbed his finger at her. "I don't care what works for you. You're not coming here by yourself."

"Well, *that'll* allow me to get a lot done on your case. Bravo!"

Most annoying woman ever.

As Brent contemplated the many ways he could lose his mind, she picked up one of the crutches and tried to lever off the floor. He took two steps before she banged the crutch against the scarred wood, the sound echoing and bouncing off the walls. "Don't help me. I'm mad at you. You're being pig-headed, and I hate that."

Pig-headed? He'd give her pig-headed. "I'll stand here and watch, then."

Hell, he'd even hum while she struggled to get up. Then, when she finally asked for his help, he'd prove to her she should listen.

He watched as she rolled to her knees, crawled to the couch and dragged the crutches upright. Damned stubborn woman. That acid in his stomach continued frying him. Eventually, using the couch for leverage, she got to her feet and rested on the crutches, staring at him with those unrelenting eyes. She wanted answers. Probably deserved them. But he wasn't going there. Not with her.

Finally, she shook her head. "Are you going to tell me what this is really about?"

Stubborn woman. "No."

"So when my boss asks me how it's going, I'll just tell her that you refuse to let me do my job. That'll go over well considering my firm is doing this pro bono. Nothing like wasting the resources of Chicago's top law firm."

That cracked it. More than cracked it. An explosion of energy shot from his feet straight to his brain. He bent at the waist, breathed in and his eyes throbbed. *Boom, boom, boom.* The pressure might blow his skull apart and he knew it, knew it would be this way. He'd spent his life avoiding this nonsense, avoiding unleashing a storm that would rip this blasted house apart. Well, hell, maybe he needed to unleash it. Why not? She wanted him to talk, he'd talk. He'd do more than that, he'd let her know exactly how he felt. He stepped closer, dipped his head and made direct eye contact.

Keeping his voice low and controlled, hoping she'd finally get the damned point, he said, "I think someone cut that gas line hoping you'd die."

Chapter Five

Jenna opened her mouth, then stopped. As much as she wanted to rail on him, the smarter, wiser Jenna took hold. This man had spent most of his life coping with trauma he'd been unable to find relief from. Now he stood in front of her as if he'd like her to vaporize. Just be gone. Everything about him—the stiff posture, the locked jaw and heavy breathing—all of it screamed anger and hurt and confusion.

"What?" he said, his tone dripping sarcasm. "No snappy comeback?"

She gripped the crutches tighter, willing herself not to take the bait. That's what he wanted. To redirect this conversation. Make it about her and not him and the emotional disaster living inside him. "No, Brent. No snappy comeback." He watched her for a second. *Yeah, big boy, I'm not giving you what you want.* "This isn't my fault. I didn't think about you walking in here and finding me…" She circled the crutch on the floor, but couldn't say it. "I'm sorry for that. But don't bait me into a fight because you're redirecting your anger."

"More psychobabble?"

Oh, he was pushing it. "I don't think someone cut that gas line. It was an accident."

"Ever consider someone might be following you?"

"No. I'm an investigator and these roads are quiet. You don't think I'd have noticed someone following me?"

Brent shook his head. "I'm not arguing with you about this. It's done."

"If you don't want me alone, fine, but with your schedule, you won't be able to pick up and go when I need to. We need a compromise."

Yes. That was it. Bring it back to the case and solving it. From his spot, he eyed her. "What do you propose?"

"I either bring someone with me or have a member of your family here. I can call ahead and make sure they're home, and they can come over with me. That way, I won't be alone and I can still get something done. In fact, Jamie gave me her cell number today. I'm sure she won't mind."

He turned back to the window and shoved the drapes aside. Dust particles flew, but he ignored them and rested one arm along the edge of the frame to stare out. Obviously, he didn't like her compromise but at least he wasn't yelling anymore.

Maneuvering the crutches, she hopped over to him and settled against the wall. "Just think about it. Please."

He rested the side of his face against his arm and dropped into a long, fitful silence. She didn't know what to do. Offer comfort? Stay quiet? Touch him? Don't touch him? What? After a minute that should have been an hour, he lifted his head and focused on her face. His gaze locked with hers and there it was, that heat, that enormous energy that made her think about all the ways she'd like Brent Thompson to be in her life. Maybe he worried too much, but when he went into protection mode, she couldn't help admire him.

"I am thinking about it," he said. "I'd have to talk to my family. I'm not sure how involved they want to be. This is my obsession. Not theirs."

She hooked her hand around his thick biceps, flexed her fingers and shifted closer. *No.* Getting too close wouldn't do either of them any good. She let go of him and instantly mourned the loss. "We can always ask the sheriff."

He shrugged and stared back out the window. "That'd work, I guess. We'd both get what we need."

Had he ever had a day when he'd completely gotten what he needed? Somehow Jenna didn't think so. Not as long as his mother's killer was free.

Boosting off the wall, he faced her, gesturing to the photos and the file she'd left on the floor. "Anything jump out at you?"

For now, she'd let him drop the subject. Emotionally, she was strung out. His exhaustion would be triple hers. So she'd give him what he wanted and return to the puzzle that was his mother's death. As twisted as it seemed, that was apparently Brent's comfort zone.

"I still need to run through all the timelines and talk to that druggie guy you said lived across town. So far, everything your family has told me is consistent with what you've said. And the reports. The druggie is the only one I can't verify a timeline on. Well, and your dad, but Jamie said she saw when your dad pulled in that night and he went crazy. I don't know why I feel this, but I don't think he did it. Can't rule him out, though. I'll need to talk to him."

Brent let out a long breath. "I know. I can give you the last number I had for him, but it's been years. He could be in the wind again."

"I'll find him. For now, let's find this druggie. We'll ask the sheriff to pull any reports of home-invasion incidents from that time. Particularly in surrounding areas. You never know. Something could be related."

"I did that."

"And?"

"Dead end. But I have copies of all the reports at my place. I can give them to you. Fresh eyes, remember?"

She smiled. "I remember. Never hurts to look. I'd also

like to meet with some crime-scene people I know and show them the photos. We need to identify the murder weapon. Or at least get an idea of what it could have been. It might lead us somewhere."

Jenna had helped on a case the prior year where their defendant was accused of killing his brother. He denied it, but their defendant was an avid bowler with plenty of tournament wins. Unfortunately for Penny, that victory wound up going to the prosecution when they found DNA on the base of one of the defendant's trophies—the murder weapon.

Heels clomped against the porch boards and Jenna angled back to find Brent's aunt in the doorway. Sylvie's mouth dropped open. "What on earth is she doing on crutches?"

"She sprained her ankle," Brent said.

"The crutches are a precaution. Your nephew is quite stubborn when he wants to be."

"Oh, honey," Sylvie said, "I could have told you that."

"Aunt Sylvie, don't start. The crutches are a good idea."

Jenna grinned up at him. He simply refused to back down. This was probably the thing that had kept him going on his mother's case all these years.

He tweaked her nose. A nice thing after the blowup they'd just had. At least he didn't hold on to arguments.

"Stop looking at me like that." He smiled down at her. "You all set here? I can run you home in your car and get a lift back with Camille and her husband when they drive out for dinner tonight. I'll drive my car home later."

Right. The family dinner his aunt had guilted him into. But she was not going to have him spending half his day running back and forth.

"That's crazy. My driving foot is fine."

"I know, but it's a long drive. I'd rather take you."

Again they were going to fight? Jenna closed her eyes. A nap would do her some good. "No."

"Yes."

"Or," his aunt said, "the two of you could stop this nonsense and Jenna will stay for dinner. Then you drive her car home, Camille drives yours and Doug drives theirs. Problem solved. We're done here."

This bossy thing must be a family trait. "I don't want to intrude."

"You're not intruding," Brent and his aunt both said. He looked at Sylvie and laughed. "Good one."

"Besides," his aunt said, "it's almost three o'clock. By the time he drives you home and they get back here—because, let's face it, Camille has never been on time a day in her life—my dinner will be ruined. If you stay, I'll get extra time with Brent. I love that idea." Not giving Jenna an inch to argue, the older woman spun to the door. "It's all settled. I'll go to church in the morning, so just pop over to the house when you're done here."

After his aunt left, Jenna flopped out her bottom lip. "Wow."

"Welcome to my life, babe."

"She's downright scary."

He laughed. "Sometimes. But here we are and we've got time to kill. Let's run through your timelines."

JENNA WAS GONE.

The dinner dishes had been cleared and the aroma of his aunt's high-octane coffee drifted into the nook of a dining room where Brent sat with Camille and Jamie discussing everyone's plans for the holidays. Camille and Doug would be gone for Thanksgiving but home for Christmas. Brent, as usual, would either be working—he liked to give the married guys the holidays off—or at his aunt's. No big mystery. Jamie would spend Thanksgiving with her husband's family downstate. Her kids didn't get to see the other set of grandparents often, so they spent the long weekend with them. They'd be back for Christmas, though.

Nope, the only mystery right now was where Jenna had disappeared to. Brent stood and tapped the table. "Be right back."

Camille glanced up, her blue eyes so big and round that it instantly brought him back to childhood and, worse, the teenage years when he'd spent too much time scaring off horny boys. With his father checked out, all of it had fallen on Brent. Someone had to protect Camille, and Brent had never minded watching out for his little sister. Still didn't.

As his sister matured, her looks had changed. Her cheekbones had sharpened and she'd cut her normally long light brown hair to chin length. When she'd done that, her resemblance to their mother had knocked Brent sideways. He couldn't tell Camille, but every time he looked at her, he thought of their mother.

"Where are *you* going?" Camille asked.

"Kitchen. Our guest has gone AWOL."

"You're trying to steal cookies."

He cracked a smile. "Since I'm in the kitchen…"

"Check the cabinet," Jamie said. "I dropped off the pies and a batch of your favorites this morning."

"The chocolate chip? With the macadamias?"

"Yep."

"I love you."

"I know you do, cuz."

He snapped his fingers and spun back in Jamie's direction. "Hey, when you left this morning, did you see anyone?"

"Where?"

"By the house."

She drew in her eyebrows. "Well, there were a few cars on the road, but it's Saturday. People were heading into town. Why?"

"Just curious."

But from the looks of Jamie's hard stare, she wasn't buying it. "Brent, what are you up to?"

Time to bolt. "Nothing. I was curious."

Making his getaway, he strode into the size-impaired kitchen and squeezed between the table and cabinets where his aunt unwrapped two pies.

Brent went straight for the cookie cabinet.

"They're on the table." Aunt Sylvie pointed over her shoulder. "I took them out for you."

There they sat, a good two dozen of his favorite cookies that Aunt Sylvie had taught Jamie how to make. He bent low, kissed his aunt's cheek. "You two are the best."

One thing about his cousin and his aunt, when he was around, they made his favorite foods. How he'd have gotten through his adolescence without their female nurturing and guidance, he'd thankfully never have to know.

"Did you see Jenna?"

"Your uncle said something about a fire. Check out back."

Again with the fire pit? "He's obsessed with that thing."

She sighed. "Don't I know it? He's been this way for years. Did you see he rebuilt it?"

This would be no less than the third time. "Get out."

"He changed out the bricks. Got some fancy ones he picked up in Kentucky."

His uncle was a long-haul trucker who picked up all sorts of junk while on the road. One year he'd come home with enough fireworks to last three years. Another time it had been folding chairs that he'd bought at wholesale prices and resold to townspeople, making a nice profit along the way. When it came to his family, his uncle always made ends meet. No matter what, his family came first.

Brent grabbed three cookies off the plate. "I'm checking out the fire pit."

"Two cookies, Brent. Save room for pie."

"Whoops. Already touched the third one. Have to take it now." Knowing her kill zone, he grinned. "Isn't that what you always told me?"

"Don't sass me." She shooed him from the cookies. "Go."

He gave her a backward wave, pushed open the storm door and found his uncle sitting across from a blanket-wrapped Jenna in front of a roaring fire. A cool wind blew the smell of burning timber toward him and he breathed in. Nice. In the two hours he'd been inside, the temperature had dropped a good ten degrees. The cooler air smacked at his cheeks. He'd left his jacket inside so his long-sleeved T-shirt would have to do. "Hey, nice fire pit."

"Picked up the bricks a couple of weeks ago. Home improvement store going out of business. Helluva deal."

To Brent, they just looked like bricks. He grabbed one of the aluminum patio chairs and, hoping to hell the thing would hold him, set it next to Jenna's. She'd propped her foot up on a cinder block that had been sitting in the yard for ten years.

"How's the ankle?"

"It's okay. Better now that it's propped up."

"That cinder block is good for something at least."

"Don't make fun of my cinder block," Uncle Herb shot back. "She's got her foot up on it, doesn't she?"

Jenna made a hissing sound. "Got you there, big boy."

At that, Brent made the mistake of looking at her and—*pow*—there it was again, that crazy feeling he got in his chest every time she came within five feet of him. And with the heat from the fire, the flames lighting up her face and shining off her long dark hair, she was nothing short of movie-star stunning. Their gazes held and, well, truth of it was, they stunk at this no-flirting thing. He knew it, his erection knew it and apparently his uncle also knew it, because Herb cleared his throat and made some lame excuse to go inside.

Brent watched him go, suddenly not sad to be alone with Jenna in front of a fire. "Coffee is almost ready. Then we'll head out."

"No rush."

"Camille likes to get out fast." He broke the amazing eye contact and studied the conjoined yards where all the open space had provided plenty of running room when he was a kid. "She's never said it, but being here throws her."

"It's understandable. I'm not family and knowing what happened next door throws *me*."

A hunk of wood in the fire snapped and they sat in silence while it crackled and broke apart. Jenna set her foot on the ground and shifted to him. "Can you get me the contact information for that other suspect? I'd like to check him out tomorrow."

"I have it at home. If you can wait until afternoon, I'll drive you. He lives about an hour from here."

"Do you have time for that?"

"Yeah. It's Sunday. Unless something comes up, I'm off. I've got a game with a bunch of guys in the morning, but we're usually done by eleven."

"That sounds fun."

"It is fun. I miss football."

"Maybe I'll come watch. Then we can go right from there. Unless it's a guy thing."

"Not at all. Some of the guys bring their kids. You can be my plus one."

Jenna sighed. "I hate that plus-one thing. And right now it feels like everyone is getting married or having some kind of function, and I keep getting these invitations with Jenna Hayward and guest."

He knew that feeling. "Annoying, isn't it?"

"Thank you! I know people are being nice, in case

there's someone I want to bring, but it's like a pressure thing. I know I'm crazy, but that's how it feels."

"It's not crazy." He jerked his thumb at the door. "I get it all the time from the crew inside. *When are you getting married? Who are you dating? I met a nice girl at the market.* It never ends."

Between his hours on the job and his mom's case, he didn't have time to date. All he had were two hours on Sunday when he played football to work off the damned stress of his life. He considered that a mental-health necessity. Football was the release valve. Well, sex too, but since he wasn't getting too much of that lately, football would have to do.

"I never get that from my family. I have four brothers, though, and a father who cleans his gun when I bring dates around."

Brent laughed. "That'll be me one day."

"I think my father and brothers would be happy if I joined a convent. They've hated all my boyfriends."

"They hate them because they love you. I hated Doug, too. And he's the nicest guy I know. I just didn't want him having sex with my sister. Hell, they're married and I still don't want him having sex with her. Ew."

Jenna reached over and poked him, her long nail digging into his arm before she backed away again. "See, I love that about *you*, but I hate it about my family."

"It's what brothers do. I've always taken care of Camille. She lost her mom."

"So did you."

"Yeah, but she's a girl and girls need a mom."

"So do boys."

He waggled his hand at her. Enough said on that front. "Tomorrow, I'll pick you up about 8:30 a.m. We'll go to my game and then head out to see one Terrence Jeffries. I'll need a shower before, but I'll buy you lunch while you wait."

"It'll give me time to study your notes. Do you think there's anything there?"

If there was, he couldn't find it. "Jeffries says he was home alone that night."

"What's your gut saying?"

"My gut says it's not him. I can't go by that, though. This is my mother. I second-guess everything."

"You're too close to it."

"That's why I have you."

Again, she leaned over, but this time touched his knee. "I'll do whatever I have to. I wanted this before, but after spending time with you and your family, my reasons are different. You all need closure. I want to help you get it."

He stared down at her hand on his knee and his pulse went ballistic. Off-the-charts ballistic. Not to mention the erection he was sporting. Female friends casually touched him all the time. This, right here, the way his body responded? It had been months since he'd felt that. Damn, he needed sex. And suddenly, his typical one-nighters that got the job done—the means to an end—wouldn't do.

He'd been thinking about Jenna Hayward in a less than gentlemanly way since the day he'd met her. And something told him if he pursued it, they'd both be willing participants.

But they'd agreed no funny stuff.

At least until her work on his mother's case was over.

Have to wait. For now. He grabbed her hand, gave it a gentle squeeze, then stood. "We should head inside."

Scooping her crutches off the ground, he held them with one hand and extended his other to help her up.

"Thank you."

He set the crutches in front of her. "You good here?"

"Yep."

He waved her ahead of him, but she stopped. "What?"

"You're always taking care of people. Makes me wonder who takes care of you."

Once again. *Pow.* Right in the chest. She hobbled to the door and waited for him to open it while he tried to string together a sentence. He got there, set his hand on the knob, but didn't open it. "I don't think about it."

"I know. Maybe, when this is over, we can change that."

Chapter Six

The next morning, after watching Brent and his over-amped friends nearly kill each other on a football field, Jenna rode shotgun to pay a surprise visit to Terrence Jeffries. Who knew if he'd be home, but she couldn't worry about that. One thing she didn't want was to alert him that they were coming so he could take off. If he wound up not being home, they'd wait. And wait a little more until he arrived.

Brent merged his SUV onto the tollway and hit the gas. Traffic was light and apparently that worked for Brent because he set the cruise control and let his fingers do the driving.

Jenna turned sideways to face him. "So, you maniacs play that hard every Sunday and no one winds up in a hospital?"

"Sometimes. But that's football."

"I mean, when you said football, I was thinking flag or touch. You boys were in full pads."

"Yeah. We're all ex college or high-school players who miss the adrenaline rush."

"That's insanity."

He made a *pffting* sound. "That's stress relief."

Oh, brilliant. "Of course. You look at the guy across from you and then slam him to the ground. And then, for kicks, he does it back."

He glanced at her and grinned. "What's your point?"

"I guess I don't have one."

Except, as much as the roughness made her wince, there was something rather delicious about seeing Brent Thompson in his tight football pants, tearing his way through a defensive line to their quarterback. Simple fact: this man possessed an uncontainable hotness. The scarf around her neck—a pretty yellow one her mom had given her— became too much and she tugged on it, letting air hit her neck. Brent shifted his grip on the steering wheel and she studied his long fingers. Talented fingers. Probably in more ways than one.

Oh, boy. She loosened the scarf a little more. This line of thinking wouldn't serve either one of them. Not after that moment by the fire pit last night when she seriously wanted to jump him. She faced front again and dug in her briefcase for a file.

"Terrence Jeffries. Have you ever questioned him?"

"Me personally? No. I've given the sheriff questions, though, and he's spoken to him many times. He's good at talking his way around an interview, which is amazing considering he's been stoned for thirty years."

"Still, huh?"

Brent shrugged. "As far as I know."

"Okay. I'm going in there playing the new-girl card. I'll tell him I'm new on the case and just wanted to hear from him where he was that night. Maybe he'll slip up."

"I'll wait outside. My presence won't help you."

"He doesn't like you?"

"He knows he's a suspect in my mother's murder. That alone makes him not like me."

She held up the file and flicked it. "Good point."

"I'll be outside if you need me."

"I know you will."

Seventy-five long miles later, Brent parked in front of

a faded white, broken-down cottage. A Jeep with rusted wheels sat in the tiny driveway. Jenna took that as a good sign.

"Nice place."

"He invests his money in drugs."

Leaving the crutches in the car, Jenna limped to the front door with Brent on her heels. He stopped at the bottom of the steps leading to the stone porch. "I don't understand why you won't use crutches."

"I am using them. Just not right now."

He shook his head. "Whatever. I'll be right here."

"I'll holler if I need you."

"Last time I saw this guy he weighed about ninety pounds. Even with a bum ankle, you could take him."

She knocked on the door and faced front so Mr. Jeffries would get a face full of Jenna and not Brent standing at the base of the stairs. She turned back to him. "Maybe you should scoot to the side so he doesn't see you. At least until I get in there."

"Nope. He needs to know you're not alone."

"I'll be fine."

"And I'll be right here."

The front door swung open and a tall, thin man with gray—literally—skin stood there. What was left of his hair stuck up on one side, and a half-smoked cigarette hung from his mouth. The notes in the evidence file said he'd been twenty-two when the murder occurred. Jeffries looked a whole lot older than forty-five, but a life of drugs did that to a body. Tore it down, weakened and aged it.

Time to put the Miss Illinois Runner-Up smile to work. "Hello. I'm Jenna Hayward."

He gave her the standard once-over, checking her out from head to toe. After Brent's comment the other day about not selling herself short with revealing clothing, she'd opted to test his theory and went with jeans, a T-shirt and a blazer. Even so, the look Jeffries gave her spoke volumes about where his mind had gone. Nothing unusual there. At least until he spotted Brent at the base of the stairs.

"Oh, come on, man," he said. "I keep telling you I didn't hurt your mother."

Needing to refocus Jeffries, Jenna took two steps sideways and blocked his view of Brent. "I'm an investigator helping out with the investigation into Mrs. Thompson's death. Your name is in the file."

"Yeah, because they think I did it. And I keep saying I didn't."

"Which is why I'd like to ask you a few questions. To see if we can rule you out."

He craned his neck to see Brent.

"He'll wait right there," Jenna said. "I'm the only one talking to you."

"Are you a cop? My lawyer says I shouldn't talk to cops without him."

A smart man, your lawyer. "I'm not a cop. As I said, I'm a private investigator. I work for a law firm, and we're helping with the investigation." That's all she'd give him. If he chose to talk to her and she discovered something to turn over to police, it was still his choice to speak with her. Even if it was hearsay, information communicated by someone else and not verifiable, a smart prosecutor could find a way to make it admissible. Jenna waited while Jeffries glanced at Brent and then back to her.

"I need to call my lawyer." He stepped back. "You can come in if you want. Or stand there. I don't care."

He spun away from her, leaving the front door open. Oh, she was going in. If nothing else, simply to eavesdrop on the conversation with his lawyer. "If you don't mind, I'll step in. It's rather windy out here."

"Leave the door open," Brent said from the bottom of the steps.

She glanced back at him, gave him a discreet thumbs-up, but he climbed the two steps and leaned against the porch pole, keeping her in sight.

Inside, the living room was a small, perfectly square room with a twenty-inch television sitting on a wooden folding tray. Across from it were a patched plaid sofa that had to be someone's great-grandma's and an end table with a cheap ceramic lamp. Above the sofa two shelves held what looked like sports memorabilia. Interesting. Jenna peeked down the hall where Jeffries's voice drifted from another room. Bedroom maybe.

Knowing Brent watched, she jerked her head toward the wall and then wandered to where the collection of sports items—broken bats, a deflated football, a yellow flag, a signed ball—gathered dust. Next to the broken bat was a hunk of cement. She snapped photos of the items. Once she was through, she glanced down the hall. No sign of Jeffries. Good, because she wanted a closer look at the cement. Using her scarf as a glove, she pulled it down and studied it for signs of dried blood. Twenty-three years later, who knew if it might still be possible, but she'd learned to note everything. She set it on the floor and took pictures from different angles. Couldn't hurt to compare the shape to the crime scene photos of the wounds on Brent's mother.

A long shot at best. This would be one dumb killer to leave a murder weapon out in the open. She placed the items back in their original positions on the shelf. The dust was disturbed, but hopefully she'd be gone by the time he noticed. If not, she'd talk her way out of it. A little eye-batting and smiling could take a girl anywhere.

Jeffries shuffled back to her, his head down. "My lawyer's service can't find him. They found his partner, and he said I shouldn't talk to anyone without a lawyer. We should set up an appointment."

Of course they should. Jenna dug into her purse. "That

would be fine. As I said, I'm just verifying a few things. Here's my card. Have your lawyer contact me."

He took the card. "We'll call you."

Liar. But if they didn't, she'd come back. And she'd keep coming back—and calling—until he agreed to talk to her. "Great."

She held her hand out and he shook it. "She was a nice lady. I didn't do it."

"Then you won't mind answering my questions. With your lawyer."

STANDING OUTSIDE TERRENCE JEFFRIES'S house was not on Brent's list of favorite things to do. Ideally, assuming the guy was the murderer who'd ripped Brent's life away, Brent wanted to crush his skull. Make the guy feel what Brent's mother had while blood had poured out of her. When she'd known her children would find her body.

But if the man was innocent, that skull bashing would be a problem. Thus, he stayed away from Terrence Jeffries. Too many conflicting emotions. Too much anger.

Too much pain.

Hearing Jenna say goodbye to Jeffries, Brent boosted off the porch pole and walked down the steps to wait for her.

She exited the house, pulled the door closed and hobbled toward him, her lush body moving as fast as her bum ankle would let her.

"Let's go. I've got photos to print and compare to the crime-scene ones."

Years of dead ends had taught him to keep his hopes in check, but the excitement in her eyes, the energy coming off her, she had something. "What photos? You found something?"

She grabbed his forearm and dragged him to the car. "I'll show you in the car. He's got all sorts of sports memorabilia. Bats, balls, that kind of stuff. But he also has a hunk of cement. I don't know what it is, but I snapped pictures."

Ah, damn. Here she was all pumped about her discovery and he'd have to wreck it. They reached his SUV and Brent opened the door, letting her slide in before propping his arm on the door frame.

"What?" Jenna said.

"The cement. It's a piece of an old baseball stadium that was torn down. In 2008."

Jenna's body deflated. *Boom.* That fast, her excitement faded. He knew the feeling.

She smacked her palms against her thighs. "Well, shoot."

"It came up when the sheriff questioned him a few years ago. There's nothing there."

Jenna grasped the front of his shirt and gently tugged. "I'm so sorry."

"For what?"

"I thought I had something. Now I've dragged you all the way out here to tell you what you already knew."

He leaned in closer and got to eye level with her. "Hey, you're doing exactly what I need you to. Fresh eyes, Jenna. I don't care if we go through every piece of evidence again. You might see something differently, and that's what we need. Don't get down on yourself. We knew going in this wouldn't be easy and you've just started. So lighten up." He grinned. "Don't be a baby."

"Hey!" She twisted his shirt in her fist and he set his hand over hers.

"I was teasing."

Untangling their hands, she played with his fingers, gently stroking each one—*hello, erection*—until she got to his pinky. What the hell had he been thinking putting his hands on her? Huge mistake. Sex-starved as his body was, he should have known better than to reach into that cookie jar. Considering he was a man who liked cookies.

He backed away, straightened up. "This is killing me. We should go."

"Brent…" she began, her voice low and husky.

He'd bet she sounded that way in the morning, when she woke up from a long night in the sack. Immediately, his mind drifted to Jenna—naked—in a bed, legs tangled in sheets. Dammit. Even her voice made him crazy. That may have been his desperate body talking, though.

"No, Jenna. We…we need to go. Before I do something stupid. Something we both agreed wouldn't happen. Let's just…" *Find a room.* "…go. We *need* to go."

Not bothering to look back at Jeffries's house, because, yeah, that would only aggravate him more, Brent made his way around the front of the SUV.

His bum luck that his surefire release of aggravation was sex. Lots of it. And right now, on his day off when he had plenty of time for that particular endeavor, his boiling attraction to Jenna, combined with not being able to crush Terrence Jeffries's skull, might turn him into a maniac.

He hopped into the driver's side and kept his eyes straight ahead. *Don't look at the hot brunette.* Three blocks later, they still sat in silence, but he was in no rush for conversation. Speaking to her, like touching her, would be trouble.

"Are you mad?" she asked.

And didn't that blow the whole not-speaking-to-her plan? "No. I'm…" He slapped his hand over his mouth and dragged it down.

Driving right now would be a mistake. He parked in front of a clump of trees, sat back and organized his thoughts. All the thinking about not having sex only made him want to have sex. Time to have this conversation. But then he'd have to look at her. Always trouble. *Suck it up.*

He released the seat belt, shifted sideways and, yep, that thumping in his chest started right up. "I don't know what

I am. I want things. None of which I can have right now and it's…frustrating."

"I know, but we'll get there."

What? Did she have any idea he was talking about them spending excessive time in a bed? If so, she was pretty damned open about it.

No.

She had to be talking about the case. The no-flirting rule was her brilliant idea and she'd better not be taunting him with the idea they'd eventually get busy. "Uh, I think we're talking about different things."

"No, it'll be fine." She tapped her phone. "Even if these photos aren't of the murder weapons, I can compare them to the pictures of your…the pictures from that night. I'll see if there are any similarities. So this trip wasn't a waste. Don't be frustrated."

Ha. Kicker, that. She thought he was frustrated about the memorabilia. *That* came and went four years ago when the issue first came up.

Unable to resist, he ran his index finger along her cheek. "Honey, I'm not talking about the pictures."

Brent waited for his meaning to penetrate. *One, two…*

"Ooohhh," she said.

And, God, her lips were perfect. Just puffy enough that he'd like to stroke his thumb across the bottom one and feel all that softness. Kissable lips. Exceptionally kissable lips.

And it hurt.

Looking at her had become an exercise in torture. He wanted her. Plain and simple. Whether that want would go away after a few hours of fun—as usually happened—he couldn't be sure. *This* wanting, the one keeping him up at night, felt different. Rooted. Like it wouldn't die with fast, primal sex.

What he didn't need was a woman getting inside his head and staying there. His adult existence had consisted of finding his mother's killer. It was, in fact, all he knew—emotionally speaking. He had no room for anything else. No room. Zero.

When he found the killer, maybe then. Now? No way. He'd blow off his own head trying to juggle a relationship with his mom's case.

But Jenna was looking at him with those amazing blue eyes and that punch to the chest ripped his air away. *Hell with it.*

He kissed her.

Not gently, either. When his lips hit hers, months of need broke loose. She didn't protest. Unless her tongue in his mouth was meant to be a protest. He didn't think so. He leaned in, nipped at the bottom lip he'd just fantasized about and she made a sound, a half groan, half moan low in her throat that set every nerve in his body blazing.

She clamped her hand around the back of his neck and held him there, angled her body closer and—uh—he didn't know what to do with his hands. He knew what he wanted to do, but his brain had stalled. Overload.

So he backed up. *Seriously?*

"Hang on," he said.

But she was focused on his lips and inched closer, moving in for round two. Had she heard him?

"Hey!" he hollered. "Unless you want me to find the nearest hotel, we've got to stop. I can't take it. I'm trying to do the right thing here. The *thing* you said you wanted. Or, in this case, didn't want, but I'm still a *guy* who *likes* sex. A lot. So I'm not sticking with this doing-the-right-thing long. Decide what you want, Jenna, and I'll give it to you."

Finally, her gaze drifted from his lips, up to his eyes. She blinked. Three times.

"I want us to be clear on what we're doing," he continued. "Are we clear?"

With the heat incinerating the car, it took her a second, but she nodded. "We shouldn't tempt ourselves, right?"

"If that's what you want, yes."

"I want both. That's the problem. I want everything."

Ha. Didn't everyone. "Yeah, well, sometimes life sucks."

"That it does." She rested her head back against the seat and stared out the windshield. "I guess we should head home, then."

"I guess we should."

"Brent?"

"What?"

"I think I'm crazy about you."

He jammed the stupid seat belt into the buckle and looked over at her. This was a message he needed to deliver while staring her right in the face. No avoidance.

"That's good, because I think I'm crazy about you, too. But I don't have room for a relationship. I don't want to hurt you. You have to know that. Every relationship I've had has ended badly. I'm too wrapped up in finding my mother's killer. Women always start out admiring that, but when I break dates or bail on functions to chase a lead, they get pissed. I don't blame them, but there's nothing I can do about it. I owe my mother this. I owe my family this. It comes first, always."

"And I'm high-maintenance."

"I didn't say that."

"I know I need a lot of stroking—it's part of me—and you don't have time for stroking."

"I did *not* say that."

And here we go. They weren't even *in* a relationship and they were arguing about the very thing he wanted to avoid.

Jenna held up her hands. "I'm stating the obvious. We don't have to debate it." She reached over and squeezed his arm. "Please. I'm not mad. Honesty shouldn't be a bad thing. The truth we can work with."

Extraordinary woman. He sat back in his seat, blew out a breath. She'd given him the out. Let him off the hook. So why didn't it feel good? The sense of relief he should feel didn't materialize. All he felt was bottled up. Like a pop needing to explode.

"I care about you," he said. "And whatever this is going on with us, I like it. It drives me insane, but I like it. We should wait until you're off my mom's case, though. Not complicate things."

"Of course. By then we'll probably be sick of each other."

Doubtful. Another thing that scared the hell out of him.

Chapter Seven

Jenna pushed through her apartment door and headed straight for her computer. Behind her, Brent trailed along so she waved him to a chair—any chair—while she downloaded the photos.

"Have a seat. If you want something from the kitchen, help yourself."

Because I'm in work mode and not playing hostess.

Despite the cement being ruled out as a murder weapon, there was something tugging at her. She needed to study the photos, compare them to the crime-scene pics and let her brain absorb it all. Sometimes, sitting in the quiet, just *being*, brought everything into sharper focus.

What she was focusing on, she wasn't certain, but it was in there somewhere. And she'd find it. For Brent, for his mom and family, for her career, she'd find it.

She plugged her phone into the laptop, booted up and waited.

From the corner of her eye, she saw Brent drop onto her sofa. He'd avoided the side chair that, when it came to his giant frame, looked like a baby seat.

"What's your plan?" he asked.

"I'm printing the photos to study them." Laptop still cooking, she swiveled her chair toward him. The man was simply huge and with all that hugeness came a sense of…

what? Not comfort because this was her space, her sanctuary that she'd decorated to the tiniest detail. Every muted color, every rich fabric, every quirky photo was her doing. Even the finish on the hardwood was chosen by her. All of it imperfectly coordinated to create a home that from the second she walked into it made her feel warmth and satisfaction and happiness. Her space.

That now had a very large man in it. A very large man she could see in it for a long time to come.

If she let herself.

Brent Thompson was a war zone. That or he was a coward, which she didn't believe. This was the guy so emotionally damaged that he closed in on himself and refused to let anyone new in.

And she wanted him. The guy she couldn't have.

Obviously, that unbelievable kiss had turned her stupid.

Her laptop dinged and she whipped back to it. Better that than thinking about Brent and her and the relationship she'd like to try.

Behind her, she heard him move, and then he was beside her. The soft, clean scent of soap from his earlier shower reached her, somehow settling her.

This was a destructive path. He'd flat out told her so. What was wrong with her? She was a walking cliché of love-the-man-you-can't-have. Well, too bad.

"I'm sorry, but I like having you around."

She kept her eyes on the laptop because looking up at the giant hunk behind her wouldn't help her current level of stupidity.

"That's a bad thing?" he asked.

"No."

"Then why are you apologizing?"

"Because you don't want me to like it." She clicked on

the series of photos to print. "You want me to push you away."

He sighed. "I never said that."

I'm such a cliché. "Ignore me. We had an agreement and I'm blowing it. I don't want that."

Humming noises came from the printer and she rolled her chair sideways to retrieve the photos. Except he moved with her and squatted beside her, that clean soapy smell right there, in her face, making her want to curl up in him.

"Hey."

Jenna focused on her photos. Underneath all her talk about waiting until the case was over, she knew she was a liar. She enjoyed his company, enjoyed the way he took care of everyone around him, enjoyed that smile he hit her with just before he was about to tease her about something. All of it. She wanted it. Even the damaged parts, because those were the parts—each annoying, heartbreaking component—that made him into *this* man.

"No, Brent."

Slowly, he swiveled her chair to face him, but she kept her gaze down, pretending to study the photos because—darn it—if she looked at him, she'd make a fool of herself.

"We said we'd be honest, right?"

Oh, such a man, throwing her words back at her. Now she *had* to look at him. Or slap him. It was a toss-up as to which would actually happen.

"Yes. I think we're both painfully clear on that. I shouldn't have said anything. It was a statement of fact that has suddenly spun out of my control because—" she threw up her hands "—guess what? I happen to care about you and I don't want to feel like I shouldn't. There. Said it. Now I'm done."

"Whoa! Who's making you feel like you shouldn't?"

"You. Me. Both of us. You don't want a relationship.

That's fine, but it doesn't mean I can't care about you and enjoy your company. If there's one message I've received it is that you *will* walk away. You said it yourself."

Oh, Jenna. So stupid.

He'd told her he'd walk, that he'd leave her, he'd set the stage for his grand exit, yet here she was, wanting what she shouldn't.

"Hang on," he said. "All I asked was if we could wait until you were done working my mother's case. That's all. I need the two areas separate so I don't get distracted and miss something."

"You don't actually believe this garbage you sell yourself, do you?"

He stood, looming over her, and she popped out of her chair, squared off with him even though she barely reached his shoulder.

"What the hell are you talking about?"

"You're so emotionally closed off, you're hollow. Or you like to think you are."

He flinched. Good. At last, an unrehearsed reaction.

"Finally using that psychology degree, huh? Beauty queen turned detective-slash-shrink. Classic, Jenna."

She stepped back, a little stung from the jab. *Wow.* "Now we're getting somewhere."

"Nowhere good. That's for sure."

He grabbed his jacket off the back of the chair and headed for the door. Leaving. Of course. The minute she started dismantling the armor, he wanted to run. Talk about a cliché.

"That's the difference between us," she said. "I see this conversation as an opportunity to talk about the hurt and anger you've bottled up for twenty-three years. You see it as an attack."

He stood in the doorway with his back to her, his jacket

clutched in one hand, his fingers working the fabric. Finally, he glanced back. "What is it you want from me?"

"That's the problem, Brent. I want what you can't give me."

"We talked about this!" he hollered. "You said you were fine with waiting until you were done on this case."

"And I am."

"Then what are we fighting about?"

She folded her arms, checked herself. Focused on not screaming, not falling into the scenario he'd obviously learned to manipulate with other women. Suddenly, she saw it all, could envision him having this argument over and over again, the woman in front of him desperately trying to break through the wall that was Brent. Each time it probably started and ended with the woman asking him to love her and him apologizing. Oh, he was brilliant. As in any football game, he'd figured out the plays that would get him the result he needed.

The one that allowed him to walk away.

Well, she wasn't giving it to him. *Sorry.* "You think this is about me wanting a relationship. It's not."

He gawked. "I'm confused."

"What I want is for you to feel something. Or at least admit you're afraid to."

"Honey," he said, loading her up on the sarcasm as he stepped into the hallway, "you're not getting either."

BRENT HUSTLED DOWN the front steps of the three-flat Jenna lived in on Chicago's west side. A few kids were messing with a soccer ball by one of the huge trees lining the sidewalk. He angled around them as he passed the tightly packed row of houses. He'd parked two blocks down because—yeah—this was Chicago and on-street parking was a challenge.

The walk would do him good. He could stomp his way

down the block to relieve his aggravation. With his luck, he'd blow out a knee. He eased up on the stomping and sucked in a deep breath. Moisture hung in the air and the temperature had dropped into the fifties, but for him, right now, he needed the cool air hitting his lungs. Perfection. He lengthened his stride—ah, to heck with it—he had sneakers on, he'd run the two blocks, get his heart rate up and bust off some anger. Perfect weather for it.

Freaking women. Always hassling him. Every time. If he was honest, it backfired on him. If he wasn't honest, it backfired. Either way, it never worked and the slew of women in his wake could all attest to it.

And now this one. She thought she could get inside his head a different way. Not happening. It all came down to the same thing. They wanted something he couldn't give.

He hit the button on his key ring and hopped into the SUV. Damn, Jenna. He'd thought he would have it made with her. She understood him. At least he thought. Until she hit him with this psyche mumbo jumbo. What the hell was that?

His phone rang. This would be her. Wanting to *talk*. He should just video these episodes and play them for the women who came into his life. He'd call it the warning video.

The phone rang again and he ripped it out of his jacket. "What?"

"Whoa." Male voice. "Your social skills need work."

"Russ?"

Special agent Russ Voight from the FBI's Chicago field office had been the agent on a fraud case involving one of Penny's clients. The same case where Brent had been assigned to provide security for Penny. In a truly bizarre—or maybe not so bizarre—way, Russ and Penny had managed to explore the personal side of their relationship and were currently in talks about an engagement. Well, Penny was talking. Russ was listening. One thing about Russ, he wouldn't be rushed into anything.

At the end of that grueling fraud case, Brent and Russ had found themselves friends. Facing death together had created a bond between them. Not that they talked about it. It just was what it was.

It didn't hurt that they were both rabid fans of any Chicago sports team and occasionally met for beers to take in a game.

"You okay?" Russ asked.

No. "Yeah. I'm good. In the middle of something. What's up?"

"Bears are getting destroyed."

Dammit. Missed the Bears game. Brent fired the engine and flipped to the game on the radio. "That bad?"

"You're not watching? Wise. Save yourself the agony."

"I've been running around with Jenna."

"How's that going?"

"Ha!"

Russ laughed. "Ouch. Bud, that doesn't sound good."

"She's a handful."

"That she is. Usually Jenna being a handful works in Penny's favor. You may have noticed, she never gives up."

Brent noticed. "That's a plus. Most times."

"Dude, what the hell is wrong with you? You sound like a whiny five-year-old."

He *felt* like a whiny five-year-old.

"I don't know." He scrubbed a hand over his face. "Women confuse me. I mean, I'm honest and I get in trouble. If I'm not honest, I get in trouble. I don't understand what the entire female population wants from me."

"You think that makes you special? You're not. None of us know. What happened?"

Brent snorted. Having this conversation with Russ? Please. He'd rather amputate his own toe. "It's stupid."

"Probably."

"Nice. Is this your sensitive side?"

"No. I save that for Penny. I have to keep it in reserve."

At that, Brent laughed. Men were easier to deal with. No hidden messages, no guesswork. If you thought a guy was dumb, you said he was dumb and everyone moved on.

"It shouldn't be this difficult to understand women. I mean, I told her straight away what the deal was."

"Jenna? What *deal*?"

He couldn't tell Russ. Couldn't. Russ would tell Penny, and she'd go ballistic and accuse him, like every other male who looked at a female twice, of being a pig. But he was so mad that if he didn't blow off some of this, he'd explode.

A guy pulled up beside him, pointed at the SUV. *Parking space.* Not happening. Brent knew his temper and driving all churned up like this would not end well. He waved the guy on and cut the engine so it didn't look as if he would be pulling out.

Theoretically, Russ might understand the Jenna situation. He'd gotten involved with Penny during a case and that had to be dicey, considering it was his case and Penny was the defense lawyer.

"Okay. But you need to let me finish. Hear me out and then—"

"You slept with her. You've got to be kidding me."

"No. I just said let me finish."

"When you start like that, where's my mind supposed to go?"

Point there. "I didn't sleep with her, although, that thought hasn't escaped me. I'm not blind. But we've got this…" He waved one hand in the air, searching for the word. "…energy. It's getting in the way."

"I know that energy."

"Exactly. But here I think I'm being a good guy by telling her my personal life doesn't exist until I figure out what happened with my mom, and it blows up on me."

"You said that?"

"In a nice way, yeah."

"Huh," Russ said. "Can't imagine why she's upset."

"Hey, I didn't say it was right, but at least I'm honest. What do these women want from me?"

I want you to feel something. That's what Jenna had said.

"Uh, your time?"

"Which I don't have."

Russ sighed. "Look, don't get agitated, but if this happens a lot—"

"All the time!"

"Then you gotta wonder if it's not you and change your approach."

Brent slammed his hand on the steering wheel. "I'm being honest."

"And I appreciate that. I'm just saying there might be more to this than you want to acknowledge."

Or at least admit you're scared.

Dammit. Every line she'd laid on him was looping in his head. He needed to break that loop. Rip it to pieces. Fast.

"Did I lose you?" Russ asked.

"No. I'm here."

"Jenna's a great girl. Penny loves her. But she needs a certain amount of positive reinforcement. She's at her best when people love her. If you choose to get involved, you'd better be able to give her what she needs. That's how this works. You get what you need. She gets what she needs. With Penny, it's easy. I keep her stocked in white gummy bears and she knows I love her. I just sat through a Bears game sorting gummy bears. If you'd ever asked me if I'd do that, I'd have flattened you. But here I am."

Brent rested his head back and dug his thumb and middle

finger into his eyes. All this talking about not talking wore him out. And he wasn't even close to done with this topic.

"Jenna *is* great. Amazing even. She's the first woman in a long time I think I could actually…" *Love.* No. Not love. Nuh-uh. "I don't know. Something."

"You need to talk to her."

"And say what?"

He knew. Down deep, in those nasty places he didn't dwell on, he knew she terrified him.

"Wha, wha. How the hell should I know? But if you didn't care, you'd have forgotten about it by now. Talk to her."

"Dude!"

"Dude!" Russ hollered back.

Despite his foul mood, Brent smiled. Once again, guys were easy. "I gotta think about how to do this without losing my man card."

Russ laughed. "You do that. I'm coming downtown to meet Penny for dinner. She's running late—shocker, that. Meet me for a beer and we'll talk sports."

That wasn't a bad idea. Sports was a nice, low impact topic that would distract him from all this other emotional nonsense.

Women.

His entire life consisted of either losing them or fighting with them. No wonder he was still single.

Chapter Eight

There had been record-setting trips to Carlisle before, but this one may have been the topper. Forty-three minutes. After his aunt had called him asking why Jenna was in Carlisle without him, Brent decided that was a great question, ditched Russ and the beer he'd been nursing for an hour and headed south. He'd hit the left lane and off he'd gone. He'd love to know what the hell Jenna was doing traipsing through his house with the sheriff. At least she hadn't gone back on her word to not go there alone. That might be the only thing keeping him from blowing his stack.

For a second, he'd considered calling her, but had nixed that. At the time, he wasn't ready for another round of arguing. Still wasn't, but if he concentrated on his mom's case, like he always did, he could keep everything in check.

He swung into the driveway and parked behind the sheriff's cruiser and Jenna's BMW. To his left, Aunt Sylvie had obviously been doing her eagle-eye routine and was now heading toward him. Great. All he wanted was to get inside and see what the hell was going on, and now he had his aunt detaining him.

He met her on the patch of grass between the two houses, and they stood in the dark where the spotlights from both homes didn't quite reach.

"Hi," she said. "You drove too fast."

He kissed her cheek and the scent of cooking meat—dinner—lingered on her, reminding him that he hadn't eaten yet. "Yell at me later. Let me see what's going on inside and I'll update you."

"Do you think they've found something?"

She's worried. Or simply agitated over the sudden activity at her sister's house. He wrapped her in a hug, gave her the good, solid squeeze she loved. "I don't know. Don't get ahead of yourself. Let me see what's what. It could be nothing."

"I'm scared, Brent."

Me, too.

He backed away, held her at arm's length. "I know."

"I don't know if I can take another disappointment."

That, he understood. All too well. "I have a good feeling this time. Maybe we'll get a break and we'll finally let Mom rest." He jerked his head. "Go inside. I'll update you in a few."

Aunt Sylvie glanced up at the house where light seeped through the drapes. A shadow crossed through the slit and Brent's stomach seized.

Combining the activity around the house with the Jenna-torment left his ability to compartmentalize a crumbling mess. He was most definitely coming apart.

Coming apart. Seriously? Was he a crybaby now? All this psychobabble worming around his head might make him crazier than he'd ever be on his own. He tilted up his head, stared at the few twinkling stars and let the quiet night settle his mind.

He closed his eyes and cracked his neck. *Get to work.*

On the porch, he hesitated. Go in? Knock first? His damned house and he was knocking? Not. At the same time, Jenna hadn't told him she'd be coming out. Whether that was because of their argument or because she didn't want him to see what they were doing, he didn't know.

And he didn't like not knowing.

Having her rifle through his life and rip it open was his idea. He'd practically demanded that she be bold and unfiltered, and he'd gotten it. Only, he'd prefer she keep that *unfilteredness* to his mother's case and not his emotional shortcomings. Some things didn't need to be analyzed.

Hell with it. He walked in.

Jenna and the sheriff stood in the middle of the living room where crime-scene photos were spread in a path to the sofa. A flash of white on one of the photos—his mother's pajama top, the one with the pink hearts—caught his eye. Sickness consumed him and he immediately brought his gaze to Jenna. *Close one.* As usual, that punch to the chest hit him. This time it was more of a kick. A solid boot right to his sternum. This woman tore him up. By the time she got done with him, all that compartmentalizing he'd done since the age of five would be shattered.

But never before had he felt that boot to the chest. There were women he'd enjoyed, in all kinds of ways, but none who did this to him. Was that good or bad?

Psychobabble. That's what it was.

Either way, he wanted her.

She hustled over to him, grabbed his jacket sleeve and angled him away from the photos. "Hi."

"What are you doing?"

He calculated the myriad of ways she could answer and anticipated her putting him off, making up excuses, *avoiding* him.

"I'm not sure."

That, he hadn't expected. "Come again?"

She waved her arms. "I know it sounds crazy, but there's something in the photos that's bugging me. I needed to walk through the house again, get it set up the way it was that night and study it."

"Why didn't you call me?"

"You were mad at me."

Had him on that one. The sheriff cleared his throat. *Thank you.* Brent glanced over the top of Jenna's head. "Sheriff, thanks for coming out."

"Sure thing, Brent." He pointed to the door. "I'll give you a second. Holler when you're ready."

Good plan. They didn't need a cheering section. Brent held the door open and closed it after the sheriff walked through.

Puckering her lips, Jenna eyed him, angling her head one way then the other. "Are you still mad at me?"

"I don't know. But guess what? Apparently there's this thing adults do that's called talking, and we should probably do it."

Suddenly, her face lit up and she burst out laughing. "Talking? You?"

Yeah, me. For a second, he stared at her, but her face revealed a whole lot of nothing. Then he leaned over and kissed her. An easy press that warmed his blood but didn't spark like the last kiss, which could have taken down a city. He backed away and ran the pad of his thumb over her bottom lip. Great lips.

"I want to apologize. About before. At your place."

Still didn't fix the problem, but hopefully she'd recognize the step he'd taken. But was recognizing it enough? She deserved more than some broken-down guy with emotional limitations. Most of the women he'd dated had. He was just never willing to give them what they deserved.

"I accept your apology. Thank you."

"I *am* scared."

Oh, damn. He'd said it. *Strong men don't do this.* Needing her out of his space, he retreated a couple of steps.

After the second step back, Jenna followed him, gripped both of his arms and squeezed. "Look at me."

Slowly, he breathed in and looked down at Jenna, concentrating first on her stormy blue eyes that changed with her moods, and then on those perfect lips.

Was she speaking? Her lips were moving, but it all sounded gibberish.

"Did you hear me?"

He shook his head.

She brought her hands up, cupped his face, and her palms were warm and steady and soft and made him think of things he shouldn't necessarily be thinking. Things involving his bed over a long weekend.

"Can you hear me?"

The fog in his head cleared. He nodded.

"I said I don't blame you. You've been through a trauma no one should experience. Especially not a child. I think you've programmed yourself to constantly self-protect. Maybe I'd do the same thing. But eventually, all this self-protecting will backfire. It might be forty years down the road when you're sitting alone on a holiday because you have no family left, but it'll catch up. And that will be ugly. You can either let people in or you can stay closed off. Personally, I think closed off would be lonely."

He brought her hands down, but not wanting to break the contact—*what am I doing?*—held on. "Before a couple of hours ago, I hadn't thought about it. Right or wrong, I'm doing what I know."

"Maybe you should let people help you so you can know something different."

"People do help me."

She jerked her hands, but not enough to break free. "You know what I mean. You have friends and your family, yes. But outside of that you have no interest in opening yourself up to anything but sexual relationships. If that's how you want your life to be, fine. We'll stay friends or business associates or whatever you want to call it, and that'll be that."

"Is that what you want?"

"It's not, but as much as I think your self-preservation theory is a crock, I'm not about to walk into an affair with a man who will slaughter me."

"Exactly why I wanted to be honest about my priorities. This case is my priority."

Finally, she tugged her hands free. "You're not ready for this. We should stick with our original plan until I'm done on your case."

Was she kidding? He'd just emasculated himself in front of her and she was turning tail? "I'm not sure what you want from me."

"Don't make me slap you. You admitted you were scared and I love that. It's a major step. But we're all scared, fella, and I can't handle you falling back on the excuse that you don't have time for a relationship. Tell me you're scared and leave it there. Don't bulldoze me with this no-time theory."

Frustration burned in his gut. This shouldn't have been this hard. "I don't know what to do with the fear."

"You do nothing with it. You—*we*—take it slow. Nobody says we're getting married. We go out. We—hold on now, don't panic—go on dates. Dinner. The movies. Ball games. If it's a disaster, at least we tried. But hey, that's just me. And, since I'm working your mother's case, you don't have to come up with excuses to break our dates. I'll probably break them before you do."

Slow. She'd said it. Not him. Usually he was the *take-it-slow* one. This woman was destroying all of his excuses. Every last one. Son of a gun. He dug his fingers into his forehead and rubbed. At some point, he'd laugh about this. Right now? *No.*

"What's wrong? I'm blowing your theories to bits?"

He laughed. "Pretty much."

"It's not a bad thing."

"Feels like it."

She smiled at him and then tugged on his shirt. "You're not used to it. Relax."

Had he ever done that? Maybe with the guys watching a game, but with women? Never. Always on guard. Waiting for them to want more of what he couldn't give. And then they'd walk away and he'd be fine—A-okay—with it.

The way he felt right now, if Jenna walked away, he'd tackle her, grab her ankles and beg her to stay. Talk about emasculating.

Man, oh, man, his life suddenly got a whole lot more complicated. "Dating, huh?"

"Yes, Brent, dating. It's a concept I know you have problems with."

He rolled his eyes. "Harsh."

She poked him. "I couldn't resist."

"Next time, try. Rome wasn't built in a day."

That cracked her up enough that she snuggled into him, wrapped her arms around his waist and squeezed. "You're a good guy, Brent Thompson."

When it came to relationships, he wasn't convinced of that. For her sake, he hoped it was true. "When we're done doing whatever it is we're doing at my mom's, do you want to have a late dinner with me?"

"Like a date-dinner?"

"Yes, Jenna. A date. I'm asking you on a date. But if you drive me crazy with this, I'm bailing."

"Wow. I was simply clarifying. I'd love to have dinner with you. Thank you."

Step one complete. And he'd survived. "Perfect. Now what the hell are we doing here?"

WHILE BRENT WAITED on the porch, Jenna collected the crime-scene photos she'd spread across the floor.

"What's next?" Sheriff Barnes asked.

The man had been here two hours and the gravelly tone

in his voice had become more prominent. He'd already worked a full day and she was peppering him with questions, forcing him to recall a murder that happened twenty-three years ago. A murder he hadn't been able to solve.

She stacked the last of the photos from the living room and straightened the pile. "Thank you for doing this."

"It's not a problem. You didn't figure out what was bothering you."

No. She hadn't. *Thanks for the reminder.*

"Not yet. But I will. It's here. I just haven't tripped over it yet."

He gestured to the remaining photos stacked on the floor next to her briefcase. "We haven't been through those yet."

"Those are perimeter shots. Some from the morning after, but most from that night."

"We're here. We might as well do it." He swung back and opened the front door where Brent waited on the porch. "You're good."

A few seconds later, Brent entered the house, his big body filling the vast emptiness. This had been his home, a place he should recall happy things, memories of playing and family gatherings, Christmas mornings and birthdays. What did he see when he stepped in here?

One day she'd ask him. Not now. Getting in touch with his feelings wasn't high on his to-do list, and she'd already gotten a win with him admitting his fears about emotional attachments. She wouldn't push it.

At least not yet.

"We're almost done," she said.

Hands in pockets, his go-to stance when he wasn't sure how he felt about a situation, he cocked his head and squinted at the photos in her hand.

She waved the stack. "These are perimeter shots. It won't take long to go through them."

He nodded. "Did you tell the sheriff about your visit to Jeffries's?"

Sheriff Barnes slid his gaze to Brent, then to Jenna. "What?"

"He called his lawyer." She scrunched her nose, thought about the wasted hours. "We're setting up a time to chat."

"I'm not surprised. We've talked to him enough that he panics when he sees us pull up."

"I thought I hit on something with that hunk of cement from his collectibles."

The sheriff smiled, but it was one of those tight-lipped smiles that stunk of failure. "Nothing doing there."

She shrugged. "I snapped some pictures while he was out of the room. If nothing else, it's something to think about."

Along with the bazillion crime scene photos she'd yet to get through. She'd studied all the interior shots, but only a few of the exterior ones. *Exterior.* Sharp, searing stabs blasted the back of her neck. "Oh, wait."

Brent was already in motion, moving toward her. "What?"

Jenna dropped to her knees and fanned the perimeter shots she held, spreading them across the floor. *Where is it? Where is it?* "Come on. I know you're in here."

Squatting next to her, Brent touched her arm. "What are you looking for?"

"I don't know. Something."

There. A photo of the back entrance taken the night of the murder. She studied the photo. Back door closed, folding chairs on the porch. A baseball bat originally thought to be the murder weapon but ruled out. A football and a baseball sat next to it. Next picture. *Where is it?*

Flicking a couple of photos aside, she scanned two others, taken in sequence and then lined them up next to each other. Together they were a complete view of the house.

The entire area had been lit up, probably by spotlights so the crime scene guys could work the area.

"Jenna?"

"Give me a second, Brent."

Go slow. Study each one. Blood stains on the porch? Displaced items? There had to be something. On the photos, she trailed her finger over the steps, and then to the side of the porch where firewood had been stored in an iron rack. "What about the wood? Was that checked?"

"Every piece of it," the sheriff said. "Clean."

"Dammit."

She moved on. Nothing but grass. Except. Wait. On the ground near the side of the porch, the edge of something peeked out. She went back to the stack of photos, snatched the next two pieces to her puzzle, lined them up and found nothing but more grass leading to the driveway. Whatever peeked out wasn't visible in the other photos. Shoot.

Glancing up at the sheriff, she tapped the photo. "Any idea what this is? Was it taken into evidence?"

The sheriff squatted beside Brent, his gaze darting over the photos and, if Jenna guessed right, his mind racing.

"It was dark," he said. "We went back in the morning to make sure we got everything. Whatever that is, I don't remember it."

Jenna hadn't seen anything on the evidence list that resembled this item. If they had it, she'd know. Brent stood tall and she looked up at him. "Any ideas?"

"Let me see that."

She handed him the photo. He analyzed it for a few seconds, clearly his law enforcement brain organizing thoughts and then, like a bomb had exploded, he dropped the picture and bolted. "I think I know what it is."

Chapter Nine

Brent tore down the porch steps as if he was chasing a loose football. *Get there, get there, get there.*

All these years his father had stored those bricks under the house. For what purpose, Brent never knew and never cared. They weren't bothering him, so he left them there. And maybe he was wishing for it, but whatever was in that photo had the faded reddish color of a brick.

In the pitch black, his breathing coming too fast—*control that*—he dropped to his knees, ripping the lattice off the bottom of the porch and sending a few hunks of wood flying. He closed his eyes. Better not to get a chunk of wood lodged there.

After a few seconds, he opened them and adjusted to the blackness. *Need light.* He pulled out his phone, shined the light from the screen. Not enough.

Jenna leaned over the porch rail. "Brent?"

"Flip that light on. I need a flashlight."

Setting his phone down, he tossed the broken lattice aside and pulled off the remaining pieces. *Ow.* He held his finger over the light. A sliver of wood had pricked his skin. At least it wasn't an eye. He tried to fish it loose, but the sliver broke, leaving half still lodged in his finger. He'd get the rest later.

The porch light came on, throwing shadows across the

trees behind Brent. Jenna came around the house, limping a little on that bad ankle—the crutches were where?— and carrying a giant flashlight that had to belong to the sheriff.

"I think it's a brick," Brent said. "In the photo. There's been a stash of them under the porch for years. I saw them last month when I had to fix the lattice."

A sudden sick feeling jabbed at him, turned his stomach inside out. All these years he'd been chasing leads and the murder weapon could have been sitting under the damned porch. No, couldn't be. All those bricks had been checked twenty-three years ago. Unless someone added to the pile after the fact. He let out a huff because—hell—he didn't know what to feel. Useless came to mind. His face grew hot and his head pounded. *Boom, boom, boom.* A swarm of pain and rage and torment devoured his system. *Coming apart.* He banged his hand against the side of the porch. "It's been under my damned porch all this time."

Jenna stepped closer, set her hand on his shoulder. "Brent, hold on."

No. He jumped to his feet, started pacing, just tearing up the ground, wanting to rip something apart because what kind of an idiot has a murder weapon sitting under a porch for twenty-three years and doesn't know it? Dammit. "Twenty-three years. Unbelievable. After the sheriff's office checked the initial stash, I never counted or bothered to check them again. There could be DNA on that thing! After all this time, who knows if there's anything decent left. How stupid am I?"

Jenna threw her hands up. "You are *not* stupid. I got lucky with that photo. Right place, right time. If I hadn't seen that hunk of cement at Jeffries's house, I may not have even caught this. And without you, we wouldn't know the bricks were under the porch."

The sheriff walked up behind Jenna, stowing his cell. "Sorry. Phone call. What's up?"

"Brent thinks there are bricks under the house. What's in that photo might be the edge of one. I don't remember any bricks on the evidence list so if it is a brick, it was missed at the crime scene."

Brent squatted again and shined the light into the general area where he'd remembered the bricks being. There they were. A dozen or so, stacked in even piles. "They're here. I need to crawl under there."

Think like a US marshal. This could be potential evidence. Evidentiary procedure had to be followed. The chain of custody alone could derail a case. It would take time, but each brick would need to be labeled with details about when it was found and who handled it. "I can't do it."

Barnes nodded. "Damn right you can't. If we find a murder weapon under there, the victim's son shouldn't touch it."

"The defense will have a field day," Jenna said.

All of this, he knew. One slipup and the bricks could be inadmissible. Ideally, they needed the State Police to send a crime scene investigator to handle evidence collection and marking.

But they didn't know if this truly was evidence. For all they knew, they had a stack of worthless bricks.

"I'll do it," Barnes said. "I was part of the original investigation, and if it comes down to it, a prosecutor can make that fly. I'll take it to the lab myself to keep the chain of custody intact."

"Perfect," Jenna said. "We have a private lab the firm uses. It'll be quicker."

That'd cost a fortune. A fortune Brent didn't have. Just as he was about to say it, Jenna turned to him. "The firm will cover the cost. Penny told me that early on."

Next time he saw Penny, he wouldn't tease her about how short she was. He wouldn't tease her about anything. Ever again. Well, that might have been pushing it, but for the next while, he'd leave her alone.

At some point, he'd figure out a way to thank her and make her understand how grateful he was. Suddenly, after all the years of no progress, maybe they'd be able to close his mother's case and give his family closure.

Closure.

He despised that word. Wasn't particularly sure he even understood it. One thing he did understand was that when they found his mother's killer, he'd have to find a way to deal with his messed up emotions. Once the killer was found, his goal would be achieved. And after spending his entire adult life—every spare second of every spare minute of every spare hour—studying his mother's case, he'd have to figure out a way to move on.

Barnes turned back. "Let me get gloves out of the car."

While Barnes chased down gloves, Jenna stepped closer. "Are you okay? You're quiet."

"You could be right about the bricks. The color is right."

"That's not what I'm talking about."

Of course it wasn't. She wanted inside his mind again. Maybe soon he'd let her in. Now? He couldn't do it. That storm of emotions already churned, filling his lungs and trapping his air. When it broke through, it would drown him.

"I know." He touched her face, ran his finger down her cheek and over her jaw, and that simple motion—the connection—centered him. "I can't go there. Part of me wants to. It's…" He shook his head. "It's too much."

There. Best he could do. Lame as it was. He just hoped she understood how difficult lame could be.

She went up on tiptoes and—*hey, now*—kissed him. Quick. Probably didn't even qualify as a kiss, but he wouldn't complain. Not when that minor peck told him that she wouldn't bug him about his emotional failings.

The damned kick to the chest happened again, pounding at him as if he was supposed to do something. Whatever *something* was. But when she backed away, he wrapped his hand around her head and held her there, kissing her the way they'd done it earlier. Fast and hard and making sure his intent was clear. He wanted her and—surprise, surprise—it was about more than sex.

If dealing with his pit of emotional garbage scared him, thinking about a *relationship* might give him a coronary.

The crunch of boots on dry leaves sent Jenna leaping backward, but her gaze was on him and a wicked smile met his.

"We'll finish that later." She spun to Barnes, already shifting to work mode. "We can compare the shape of the bricks to the wou—"

She glanced up at him, brought her fingers to her mouth and tapped. Still, she was protecting him. Noble, but a problem.

"Unfiltered, Jenna."

She dropped her hand. "Wound. If we can match the shape of the wound to one of these bricks, we have the murder weapon."

"And possibly DNA," Barnes added.

Could they get that lucky? Brent didn't think so. This exercise, like all the ones before, could be a bust.

Jenna stepped forward, tugged on his shirt and met his gaze. "It's okay to be hopeful. I'm hopeful."

"I know, but…" He waved his hand. "All the disappointments."

Barnes handed them each two pairs of gloves. "You won't be touching anything, but we all wear them. Double 'em up. No chances."

"Yes, sir."

Barnes dropped to his belly. "Here we go. I'll take photos before I bring anything out."

Overhead, a bird chirped and Brent looked up. Wind rattled the almost barren tree branches. Slowly, he walked to the back end of the house, turned and came back. This could be it. A murder weapon. *Don't go there.* Not yet. But…maybe. Jenna watched him. *No talking.* Please. No talking.

After fourteen laps and some serious mind-shredding later, Brent saw Barnes crawl from under the porch. The sheriff, straightened and brushed moist dirt from his clothing. "I got a broken one."

"Ooh," Jenna said. "Let me see."

Stooping low, he grabbed the broken brick from the pile. "Don't touch it."

"I won't. Let's take it inside." She turned to Brent, making hard eye contact in the dark. "I'll compare it to crime-scene photos."

Translation: *I'm going to look at photos of your mother and don't want you to see.*

He could live with that. Even if the waiting might kill him. Then he wouldn't have to live with anything.

She left him standing beside the house, but he strode to where he could see part of the porch and Jenna just inside the front doorway. She held a photo, the overhead light shining down on her. "What is it?"

"I think we've got something."

"What?"

From her spot, she looked down at him. "I had the sheriff line the brick up with the wound on your mom's head. The corner of the brick looks like a match. We could have our murder weapon."

JENNA OPENED THE outer front door of the building and stared into the dimly lit hallway leading to her apartment. Two hours earlier, they'd found that stash of bricks, all of which were now at the lab. Maria, her scientist friend, didn't appreciate being called on a Sunday evening, but as Jenna often did, she talked her way around it.

Even if she now owed Maria a huge favor.

"Everything okay?" Brent asked from behind her.

After the kiss he'd hit her with earlier? No. Everything was not okay. And now he had to go and be a gentleman and walk her to her door. She was no fool and her no-fool self knew his protective instincts ran deep. After that kiss, there was definitely something else running deep.

On both their parts.

She angled back to him. "What are we doing?"

"I don't know about you, but I'm pretending we didn't make an agreement about the…uh…*physical* aspects of our relationship."

He was no fool either. "We said we'd go slow."

"What's your point?"

She laughed. Then to her great horror, stepped inside, waving him in while her brain and body sent conflicting signals. *Do it, don't do it, do it, don't do it.* Her brain may have known what it wanted, but her body was buzzing in a way she'd only felt…well…never. That's what this was. A first. Firsts didn't happen often and she wasn't exactly one to let an opportunity slide by.

"Don't ask me if I'm sure. I'm not. My brain is saying one thing, but my body is definitely saying another. And I like what I'm hearing."

Brent cracked up and the sound of it—the newness and unexpected pleasure of this tormented man lightening up— filled her. Sure, she'd heard him laugh before, but he'd held back, muffled it under the weight of grief. This laugh came right from his belly, and she'd made it happen.

I'm a goner. "Let's go."

She left the front door open and darn near sprinted to her apartment, glancing back to make sure Brent followed. Yep. There he was, marching toward her, his gaze on her as she reached the door and jammed the key in the lock. Or at least tried to. Wrong key. *Shoot.*

"I'm stupid with lust right now." Again he laughed that amazing belly laugh and—oh, my—she wanted to hear that over and over. "Brent Thompson, if you ever fake laugh in front of me again, there will be hell to pay. That's a promise."

Finally, she shoved open the door, reached back and grabbed his jacket, hauling him inside. The timed lamp on the end table had switched on and threw soft shadows across the room. "You promised me a late dinner, by the way."

"We can order."

And even as he said it, he ditched his jacket and tossed it on the chair by the window where she'd forgotten to close the drapes. Forget it. Her plan didn't include the living room anyway. She slid her jacket off and dropped it. Brent inched closer, sending her body into sizzle land.

"Pizza. Later."

"I like pizza."

"Excellent. Follow me."

Walking the narrow hall to her bedroom, she stripped off her shirt, tossed it back to him and he laughed again. "Is this some twisted stripper act? If so, it's working."

Her bra came next and she threw that back as well. A few more feet and they'd be at her bedroom where he'd see her naked from the waist up. Her body had been judged countless times, from all angles in all sorts of outfits. But that was fifteen pounds ago and never naked. Now that extra fifteen pounds spooled into nervous tension and gripped her. *He said he likes my curves.*

She stepped into her darkened bedroom and stopped. When his arm came around her, she didn't flinch, just settled back against him where his erection poked her lower back. Oh. Boy. He dragged his hand up, gently cupping her breast, and heat shot to her core.

"You're beautiful, Jenna."

In all the times and ways people had told her that, it was never more than words simply coming at her. She'd heard it so much, somewhere along the way, it became meaningless. Except those words never sounded like this. So filled with meaning and…and…truth. When Brent said it, her heart opened up and took it in.

And she believed it.

BRENT COULDN'T STAND IT.

All he wanted was to strip Jenna naked and spend the entire night exploring her lush body. Pure torture. When she went for the button on his jeans, he didn't stop her. He also didn't stop her when she shoved them down to his ankles, letting her fingers skitter over his hips—and other places.

If she'd had any doubt about his level of interest, he'd just blown that away. Far away.

He stepped out of his jeans, kicked them to the side and dealt with the condom from his wallet. He ripped his shirt off and stepped forward, nudging her against the bed until she fell backward and scooted to the center. Needing his hands on her, he grabbed her ankle to hold her still, and then dropped next to her.

Lowering himself on top of her, he took a second to let that skin-to-skin heat absorb. Damn, he loved that. Loved that the woman under him was no beanpole and he didn't have to worry about snapping her in two. He kissed her neck, nipped at her chin and smiled when he coaxed a tiny moan from her.

All these months of picturing her naked and sprawled under him, on top of him, beside him—any way he could get her—and it had finally happened. Yeah, he'd take his time. Not rush to the end and that big bang that cleared his mind. This time, he wanted slow, then fast, then slow again. Endless minutes to memorize every place he touched and kissed and nibbled.

With Jenna, that's all he wanted.

Another moan. *She's mine.*

He buried his face near her ear. "I like that sound. Is that what you do when something feels good?"

Slowly, she slid her fingers along his back and—*whap!*—smacked his butt. "I guess it is because what you're doing feels good. *You* feel good."

He nuzzled her ear, trailed kisses along her jaw, anticipating that first second, the ultimate pinnacle of his fantasy when he entered her. Months of thinking about that moment, and here it was. Waiting for him.

Jenna arched against him, prodding him to make a move. To do *something*.

"You don't have to get pushy about it," he said.

"You're teasing me."

"I'm enjoying you. Big difference."

And something he hadn't done in a long time.

"Enjoy me later."

Certain things in life had become clear in the past few days. Jenna being brutally honest was the first. The second was he hadn't laughed enough. Until Jenna, he hadn't laughed nearly enough.

He kissed her again, lingering a second while she hooked her legs around him. He pushed and—*oh, man*—the shock of those first few seconds of being inside her made him gasp. He dropped his head, breathed in and she arched against him, urging him on. Locking her legs, she held on while they moved together in that first-time rhythm that would—if he had any luck—move to second- and third-time rhythm.

Another moan, this one louder, came from Jenna and he moved faster, wanting to hear it again and again and again. So close. He was so close to that edge and hanging on, just ready to go over, but for once not wanting it to end.

Damn, he'd turned into a sissy. *Who cares?* When it came to Jenna, he didn't care.

Her body bucked and she arched up, gasping and—*zap*—his mind fried. He looked down at her, took it all in. The way her mouth tilted up, her long hair spread across the pillow, her closed eyes—*beautiful*—and his world came apart.

Sprawled on top of her, his breaths came out short and shallow. Cripes. He needed to pull himself together. Get control of his mind and body because—hell-to-the-yeah—every Jenna fantasy he'd ever had needed to be explored. Every damn one of them. And he'd do it. Slowly.

She ran her hands over his back in a sweeping motion that if she kept up he'd drop to a dead sleep. "That feels good," he said.

"*You* feel good. I knew you would. Knew it."

"Good," he said. "Because I love you."

Chapter Ten

He *loved* her? He did *not* just say that. Not now, when things had been so perfect. So fun. But no, Brent had to remind her just how emotionally twisted he really was.

As much as she'd fooled herself into thinking they could have a fling, a physical release that would satisfy both their curiosities, she should have known better. She cared too much. About him. About his family. About his mother.

Now he claimed he loved her, and she was just needy enough—and smitten enough—to believe it and get her heart stomped on when his infatuation cooled.

Brent rolled off her, his big body landing precariously on the edge of her queen-size bed. *Need a bigger bed.* Great. Already buying king-size furniture for the king-size man she had no business buying anything for. With his need to close himself off and her need for constant approval, they'd be New Orleans the day after Katrina. One heck of a mess.

But she had yet to respond to his big announcement. What was a girl supposed to do with that? *Thank you? Back at ya?* No.

He rolled to his side, kissed her bare shoulder. "I promised you pizza. I'm starving."

Pizza. Really? She shook her head, smacked her palm against her temple and shook again. Yep. Fully awake. "Um, did I miss something?"

"I said I'm hungry."

"Before that. The thing you said."

He cocked his head, closed one eye. Thinking. *He must be joking.* How could he forget something that important?

"The I-love-you thing," she said. "Did I hear that right?"

Brent laughed and in one quick move was on his feet, dealing with the damned condom and collecting his clothes, all those yummy muscles and hard lines of his body kicking up her pulse.

"You heard it. We don't have to talk about it."

Oh, now she got it. People said all kinds of nutty things during an orgasmic high—not that she'd ever been afflicted with that particular problem. But obviously, Brent had.

And now he needed to backpedal because he was afraid she'd start dropping the "L" word also. *That* made total sense. A weird sense of relief set in and the sudden tension in her shoulders eased.

"It's all right. I just didn't know what I should do."

Brent zipped his jeans, checked that all was in proper order and shoved his T-shirt over his head. "About the fact that I love you? Or that I said it?"

"Uh…both?"

Again, he laughed. "You're funny. You don't need to do anything. I said it. I meant it and we can be done."

"You can take it back."

He gave her an *are-you-on-medication?* look. "Is this third grade? Why would I take it back?"

She grunted—*take a second*—and rolled to the opposite side of the bed where her bathrobe hung from a hook on the wall.

"You know what I mean. We were caught up. It was fun. A great stress reliever. Even if you think you're in love, you're probably not."

Propping his hands on his hips, he stared up at the ceiling and blew air before facing her again. Everything about him, the stiff stance, the squinty eyes, the locked jaw, screamed impatience. Well, excuse her for wanting to clarify. Any woman would.

"Jenna, I know you were a psychology major, but last I checked I know how I feel. I may stink at sharing it, but I know. And I sure as hell don't need you telling me. Thanks for that, though. I'll be in the living room."

Darn it. Knotting the belt on her robe, she followed him down the hallway, his long strides fast and purposeful. Mad again. Too bad. He would not goad her into a fight so he could deflect the subject. No chance. *Snap.* Her brain clicked into gear. How had she not realized that when he didn't like a topic, he picked a fight? The best defense is a good offense. Brilliant.

"Brent, that's not what I meant and you know it."

He stopped, just halted in his spot and stared straight ahead. "What did you mean, then?"

She scooted by and swung to face him. "I was giving you the out, in case you didn't mean it. You just sprung this on me after great sex. What was I supposed to think?"

"You weren't supposed to think I was lying about it. You're the one always on me about talking, so I talked. What, in your experiences with me, makes you think I casually throw that phrase around?"

Big fella had her there. She opened her mouth, thought for a second, got nothing and blew raspberries.

"Okay, well, can we hit the reset button here? I was surprised. And confused. I didn't mean for it to become war."

He squeezed his eyes closed, scrunched his face and dug his hands into his hair. "I'm horrible at this. I've had this…I don't know…thing…for you. For months now. Every time I see you I get this crazy feeling in my chest. I've never had that before. Maybe I got caught up in the moment or whatever, but I don't say things I don't mean."

She waited, desperately hoping some revelation would

hit her. Nope. Nothing. But the panic was there, shooting up her arms and into her neck, making her face hot because she'd had a thing for him, too. Since that first day she'd seen him in Penny's office, they'd simply *clicked*.

Wait. She couldn't do this. Couldn't let herself believe he actually loved her. If she believed it, she'd start to want things. Things like the two of them sharing meals and secrets, grocery shopping, lazy Sunday mornings. A backyard with a swing set. The two of them making a life together.

Worse, she could *feel* it. Those little moments when he smiled at her or teased her. That settled feeling she got when he touched her. All of them firsts. Firsts she hadn't wanted to read too much into.

Until he told her he loved her.

"You don't have to say anything, Jenna. I don't expect that." He shrugged. "Let's see where it goes."

Oh, this had to be a trap she was about to step in. It couldn't be that simple. "I feel it, too. Whatever that something is. I'm not ready to say it, though. It's too important, and when I say it I want to know, without a doubt, what it means."

"It's okay."

"Well, this is crazy. Usually I'm the one needing the positive reinforcement."

He snorted. "Well, it's new territory for me, too. I need to get used to it. Maybe enjoy a relationship for a change. Can we do that?"

Relationships, even good ones, were never easy. Throw in a man with repressed feelings and a needy ex-beauty queen and it might be the worst combo ever. But what if it weren't? What if, in some backward way, they balanced each other?

That might be the biggest and most welcome surprise of her life.

Brent waved a hand in front of her eyes. "Have I turned you to stone? You're not saying anything."

"Yes. We can do that. It will require you to feed me, though."

She reached for the phone, but he brought her into his arms and kissed her. Nothing crazy and definitely lacking the intense heat they'd shared earlier, but these soft, gentle pecks promised more. These were the kisses of coming home at night, leaving in the morning, rushing to do an errand. Those wonderful and comforting everyday kisses she sorely missed.

She backed away, setting her hand on his cheek. "I thought you were starving."

"I am. Just thought it was important to wait on it a sec." He grinned. "Now order my damned pizza, woman."

"That'll be the day."

Still, she ordered the pizza. The extra-extra large. Just in case. She set the phone on the side table, and then glanced at the front windows and the open drapes. Perfect. At street level, in her bathrobe, groping a man. Great show for the neighbors.

She moved closer, grabbed one of the drapes to flick it closed and—*crash!* She spun toward the window and all at once her mistakes hit her. *Other way. Turn. Now.* She swung her head to the right and covered her eyes, protecting them from the prickling shards of flying glass. Something hard and heavy bounced off her shoulder and skidded across her jaw, ripping at the skin before thunking to the floor. Memories of her brothers' teasing—*protect your face, beauty queen*—roared back. *Not-my-face, not-my-face, not-my-face.*

She staggered for a second, her head looping and spinning. Sudden warmth seeped down her cheek. *Please, no blood. What if it's blood? No blood.*

She brought her gaze to Brent, shook her head wildly because—dammit—her life had been spent primping, playing up her looks, using them to get ahead and...*I'm bleeding.* Pathetic, pathetic Jenna. Nausea consumed her and she held her arms out. *Hold on. Hold on.*

"Jenna!"

Brent's voice. Eyes shut, she focused, listened for any sound other than his voice. No shattering glass, no thunking objects, nothing. Safety. She opened her eyes as Brent lunged for her, reaching for his gun while watching the window.

Liquid warmth trickled over her jaw and she lifted her hand.

"Don't," he said. "You're bleeding."

Her face. Bleeding. *How bad, how bad, how bad?* Her looks were everything. Her first foot in any door, her ultimate weapon and now, if the seeping blood was any indication, she had a gash down the side of her face. One that might scar.

Scars meant her mother would stand in front of her, checking every inch of that gash. Normally, she'd beam. *Oh, look how beautiful you are. Perfection.* What would her mother see now? Now she'd mourn perfection. She'd see the marring and the pain would be too much.

"Are you okay?" Brent asked.

Was she? No way to know. "Yes. Go."

He charged for the door. "Call 9-1-1 and lock this door after me."

She nodded, her head bobbing like some dumb waif. "Be careful."

Great. She'd just told a US marshal to be careful. Suddenly, she was his caretaker? He'd *love* that. Not that it mattered because she'd just been hit by—what?—she glanced at the floor and there it was, of all things, a brick.

BRENT HAD HAD ENOUGH. Whatever Jenna thought about that was too damned bad because she was done. Off this case. Now maybe she'd be convinced the gas-line incident wasn't a fluke.

After checking the perimeter around Jenna's house, he hustled down the short hallway leading to her flat and rapped on the door. "It's me. Brent."

The door swung open and there she was, still in her silky bathrobe, holding a washrag to her bleeding cheek. He checked her feet. She'd thrown on his sneakers, probably because they were the closest to her and she didn't want to step in glass. The way he'd torn out of the house, he may have a shard or two in his feet, but right now enough adrenaline flooded his system to numb any pain.

"I called 9-1-1," she said. "Police are on the way. Did you see anything?"

"By the time I got out there, they were gone."

She pointed. "It was a brick."

"I saw it."

And hadn't that been a life-shortening experience? Standing there as all those shards, like airborne ice picks, flew at her. And the brick. That one freaked him out good. His pulse hammered and he locked his teeth together. A few inches higher and that brick would have clocked her on the temple.

"Brent, don't go there."

He straightened up, met her snappy gaze. "Someone just threw a brick at you. You could have gotten your head bashed in."

And he'd stood there watching, half-frozen.

"But I didn't."

Sirens drew closer—cops. Any second they'd come storming in and see Jenna in a thigh skimming, silky bathrobe that now hung open at the neckline to reveal a substantial portion of her mind-blowing chest. Distracting himself from his own imagination and thoughts of her dead on the living room floor, he waggled his hand.

"Uh, you might want to put clothes on."

She glanced down, gasped and kicked out of his shoes. "I'll just throw something on."

"Yeah. And I need to look at that cut. You may need a couple of stitches."

If they were lucky, that would be the worst of it. This time.

No. There'd be no next time. Whatever argument she'd hit him with, he'd be ready. One thing was for damn sure. He was pulling Jenna off this case.

Two hours later, Jenna sat on an ER gurney waiting for the doc to stitch up the gash on her cheek while Brent leaned against the wall, stewing. Every inch of him burned. Continuous blood from Jenna's face combined with the closed-in, putrid hospital odor didn't help his foul mood.

"Brent, you look fierce."

"Maybe because someone just tried to kill you. Or do you think that was a random act, too?"

"Oh, my God, please tell me you're not picking a fight with me after someone just trashed my house."

He paddled his hand in her general direction. "I wouldn't have to pick a fight if I thought you'd be reasonable."

"How was I supposed to know someone would toss a brick through my window? And, if you'd relax, you'd realize someone is upset, which means we're making progress."

Unbelievable. As much as he wanted to rip into her, he'd remain calm. *Calm.* "Do you not get that someone just hurt you?"

With her free hand, she pointed to her cheek. "Trust me, I get it. Not only was my home violated, but I have to sit here and get my face, my ultimate tool, stitched up. So, don't tell me I don't get it. I assure you, I'm feeling everything I'm supposed to."

Great. Finally. Common sense. "Then we won't have any problems. I'll take you to my place or to your folks or wherever, but you're not going home. By the way, your landlord is boarding up the window for you."

She jerked her head. "Already?"

"Yeah. Your neighbor came over to check on you when you were with the cops. I gave her my cell number. She texted me a few minutes ago and said the landlord was there. Your place is secure, but I'm not taking you back there."

"So, that's it?"

Not in this lifetime did he think Jenna was giving in this easily. "Pretty much."

"You're going to tell me where I can go and when. Are you going to change my diapers too?"

If he were in a better mood he'd laugh. "I'll do whatever it takes to keep you breathing, Jenna. Including taking you off this case."

Still holding the bandage to her cheek, she hopped off the gurney, marched over to him and squared off. "Don't you dare. You cannot take this from me."

He stared at the wall behind her, focused on the sign explaining patients' rights. If he looked at her, he'd probably find those baby-blues pleading, working him like she worked every other man with a pulse.

"I can and I will."

"Look at me."

He glanced down, then away again. As good as she'd get.

"Fine. Don't look at me, but on a purely professional level, if this were anyone else, you wouldn't do this. If I were a man, you wouldn't do this. If we hadn't slept together, you wouldn't do this."

"I'm not going to argue that."

"Damn you!"

Finally, he looked into those firing blue eyes that should have peeled flesh off him. *Settle her down.* He reached for her, but she snapped her arm away.

"Hey, I refuse to let you wind up dead. Simple as that. Be mad at me if you want because, in this case, I don't care."

"You are so stubborn."

Again, he wouldn't argue. She stomped back to the gurney, hopped up and pulled the bandage from her face to check it.

"Still bleeding," he said. Precisely why he'd talk to Penny and pull her off this case. "This is too dangerous now. It's no coincidence you got hit with a brick."

"You're firing me because I got hit with a brick?"

Simple as that. "Yes. I'll take it from here."

"Oh, of course you will. You get my help in making progress and now you want to shove me aside."

"No, I want to keep you alive."

Outside the room voices erupted, something about a GSW—gunshot wound—and Brent figured they'd be waiting awhile yet.

Time to fix this. This time, he'd go for the softer approach and hope that her level of fatigue would get her to back off. He wandered over to her. "Honey, listen to me."

"Don't *honey* me." She poked him—hard—right in the chest. "You." Another poke. "Can't." Poke. "Do this to me."

Yes, he could. He wouldn't stress that. With the look on her face, he might be the next gunshot victim here. "Jenna—"

"Please," she said, her voice tight and strangled, life dripping out of it. "Please, don't do this to me. I haven't craved a lot of things professionally. Joining the FBI was the only thing, and I fell short. After that, it's been tiny victories. Little milestones. Until your mom's case." She focused on him, those blue eyes not nearly as hard. "I need to see this one through, Brent. Please."

I'm burned. Done. He dropped his shoulders and stared down at the floor. Option one: give in and let her finish this. Option two: don't give in and have her never speak to him again.

Option two stunk.

It would also keep her alive.

Gotta do it. He faced Jenna again, took in her sad eyes and knew this would hurt.

"I handled that wrong. I'm sorry. I'm worried about you. And you getting hurt was not part of this assignment." He tugged on the ends of her wild hair, then swept the long strands back over her shoulder. "I want you in one piece. That's all."

"I know. And I love that about you. But I need this."

"I'm sorry, Jenna. I'll call Penny and have her go to your place. Pack you a bag. Or I can do it. Not sure you want me rifling through your stuff, though."

The curtain flew open and Penny and Russ stepped in. Jenna leaned back and Brent dropped his hands. Penny's laser-sharp gaze whipped between the two of them. For once, considering it was ten o'clock at night, she wasn't wearing one of her power suits. For this trip to the ER she'd dressed down in slacks, a crisp white shirt and heels. Russ stood behind her in jeans and a sweatshirt.

"I heard my name," Penny said.

Jenna threw up her hands, revealing that still-bleeding cut on her face. "Really, Brent?"

"Hey," he said, "she's your boss and your assignment put you in danger. You can bet I called her."

Penny marched over to Jenna and inspected the cut. "Jenna, that's nasty."

"Gee, Pen, thanks."

"Sorry."

"She needs stitches. They've got a GSW down the hall. Guessing we'll be a while."

"Penny," Jenna said, "he's going to try and talk you into

booting me from this case. I'm telling you right now, I won't be happy if that happens."

Brent drew air through his nose before his mind left him and he started yelling.

Women. Always hassling him. His phone rang—*thank you*—and he dug into his pocket. "I'm taking this. It'll give us a second to cool off."

On his way out of the room, he gave Russ the *shoot-me-now* look.

If he got her out of here and she was still talking to him, much less having any interest in pursuing their personal relationship, it would be a minor miracle.

Barring that miracle, at least she'd be alive. He'd be okay with that.

Even if Jenna wasn't.

THE SECOND BRENT stepped into the hallway, Jenna went to work on Penny.

"He's freaking out because I got a brick through my window. You and I both know I've been in much more dangerous situations than this. We know it. I can take care of myself. All this incident means is we're getting close to something we're not supposed to get close to. The fact that it was a brick can't be ignored. I've scared someone, possibly the killer and when people are scared, they make mistakes. Mistakes that leave evidence to convict them." She looked at Russ over Penny's shoulder. "Tell her."

Russ held up his hands. So much for him helping.

She went back to Penny. "Please. Don't pull me off of this. I'll take precautions. I'll make sure I always have someone with me. I'll even stay with my folks. Well, maybe not them because my dad will freak, but I'll find somewhere safe to stay. Please, Penny. I need this."

Penny stared right into her eyes. Assessing. Good. If she'd already made up her mind, she would have said so. Hesitation from her boss might be the opening Jenna needed. One she could exploit.

"Give me another week. Earlier tonight we dropped a brick off at the lab. I think it's the murder weapon. It's unlikely we'll get prints off of it, but DNA is possible and maybe we'll have our murderer."

"Nice work, Jenna," Russ said.

"We found it under the porch at Brent's mom's. The sheriff came with us to keep the chain of custody intact."

Russ moved closer. "That's why you got a brick through your window."

But Jenna kept her focus on Penny, who continued to stare at her. "Yes. I can handle this. Please. Tell him I can handle this."

Apparently, that was all her boss needed. Penny turned to Russ and he gave her the all-purpose *eh* face. *Distract them.*

"And, Russ," Jenna said, "I'd planned on calling you earlier. Can you help me track down Brent's father? I tried the number Brent gave me, but it belongs to someone else now. I could dig around, but it'll be faster if you do it."

"Now you want the big man mad at me, too?"

"Sorry."

"What about the junkie?" Penny asked.

Now they were back to Jeffries. Jenna was fairly certain he was a dead end.

"I'm not ruling him out yet. I need to talk to Brent's father and see how I feel about him. Then I can start focusing on one or the other. If we get DNA off that brick, we might have a slam dunk, but that might take a few days, and I don't want to lose momentum."

Brent stepped back into the room and they all shut up.

"Suddenly everyone gets quiet." He glanced from Jenna to Penny and then to Russ. "What momentum?"

For whatever reason, Jenna didn't want to talk about this

in front of him. Call it survival, call it protective instincts, call it whatever, but she didn't think he needed every detail. He'd said himself that he couldn't wrap his mind around his father hurting his mother. "We're talking about the brick."

"Huh, I'm sunk now if even Russ is quiet. No way I'll win against all three of you. Even if I am the client and want you off this case."

"Brent," Penny began. "You *are* the client here. I'll do whatever you want, but your goal in this was to heat up the case. Obviously, you and Jenna have done that."

No kidding there. As if he'd read her mind, Brent slid his gaze to Jenna and their eyes held for a long moment while her mind flashed back a few hours to her bedroom and how they'd made each other smile.

No one was smiling now.

Brent gave in first and turned to Penny. "I'm worried about her."

"I know. I worry about her all the time. But this is her job, and if she wants to see this through, it should be her choice."

"And what if something happens to her?"

"We'll make sure it doesn't."

Brent scoffed, shook his head, then scratched the back of his neck. Killing time. She had him. Time to move in.

"Please, Brent," Jenna said. "I'll be careful."

His eyes were on her again, growing darker by the second, and she held her breath. The tension between them ran so thick an ax couldn't penetrate it, but she sat tall, challenging him. He wanted her to give in. To crumble. To let him have his way. Well, she wouldn't. Not this time.

Being the smart woman she was, Penny swung to Jenna and then back to Brent before turning to Russ. "Am I missing something here?"

"What are you asking *me* for?"

"You had a beer with him earlier. Maybe you know something."

"He doesn't," Brent said.

Jenna didn't believe it any more than Penny did, but that was between Russ and Brent. If Brent had shared his thoughts about his relationship with Jenna, good for him. At least he was talking to *someone*.

Even if it did sting a little bit that she wasn't that person. *Later.* There'd be time to worry about that later, when she and Brent actually figured out what the hell they were doing with each other. Aside from having multiple orgasms.

Jenna puffed up her cheeks, felt the tug of skin on her still-seeping wound and winced.

Brent moved to the bed, got right into her space. "You can't go home. We find you somewhere else to stay and you don't go anywhere alone. Whatever we have to do, I don't care. You can't be alone. Those are my terms. You agree to them and you stay. If you argue, you're fired."

At once, her toes, her fingers, her arms, everything tingled. *Yes!* Victory. He wouldn't see it that way, and she definitely wouldn't point it out, but she had most definitely won this round. Maybe there was hope for them yet, because stubborn Brent Thompson hadn't sacrificed her. He could have, but he hadn't.

Penny rolled out her bottom lip and studied the two of them for a few seconds. "I don't know what's going on and I'm not sure I want to, but, Brent, if you need to be somewhere, I can drive Jenna wherever she needs to go."

"I'm good," he said. "I'll make sure she's safe."

Penny clucked her tongue. "I'm sure you will." She spun to Russ. "Russell, shall we go?"

Oh, boy. She'd busted out the *Russell* business. Poor Russ would get a grilling in the car. Any other time, Jenna would have jumped in and asked to speak to Penny alone. To tell her that Russ was an innocent in this mess and even if Brent had confided in him about their relationship—or whatever the subject was—Penny should leave him alone. But, as confused and tired as Jenna was, she didn't have it in her tonight.

Even if she did, she wasn't sure what she'd say to Penny. *Hey, boss, you know how I'm not supposed to get up-close-and-personal with clients? Well, Brent is amazing in bed. In case you were wondering.*

Before Penny and Russ could leave, shoes squeaked from outside the room and a female doctor, who looked about twelve, stepped in. "Sorry for the wait, folks. Let's get this problem fixed up."

Jenna didn't want to be a whining patient, but this was her face. One she'd have to see in mirrors for the rest of her life, and a twelve-year-old wanted to stitch her up? The doctor shoved her hands into gloves and smacked open a cabinet where she messed with items, ripping open packages, fussing with gauze. Little by little, panic climbed in Jenna's throat. She knew nothing about this doctor, and the woman was about to shove a needle into her face. Her no-fail, always-come-through-for-her face.

She's going to make me look like Frankenstein's monster.

Brent moved to the side of the bed, hands propped on hips. "You okay?"

No. She shot another look at the doctor, and then came back to him.

And then, as if something clicked, Brent nodded. "Uh, doc?"

The doctor set supplies on the tray near the bed and turned, her gaze shifting to the butt of Brent's sidearm that stuck out from the hem of his shirt. "Is that a weapon?"

He dug into his pocket for his wallet and badged her. "Brent Thompson. I'm a US marshal."

"I see. Did you have a question for me?"

"I do. No disrespect here, but are you by any chance a plastic surgeon?"

Thank you. Jenna hadn't said one word, but he knew.

The doctor glanced at her and Jenna turned her face, putting the vertical gash on display.

"No, sir, I'm not. But I can stitch up a wound."

"I don't doubt that and, again, no disrespect here." He tucked his finger under Jenna's chin and inched it up. "But look at this face. Tell me you can stitch it up and it'll be as perfect as it was before she got cut."

About to follow Russ out the door, Penny took it all in and Jenna dared no eye contact. Her boss wasn't stupid and Brent jumping into the fray, putting his hands on Jenna in such an intimate way was sure to have her perception-radar blinking.

The doctor studied the gash again. "I can't guarantee that. A plastic surgeon couldn't, either."

Brent nodded. "I understand and appreciate your opinion, but we'll take our chances with the surgeon."

"Sir—"

"I want the surgeon," Jenna said. "I'm sorry, but you're a woman. Please understand."

Voices erupted from the hallway. "Coding!" someone shouted.

Snapping off her gloves, the doctor tossed them in the trash and spun to the door. "I have to go. I'll see who's here."

"Thank you," Jenna called.

Penny smacked her hands together. "Okay. Well, that was…interesting. You're in good hands here, so Russ and I are leaving. Call me in the morning. We'll talk. Count on it."

Chapter Eleven

First thing Monday morning, Jenna hunkered down in the Hennings & Solomon boardroom with a whiteboard, the box of files she'd made Brent retrieve from her apartment and all of her notes.

Avoiding the bazillion questions that would come from her family, she'd opted to spend the night in a hotel. Plus, if she knew anything about her boss, Penny would ask, in no uncertain terms, where Jenna had slept the previous night and Jenna wouldn't have to lie. She wanted to truthfully tell Penny she'd slept in a bed alone.

Of course, Brent had insisted on playing bodyguard and slept on the hotel room's sofa, which was rather heartbreaking since he was twice as big as the thing and couldn't have gotten any decent sleep. But there were only so many battles she could win with him, and, as tough as she'd played it, his presence calmed her. It let her feel a little less wary.

None of that could be admitted. All that would do was ignite the argument that she should walk away from his mom's case. Instead, they'd found a compromise with Brent following her to work and escorting her upstairs after which he went off to make sure a federal witness got to the court- house unscathed. Right now, that witness—bless him—got

Brent out of her space so she could make sense of her notes without her personal feelings interfering.

Penny popped her head in the door. "Good morning, sunshine."

"Hi."

"How's the face? I'm assuming the big, bad marshal got you a plastic surgeon?"

Jenna turned her head, revealing the bandage running from her jaw to midcheek. "Yes. He did. Eleven stitches."

Penny rolled out her bottom lip and narrowed her eyes in the way she did when focusing on a potential witness. "That was something, seeing Brent take over like that. He has a protective nature about him though, so I'm not sure why I was surprised."

Anytime now, Penny would find a way to pry about what she'd witnessed at the hospital. "He's a good man."

"He is indeed. Where did you sleep last night?"

Good old Penny. "I was too tired to deal with my family so I went to a hotel. Got the highest floor and double locked the door."

"Uh-huh."

"What?"

"Are you lying?"

"Nope. Want to see my receipt?"

Penny circled one finger in Jenna's direction. "You better not be lying."

"I'm not. Promise. Why would I lie?"

"Because Russ has gone into Band of Brothers mode and clammed up. That tells me Brent told him something, and he's refusing to betray his confidence. I love that about Russ, but when he uses it against me, I could stab him and dump his body."

Jenna cracked up. Penny, all five-foot-one of her, didn't pull any punches. "Thanks for the laugh. I needed that."

"Tell me not to worry about whatever is going on with you and Brent. This is business, Jenna, but he's my friend and I care about him."

"You don't have to worry. We're fine. We're both adults and we know what's at stake. I promise you. We're fine."

After a solid thirty seconds of silence, Penny waved her off, then gestured to the papers spread on the table. "What's this?"

"I'm working on a murder board."

"Ooh, can I help?"

As a defense lawyer, the most morbid things excited Penny. Jenna supposed the constantly thickening skin came with the job.

"Sure. I'm adding suspects to the white board. It helps me sort everything."

Penny grabbed a marker out of the fancy oak pencil box on the credenza. "You tell me what to write."

"I have this Jeffries guy and Brent's father. The sheriff is double-checking on any home invasions in the surrounding areas around that time. So far he's come up with one person. The guy was nineteen at the time and didn't have a history of violence. He was a petty thief looking for jewelry and small items to hock."

"Where is he now?"

"Lives in Indiana. His name is Carlton Boines. He did a two-year prison stint the year after Brent's mom died."

Penny made notes on the board as Jenna babbled. "Here's a photo of him." She handed Penny the picture and tape.

"That could be something. What else?"

For the next thirty minutes, Penny made notes on the board. By the time they were done, they had a lineup with three photos. Boines, Jeffries and Brent's father. That was it. Three suspects. Not a lot, but a start.

Jenna shoved her notepad away and sat back. "While

we're waiting for DNA on the brick, I'll find Boines and then start working on family members and acquaintances of his and Jeffries. Anything from Russ on Brent's father?"

"That's what I came in here for." She held up a note. "Russ got you this number and an address in Severville. It's near the Kentucky state line."

How interesting that Brent's father lived just over seven hours south and hadn't taken the time to let his children know. "Thank you. I'll call him."

"How does Brent feel about you questioning his father?"

Jenna set the note on the table. "He hasn't said. Not a shock since he doesn't say much about anything."

"You've read the evidence, what do you think? Did Mason kill his wife?"

"Penny, I honestly don't know. He's still considered a suspect. They just don't have any solid evidence. But after meeting Jeffries and finding out the sheriff doesn't have diddly on him, I have to start looking elsewhere. And that means questioning Brent's other family members about the relationship between Brent's mother and father."

"Did they get along?"

Jenna scrunched her nose. Somehow it felt like a betrayal sharing what Brent had told her, but this was Penny. His friend. Someone he trusted. "He said they yelled. Plenty of couples yell and it's not abusive. It's simply the way they communicate. Brent may have been too young to know the difference."

Still holding the marker, Penny tapped it on the table. "And you're afraid of what you'll find."

"And I'm afraid of what I'll find. From what I've gathered, Brent's dad doesn't have it in him to kill someone. He's weak. Evidenced by his walking out on his children. But we've seen crazier."

"We sure have. You have to question him. If nothing

else, to rule him out." Penny leaned forward and spun the phone toward Jenna. "Let's call him."

Yes. Let's. She eyeballed the number, grabbed the phone and dialed.

By the third ring, her hopes were dying fast. *Come on, be there.* Voice mail. Drat. Maybe she should just drive down and surprise him? Always an option. A long beep sounded and Jenna left a generic message telling Brent's father her name and that she was calling from Hennings & Solomon. That was it. If nothing else, he'd be curious why someone from a law firm would call him.

She dropped the receiver into the cradle and pushed the phone back to its original spot. "Now we wait. I'll talk to Brent's cousin. His aunt isn't comfortable talking about her sister. At all. She gets that deer-in-the-headlight look every time I'm around. Plus, Brent adores her and I don't want him annoyed if I push too hard. Jamie and her father are easier to get information out of."

"It's like walking through a minefield."

"Let me tell you, my psychology degree is coming in handy. I could do a thesis on this family. They were all questioned and apparently ruled out years ago, but they're still traumatized and no one wants to admit it. Instead, they stare at an empty house and watch Brent drive himself crazy. Tragic. Any way you slice it."

Penny checked the clock on the wall. "I have a client call in five minutes. Mike will go with you to track down Boines. Don't go alone."

For once, Jenna wouldn't argue about taking her rival, a retired detective and Hennings & Solomon's other investigator, with her. The itchy stitches on her face were all the convincing she needed. The irony of her marred face was not lost on her, because suddenly the beauty queen couldn't use her looks to get information out of men.

This she'd have to do on skill alone.

THERE WERE PLENTY of things about this case that bugged Jenna, and sneaking off to Carlisle without telling Brent might be the one that bugged her most. Even if she'd planned on telling him—after the fact—she was defying his request that she inform him when contacting his family. Plus, her goal today was to garner information about his father, about whom he clearly had conflicting emotions.

But he wanted his mother's killer caught, and that meant poking around in his parents' marriage.

The only thing she knew for sure was that she despised the knot of fear stuck in her throat. Someone had put a brick through her window and whoever that someone was, they didn't want her poking anything. Well, too bad. The stitches on her face alone were enough to push her forward. If she had a scar, when she found the person who did this to her, she'd beat them senseless.

So, with time ticking and Brent working, she'd recruited Mike to play chaperone. She also brought along her .38 for added protection.

Jenna exited the tollway with the midmorning sun shining through her windshield. Great day. Days like this weren't made for fear. They were made for strolling the lakefront, snuggling up with a sweetie, holding hands. All the good stuff. Maybe at some point, she and Brent would do that. Was he even the strolling type? So much to learn.

She let out a small sigh and hooked a right into the truck stop where Jamie had agreed to meet her. Wanting to keep this meeting out of eagle-eye Aunt Sylvie's range, Jenna had concocted some nonsense about a time crunch and asked Jamie to meet her at the truck stop to save her thirty minutes of driving.

The entire thing might be a joke because these people were so tight that Jamie probably had hung up with Jenna and called her mother. Still, if they met at the house, Sylvie would be all up in their business and calling Brent wanting to know what was going on. And considering Brent didn't know, well, enough said.

Complicated. Not so much the professional aspects, but the emotional ones. On a professional level, she had no problem going rogue and hunting down witnesses. Brent was different. The double orgasm the night before proved that. Now she'd slept with him, gotten emotionally involved and—*voilà!*—immediately began hiding things. How would that look to him?

If the roles were reversed, she'd think she was being used.

Which he would despise. And couldn't be further from the truth. For a second, she considered calling him, just admitting the whole damned thing. For a second. Then the investigator in her grabbed hold and smacked her upside the head. This was her job. Emotions must be removed. That meant Brent and her feelings for him, that comfort she felt when around him, the way her body responded when his big hands touched her skin, all needed to be set aside.

"Jenna Hayward, cliché of the year," she muttered. "That's me."

"What?" Mike asked.

"Nothing. Talking to myself. You can wait in the car. I don't want to spook her. Just keep an eye out, okay?"

"Sure."

She parked and glanced around the parking lot. To her right, a few truck drivers stood gabbing in front of their rigs. The fuel pumps were relatively quiet with only two cars in need of their service. No Jamie. Jenna checked the time on her phone. Five minutes early. She'd wait. Maybe grab a cup of coffee from inside.

But that meant walking around with this hideous bandage on display. She flipped the visor mirror open, fluffed her hair a bit, pulling it forward. Nice try. Even with long hair, the bandage was visible.

Eh, who needed coffee?

She'd just wait. Maybe answer some emails. Call her family. File her nails. Anything to not think about Brent and the multiple orgasms.

Heck of a mess. *He'll be steamed at you now.*

Out of the corner of her eye, she glimpsed Jamie's Jeep pull up. Perfect. No more stewing about Brent. She grabbed her purse and hopped out. Jamie did the same, but Jenna was hoping they could talk in her car.

"Hi," Jamie called. "Who's that with you?"

"Just a coworker. We have a meeting after this."

Total lie, but it would do.

"Ah. It's a beautiful morning. How about we get coffee and sit at one of the picnic tables?"

Coffee and an outside table. *Terrific.*

"Great," Jenna said, finger-brushing her hair forward.

Jamie came around the front of the car, moved in to give Jenna a hug and stopped.

Yep. Here we go.

"What *happened*?"

"Just a cut."

"How on earth?"

How much to tell her? Obviously, Brent hadn't shared last night's drama with his family, and Jenna wasn't sure it was her place to do so. On any other case, she wouldn't even consider talking about it. In her mind, it fell under the rule of privileged information. But Jamie was a friend, right?

Sort of.

Again with the emotional entanglements. Friendships had no place in an investigation.

Jenna waved it away. "I'll tell you about it later."

They marched by the truckers, a couple of guys in their forties wearing jeans, ripped T-shirts and filthy baseball caps.

"Hey, ladies," one of them said.

"Morning," Jenna chirped.

Wait for it.

"What's your hurry?" the bigger guy cracked. "Come over here and let us have a look at you."

Jenna grabbed Jamie's elbow. "No, thanks. You boys have a great day."

"You could make it better," the other one yelled.

She sure could. By showing them her .38. Idiots. Jenna sighed. "Keep walking. They won't bother us."

"You get that a lot, huh?"

Sure do. Sometimes, when it served a purpose, she encouraged it. At least she used to before she had the blasted ugly stitches. "If being objectified by men is the worst of my problems, I can handle it."

Inside the truck stop, they bought coffee and Jamie added a donut—this family loved their sweets. Jenna paid for the items, keeping her head partially cocked so her hair would feather over the bandage. What was she doing? People stared at her all the time. Why did this have to be different?

This time your face is a mess.

That's why.

Hurrying out of the shop, Jenna led Jamie to a group of picnic tables near the grassy area. She glanced to her right and noted the truckers saddling up. Good. What she didn't want was them wandering over and harassing them.

Jamie dove into her donut while Jenna creamed her java and then retrieved her notepad. That donut looked pretty good. Had to be five hundred calories. Had to be. She loved a donut every once in a while and the proof of that was in the fifteen pound weight gain since her pageant days.

"So what's up?" Jamie set down the donut and licked frosting off her thumb.

Go to work. "I mentioned on the phone I have questions about your uncle Mason."

Jamie flicked her glance to the donut, then came back to Jenna. "Did Brent say it's okay?"

Something in Jamie's tone, that squirrelly hesitation, sparked a nerve. Jamie had something to say and it wasn't necessarily good.

"I haven't told him yet. I wasn't sure how to handle it, and I don't want to upset him. But he wanted me to investigate and that means digging into his parents' marriage. No way around that. If you're concerned about it, I can keep this conversation between us. As much as I can anyway."

Because if Mason Thompson was a murderer and went to trial, they'd probably all be called to testify.

Jamie winced. "I hate talking about his family without him knowing it. It feels like a betrayal and I love him. I don't want him hurt anymore."

I know how you feel. All too well. Brent and his brooding, nontalking self had wormed his way into her life, and she wasn't letting him go. It might devastate her, because men like Brent were tough. They had those steel exteriors that wouldn't let people in.

And she wanted in.

Jenna reached across the table and squeezed Jamie's hand. "If it helps at all, I know how you feel. I probably shouldn't admit this, but I'm pretty crazy about him myself."

"I knew it. When he went searching for you at dinner the other night, I could see it. Plus, he's anxious when he's around you. With the way he's acting, he could be a male dog waiting on a female in heat."

Only half-horrified, Jenna snorted. "I'm definitely not telling him you said that." She drew her hand back, picked up her pen. "I just wanted you to know I won't hurt him.

Whatever you tell me, I'll protect him. As much as I can, anyway. I promise."

Jamie squared her shoulders. "Okay. Ask me your questions."

"Thank you. Can you give me an idea of what Brent's parents' marriage was like? Did they fight a lot? Were they happy?"

"All parents fight."

"So, nothing crazy. No domestic violence?"

Jamie stayed quiet, her big green eyes on Jenna, but not necessarily sharp or focused. *Mind wandering.* "I never saw him hit her."

Hit her. Quite specific. *Too* specific. And Jamie was still staring in that strange way that begged to be questioned. "I feel like you want to say something." More silence. *Move on.* "Brent's father worked evenings, right? Was that ever an issue?"

"Not that I know of, but he didn't like people at the house when he wasn't there."

From inside her purse, Jenna's phone chirped. Bad timing. She ignored it. "Like who?"

"Female friends were fine, but no men. If they needed work done on the house and repairmen had to come, he had to be there."

"Was there a reason? Did he have trust issues?"

Sure sounded like a jealous husband. In Jenna's line of work, she saw a lot of that.

"I don't know. Maybe. I overheard my mother complaining about it one night. Mason didn't like my dad going over there when he wasn't home. My mom was appalled. It wasn't like they were having an affair or anything."

Oh, hey, now. *That's fascinating.* Jenna set her pen down hoping the lack of note taking might loosen Jamie's lips more. "Do you know if there was a history of adultery? Either of them?"

"Heck, no."

"You seem pretty sure."

"Well, I…huh."

"What?"

She shrugged. "I guess I don't know. I mean who really knows what goes on in a marriage?"

Indeed. "So nothing comes to mind?"

"No. Aside from him not wanting men in the house. That was always a big deal."

"Who were her male friends?"

"You think she was having an affair?"

Here, Jenna needed to be careful. This was Brent's mother, his protective aunt's sister. One slipup and Sylvie would be on Brent about it and Jenna's life would get a dose of misery.

"I don't think anything. I'm trying to get an idea of what the marriage was like."

"I've never heard any rumors about an affair. I think I would know."

"With affairs, it could be a love triangle gone bad. Sometimes the boyfriend wants the woman to leave her family and when she refuses, he gets angry."

"Like I said, I think I'd have heard about that, but if you want a list of the men they were friends with, it's easy. Just look at the phone listings for Carlisle. Everyone knew everyone. And Aunt Cheryl was loved."

Jenna nodded. This trip couldn't be considered a success, but this jealousy thing might be a lead. Brent, in his eternal I-refuse-to-talk mode hadn't mentioned his father having control issues.

"I think that's all I need. If you think of anything else, would you call me?"

"Sure."

Jenna rose from the bench, grabbed her still-full coffee cup, the contents now cold, and tossed it in the garbage can.

"Jenna?"

"Yes?"

"He yelled a lot. Mason."

Ah, this was what Jamie had held back. "What did he yell about?"

"I don't know. Stupid things. If the house wasn't spotless, a dirty dish in the sink, whatever. When it was warm out and the windows were open, we'd hear him. I never saw bruises on her or anything, though. I don't think he hit her."

Jenna set her hand on Jamie's arm and squeezed. "Not hitting doesn't mean he wasn't an abuser."

"I know. He just liked things a certain way and he'd get mad if they weren't."

"I see."

Controlling husband, men not allowed in the house, a lot of yelling. Sure sounded like an abuser. *Dammit*. Part of Brent, the part that had witnessed the yelling and control issues, probably could believe his father was a murderer.

When they reached Jenna's car, she turned to Jamie. "Thank you. I know this was hard."

"I don't want to be starting rumors is all."

"You're not. I need the puzzle pieces and you've helped. Thank you."

After saying goodbye, Jenna slid into her car, waited for Jamie to pull away and, without a word to Mike, retrieved her phone from her purse. One missed call. She clicked on it and the number she'd dialed earlier from the conference room popped up.

Brent's father had returned her call.

Chapter Twelve

"Sometimes I wonder if I'm speaking a foreign language," Brent said.

He stood in the doorway of the executive conference room at Hennings & Solomon trying—really trying—not to lose it on Jenna. She spun from writing something on a whiteboard plastered with photos of Jeffries, another guy and…his father. Her list of suspects. A sick feeling settled in Brent's gut.

Marker still in hand, she scrunched her face, clearly insulted by his tone. She didn't like it? He could give her a list of things he didn't like.

Starting with her going back on her word.

She capped the marker and tossed it into a box on the cabinet beside her. "If that's your greeting, maybe you should try again. And you can start by closing that door so half the office doesn't hear you."

Right. Mad as he was, making her bosses an audience wouldn't help her career. He stepped in, smacked the door shut and crossed his arms.

"Oh, you're definitely about to pick a fight."

Ya think? But no, he wasn't owning this one. *This* one fell squarely on her. "Actually, you started this one."

"Me?"

But the way she looked at him, a little pouty and

innocent, wasn't jibing. He eyeballed her, shook his head
at her dramatics and walked to within a couple of feet of
her. Jenna held his gaze, her body unmoving, but in all that
stillness, they both knew she was busted.

"Brent—"

"I had two requests." He held up a finger. "That you not
go anywhere alone." The next finger. "And that you give
me a heads up when talking to my family."

"Right. I didn't go alone, but I did talk to Jamie."

"At least you're honest about it."

"I can explain."

"Terrific."

She rolled her eyes. "I hate it when you're a jerk."

"And you don't think you were a jerk today? Sneaking
off to talk to Jamie?"

Her shoulders dipped forward, deflating like one of
those giant air balloons he saw in front of stores having
blow-out sales.

"If I was, then I was a jerk doing my job."

This is where he had to be careful. When she hit him
with those sparkly blue eyes, his system went wacky, and if
he didn't keep that in check, she'd talk her way around him.

"I don't understand why you kept this from me."

"Because I wasn't sure what she'd tell me. I wanted her
to feel like she could talk to me without hesitation. I'm
fairly stunned she told you. She seemed concerned that
you'd be upset."

"She didn't tell me."

"Well, she was the only one there."

Having spent even a minimal amount of time around
his family, she should have anticipated how this worked.
Instead, she chose not to give him a heads-up and left him
blindsided. Something he hated above all else.

"Jamie told my aunt and, guess what, babe? I had *her*

all over my butt. Getting hysterical because we're digging up skeletons."

"Then maybe you should be having this conversation with Jamie, because she's the one who opened her mouth."

"How about we get back to the fact that you lied to me?"

Jenna bunched her fists at him. "I didn't lie to you."

"Lying and lying by omission are the same."

Bottom line: he'd trusted her and she'd blown it. The one time in his life he'd given in, let down his guard and—*whomp*—he got burned.

Coming closer, she held out her hands. "No, Brent, they're not."

He didn't care. Why should he? If he couldn't trust her, what was the point? "I need to be able to trust you."

"You *can* trust me."

Her eyes were so big and blue a man could lose himself in those suckers. Dive right in and never come out. He should walk now. Get it over with and maybe they could stay friendly when they saw each other.

Except she latched on to his arm, the beauty queen with an iron grip. "Whatever you're thinking, we will talk this through."

No talking. Talking was the hell that burned inside him. If he let that out, game over. He'd never recover. Fighting his urge to bolt and leave this nonsense, the emotional chaos and stress behind, he locked his knees.

"Tell me I can trust you."

Where'd that come from?

She moved closer, and squeezed his arm. "Yes, you can trust me. I wasn't trying to hurt you. On a personal level, I'm protecting you. Part of that means not telling you things. If there's something you should know, I'll tell you. Otherwise, let me do my job."

One at a time, she uncurled her fingers. Maybe in case he tried to bolt. To test his theory, he flinched and she latched on again. Despite himself, he half-smiled. Somewhere in this mess, her holding him hostage was funny.

He patted her hand. "I'm not going anywhere."

Still, she hung on. "You can trust me. Please know that."

He tilted his head, ran his finger along the edge of the bandage on her cheek. All because of his mother's case. He'd put her in danger, unintentional as it was. He'd gotten her into this.

"I'm usually the one in charge," he said. "Everyone comes to me for answers. When my aunt called me, I didn't have any and I felt…weak."

"Feeling weak doesn't make you less of a man. It makes you human. If you don't have answers, maybe I do. Give me that chance. Ask me before you get mad. That's the only way this will work. Your family is great, but they know how to work you. I told Jamie you didn't know we were talking."

"And she turned around and told my aunt."

Jenna touched her finger to her nose. "Jamie didn't want to be the one to spill the beans on me so she went to your aunt. Why she did that, I don't know."

"She probably felt guilty keeping it from me." He shook his head. "She stinks at secrets."

"Whatever her reasons, she pitted us against each other and we can't have that. Professionally or personally." She twisted his shirt in her fist and tugged. "I need you on my side. Can you do that?"

He turned it over in his mind, stretched it in all directions. Instinctively he knew the answer, but communicating it didn't come so easy. Being on her side meant being on no one else's. That steadfast, unconditional acceptance. He'd never had that with anyone outside of his sister and his aunt's family.

Time to try it.

He nodded. "I can do that."

She went up on tiptoes and hit him with a lip-lock. Right

there in the conference room where anyone could walk in. He dipped his head lower, skimmed his hands over her waist and settled them in that groove at the base of her back. The tips of his fingers skimmed her butt and his chest went crazy again. Damn, he loved that.

Loved her.

He backed away, nibbled her bottom lip. "Where are you sleeping tonight?"

"Hopefully wherever you are."

"I think we can make that happen."

The following evening, after depositing his witness at a safe house, Brent checked his dashboard clock. 6:30 p.m. Early. Any other night, he'd hit the gym and grab a bite. Plus, it was the first of the month, a time he usually made the rounds of his law enforcement friends asking for any and all updates on cases similar to his mom's.

Tonight, he didn't have it in him. For the first time, even more than chasing down his mother's killer, he wanted to go home to someone.

Specifically, to Jenna. After a life spent numbing himself to emotional attachments, a high-maintenance ex-beauty queen suddenly made him want to mix things up. He rested his head back and his stomach rumbled. Dinner first, gym later. But that didn't sound like a banner evening. He checked the clock again. 6:32 p.m.

When he'd called Jenna earlier, she'd said she'd be at her parents' for dinner until eight. Where she was sleeping tonight, she hadn't said. She'd spent last night with him and he was definitely hoping for a replay. All Brent knew was he hadn't seen her since that morning and didn't like it.

He grabbed his phone from the cup holder and shot her a text.

SLEEPOVER?

No one would ever call him a romantic with that line. Eh, he'd find other ways to please her.

The text buzzed back.

PENNY WOULD CALL YOU A PIG.

No doubt. And it made him laugh as he typed.

I MISS YOU.

Come on. First I announce I love her and now this. Definitely losing my man card.

But what the hell? He pushed send.

Seconds later came her reply.

OMG! LOOK AT YOU ADMITTING YOUR FEELINGS. I'M SO PROUD. I MISS YOU TOO. SLEEPOVER=YES

"Score," he whispered, grinning like an idiot.

His phone buzzed again.

WINDOW AT MY PLACE IS FIXED. I NEED CLOTHES. MY BROTHER WILL DRIVE. MEET ME THERE.

She was sticking to her word of not traveling alone. Finally, they were in sync.

In many ways.

He responded to her text, telling her that he'd pick her up and they could go to his place. He lived in a high-rise with better security.

Plus, he wanted her in his space again. To give it life and energy rather than it being the place where he spent hours studying homicide cases. He dragged his hand over his face, and then rubbed it over his chest where that damned Jenna explosion wouldn't let up. He had a woman in his life and it wasn't just about sex and the release that came with it. Sex for the sake of sex never hurt, but this was different. Now, he wanted her around. A lot.

"Yeah, dude. Things are changing."

Whatever. All this thinking wouldn't solve his problems. For now, he'd take it as it came and hope like hell they found a killer.

At 8:25 p.m. on the dot, he buzzed Jenna's apartment. Seconds later she swung open the door. "We have to go."

"Where?"

She stepped around him, hobbling on that bum ankle.

"Are you limping? Where are the crutches?"

"It just hurts. We have to go."

There went his plan for the evening. "Uh, where?"

"Carlisle."

"Now?"

He had yet to move so she latched on to him, dragging him out the door. "Yes, I just heard from my friend at the lab. She sent the report to the sheriff. Now move so I can lock this door."

In the world of law enforcement, getting a forensics report back in forty-eight hours took a minor miracle. Or some serious butt kissing. "How? It's only been forty-eight hours."

"Welcome to the world of private labs, Marshal Thompson."

Gnarly, paralyzing tension rocketed into his neck. For years he'd been chasing leads on his mom's case, and in a matter of days Jenna had uncovered possible evidence and gotten a forensics report. A damned forensics report. He should be thrilled. Or at least hopeful.

What the hell was wrong with him?

Jenna locked the door and turned to him, all blue eyes and a not-so-tight T-shirt. She held up her hands and kept her gaze glued to him. "I can see you're freaking. That's normal. It's been years and suddenly we have movement and you don't know what to think. There's nothing to think. Let's see what the report says."

Made sense. But Brent's feet were cemented to the floor. *Get going.* He should have been sprinting to his car, but nope. Standing stock-still like a pansy.

"Brent?"

"I'm…" He dragged his hand over his face. "I don't know." *Tired.*

Jenna stepped back, tipped her head up to look at him. "You're scared."

Yes. "No."

"You're afraid your mother's blood and your dad's DNA will be on that brick. I don't blame you. But if we don't get there, we'll never know. Whatever that brick tells us has been there for twenty-three years. The only difference between yesterday and today is that we'll know."

That was a good way to look at it. He took that in, considered it. "If my father's DNA is there, I'll lose my damned mind. I'm still hacked that he bolted on us. He's always been a suspect, but I don't go there."

She grabbed his hands and squeezed. "I know. So how about I do it for you? I'll go to Carlisle and meet with the sheriff."

Did he want that? He'd always been the one funneling appropriate information to his family and—yeah—that job stunk. But he had to do it. His mother deserved it and he wasn't willing to let her case die. Not ever.

But someone else being the funnel for a change, giving his tired brain a rest, he could get behind. "You can't go alone."

"I'll be fine."

"No. I'll go with you. I'll sit outside while you look at the report. Then you tell me. Good or bad, you tell me. You good with that?"

"Are *you* okay with that?"

He nodded. "I am. For once, I'm okay not being in charge."

BRENT HELD THE door to the sheriff's office open for Jenna, but she stopped and hit him with those crystal blue eyes that—*whap!*—hit him square in the chest. How the hell did she do that? Even the ugly bandage couldn't smother how gorgeous she was.

"I feel like I should say something," she said.

"Nothing to say. After twenty-three years, I'm about to find out if my father used a brick to kill my mother."

Jenna winced. "It could be nothing."

"Or it could be something. Which we won't know unless you get your beautiful behind in the damn building."

She shook her head, but laughed. "Remind me later to show you how much I appreciate the man you are."

"Oh, honey," he said. "Way to distract me."

"Is it working?"

"Yep." He smacked her on the rear. "Now go."

The sheriff came out of his office, spotted them standing in the doorway and waved. "Hey, gang."

Jenna strode through the small reception area, her low heels clicking on the linoleum. He inhaled the musty smell of a building vacant of fresh air and realized certain things never changed. The institutional feel of the sheriff's office was one of them. This time, though, he had Jenna with him, and he could study the fit of her jeans and the lack of a short skirt. Couple that with the looser fitting shirt and Jenna had made changes in her wardrobe.

Brent shook hands with Barnes. "Sheriff, thanks for seeing us so late."

It had been twenty-three years of gut-shredding for him, as well. It wouldn't be a shock if he'd already looked at the report.

"I have the report in my office."

Brent took a step and Jenna grasped his arm. "You wanted to wait outside."

Right. He had to get used to this. "Yeah. Sorry."

"Don't apologize. If you've changed your mind, it's fine. I want us to be on the same page, though."

"Something wrong?" the sheriff asked.

Brent patted Jenna's hand and backed away. "No, sir. Jenna will take this one. I'll wait out here."

The sheriff's eyebrows hitched up. "That's…different."

"Yeah, it is."

Into the office they went, closing the door behind them. The next few minutes would be torture, and it wouldn't end when Jenna came out, because after this, whatever the news, he'd have to have a conversation with his aunt. He dropped into one of the cheap waiting-room chairs that had been there for ten years. The cushion sagged under his weight, reminding him just how sick of this place he was.

He slid down, rested his head against the top curve of the chair and closed his eyes. *Mom, I hope this is something.* Failure wouldn't do. He had to get this done.

Eyes closed, he waited, listening for the squeak of hinges when the office door opened. He counted to sixty and when he got there, he did it again. On his fifth cycle, the door finally squeaked and he popped to his feet.

Jenna stuck her head out. "Come in."

Their eyes met and held while he walked, but she wasn't giving him any clues. Nada. Then he remembered she spent her days around liars and lawyers and there you go.

"Have a seat," the sheriff said.

Brent leaned against the door frame, folded his arms, and then let them drop. "I'll stand."

"The short of it is that your mom's DNA was found on the brick," the sheriff said.

They had a murder weapon. Brent's breathing hitched and he straightened, set his shoulder blades. "What else?"

"Nothing. No other identifiable DNA."

His father's DNA wasn't on there.

"So," Jenna said, "we have a murder weapon, but nothing else that will help us identify the killer."

Chapter Thirteen

Didn't that make Jenna crazy? Damned DNA. Everyone talked about how great it was. Well, yeah, but not when you didn't have any. The reality was DNA only broke a case a fraction of the time, and this case wouldn't be included in that fraction.

Brent was leaning against the door frame, his shoulders back, his gaze steady, taking this news like the solid man he was.

"I'm so sorry," Jenna said.

"For what? You found the murder weapon. We hadn't done that in all these years. Add this to the brick that went through your window and someone is scared."

"Whoever it is, we have to catch him before he takes off on us."

Barnes rocked back in his chair. "What's this about a brick?"

"Someone tossed a brick through her window the other night. No coincidence."

He tapped his cheek. "Is that what the bandage is?"

"Yes," Jenna said. "I needed stitches."

Hopefully it won't scar. And once again, she was thinking like a beauty queen. No. Not like a beauty queen. Like a woman who didn't want an ugly scar on her face.

"Well, shoot. I'm sorry about that."

"Don't be. As Brent said, we're getting closer."

Brent boosted himself off the door frame and took a step closer. "What's next?"

Needing to move, Jenna stood. "I think Russ can help." Barnes didn't know Russ, though, so this might take convincing. "He's FBI and he's good. I'd like to see if there were any other similar cases around that time."

Barnes pulled a face. "Like a serial killer?"

"I don't know. I'm looking for anything."

Silence ensued while Barnes mulled it over. He'd been agreeable all this time; she couldn't imagine him not wanting FBI help. "Sheriff?"

He finally nodded. "If you think it'll help."

"I do. I'll talk to him."

Another thing she'd be dragging Russ in on. Which, after the fight about meeting with Jamie, reminded Jenna that she needed to bring Brent into the loop that she'd called his father. In this situation, she hoped to travel to Mason Thompson rather than him returning home and causing more upheaval.

Jenna tugged on the hem of her shirt and smoothed it. "We should go. Sheriff, thank you. I'm sorry the brick didn't pan out."

"We have a murder weapon. I'm satisfied."

Well, she wasn't.

Outside, Jenna leaned on the porch rail and breathed in the cool evening air. Building lights illuminated the walkway, breaking up the blackness just beyond. Had she been alone, the creep factor might be too much. But the quiet soothed her busy mind.

Brent rested against the opposite rail and crossed his legs at the ankles. "I wanted more."

"Me, too."

"At the same time, I was terrified my father's DNA would be on that thing."

This is it. Time to tell him about his father. "I know you were. This has to be incredibly difficult."

He shrugged.

"I need to tell you something."

Immediately, his shoulders flew back. "Uh-oh."

"No uh-oh. You asked me to keep you informed. That's what I'm doing. The number you gave me for your dad didn't work. I asked Russ to help me and he gave me a number for your dad in southern Illinois. We're playing phone tag and have exchanged voice mails. I was waiting until I talked to him to tell you, but this seems like the right time."

"This came out of your conversation with Jamie?"

No-win situation. If she said yes, Brent would want to know what his cousin had said. Regardless of Jenna craving a little payback when it came to Jamie's loose lips, Brent didn't deserve to hear nasty things about his father.

"We've known he's been a suspect and I'm talking to everyone, right? Fresh eyes and all that. I just need to talk to him. Then we can rule him out."

"Or not."

Jenna chose not to respond. Cases could go either way and predictions were often wildly incorrect. "When I speak to him, I'll let you know."

He grinned. "So I don't yell at you again?"

"Yes, so you don't yell at me again." She levered off the porch rail, walked the few feet to him and grabbed a handful of his shirt. Her knuckles skimmed his rock-hard abs. *He must kill himself in the gym.* "I don't ever want that to happen again."

He glanced down at his mangled shirt and puckered his lips. "Getting a little rough for someone who needs a place to stay tonight."

"I can always sleep in my own bed."

"Not a chance. Besides, I've got a great bed."

"I know you do."

He tugged his shirt free and slipped his arm over her shoulders. "Then let's go home."

AFTER ANOTHER NIGHT with the incredibly irresistible Jenna—he could use more of that in his life—Brent spent the early part of his morning dealing with the processing of a federal fugitive. He strode through the lobby of the Chicago US Marshals' district office and headed for the stairs that would take him to the fifth floor. The morning rush had dwindled, leaving the cavernous lobby with less than a dozen visitors and employees coming or going. As he approached Lenny, the guard at the reception desk, Brent tossed him a small bag of Aunt Sylvie's cookies. Like Brent, the guy had a thing for the killer salty-sweet combo of chocolate chips and macadamia nuts.

"You're a good man," Lenny said.

"Remember that when I run out of my own stash and raid yours."

Brent's phone rang and before he got to the stairs he ducked to the side to check it. Speaking of the devil. He hit the button. "Hey, Aunt Sylvie."

"Where are you?" The rough-edged tone she used when something had hit the fan immediately put him on edge.

"Just walking into my office. What's up?"

"He's back."

A woman wandered by, giving Brent a long look as she passed. Thanks, but no thanks—that was the last thing he wanted. "Who?"

"Your father. He just showed up."

It took a solid ten seconds to absorb the words, but Brent's body finally stiffened and his ears whooshed. *Concentrate.* He gripped the phone tighter and squeezed his eyes shut. The whooshing stopped and the lobby sounds—dinging elevator, the swish of the revolving door, clicking heels on marble—came into sharper focus. "Wait. What happened?"

"He's here. Right next door walking around like he owns the place."

Jenna was so dead. Just last night she'd assured him that she'd warn him if she'd made contact. "He does own it."

And didn't that stick in his craw considering Brent had been paying the taxes and other expenses on the place since his father had bolted.

"What's he doing here?"

Excellent question. "I don't know. Did you talk to him?"

"Of course not," she huffed. "I saw a strange truck in the driveway and sent your uncle over. He came back looking as if hell had swallowed him and told me the truck was Mason's."

Already, Brent was checking his watch, figuring how long it would take him to tell his boss he had an emergency, get someone to cover transporting his witness this afternoon and get to Carlisle. "Is he still there?"

"No. He and your uncle had words and he left. He told Herb he wanted to see the old place. Good Lord, what if he's staying? I can't do that, Brent. I just can't."

Already with the hysterics. "He's not staying. Trust me on that. Did he leave a number?"

"No, but he asked for yours and your uncle gave it to him."

Good. Let him call. "Okay. I'll clear my day and head out there. If he comes back, stay away from him. Don't upset yourself anymore."

He clicked off and sucked huge gulps of stale lobby air into his lungs. Damned Jenna. She had to have spoken to his father. Why else would he be here? Again she had blindsided him. The woman made him insane. Every step forward, she snatched him back. How many times would she go rogue on him, and how many times would he allow her to talk him out of being angry?

Out of walking away.

And if she thought she was going to give him any BS about wanting to tell him in person, he didn't want to hear it. No chance. The elevator dinged and the doors slid open—hell with the stairs. He'd go upstairs, clear his schedule and then hunt Jenna down.

Within the hour, Brent strode through Hennings & Solomon's fancy waiting area to the desk where Marcie, the young receptionist, greeted him. After his stint on Penny's protection detail last spring, Marcie readily recognized him.

"Please hold," she said into her headset. She connected her call and hit Brent with one of her cheery smiles. "Hello, Marshal Thompson."

Not feeling too cheery, the best he could summon was a nod. Damned Jenna, aggravating him. "Hey, Marcie. Jenna around?"

"One moment."

Marcie located Jenna and directed him back. The Queen of Blindside stood in the hallway outside the bullpen looking nothing short of fantastic in a black skirt and not-so-clingy sweater, and that stupid punch to the chest walloped him. No time for that when his mission right now might include killing her.

She unleashed one of her beauty queen smiles. "Well, hey there. This is a surprise."

It sure is. His steady, direct approach must have been a clue to his mood because her smile melted like snow on a ninety-degree day. "Conference room. We need to *talk.*"

"Um, sure." She scooted up to him, balancing on her high heels while he burned treads in the carpet. "What's wrong?"

He ducked into the conference room Penny had used

months earlier to escape from him—her protection detail. Great choice considering his already irritated status.

Jenna followed behind, closed the door and immediately reached for him. *No touching.* Hands up, he halted her. "After everything we've talked about, you blindsided me again."

Her head snapped back. "I'm sorry?"

Not an apology, but a question. As if she misunderstood his meaning. He stepped closer, refusing to let those blue eyes distract him. Not this time. "Let me clarify. I asked you one simple thing and that was to keep me in the loop when you spoke to my family."

"Yes. And I have."

"My father doesn't count? You didn't think it was wise to tell me he was coming here today?"

"What are you *talking* about? He's coming here tomorrow. Not today."

And there it was. She knew and she didn't tell him. "You talked to him and you didn't tell me?"

"I was about to call you."

"You didn't think that was important enough to disrupt my day?"

"Brent, I spoke to him barely thirty minutes ago and then Penny called me into her office. That's where I was when Marcie paged me. As far as your dad, he said he'd be here tomorrow. I was going to call you when I finished with Penny."

Brent figured he must have been from some other planet because he thought it was pretty damned clear he wanted to hear this stuff ASAP. Penny was a reasonable boss. She wouldn't have minded Jenna taking a minute to call him. What didn't she get about that? "He just planted his tail at the house. My uncle talked to him and my aunt is having a damned stroke."

"And that's my fault?"

"Wanting you to call me the second you hung up with him isn't a lot to ask."

She stepped closer, reaching for him, but he backed away, shrugging loose of her hold. Her bottom lip wobbled and she swallowed a couple of times as her blue eyes filled. Jenna crying. That was new. As much as he hated the sight, he couldn't help her. She'd blindsided him for the last time.

"Brent, please, he told me he'd be here tomorrow. Not today. He must have come up here and *then* called me. He lied to me."

"Why would he come here before he even spoke to you?"

"He lived in Carlisle for years, maybe he's still in contact with someone who knows I'm poking around. I don't know, but I didn't talk to him until thirty minutes ago."

Brent jammed his hands into his hair, dug his fingers into his scalp. Blood barreled into his skull, pushing, pushing, pushing until his eyes throbbed from the pressure. Insanity. That's what he had here. All of these people yapping at him and he didn't know what was truth versus fiction.

"My aunt is hysterical. They all come to me. Every damned issue becomes mine to fix." He breathed deep. "I asked you to do one thing. Just give me a flipping heads-up so I can manage the spin. How was that not clear?"

"It was clear. But I don't control what your father does. How was I supposed to know he'd show up today instead of tomorrow?"

"You couldn't, but again, a heads-up about the conversation would have helped. Now I'm stuck with chaos and hysteria. I don't even know where the hell he is right now. He could be on his way to Camille's. I've gotta get over there and tell her before she finds out and goes nuts. That thirty minutes you waited would do me a whole lot of good right now."

"This is not my fault!"

The conference room door flew open and Brent swung

back to find Penny in the doorway, her lips pressed tight. "Whatever you're fighting about, take it down a notch." She scooted in and closed the door. "What's going on?"

"Nothing," Jenna said.

"Doesn't sound like nothing."

"My father showed up," Brent said. "I didn't know."

Penny whirled on Jenna. "You didn't *tell* him?"

And now Penny knew. Brent bit down, waited for his teeth to scream from the agony of all this pent-up anger and hurt and…and…rage. "*You* knew?"

"No, no, no," Jenna said. "She only knew because she called me into her office. I swear to you. She's the only one who knows. I wouldn't do that to you. Brent, I know what you're doing. Please, don't do this."

But Brent was beyond that. To hell with it. All this emotional upheaval surrounded Jenna. She made him crazy. No matter how much he cared—and constantly craved her lush body—he didn't have the stamina for this. He needed calm and quiet. Jenna didn't provide calm and quiet. She was excitement and lust and attachment. All things for him to obsess about, and he had enough to obsess about. *Time to go.*

Turning his back on Jenna, he faced Penny. "I'm concerned for her safety. Great job finding leads, but we've got a killer unhappy with her. I'm pulling the plug. You're fired."

There. Done. Enough said. Without looking at Jenna, he walked out.

Fired? Fired. The word left Jenna more than a little dumbstruck. He'd actually done it. Later, when she got over this mind-frying anger, that loss would tear right into her chest and drill through her heart. At this moment, chasing him down the hallway, she was too incensed to feel the pain.

"You are not firing me." She made sure to keep her voice

low, but loud enough that a retreating Brent would hear. "We will take this outside, but we're not done."

"We're done."

They stepped into the elevator and Brent smacked the button, ignoring her. Of course he was. Because if he looked at her, she'd see all his terror carving him up, eating away at him like acid on skin, and God help him if he showed any weakness. Instead, he picked a fight and here they were back at the beginning.

"Putting aside our personal involvement, are you going to jeopardize my career by firing me?"

"I told Penny my reasons. I *told* her you did a good job. If there's any fallout I'll fix it, but I can't do this with you anymore."

So stubborn. All these years he'd been trying to find his mother's killer. Finally, some progress was made and he wanted to end it. He'd have his life back and be able to heal, and he wanted to stop?

Wait.

She looked up at him, the man who pretended to ignore her by staring at the elevator doors. *Locked up tight.* As usual. Because this was his MO. To stay distant and unattached so he could focus on his mother. Avoid emotional conflicts with women. *I'm so dumb.*

"Now I get it."

Finally, he glanced at her. "What?"

The elevator hummed and Jenna glanced up at the flicking numbers. Five, four, three—she hit the stop button and the alarm sounded, a loud, blaring that rammed her eardrums.

"Brilliant," Brent said, reaching for the button.

"Don't touch that button."

He stopped, grunted and turned to her. "I'm not doing this. I'm done."

"Of course you are. Because you're terrified of solving this case. Without it, you'll have to find a way to deal with the emotions you've packed into yourself. You've said yourself you're a bomb waiting to go off. Without your mother's murder, you'll have nothing but that bomb. So, instead, you'll push me away, like you've done every other woman in your life, and then you'll be alone and miserable. Which, oddly enough, seems to be your comfort zone." She flung her arms. *"Bravo!"*

In that annoying way of his, Brent snorted. "Here we go with the psychological evaluation again."

He turned back to the closed doors, focused on them as if they were the most fascinating thing he'd witnessed. *Locked up tight.* This would get her nowhere. That thick skull of his would not be penetrated until he calmed down. She'd have to wait. She hit the button again and the alarm stopped. The elevator jerked and began its descent. Two, one. The doors slid open and he stepped off.

"Don't do this, Brent. Let's chalk it up to an argument, a misunderstanding, whatever, but don't fall back on being a jerk because it's easy. You're better than that."

He paused and a woman, someone from the fourth floor Jenna had seen before, angled around him. Given the late morning hour, the lobby was quiet. At least she'd gotten one break. She waited for Brent to turn around. Waited for him to admit that terror had consumed him. Waited for him to apologize.

A full twenty seconds passed and nothing. Not a word. Just this big, hulking man standing with his back to her. In that deepest part of her where she'd grown to admire him, to care for him—no, to *love* him—that stung. Finally, Brent took a step, hesitated, but no, kept moving, his strides long and fast and heading straight for the door. Away from her.

Jenna didn't move. Maybe, after she'd spoken to his dad, she should have called him on the spot or rushed to wherever he was. Her mistake. One she'd never make again, but she'd thought she'd had time. Simple as that.

She'd thought she had time.

Apparently not.

Well, she did now and Brent had just announced he didn't know where his father was. She'd find Mason. Fired or not, she'd find him. What she did on her own time was her business, and she suddenly felt ill. Not actually a lie since her stomach flip-flopped like an Olympic gymnast. *Pseudo sick day.*

She'd head upstairs, avoid her boss, grab her keys and purse, and take a trip to Carlisle to find Mason Thompson.

She hadn't worked this hard to walk away.

No, sir. Fired or not, she had a murder to solve.

JENNA PULLED INTO the driveway of Brent's home, well, the Thompson home, because now that his father had shown up, who knew what to call it?

Above her, dark clouds swirled, their blackness threatening and ugly. A storm rolling in. How appropriate. She parked and then marched next door, fighting to keep her heels from sinking into the soft grass that separated the two homes. Hopefully, Sylvie or Brent's uncle could fill her in on what had gone on with Mason. She needed to find the man, question him and compare his story to what she'd heard from the rest of Brent's family. All before Brent tracked her down.

If she thought he was mad now, all she needed to do was wait until he found her still working the case. And doing it alone. But after sneaking out of the office to avoid her boss, who would most certainly remind her that she'd been fired, Jenna and her .38 were flying solo. Besides, his family lived next door and they'd play chaperone.

Although her reasonable self warned her not to pursue this, part of her couldn't walk away. They'd come too far and it had become too personal. Proving herself wasn't the issue anymore. Now she wanted to help Brent figure out who had taken his mother from him.

She simply needed to do this one last thing and talk to Brent's father.

Then she'd either rule him out or have the sheriff question him again. And again. And again. With what Jamie had shared, it was time to pressure Mason Thompson.

Eventually, if guilty, he'd break. The man was too weak to withstand an interrogation—an *interview*—as her father called it.

Then she'd leave Brent and this case behind. For her own sake, she had to. But, darn it, the thought of that squeezed her chest, like a fist curling at the base of her throat. She heaved out a breath and pinched her eyes closed. *Don't cry.* She couldn't. Not now.

Heartbreak. That's what this was. It had been a long time since she'd felt it and—*darn*—had she ever truly understood its paralyzing presence, its savage way of sucking away every ounce of happiness? She didn't think so. Her aching body didn't either.

But she and Brent couldn't live like this. He used every disagreement as an excuse to run from a relationship, and the chaos and pain would be too much.

Just finish this. The rest she could do later. For now, she'd pull herself together and get through this last task. She tugged on the sleeves of her trench coat, smoothed the collar, took a breath and banged on Sylvie's door.

Behind her, the wind whipped up again, rattling the branches on the big oak beside the porch.

No answer.

The absence of their cars didn't bode well, but Jamie's car was here. Maybe she'd gone somewhere with Sylvie?

She banged again and waited. Still no answer. Fine. She'd try next door. Maybe Mason had returned and they were all in there having a powwow. If they weren't and Mason was there and she wound up alone with a suspected killer, well, she had her .38. That was all the reasoning she needed. She tromped down the stairs and across the lawn, her heels once again sinking into the grass. Mud on her favorite shoes. Great. Just another annoying thing on an already annoying day.

Brent had actually *fired* her. After everything they'd talked about and knowing how important this was to her, how she hungered to make a difference, he'd ripped it right out of her desperate, clutching hands.

If she could go back, maybe she'd make a different decision, ask her boss to hang on a second and call him immediately rather than waiting.

But beating it to death wouldn't fix it.

She climbed the porch and a noise—scraping—drew her attention. She peeked around the side of the house and saw the lattice Brent had torn off the other night sitting on the ground.

Hadn't he replaced that? Yes. Definitely. He'd told her that he'd only tucked it back in and would nail it in place the following weekend.

So why was it sitting on the ground? She supposed this howling wind could have knocked it off.

Unease creeped up her spine, tapping each vertebra on the way up. With each tap her heart rate kicked up. A warning? Paranoia? She continued to stare at the opening under the porch, waiting. Anticipating.

Don't.

Yet, like a lure she couldn't resist, she tiptoed off the porch to investigate. Slowly, she eased her .38 from her purse, held it just the way her father had taught her—two hands, thumbs along the side, grip tight.

She moved silently, avoiding a pile of leaves that might crunch when stepped on. No movement from under the porch. Step over step she approached. Just before the opening where the lattice should have been, she squatted.

Something flew at her—*jump*—and her pulse hammered, sending blood rocketing into her brain, slamming its way in. She reeled back. Trigger. *No.* Could be nothing. Someone clearing debris from under the house. She couldn't know. *Pull the trigger.*

Too late. A brick—another damned brick—hit her square in the chest, knocking the wind out of her. She fell backward, landing on her butt, and pain shot down both legs. Gasping, she forced air into her lungs. Gun. *Don't drop it.*

Before she could look up, another brick smashed down onto her hand. Grinding hot pain lanced into her fingers and she cried out. Looming over her was Jamie—*Jamie?*—brick still in hand, readying for another swing. *Fight.* Jenna kicked out, connected with Jamie's hip, knocking Jamie sideways.

Somehow, her gun was still in her hand, but her grip was no good. She tried to curl her fingers and a second bolt of pain shot through them. Useless fingers. She rolled, grabbed the gun with her left hand and—*boom!*—something clocked her on the back of the head.

Ahead of her a tree swayed, its edges blurring against the gray sky. Using a branch as a focal point, she got to her knees. Nausea filled her belly. *Feel sick.* Cold, wet moisture from the dirt seeped through her tights to her knees, and her head looped and spun right along with her rebelling stomach. *Too much.*

She lay back down and closed her eyes. *No sleeping.* She fought to open her eyes but the lids were so heavy.

"Stupid beauty queen," Jamie said. "My cousin loses his sense and look where we are. So stupid." Something poked Jenna's side. "Get up."

Up? No. She closed her eyes again. Sighed at the relief. And then, finally, the blackness came.

"HE'S BACK?" CAMILLE asked, her voice cracking under the strain of hearing that their father had appeared as suddenly as he'd abandoned them nine years earlier.

Brent sat back on his sister's giant sofa and forced his shoulders into a relaxed position. In the time he'd been working his mother's case, this was one conversation he never wanted to have, but if he appeared calm, Camille might believe it.

Typically, he could talk motives and suspects with no problem. Telling Camille their father had returned would open the gaping wound she'd spent years of therapy gluing shut.

Brent nodded. "He showed up at the house today. Uncle Herb talked to him. Sylvie is a mess and I'm heading out there. I wanted you to know."

At least *she* wouldn't be blindsided.

Get over it. He couldn't dwell on the fact that he and Jenna, despite their raging sexual attraction, didn't mesh. If they had, she would have notified him lickety-split about his father. Even if she didn't know the old man was moving up the time frame, she should have told Brent he was coming. Sure, the guy showing up a day early would have been a surprise, but Brent would have at least known he was coming.

Instead, he got smacked upside the head with it and still didn't understand why.

Women. Always complicating his life.

His phone rang. *Ignore it.* He drummed his fingers on his leg and Camille's gaze shot to the coffee table where his phone continued to ring.

"Is that him?"

"I don't know. Could be. Uncle Herb gave him my number."

"Can I look?"

Third ring. "Sure."

Shaking her head, Camille scooped the phone up and glanced at the screen. "Penny Hennings."

Brent blew air through his lips and gave the relief its due diligence. Facing his father was imminent, but he didn't have to rush it. Had it been Mason calling, Brent would have ignored it. Let the old man wait on him for a change.

The phone went silent and Camille set it down. "Isn't she Jenna's boss?"

"She is."

"Maybe they have news. Shouldn't you talk to her?"

"I fired them."

As expected, because his sister's mannerisms hadn't changed since her seventh birthday, she wrinkled her nose and pursed her lips. Total pig face. "Why?"

Where should he start? "Jenna sat on telling me about Dad. He wasn't due until tomorrow."

Camille shrugged. "And?"

And nothing. "She should've called me ASAP."

"But…" She cocked her head. "You just said he wasn't due until tomorrow. You're mad because she didn't call you?"

When she put it that way, it didn't sound reasonable. "It's not that simple."

"Brent, you're my big brother and I've always been in awe of you, but that's dumb."

"Hey—"

"No hey. If it had been me having to deliver that message, I'd have needed a few minutes to figure out how to tell you our deadbeat father was back. I'd have been worried about your reaction, and I know you better than anyone. She cares about you and you fired her." Brent leaned forward, but Camille held her hands up. "I'm not saying she was right, but she's done a lot for us. That's all."

Camille was taking Jenna's side. What the hell was with his family?

"I *don't* like being blindsided."

"But she didn't blindside you. Dad did. It's his fault, not hers."

His voice mail chirped and that reprieve couldn't have come at a better time considering that Camille and her ever-efficient mind were aggravating him. He picked up his phone, checked the screen because why not? This conversation was definitely skidding off the rails.

"You want to run from her," Camille said.

He'd scroll through his emails while he was at it.

"Brent, you know I love you, but there's a reason you're not attached, and running won't cure it."

Enough. He met his sister's gaze, gave her the hard look he knew she'd understand. "Shut up about my life."

His normally agreeable sister shrugged. "You've never shut up about my life."

Hello? Someone had to take care of her. He hit the button to dial Penny.

Camille rolled her eyes. "You're messing this up. And that would be a shame because I think you care about her. I never butt into your business when it comes to women, but this time it won't be so easy for you to walk away."

Brent held the phone up. "It's ringing."

And I'm ignoring you. At least trying to. When had his sister gotten so smart about people? About *him*? He'd give her credit for one thing, she had him nailed. Yes, he'd walk away from Jenna, and no, it wouldn't be easy.

Nothing was ever easy when it came to Jenna. Especially that crazy feeling he got every time she stepped into his orbit. When she was close, he wanted closer. There was comfort there. A connection he'd never had and...*forget it.* No sense in tormenting himself.

Penny picked up. "Hey," he said into the phone. "What's up?"

"Is Jenna with you?"

His fingertips tingled. Weird. He curled and uncurled his free hand. Brent stood and paced the small area behind the sofa. "Uh, no. I left her in the lobby. Why?"

"Because she's gone."

"Gone where?"

"Well, Brent, if I knew, I wouldn't be asking you. She's not answering her cell. You said she's in danger and now she's gone."

He stopped pacing, stared straight ahead while his pulse jackhammered. *She's gone. AWOL.* He wouldn't panic. Not yet. Jenna liked going rogue and he wouldn't put it past her to continue investigating. Even after he'd canned her. Her relentless ambition, her quest to find answers, were things he loved about her. Chances were she'd bolted to avoid Penny asking questions.

"I'll find her."

He hung up on Penny and dialed Jenna's number.

"Problem?" Camille asked.

"Jenna went AWOL."

"After you fired her."

He adored his sister, but right now she was hacking at his last stable nerve. "You need to back off."

She hopped off the chair, walked to the entryway of the tiny apartment and grabbed her coat off the hook.

Jenna's voice mail beeped and her voice, the breathy one she layered on when she thought she needed it, came through the line.

"It's me," he said. "Call me."

Camille shrugged into her coat. "No answer?"

"No. Where are you going?"

"Wherever you are. It's time to find our father."

Chapter Fourteen

"Wake up, beauty queen."

Still with her eyes closed and fighting the need to come fully awake, Jenna focused on the voice. *Who is that?* Piercing light flashed behind her eyelids and a shattering stab blazed down her neck. She peeled open her eyes, met the darkened living room of the Thompson's house and silently thanked whatever god had gifted her with dim lighting.

Ratty sneakers appeared in front of her. Jenna slid her gaze upward, along the jean-clad legs, over the zip-up jacket—Jamie—to the .38 in the woman's hand.

My gun.

Jenna, the FBI reject, had made the most critical of all critical errors and let her weapon leave her. *So sorry, Dad.* Worse, she didn't understand any of this. She rolled to her back and her vision loopy-looped right along with her stomach. *Gonna be sick.* "Bathroom."

Jamie squatted in front of her. "What?"

"I'm…sick."

"Yeah. Expected that when I dragged you in here." She dropped a small pail next to Jenna. "Here you go, beauty queen. Do your thing."

Swallowing back bile, she clutched at the pail, waiting. She exhaled, then inhaled again and still vomit threatened.

After a few more breaths, she opened her eyes and slid her gaze sideways. Jamie stood by the window.

"What are you doing?" Jenna asked.

"You don't want to know."

Get up. If she could just sit up, maybe she'd have a chance to get the gun back. *Fool.* She could barely see straight, much less fight for a gun big enough to knock a decent-sized hole in her. Still, if the alternative was lying on this floor waiting for someone to save her, she'd better figure out a plan.

Jenna levered up and found herself on the losing end of her own gun. Vomit lurched into her throat and—*oh, no, oh, no*—she grabbed the pail, heaving into it, gagging until her eyeballs wanted to burst.

Maybe she'd need that hero after all.

She lolled back against the sofa and her stomach contracted, released and contracted again. Now that her stomach had emptied, maybe the nausea would subside. Let her at least get to her feet.

She stared down at the plastic bucket Jamie must have retrieved from next door. The pungent odor of pine needles invaded her already vulnerable system and she sat back, held her arm against her nose to block the smell.

Her fingers throbbed from the bashing they'd taken with the brick and she flexed them, wincing along the way. None broken. One good thing. "Jamie, please. Tell me what's happening."

"That idiot uncle of mine came back. That's what's happening. He's been gone all this time. You come along and suddenly he's back. You love that, don't you? Men falling at your feet. Following your every command." She let out a frustrated grunt. "Stupid beauty queen."

Jenna studied her movements. Stiff, jerky, nervous.

And holding a gun.

She met her gaze and those eyes that were almost the

exact color of Brent's and Sylvie's and all she saw was death. "I don't know what you're doing, but please, put that gun down before someone gets hurt."

"Shut up."

Setting the pail next to her, Jenna hung on to the edge in case she needed to swing it. "Can I get off the floor?"

Jamie held up the gun, gestured to the sofa. "Fine. On the couch. Move slow. It won't be much longer."

"For what?"

"For our visitor. My uncle is coming. He will confess to murdering my aunt and after I catch him with your dead body, I'll shoot him in self-defense. Then it's all over. Everyone goes back to their lives."

Prickles of panic cruised along Jenna's skin.

Unglued.

This whole setup was to get her uncle here so she could stage a murder. Jamie's hand shook and her gaze bounced around.

Jenna eyed the door, calculated the time it would take to get there.

"I need this to end," Jamie said. "This house should be razed so we can get on with our lives and stop thinking about Cheryl. It's all anybody cares about. This empty house and Cheryl. Now I'm going to end it. Once and for all."

Jenna's panic took hold and she pictured the scene. Bodies in front of the sofa, blood everywhere. Brent would find them. He'd walk in, see the bodies and it would be a miracle if he didn't go insane. A fierce protective instinct whipped at her.

"This isn't the way. If your uncle murdered your aunt, let the sheriff deal with him. *This* will not help you."

"Yeah, it will. You have no idea."

And the look in her eyes, that cold, deadly calm left Jenna wondering if a killer stood in front of her.

Next plan. Jenna pushed off the floor, her stomach flopping like a fish on land. And dummy her, she'd come out here and not told anyone. So many mistakes.

At the entryway, her purse had been thrown against the wall. Jamie must have put it there when she'd dragged her inside. Some of the contents, the tools of her trade—hairbrush, lipstick, notepad—had fallen out and lay scattered on the floor.

"Forget it," Jamie said. "I took your phone. My cousin keeps calling. He hates when people don't return his calls."

She didn't know that, but could use it. "I do know. I should call him. He's such a worrier. I told him I was coming here. If I don't call him, he'll break speed records."

Jamie waved the gun. "I listened to your voice mail. He's mad at you, beauty queen. Demanding to know where you are."

Caught. "He'll figure it out."

"Maybe." She shrugged. "By the time he gets here, all he'll find is another dead woman. And his dead father." She spun to the window and stormed around, jabbing the .38 once, twice, three times in Jenna's direction. Each time, Jenna flinched, waiting for the bang of an accidental—or not so accidental—shot.

"Jamie, please. I don't understand. If Mason is guilty, you committing a double murder doesn't accomplish anything. All it does is get you a life sentence."

Even if her plan was to make Mason look guilty.

"And dispose of a killer."

"But at what cost?"

"Doesn't matter."

Totally snapped. Not a pinch of rational thought to be found. Jenna rested her pounding head against the back of the sofa and faced off with her own gun. Her thoughts whirled and she analyzed her errors, picking them apart with brutal accuracy. Coming here alone, not alerting anyone, her failure to move when the brick flew at her.

But wait. Jamie hadn't been here when they'd found the bricks. Jenna ticked back to their conversation at the truck stop. She hadn't said anything. She had, in fact, put her off.

"You tossed the brick through my window, didn't you?"

No answer.

"Why, Jamie?"

Again no answer. *Push her.*

"To scare me off, right? Only I didn't go. Then I found your uncle."

"And brought him back here. As if we needed that filth here after he left his children? What kind of man abandons his children after their mother is murdered? *Not* my father. That's for sure."

The way she said it, accentuating the *not*, caught Jenna sideways. *Odd.* "What does that mean?"

"*My* father is a good man. He takes care of us. Whatever his faults, he never walked away. So I'm going to fix things. Finally make them right."

Jenna's vision blurred again and she swallowed another surge of bile. Her stomach protested and she grabbed the bucket, heaving into it. Sick as a dog, head spinning and Jamie off her rocker. With Jenna's gun. Outside, a clap of thunder sounded and the boom rattled the windows.

Banner afternoon.

Jenna finished with the bucket and, short on options, dabbed the cuff of her sweater against her mouth. "I could use a napkin. I have some in my purse. Please?"

"Is this a trick?"

It wasn't, but the idea had merit. If she could distract Jamie, she might get a few seconds to attack. But with the way her head spun, she'd probably fall on her face. "Please. I'm so sick."

Jamie rolled her eyes. "Now you're a drama queen on top

of a beauty queen. I expected more from you." She stomped to Jenna's purse and kicked it toward her. "You get them. And don't try anything. I *will* shoot you."

Jenna didn't doubt that.

A car door slammed, the sound muffled by the closed door. "Finally," Jamie huffed. Keeping the weapon aimed at Jenna, she peeked out the window.

"You're about to meet Brent's father."

Jamie cracked the door ajar, waiting for Mason to push it open. *This is it.* Heavy footsteps—boots—thunked against the wood and Jamie inched back, raising the gun. *Do something, do something, do something.*

"Run!" Jenna screamed. "Run!"

Jamie swung right, the .38 looming in Jenna's direction and—*don't shoot, please don't shoot*—Jamie's finger moved over the trigger. *Go.* Jenna rolled sideways. *Boom!* The shot ripped into the arm of the sofa where Jenna had just been sitting. *Stone-cold crazy.*

Jamie swung the gun back to the doorway. Standing there, a look of terror and panic tightening his cheeks, stood Brent's father. It may as well have been Brent in thirty years. Same big build, same hair color and bone structure.

Bone structure she definitely wanted to see in thirty years.

No dying today.

Jenna scrambled to her feet, the soles of her shoes slipping on the damned wood and her bad ankle barked. No traction. "Run!"

"Don't move," Jamie said, calm as could be. She backed up. "I don't care which one of you I kill first. Anyone moves, they get shot." She jerked her head at Mason. "Get inside."

The idiot stood in the doorway, hands raised. This man was Brent's father? Something went fluky in the gene pool. Brent would have disarmed her in four seconds. Maybe three. His father? He froze. She supposed Jamie was right about one thing: Mason Thompson was a weak man.

"Inside or I shoot you. I don't care. You're worthless anyway."

Run. Please, run. Get help. This time she hoped he'd run for the right reasons.

He stepped inside and Jenna gasped.

"Shut that door and lock it," Jamie said.

Again, Mason did as he was told.

"What the hell's going on, Jamie?" he asked.

Jamie tilted her head. "Oh, Uncle Mason, we're going to play a little game. It's called Let's-Make-Everything-Right. Now get in here and shut up."

BRENT SWUNG INTO the driveway, spotted Jenna's car parked in front of a blue pickup with a missing tailgate and let out a stream of curses that would put Aunt Sylvie in a straitjacket.

His father always drove pickups and although Brent had never seen this one, he didn't doubt who it belonged to.

So, yeah, Jenna was inside the house, probably interviewing his father. After Brent had fired her.

"I see Jenna took that whole you're-fired thing seriously," Camille cracked.

Another smart-mouth. Lucky him. He jammed the SUV into Park and eyeballed his sister. "You about done?"

"Not nearly. I always let you take the lead on things, but this time, I think you're in over your head. It doesn't matter at this minute, though, because I'd like to see what our father is up to."

"You want me to do this? I could talk to him and then bring you in."

Camille's dark blue eyes clouded and grew darker. Intense. *Stronger.* Normally, he'd insist on handling this himself. But hadn't that been one of Jenna's observations? That he never let anyone help him?

"No," Camille said. "I'm tired of being afraid to face him."

Brent reached over and tugged on her hair the way he used to when she was a kid. Those were the good memories, the memories that reminded him that their childhood hadn't been a complete loss. "Let's do it, then."

He slid from the SUV, contemplated throwing his suit jacket on again. Nah. Why make an effort for a guy who'd walked out on them?

In the distance, thunder rumbled. Wicked storm heading in. They'd make this quick and get back on the road again.

He stopped in front of the car, grabbed Camille's arm and looked her in the eyes, searching, making sure this is what she wanted.

His sister patted his hand. "I'm okay. I've got you and you've got me. That's all we need. We take care of each other."

Yes, they did. Whatever their childhood had tossed at them, they'd survived. "That we do, sis."

Camille pointed to the driveway next door. "Jamie is here. I wonder if they're all inside with him."

Him. Brent didn't expect a lot from his life, but he never wanted to reach a place where his children would refer to their father as *him* rather than Dad. A sad state all around.

Brent dragged a hand over his face. "I can't handle all of them. Not in this lifetime. It'll be a free-for-all. We have to clear the place so you and I can talk to him. Back me up on that."

"You know I will."

Camille tucked her arm into his and the two of them walked toward the porch. "Don't be mad at Jenna. She's invested. You can't hold that against her."

Brent snorted. "Is this some twisted female unity?"

"Maybe. I like her. She'd be good for you. If you pulled your head out of your rear."

"Don't start."

He unhooked his arm, dragged his key from his pocket and tromped up the stairs. He wouldn't knock. Never. He'd maintained this house for years. His name wasn't on the deed, but he'd assumed responsibility. Whatever was going on in that house, it involved him. And Camille.

He shoved the key in the door, flipped the lock and grabbed the knob. For a brief second the cold metal against his sweat-soaked palm shocked him. When he opened the door, he'd put eyes on his father for the first time in over nine years. No visits or calls or wondering if they were all right.

Nine years.

A fresh bout of anger hissed at him, coiled around his neck and he stiffened. *Stay calm.* That's what he needed now. Not to blow his top. To treat his father with respectful indifference. That's all the old man would get. Brent cracked his neck, rolled his shoulders and all that coiling anger loosened its grip. *Better.* He turned the knob and gently pushed open the door.

"Gun!"

Jenna's voice. One second. That's how long it took the word to register. Gun. Someone inside had a gun. And it wasn't Jenna. *Cover.* He shoved Camille sideways, drew his weapon and spun away from the door. Breathing deep, he zeroed in on a tree branch smacking around. Inside, Jenna's yelling mixed with another female voice, the words muddling together. *Don't shoot. Back up. It's Brent.* What in hell was going on?

Drowning in a blood rush, he glanced at the gun in his trembling hands. Dammit. Between practice and even discharging it while on duty, he'd held this gun countless times. Never once had his hands shook.

"Shut up!"

Jamie.

"Brent," Jenna yelled, "Jamie has my gun."

A shot, loud and booming went off. *No, no, no.* Who the hell was Jamie shooting at? The front window shattered and glass flew, sprinkling down on Camille, who was still stretched on the worn porch floor. *Please, don't let her be hit.*

Camille covered her head with her hands. *She's moving.* "Are you hit?"

His sister looked up at him, her normally big eyes even wider and…spooked. Shock. "Camille," he snapped, "are you okay?"

"Yes."

Another burst of adrenaline, relief this time, flooded his system. "Get off this porch. Run."

"I'm not leaving you."

"Brent?" Jamie's voice came from inside.

He rested his head against the house, his blood still barreling, scrambling his thoughts. What the hell was going on? *Disarm her. No. Hold perimeter.*

How?

He couldn't deal with it alone. He'd need backup. *Wait for the sheriff.* No chances. Not with Jenna and apparently his father inside.

Being held at gunpoint.

By his cousin.

Couldn't be.

"Jamie, please. Tell me what's happening."

"I'm sorry, Brent. I'm so sorry. I didn't mean for it to go this way."

Three seconds ago, he'd doubted his cousin could be holding that gun. Three seconds ago, he wouldn't have believed that his sweet, caring cousin, who'd helped him through countless jams in his lifetime, could fire a weapon. Three seconds ago, he'd thought he knew all there was to know about Jamie.

In three short seconds, his illusions had disintegrated and this thing launched to another level.

He dialed into his law enforcement training and blocked out his emotions. There was no room for them. Now, he was a stranger, a US marshal doing his job and addressing this situation.

To his right, Camille had moved to all fours. "Get off the porch. I need backup. Go call 9-1-1. Do it. Now."

Her gaze ping-ponged between him and the door. "Go," he said.

Finally, she crawled to the porch steps, staying clear of the open doorway. "I'll get help and come back."

Not in his lifetime. "No. Stay clear. See if Aunt Sylvie and Uncle Herb are home."

All he needed was his aunt and uncle barging in on the middle of this thing, wanting answers. Hell, he wanted answers. "If they're home, make sure they don't come here. Now go. Stay low in front of the house."

Brent watched her, his heart banging, slamming against him as his baby sister, who he'd protected from childhood, duck-walked across the lawn and out of a bullet's path. *Stay low, please stay low.* She cleared the lawn and Brent let out a small breath. *Little farther.* Driveway clear. *Check.* She made it to his aunt's house and he rested his head back. The blood rush turned to a trickle and he cut his gaze left and right.

"Jamie?" he yelled.

"Come inside, Brent."

Instinct pushed him forward. Nothing odd there, given his protective tendencies. Jamie knew this about him. She *expected* it. Law enforcement training and all those hard-fought lessons about never entering a situation like this alone kept him still.

The sheriff would show up in minutes. Before that, Brent needed to keep everyone calm. And get Jenna's .38 out of

Jamie's extremely unskilled hands. He breathed in and focused on the banging tree branch. *Go time.*

"James, put that gun down." Using his cousin's childhood nickname couldn't hurt. "I'm not coming inside until you put the gun down. Or you come out here and let me see you."

"No."

Another wind gust blew the tree branches sideways, smacking them against the house—*crack*—and making him flinch. Then came another round of thunder, closer this time and booming. Brent glanced at the sky where thick black clouds rolled in. Anytime now the sky would open up and soak the place. If it kept Camille and his aunt and uncle next door, he'd deal with it.

"Brent?" Jamie hollered.

"Let Jenna and my dad come out. They come out and I come in."

"No."

"James, come on."

"No."

"Who's in there with you?"

"Just the beauty queen and your useless father."

How the hell had things gotten so out of control that it had come to this? The woman he loved was trapped inside. Trapped with his father, a man Brent hadn't yet reconciled his feelings about and now they could both die.

Brent leaned his head against the house. *Diversion.* If he could distract Jamie, he'd get a chance to disarm her and figure out what happened.

"Okay," he hollered. "We don't want your folks in the middle of this, right?"

"Brent! You keep them out of here."

"I will, James. I will. Give me five minutes, okay?"

"Five minutes!"

"Promise me you won't do anything stupid."

Anything else stupid.

"I won't. As long as the beauty queen and your father stay put. Do not call the sheriff, Brent. I'll kill them both if you do."

Kill them. What? Jamie? He squeezed his eyes shut, felt the pressure in his forehead. Work the problem and fix this. He gripped the gun again—too tight—then loosened his hold. "Nobody will come in there that you don't want. I promise."

Brent tore off down the porch steps, keeping low as he crossed the lawn. Camille came from the front of Aunt Sylvie's, met him by the driveway, and he steered her around the side of the house. "They home?"

"No. I called the sheriff. He's over by Johnson's farm dealing with a wreck. He and a deputy are on the way, but it'll be fifteen minutes before they get here. Where are we going?"

"Basement."

"Why?"

"We're creating a diversion."

Chapter Fifteen

On the list of things to be thankful for, an outside basement entrance just flew to the top. Brent holstered his gun and hustled down the concrete steps where, using slow, silent movements, he turned the knob on the door.

"What—" Camille whispered.

"Shh."

She closed her mouth and Brent held his fingers against his lips. Above them, thunder boomed again. Using the noise as cover, he pushed open the door. The musty smell hit him full force.

On one side, his father's old tools still littered the top of the workbench. Next to the bench was the rolling tool chest. He'd need that. The furnace, with its newly installed gas line, was in the right corner. Beside it was his target. The hot-water heater.

He spun back to Camille. "Get me the wire cutters from the tool chest. And a hammer. If there's no hammer, give me something I can bang on this safety valve with. Do it quietly."

The floors were thin and any odd noise would echo right into the upper floor. He glanced around looking for a rag, a garden bag, anything that would muffle the sound when he jammed the safety valve. Nothing. He started unbuttoning his shirt, stripping down to his undershirt.

Camille gave him a look. "Uh, what are you doing?"

"I'm about to crush the safety valve so it won't work and I need to muffle the bang."

"What?"

"Shh."

He balled his shirt, set it on top of the valve and felt through the fabric to make sure his aim was square. She handed him a hammer. *Whack.* He blasted it. One good muffled shot. Excellent. He set the hammer down and shut the cold-water valve.

"Brent?"

"Give me a sec. I helped Dad replace a hot-water heater once. He told me all the things I shouldn't do. I'm doing them."

He squatted, gave the water-release valve a spin and water sloshed out, pouring over his shoes and the floor. Soaked. Dammit.

Camille still held the wire cutters and he waggled his fingers. Better than any surgical nurse, she slapped them into his hand. He grasped the red wire linking the temperature control knob to the sensor. *Snip.* That's gone. Quickly, he whipped the temp-control knob to its highest setting and the burner flamed all the way open.

He checked the water still pouring out of the tank. *Not enough.* But he had to get back upstairs. Camille.

He jumped up and faced his sister. "I need your help."

"Anything."

"Wait another five minutes, then shut the water valve. We need this thing half full. It usually takes ten minutes. If you wait another four or five, it should be good enough. Then you need to get the hell out of here because the top of this water heater will blow straight off. Hopefully, it'll scare the hell out of Jamie and I can disarm her."

"Are you insane?"

He had to be because he was leaving his baby sister

down here to practically set off his homemade bomb. God help him if something happened to her. He'd never live with it.

He stepped back. "Forget it. You can't do this. Too dangerous. I'll think of something else."

"What?"

"I don't know."

Camille glanced at the hot water heater.

"Forget it, Camille."

But she waggled her head. "It's the only option. Besides, you've done most of the work. If we do it this way, in a few minutes, this will all be over. I can do it."

"Camille—"

She spun on him and pointed. "Stop. I can do this. It's the only way everyone gets out safely. Just tell me what to do."

Dug in. When his sister got like this, it took a bulldozer to move her. And short on options, they'd have to go with it.

"Get your phone out," he said. "Watch the time. No longer than five minutes. I don't want you in here when this thing blows. I'd do it myself, but I gotta get back up there."

She shooed him away. "Leave. I'll find you."

"When you leave here, go next door. If Sylvie and Herb come home, make sure they stay there. That's what I need from you. Got it?"

His sister hesitated. *Nuh-uh.* "Camille?"

Finally she nodded. "I've got it. We can do this."

KEEPING HER GAZE pinned to Jamie—and the .38—Jenna leaned her head against the arm of the sofa. *I need to do something.* Clearly Brent's father was content to do nothing. Total gene-pool malfunction. And thank God for that because if she knew Brent even a little bit, he had a plan.

Only problem with that was Jamie knew Brent better than Jenna and had probably come to the same conclusion.

"James?" Brent shouted from the porch.

Jamie swung her head to the still-open door and immediately came back to Jenna.

"Hey," Jenna said. "Stop swinging that gun around before it accidentally goes off and hits one of us. Then your problems get a whole lot worse."

"Shut up!"

"Jamie," Brent hollered, "I'm coming in."

Jenna sat up, half relieved, half terrified. Growing up with a houseful of cops she knew an officer should never—ever—enter a situation like this without backup. Which meant either Brent had backup or he'd chosen to wing it.

Then he was in the doorway, feet spread, arms up, gun aimed at Jamie. This family. Tragic from the get-go.

The back of Jenna's neck itched and her arms tingled. Add that to the pounding headache and her body went more than a little berserk. Jamie stood faced off with Brent. If he could keep her occupied, Jenna might be able to lunge and draw her attention. Between the two of them, they'd get that gun. Hopefully before someone wound up with a hole in them.

Jamie looked back. "Don't move."

Jenna held her hands up. "Sorry. Sorry."

"Sit still, Jenna," Brent said.

Mason was beside her, his long legs stretched in front of him, arms at his sides. Brent glanced in his direction but quickly averted his eyes. "Anyone hurt?"

"We're okay," Jenna said.

There were hundreds—thousands—of ways this situation could end. Another shot being fired was only one of them. *Get the gun.*

Brent took a step into the room.

"Stay there," Jamie said.

"Talk to me. Whatever this is, we can fix. No one is hurt. James, please, we can fix this."

"I didn't want it."

"I know," he said. "Whatever happened, we'll fix it. Put the gun down."

"Brent!" a woman shouted from outside, her voice edged with crackling panic.

Camille.

Footsteps pounded against the porch—*thunk, thunk, thunk*—and in stormed Brent's aunt and uncle.

Included in those thousand ways the situation could go bad would be Brent's aunt and uncle rushing in.

"Get out!" Jamie shrieked, the high-pitched wail tearing through the tense air like a buzz saw against cardboard.

Gun still on Jamie, Brent jerked his head. "All of you, out."

Herb stepped forward. These people. Insanity.

"What in the hell are you doing?" he asked his daughter.

"Leave, Dad."

"I will not. Put that thing down."

Boom! Something under them—not close, by the kitchen—exploded and Jenna glanced through the archway following the sound. A loud scream mixed with the explosion. Jenna's ears whistled. Thirty feet away, an object blasted through the kitchen floor, sending the old linoleum flying, hunks of it showering down.

Jamie stood in front of her, mouth agape, her body angled toward the mess. *Get the gun.* Scrambling to her feet, Jenna lunged. Brent was faster. Her gaze cut to him and she leaped out of the way as his big body crashed down on top of Jamie. The gun hit the floor with a *thwack*. Brent swatted it, sending it in Jenna's direction.

She scooped it up. "Got it."

Under Brent, Jamie bucked and kicked and hollered.

I'm done.

Jenna trained the weapon on Jamie. "Stop. Right now."

"Shoot me. Do it. Please."

Oh, she'd like the chance. Yes, she would. And in that

moment, in her state of mind, she'd do it. She'd let go of any inhibition because this woman had planned on killing her. And leaving her body for Brent to find. How she—someone who supposedly loved this man—could allow him to walk into this house and find more bodies, Jenna couldn't grasp. The terror it would have inflicted upon his already shattered world would have driven him mad. And that, Jenna wouldn't stand for.

"If you don't stop moving I will. And don't think I won't. You were going to let him walk in here and find us. That makes you a monster. I hate monsters."

"Everyone, shut up," Brent said, his huge body still locking Jamie down. "Jamie, I will lay here all night if I have to." He grabbed both her wrists and pinned them. "Stop."

Under his substantial weight, she finally gave in, succumbed to the idea that she couldn't fight him off. "Dad, help me."

"Help you?" her father screamed, his eyes fixed and horrified. "I don't know what you're doing. How am I supposed to help you?"

"Uncle Herb," Brent said, "take Aunt Sylvie outside. Check on Camille and stay with them. Please."

Turning on his heel, Herb grabbed Sylvie by the elbow, ushering her out. Jamie's eyes bulged as her cheeks hardened.

"You're turning your back on me?" she shrieked as her parents left the house. "After what you did to those women?"

What women? Something prickled at the base of Jenna's neck.

"Dad, please."

And then the tears came. Jamie dropped her head, laying her cheek against the wooden floor, shrieking as if a limb had been severed. "I did it for him. Whatever he did to those women, I did it for him."

Jenna moved closer, keeping the gun on Jamie, but glancing at Brent. He met her gaze, but his eyes, the look there, all that nothingness—just lifeless—slammed her, made her ache for him. She set her hand on his shoulder and squeezed. "Baby, you need to get up. I've got this."

Brent eased off his cousin, but kept one knee on her back.

"It's okay," Jenna said. "I have her. Take a breath. I have her."

In his life, there had been moments of bewilderment, moments of disappointment, moments of life-shattering agony that cut so deep he knew he'd never recover.

This would be all of those moments combined.

Lifting his knee from Jamie, Brent backed away, his mind spinning, working, considering. All of it coming at him in a rush, making him dizzy and...confused.

"Brent?"

Jenna. She stood, gun in hand, making sure the situation stayed calm. She drove him crazy, but how many women could go through what she'd just experienced and still manage to stay in control.

"I'm okay," he said.

A lie, but he'd lied about his emotional state before. His cousin continued to wail on the floor and his mind reeled back twenty-three years. The back door. No one but family ever used the back door. *I did it for him.* Jamie's words lingered, but like a language he didn't understand, a disconnect existed.

"Jamie, why are you crying? What did you do?"

"The clothes," she shrieked, tears streaming down her face. "The clothes in the basement. I saw them. Your mom saw when he burned them."

A frigid grip took hold and Brent shivered. He stepped back, steadying himself. *Let her talk.*

"I heard her ask about them. She wouldn't let it go."

"Oh, God," Camille said.

Camille. Brent spun, saw his sister in the doorway. Whatever this was, she didn't need to hear it. "Out!"

"What did you do?" Camille repeated.

"I wanted to protect him. That's all. I didn't mean…"

"Everyone stop talking," Jenna said. "Right now."

She's right. Brent didn't care. He could do this. With Aunt Sylvie and Uncle Herb outside, he could control the emotional chaos in the house and get answers. He squatted next to Jamie, reminded himself that she'd been a constant supporter since his mom died and set his hand on her back. "Sit up and talk to me. Tell me what happened. What clothes in the basement?"

Facing away from him, Jamie rested her cheek against the floor, her hair fanning out. "The women's clothes. When he comes home, he hides them behind the pipe in the basement. Then he burns them. He gets rid of them. I didn't know why and then I figured it out. He killed the women and burned their clothes. It's always when he comes home from a trip. I used to watch for him. He'd come home and go to the basement first. I went down there one morning and found the clothes. When I got home from school, they were gone and he was cleaning the fire pit. He'd burn them in the fire pit when we weren't around."

"Brent," Jenna said, "please stop this. She should have a lawyer. You need to do this the right way."

"Yes. Stop this." The sheriff strode through the door, gun drawn, a deputy on his heels. "All of you, outside."

"I didn't mean to kill her," Jamie said, still on the floor. "But she caught him. She caught him burning the clothes and I got scared."

Someone latched on to the back of Brent's shirt. Jenna. "You shouldn't be in here," she said.

He squared his shoulders, but inside the torture ran hot

and deep, ripping into him, making his mind burn with visions of his cousin, his beloved cousin, swinging that brick at his mother. All to protect his uncle.

Leave. This house was a curse. Every sickening inch of it. *Leave.* He glanced at his father, sitting on that damned floor and the fury Brent had kept under wraps for so long unraveled, whipping inside him like a live wire, its tip singeing him. As much as he didn't want his father dead, the man had left them. Left *him* to care for a teenaged girl. How the hell would they fix this?

Could they fix it?

Jenna gave him a not-so-light shove and his feet moved. One foot, then the next, heading to the door where there would be fresh air and the howling wind and hopefully a ton a rain. Enough rain to wash away this house and the horror that it kept ramming down his throat.

I'm losing it.

He got to the porch and—yes—violent, fat raindrops poured from the sky. Rain so hard that it pounded against the roof—hammering and hammering—like it would drill through the shingles. Let it. Let it soak the house. Drown it.

He jogged down the stairs, swung a left and stormed to the backyard.

"Brent?" his aunt called from somewhere behind him.

"No," Jenna hollered back, pausing to turn back. "Give him a minute."

His aunt screamed, her hysterics registering and Brent stopped.

Jenna nudged him forward. "Keep moving. I just looked and there's a deputy with them. Camille is there, too. You need a break."

Protecting him. His feet kept moving, his shoes sinking into the already soft grass. He needed out. That's all he knew. A few minutes of peace and no one depending on him to save them.

He reached the backyard and hooked another left, pacing the rear of the house praying to God his family wouldn't come back here and see him like this.

When he reached the far end of the house he turned back and his gaze connected with Jenna's. She stood by the tree outside of his old room, the rain dousing her, making her normally pristine hair cling to her head. She took one step and her heel stuck in the mud. She kicked off her shoes—*I love this woman*—and walked toward him, her feet sinking in the muddy grass.

"It was her," he said, sliding a sideways glance at Jenna as he stomped by, continuing to pace, just burning off the energy searing him from inside out. "She sat with us at every holiday knowing what she'd done. That she'd wrecked us. All this time."

At the edge of the house, he turned again, did another lap. Jenna struggled to keep up and finally stopped in the middle by the back porch.

"Let it out, Brent. Please. Just let it fly. You'll feel better."

He'd feel better? Really? He didn't think so, because all that fire and rage and pain was tearing through him. His arms, legs, stomach. Each body part shredding. He'd trusted Jamie, looked up to her for helping to care for them. For showing them how loving families stepped up and gave shelter when all else failed. He *loved* her.

And she'd murdered his mother.

A fifteen-year-old murderer. How the hell?

He turned for another lap, slid a glance at Jenna and his throat started to close. Jamie had held on to this secret, letting him obsess and give up his life to search for a killer. She'd watched him torment himself and never cared.

Breathe, breathe, breathe.

He walked faster. *Keep moving. Breathe.* The shredding continued. No escape. Nowhere to put it all.

"Brent, let it out."

He spun and faced Jenna and his mind went all kinds of crazy. "What was she talking about? My uncle killed women? *She* killed my mother?"

The words—were they even words?—turned into a howl. Like a hole had been blown open and all that rage poured out of his mouth. Agony, every second of it, and the pressure behind his eyes became too much. He dug the palms of his hands against them and continued the insane screaming. *I'm cracking up.*

"I'm going to touch you," Jenna said, somehow penetrating his yelling.

A second went by and she rested her hand on his back. It stuck to his now soaked shirt, but she rubbed back and forth. "It's okay," she said. "Let it out."

Maybe it was the softness in her voice or that magic touch of hers, but the howling stopped and the air went silent. Over. That fast, just done.

A crack of thunder boomed again, but Jenna kept rubbing. "You're okay. Come sit on the porch."

She took his hand and led him to the porch. Her feet sloshed in the wet grass, but she kept moving until she shoved him to a step. Exhaustion leveled him and he dropped his head, allowing himself a few seconds. A few more.

Breathe.

Jenna sat next to him and rested her head on his shoulder. "You'll be okay," she said.

He glanced at her, soaked to the skin, her makeup dripping down her cheeks into the wet bandage on her face—she'd need a dry one—and he knew she was right. For the first time in twenty-three years, looking down at this beautiful woman who'd probably drive him to madness, he knew he'd be okay.

Chapter Sixteen

By 7:00 p.m. Jenna was still at her desk supposedly working on an expense report that should have taken her ten minutes. Ten minutes was up an hour ago when the other associates had all headed out for happy hour. *Woo-hoo.*

Two days ago, Brent's world had fallen apart. And hers had almost gone with it. Whether she was suffering from some post-traumatic stress, a broken heart or a combination of both, she didn't know, but her entire body hurt. Physically and emotionally.

Tears bubbled up and she shook her head. No. No more crying. Never in her life had she cried this much. She loved this man, without a doubt, but she wouldn't be the whipping girl because he refused to face the hurt and anger he'd buried. That, he'd have to do on his own. She was more than willing to help him, any day, any time, but he had to own up to it. Something he refused to do.

Penny's head popped over the top of the short cubicle wall. "Hey. You're here late. What are you working on?"

Jenna blinked away her tears and looked up. "Expense reports."

Whatever Penny saw on Jenna's face, she didn't like it. "Oh, no. What is it? Do you need to talk about what happened?"

God, yes. But that included talking about Brent, and

Brent was Penny's friend, too. Somehow, it didn't seem fair to him. "I'm okay."

Penny wheeled a chair over from one of the other desks and sat beside Jenna, gently rubbing her back. "Clearly, you're not."

Jenna swiped at her wet eyes. "He's so quick to blame me."

"Brent? For the other day? He *blamed* you for his cousin going nutso?"

Jenna gasped. "Of course not."

"Whew. You scared me. I couldn't imagine him doing that."

"He wouldn't. He just…" Jenna stared at the cubicle wall in front of her, focusing on the picture of her niece and her adorable toothless grin.

"What?"

She swirled her open hands in front of her chest. "He has all this pain and he won't deal with it. And the minute he starts to get emotionally attached, he figures out a way to end it because he doesn't want to get hurt. He used the case to push me away. Every time I did something he thought I shouldn't have done, he went off on me before asking me about it. And I know it's because he's afraid of the emotional fallout. I won't deal with him doing that. It's too hurtful."

"I'm sorry."

"Me, too."

"Has he called?"

Jenna finally sat back and spun her chair to face Penny. "Yes. Several times. I can't talk to him right now. Unless he's going to deal with his emotions, there's nothing to say. I can't live like this, constantly worrying something I do will make him run. It's not fair. To either of us."

The stitches on her face itched and she reached up, pressed on the bandage. *No scratching.* "And these damned stitches are driving me crazy. I just want to rip them out so I can see what my face will wind up being."

After everything that had happened, her face, her no-fail tool to getting her job done, might be permanently scarred. Now instead of seeing a pretty brunette, people would see a scarred one. All because she wanted to prove she was good at her job by cracking a cold case. And look what it had gotten her.

"It doesn't matter," Penny said.

Jenna glanced up, met her gaze. "What?"

"Your face. I know you think you're good at your job because of how you look. Maybe it helps, sure, but your investigative skills and your instincts are what make you good. I promise you that. Frankly, you solved this case and your looks had nothing to do with it."

Jenna cocked her head.

"Yes," Penny said. "I'm right. You didn't solve this case by falling back on low-cut shirts. Accept it."

Holy cow. She thought back. From that first day, it had been all about chasing leads, figuring out what had been missed, discovering evidence. She'd even chosen more conservative clothing after Brent had told her how smart she was.

She let out a strangled laugh. "This is horrible. It took me getting my heart ripped out to realize I'm good at my job and it's not about my boobs."

"No, it's not. And I think you and Brent have a lot to talk about. Maybe you should call him back. See where this thing goes. Obviously, you care about each other."

"I care too much. That's the problem. We're stuck. And until he's ready to make changes, we'll stay that way."

With that, Jenna sat forward, covered her face with her hands and finally let the tears fall.

BRENT STOOD IN the now-empty living room of his child-hood home staring at the wood floor where his mother had died. All the years he'd lost with her crashed down on him and he sucked in a breath.

No doubt, the house, the memories, all of it had tormented him and altered the course of his life. Made him hard inside. Hard and alone. Sure he had his family, what was left of it anyway, but for himself? Nothing. Nada. For years he'd chosen to be the lone wolf. Now, with his family blown apart, he envied his sister for the life she'd built and found solace in. His life had been his mother's case.

And look where that had gotten him.

Outside, a car door slammed and he wandered to the door, his insides grinding like rusty gears. His own fault for burying his agony. When he got to the doorway, he glanced back at the living room. This was it. He had to let it go. Let his mother go. How he'd do it, he wasn't sure, but he had a starting point.

He hoped.

Brent stood with his feet just inside the threshold. *Go.* The porch was right there, the overhang blocking the bright sunshine. If he stepped out now, that would be it. Thousands of times he'd left this house. Today would be different. Today he had answers.

"Brent?"

Jenna stood at the base of the stairs in jeans tucked into boots, and wearing a flowy white shirt and a black leather jacket.

He'd called her each day for the last three days, but her only response had been a text telling him she'd call him soon. Which she hadn't yet done. Couldn't blame her. He'd shoved her away enough. Now he had to throw himself on her mercy.

And alter his plan of attack.

"Hi," he said.

"Hi."

"Thanks for coming."

"Your text said it was important."

"It is. How's your head?"

She shrugged. "Not bad. Still hurts a little."

She started to climb the steps, but he held up his hand. "I'm coming out."

And he did. He stepped over that threshold and—*how about that?*—it wasn't the torture he expected. Really, the only thing he felt was...relief.

He turned, closed the door behind him and met her at the bottom of the stairs.

"You didn't lock it," Jenna said.

"Don't need to."

"You're going back in?"

"No."

She stared up at him, her normally sparkly blue eyes flat, and that punch to the chest he always got made him realize all over again that he had major work to do. "I'm sorry."

"For what?"

"All of it. Pushing you away when you wanted to help. Firing you because I was scared. I'm a mess and you figured that out."

"Everyone is a mess, Brent. If everyone were perfect, life would be boring. The trick is to find people who accept the mess. I accept your mess. What I can't deal with is you taking your mess out on me. And, frankly, we could have talked about this in Chicago. Why drag me out here?"

He waved a hand toward the house. "I cleaned everything out."

"The house?"

"Yeah. It's empty."

She reached for him, squeezed his wrist and that feeling, that connection, shot clear up his arm. He wanted her. Even the high-maintenance parts that would drive him insane because she'd always want to talk. Talk. Talk. Talk. But he wanted it. All of it.

"Why?"

"It's over now. Did Russ tell you?"

She nodded.

"Sixteen women so far. That's the number they know about. Over twenty-three years, who knows how many more my uncle killed while on his road trips." He tipped his head back, let the sun warm his face and chase the chill from his body. "He doesn't even know why he did it. It's…"

"Twisted," Jenna said.

"Yeah."

"I'm so sorry."

Jenna wasn't the only one. "I don't know where we all go from here."

"How's Sylvie?"

"She's in Florida. Camille and I forced her to go visit her friend. We're hoping she stays a while. Right now, there's no reason for her to be here. Her daughter and her husband are in custody. Her family was blown apart too, and as bad as this situation is for Camille and me, as broken as we are, I can't even go where my aunt has to. How the hell does someone recover from that?"

Jenna sighed. "I wish I knew."

On the road, a flatbed carrying an excavator came to a whooshing stop, and Brent used his free hand to wave.

Jenna angled back. "What's with the tractor?"

"That's why you're here."

"Pardon?"

He pulled his wrist loose and grabbed both of hers. "We're tearing it down."

She made a tiny gasping noise. He'd surprised her. Good. "I don't understand."

"The house. It's coming down. We talked to my dad. We reminded him he walked out and, for once, he needed to do what Camille and I wanted. That shut him up."

Jenna continued to gawk at him. "He *agreed* to this?"

"After I told him I'd handle selling the property and would give him the money. He can have it. I don't care. I want it over. I need a life."

"Are you sure you're ready for this? It's awfully fast."

"Twenty-three years is fast?"

She squeezed his hands. "You know what I mean."

He smiled. "Yeah, I do."

"So, your father is gone again?"

"Left yesterday. Probably better that way. At least I have his number. He said he'd call me. We'll see. I'm not counting on anything. Maybe I'd like to try talking once in a while. We'll never be close, but…I don't know. I guess I need to tell him how angry I am that he walked out." He waved it off. "Anyway, I'm tearing this house down and I wanted you here. Not because I couldn't do it alone, because I can."

"I know you can. You, Marshal Thompson, can do anything you set your mind to."

Hopefully, she truly believed that. He squeezed her hands again. "I'm ready. I thought letting this house go would be the hardest thing I'd ever do, but it's not. And, hold on to your beauty-queen panties because I'm about to say something that will blow your mind."

She rolled her eyes. "Uh-oh."

"No uh-oh. I hope—*I hope*—you'll be happy. Or at least open to it because letting this house go isn't the hardest thing I've ever done. These last few days without you made me realize that letting you go is worse. Way worse. And it hurts. Every time I see you I get this crazy banging in my chest. At first, it baffled me. Now, I think it's my mother poking me, telling me you're the one. Even if I didn't want to admit it in the beginning, I know it now, and I'm asking you to let me try again. To make this right. And I'm starting with tearing this house down. It's an albatross and—"

"Stop talking."

Come again? Always begging him to talk and now she wanted him to shut up. Women. "You want me to stop?"

"Yes."

This didn't sound good. Too late. That had to be it. She was done and, if he knew anything, he knew what that felt like. When he was done with something, it was over, no going back. Ever.

"So, you're done?"

"With?"

"Uh, me?"

"Why would you think that?"

And—hell in a handbasket—could he get a break here? Relationships being the last thing he understood was not helping him. At all. He breathed deep. "Because you told me to stop. Generally that indicates something is over."

"You don't have to skin yourself for me. All I want is for you to be honest. If it means not talking, fine. But don't use excuses to bury what you're feeling. I won't hurt you and I won't think you're weak. I need you to deal with your emotions, though. That's the only way we'll survive."

He nodded. "Leave it to me to find a psychology major."

She snorted. "A psychology major who loves you."

She loved him. Somewhere in his miserable life he'd become the luckiest guy walking. The stress of the last few days dropped from his body. Just gone. He stood for a second, for once, not stressing. About anything.

"I love you, Brent. And I want us to have a life together. I think it would be a good life. I know what I need, and I think I know what you need. But you have to know, too. You have to meet me halfway and not close up on me all the time."

He could do it. Surprise, surprise. Typically, if a woman had said that to him, he'd have made his exit. Now, not only did he believe he could do it, he wanted to do it.

"I can do that. It won't happen overnight, though. I've

spent years conditioning myself. But, I'll make it happen. I have to." He gestured to the house. "This is no way to live. I need a life. And I want you in it. I think I've loved you from the second I saw you in Penny's hallway. You see beyond the nonsense. I mean, you're a pain in the neck sometimes, and you definitely broke our agreement by coming out here and chasing after my Dad alone."

"I know. I'm sorry. I thought if your aunt or uncle were here it would be okay. I didn't think it through." She tugged on his shirt. "I didn't think like you would."

He shrugged. "You're bold. Sometimes, I like that about you. *Sometimes.*"

She rolled her eyes, but ruined it with a grin. "So romantic."

Then he kissed her, brushing his lips slowly over hers, taking it all in and enjoying the connection. Jenna created chaos, he'd always known that, but her chaos was the good kind. The healing kind.

"Ahem."

He backed away. The truck driver shuffled behind Jenna, checking out her rear. Brent imagined he'd have to get used to that.

"Hi," he said to the guy. "In case you're wondering, she's mine."

Jenna cracked up. "Ooh, cave man. Nice."

"This the right address?" the guy asked, ignoring Brent's comment.

"Yep," Brent said. "We're knocking down this house."

"Okay."

That simple. If this guy only knew. He lumbered off and Brent turned back to Jenna. "Will you stay with me? Watch it go down? Then we'll leave. The cleanup might be too much, but the going down part, I need to see it."

She grabbed hold of his hand, linking her fingers with

his and snuggled into him. "I'll stay. Then we'll go somewhere and, I don't know, just have quiet time, I guess."

Quiet time with Jenna. He'd like that. "Thank you."

"Sure."

"Not for staying. For not giving up on me. For forcing
me to bust out of that stupid emotional cage. You could have
walked away and you didn't. For that, I'll love you forever."

* * * * *

"You've got to calm down. I'm not going to hurt you," the voice said, but his words barely penetrated Sophia's terrorised brain.

She was desperate to get his hand off her mouth. She allowed her knees to give way so all her body weight fell. He didn't let go of her face, but he did let her hands go so he could grip her weight with his other arm.

Sophia reached up and grasped the hand covering her mouth with both of her hands—her need for air overwhelming all other thoughts.

"Are you trying to get us both killed?" the voice hissed.

Now there was no doubt in Sophia's mind that the voice was familiar. She shook loose from the arm that held her and turned to face the source of the voice. When she saw him clearly she almost stumbled again.

Just as tall, dark and handsome as ever—a walking cliché. The man who had walked out of her life five years ago. Without one single word.

"Cameron?"

INFILTRATION

BY
JANIE CROUCH

Published in Great Britain 2015
by Mills & Boon, an imprint of Harlequin (UK) Limited,
Eton House, 18-24 Paradise Road, Richmond, Surrey, TW9 1SR

© 2015 Janie Crouch

ISBN: 978-0-263-25292-7

46-0115

Harlequin (UK) Limited's policy is to use papers that are natural, renewable and recyclable products and made from wood grown in sustainable forests. The logging and manufacturing processes conform to the legal environmental regulations of the country of origin.

Printed and bound in Spain
by CPI, Barcelona

Janie Crouch has loved to read romance her whole life. She cut her teeth on Mills & Boon® romances as a pre-teen, then moved on to a passion for romantic suspense as an adult.

Janie lives with her husband and four children in Virginia, where she teaches communication courses at a local college. Janie enjoys traveling, long-distance running, movie-watching, knitting and adventure/obstacle racing. You can find out more about her at www.janiecrouch.com.

To my sweet coz, the real "Sophia."
Thanks for providing the strength, charm and beauty
to model a character after (although the rest is
sheer drama and not you, I promise).
I am thankful beyond measure to have you
in my life—a cousin by birth, a sister in
every other way. 143, FC1!

Chapter One

Cameron Branson had been telling the lies so long he was afraid they were becoming truth to him.

"Look, Tom, I don't have a lot of time," Cameron barked quietly into his cell phone as he sat on a bench and looked out at Washington, DC's Potomac River. Joggers ran by in front of him and a mother chased a squealing toddler, but Cameron paid them no mind.

He especially paid no attention to the man sitting on the other side of the bench next to him who was also on his cell phone while glancing at a newspaper.

Except neither man was actually talking on his cell phone. They were talking to each other.

"Protocol dictates that we meet twice a week unless circumstances prove it impossible," Cameron was reminded by "Tom."

"Yeah, well, I don't have a whole lot of concern about protocol right at this moment. What I care about is bringing down the SOB who killed Jason."

Tom sighed and turned the page on his newspaper, without ever looking at Cameron. "You've been under a long time, Cam. And you missed our last two scheduled meetings. I can only cover for you so much before higher-ups start noticing."

"Well, it's not always easy getting away from the bad

guys so we can have our chats," Cameron all but sneered. He knew his anger at Tom was misplaced, but couldn't seem to keep his irritation under control. He just wanted to get back to work.

"Everybody knows your undercover work in DS-13 is critical for us and for you personally. But it's important for us to do things by the book."

Cameron sighed but didn't say what was on his mind: doing things by the book was probably what had gotten Cameron's previous partner killed.

"All right. I'm sorry. I'll try to do better." Cameron almost believed it as he said it.

"Is everything still on for tomorrow's buy?"

"Yeah. It should go without a hiccup. Just make sure the warehouse stays clear."

"Cameron, I needed to meet with you about something else." Tom closed his newspaper and then reopened it. He seemed to be hesitating. Cameron knew this was bad. He'd never known his handler to be at a loss for words. "The parameters of your mission have changed."

Damn. "How so?"

"Taking the members and leader of DS-13 into custody is no longer your primary objective. For neither their black market activities nor their presumed part in your partner's death."

"Dammit, Tom…"

"I know, Cameron. But recent intel notified us that DS-13 has obtained new encoding-transmitting technologies that they'll be selling to terrorists."

Cameron sighed and waited for Tom to continue.

"It's called Ghost Shell. This technology is like nothing we've ever seen—it could cripple communication within government agencies. It would give multiple terrorist groups the edge they've been looking for, and open us up to attacks all over the country. It's critical that this technology doesn't make it to the black market."

"Why isn't the cyberterrorism unit on this?" Cameron murmured with a sigh.

"It's beyond cyberterrorism now. Straight into terrorism. Besides, it's already out in the open. And since you're already neck-deep in DS-13…"

Cameron just shook his head. He knew what Tom said was true. Technology like this in DS-13's hands—the group was solely focused on financial gain—was bad, but in the hands of terrorist groups who were intent on destruction and loss of life, it would mean disaster.

"Roger that, Tom. Change of primary objective confirmed. I'll be in touch when I know something." Cameron got up from the bench and walked away. Tom stayed, as Cameron knew he would, pretending to talk on his cell phone a while longer as he looked at the paper.

Yeah, Cameron's primary objective had changed. But he'd be damned if he'd let justice for his partner's memory suffer because of it.

THE NEXT DAY, sitting in the back of the extended SUV with windows tinted just a bit darker than what was probably legal, Cam Cameron, as he was known to DS-13, pretended to chuckle at a filthy joke told by one of the other riders. When a second rider chimed in with another joke—something about a blonde, a redhead and a brunette—Cameron just tuned them out. He stretched his long legs out in front of him. At least there was room to do that in this vehicle.

One thing he had to give DS-13: they may be an organized crime ring with ties to almost every criminal activity imaginable—weapons, drugs, human trafficking, to name a few—but they knew how to travel in style.

Cameron had been undercover with them for eight months. Eight months pretending to be a midlevel weapons dealer. Eight months of trying to move up in the ranks of DS-13, so he could meet the boss.

The man who had ordered the execution of Cameron's partner over a year ago.

Cameron had made very little progress in the meeting-the-boss area of his work. Instead he'd been stuck with lower-level minions, who evidently thought a punch line about high heels and a sugar daddy downright hilarious, given the guffawing coming from all corners of the vehicle. Cameron chuckled again, just so it wouldn't be obvious that he wasn't laughing.

Blending in was key. Cameron's looks—black hair just a little too long, dark brown eyes, a perpetual five o'clock shadow—made him particularly suited for blending in with bad guys. Cameron had specifically cultivated the dark and unapproachable look. His six-foot frame was muscular—made even more so over the past few months since a favorite activity of the DS-13 minions was lifting weights—and he was light on his feet.

All in all, Cameron knew he came across as someone not to be messed with. Someone who could take care of himself. Someone menacing. It had helped him in undercover work for years, this ability to blend in physically.

The problem was, he felt his soul starting to blend in, too.

"Cam, don't you know any good jokes, man?" the driver called back to Cameron.

The best joke I know will be on you guys when I arrest all you bastards.

"No, Fin. I don't know any jokes. I can't be this beautiful, able to outlift all you princesses *and* be able to tell jokes. Wouldn't be fair to the rest of the world." Cameron smirked.

This led to an immediate argument over which of the four people in the SUV could bench the most weight, as Cameron knew it would.

Cameron was tired. He was tired of the lies, tired of keeping one step ahead of everyone else, tired of spending every day with these morons. And yesterday's meeting with Tom had confirmed what Cameron had already known: he wasn't checking in with his handler at Omega Sector as often as he should.

But since Cameron worked for Omega—an elite interagency task force—there was a little more leeway about check-ins and staying undercover longer. Omega agents had more training, more experience and the distinct mental acuity needed for long-term undercover work, or they never were sent out in the first place.

They were the best of the best.

God, it sounded so *Top Gun*. And Cameron certainly didn't feel best of anything right now.

"Two-ninety clean and jerk, two-seventy bench," Cameron responded to one of the guys asking about his top weight-lifting ability.

A round of obscenities flew through the vehicle. Nobody believed him.

"I'll take any of you pansies on, at any time." Cameron looked down at his fingernails in boredom. "But you better call your mommies first."

Another round of obscenities about what they would do to his mother, then arguments resumed about lifting, leg weights this time. Cameron zoned out again.

Cameron had promised Tom he would check in with the handler more often. He wasn't particularly worried about what Tom or the agency would do if he didn't. But he was worried his brothers, one older, one younger, both with ties to Omega Sector, might decide to storm the castle if they thought Cameron was in trouble. Not to mention his sister.

He wasn't in trouble, at least not the type that required help from his siblings.

He knew he was starting to make some progress in the case; there were talks of taking Cameron to the DS-13 main base, wherever that was. That's what Cameron wanted. That's where he would meet the man who ordered his partner's death. And as soon as Cameron could link him with that or any other felony, that bastard was going down.

Oh, yeah, and Cameron would recover Ghost Shell, as ordered.

Cameron didn't take the orders about the technology acquirement lightly. He would get it. But he would bring down the bad guys while he was at it.

And then Cameron could get out of undercover work for a while and try to find himself. Get away from lies and filth for an extended period. Try to remember why he started this job in the first place.

As the SUV pulled up to an abandoned warehouse in a suburb far outside of Washington, Cameron got his head back in the game. No point whining about how hard this job was; he'd known that for a while now. Five years to be exact. Cameron immediately pushed that thought out of his head. This wasn't the time or place to think about her. Or any of the disasters that had happened since.

Opening his car door, Cameron stepped out. "All right, ladies, everything should be in the back office, upstairs. Use the east entrance since it's least visible."

The driver, Fin, was the leader of the group. Cameron walked around the car to him. "How do you want to set up security, Fin?" Cameron knew it was important to make Fin feel as if he was in charge.

"Yeah, let's leave someone at the back door outside and someone walking around inside, just in case."

Cameron nodded. "Great." He knew there would be no raids by authorities or attacks by a rival organization—thanks to Omega Sector—but nobody else knew it. As a matter of fact, nobody but them should be around this area at all. "You're coming in with me, right? So we can get it all counted and tested?"

Cameron was the one who had set up this sale, in an attempt to prove his usefulness, again, to DS-13. The men inside the warehouse—bad guys in their own right—were business associates of Cameron's. They were going to buy the weapons, ones Cameron had gotten for DS-13 at a hugely reduced price, thanks to them actually coming from the Omega Sector armory. All in all, DS-13 would make a nice little profit for very little work. Cameron would come out looking like the golden boy and would hopefully be one step closer to meeting the man in charge.

Nobody in DS-13 would ever know that the scumbags buying the weapons would be picked up by local law enforcement a few miles down the road after leaving here. The weapons would go back into government lockdown.

Fin barked orders to the rest of the men then walked with Cameron up the outdoor stairs to the second floor of the building. Inside was an office that looked down on the expanse of the warehouse, except seeing through the windows was nearly impossible due to years of cleaning neglect.

Cameron introduced the buyers to Fin and then stepped aside to let Fin talk to them so the guy could feel as if he was in charge. Cameron walked over to stand by a window that looked out onto the road. He rubbed a tiny bit of the filthy pane with his finger so he could see out, all the while keeping his ear on the conversation between the buyers and Fin, making sure Fin didn't screw things up.

Looking out his tiny hole, Cameron noticed a car moving slowly from the warehouse next door toward them. He cursed silently. Nobody was supposed to be in this area at all except for them. Omega Sector should've seen to that.

When the car got out of his line of sight from that window, Cameron casually moved to another window. He leaned back against the wall for a few moments before turning nonchalantly to the window and once again creating a little peephole in the dirt. Cameron was careful not to make it look as if he was studying anything. The last thing he wanted to do was draw attention to that car.

Sure enough the vehicle stopped right in front of the warehouse. Cameron cursed under his breath again. He hoped Marco, the man Fin had left as guard, didn't see the car. Maybe he wouldn't. The minions tended to be a little slack when Fin wasn't watching. Marco may be out smoking by the SUV or something. Cameron desperately hoped so. The last thing he needed was some civilian caught up in this mess.

"Isn't that right, Cam?" Fin called out to Cameron.

Cameron racked his brain trying to figure out what they were talking about. He needed to be paying more attention to this sale. Cameron wasn't sure how to respond. He didn't want to let on that he hadn't been listening to the conversation when he was the one who had set the whole thing up in the first place. Cameron decided to take a chance.

"If you say it, then it must be true, Fin."

Both the buyers and Fin burst out laughing, so Cameron figured he had said the right thing. He watched as Fin began showing the weapons to the buyers.

When he turned to the window again, the driver had gotten out of the car. He couldn't see much, but it looked as if it was a lone woman.

Damn.

Cameron knew he had to get down there and try to divert disaster before it hit full force.

"Fin, I've got to take a leak. I'm sure there's a can downstairs somewhere. I'll be back in a sec."

Fin and the buyers barely looked up from their exchange. Fin shooed in Cameron's general direction with his hand. Normally this lack of regard would've irritated Cameron, but now he was thankful for it. He headed out the door leading into the main section of the warehouse.

He hoped whoever was in the car was just some poor idiot who had gotten lost and would soon be on her way.

SOPHIA REARDON WAS lost and felt like some poor idiot. She rolled her window down farther and took a few deep breaths of air, trying to refocus.

Was this warehouse really the place? All of them looked the same. If she could read her own handwriting that would help. Of course, if people would do their jobs correctly in the first place she wouldn't have to be here at the corner of Serial-Killers-R-Us Street and Shouldn't-Be-Here-Alone Avenue.

Sophia looked down at the napkin where she'd scribbled the address. Yeah, that was definitely an *8* not a *3*. Which meant it was *this* warehouse she was supposed to be at, not the just-as-scary first one she'd gone to.

All Sophia needed were a few pictures of the interior ceiling frame and doorway of the warehouse to help finish a computer rendering of the building. This warehouse was identical to one that had burned down in an arson case two weeks ago—the work of a serial arsonist who had hit buildings in four different states. The FBI had been called in to help local law enforcement.

Sophia muttered under her breath again as she grabbed her camera gear and purse. She put her FBI credentials in her pocket, in case some poor security guard needed to see them. She pushed open the door to the warehouse and walked in slowly, giving her eyes time to adjust. She cursed her office mate, Bruce, who had begged Sophia to take these pictures.

"'The new girl at the coffee shop said yes to lunch, Sophia,'" Sophia said in her best mimicry of Bruce's voice. "'But today's our only chance this week. Please, please, please go take pictures at the horror-film warehouse for me. I'm worth getting mutilated for.'"

Sophia sighed. Bruce owed her. Big-time. Sophia hated this cloak-and-dagger stuff.

Sure, she worked for the FBI, but would be the first to tell you she wasn't an agent. She didn't even do CSI stuff usually, although she was part of the forensic team. She was a graphic designer, for goodness' sake. She designed brochures and fliers and posters. Safe in the comfort of her office in DC, not in some warehouse in Scaryville.

As the door closed behind her, Sophia took a deep breath and reminded herself there was plenty of air in this building and nothing to be afraid of. She was not trapped back in that car like during the accident five years ago. Sophia went through a couple of the mental exercises Dr. Fretwell had taught her to get her brief moment of panic under control. Once it had passed she grabbed her camera and began getting the shots she needed.

The doorway posed no problems so she got those first. But the beams in the ceiling area were going to be more difficult to film. Looking around she realized the office in the back would give her much better access to the shots she needed of the ceiling framing.

Sophia cautiously made her way back to the steps leading up to the office. It didn't look as if there were any serial killers or cyborgs living here, but the place still gave her the creeps. Wooden crates and boxes were piled all along the stairs and landing, making getting up them precarious. Sophia kept a firm grip on the railing for as long as she could until she had to let go to step around a huge crate.

As she began climbing the second set of steps, Sophia caught something moving out of the corner of her eye. She turned to see what it was just as an arm reached out from behind her and covered her mouth, pulling her up against a hard chest and silencing her startled scream.

A deep voice breathed quietly in her ear, "What the hell are you doing here?"

Chapter Two

Sophia was shocked into complete stillness for a moment then burst into a flurry of action. She elbowed the abs behind her and swung her legs backward at his shins. Although she heard a couple of grunts, the hand over her mouth didn't move.

Terror completely overwhelmed her. The hand was cutting off her air and she couldn't breathe. Panic made her blows even more frantic and she heard more grunts, but he still didn't release her. She reached back and tried to scratch his face, but he caught both her wrists with his free hand before she could do any damage. He pulled her closer to his chest so her kicks couldn't do any harm, either.

"You've got to calm down. I'm not going to hurt you," the voice said, but his words barely penetrated Sophia's terrorized brain.

She was desperate to get his hand off her mouth. She allowed her knees to give way so all her body weight fell. He didn't let go of her face, but he did let her hands go so he could grip her weight with his other arm.

Sophia reached up and grasped the hand covering her mouth with both of her hands, her need for air overwhelming all other thoughts. Somewhere in the back of her mind she could hear Dr. Fretwell reminding her that there was plenty of oxygen, that there was always plenty of oxygen, but she couldn't make herself believe it.

"Listen, I don't want to hurt you," the voice said again in little more than a whisper in her ear. "But I need you to calm down."

Sophia didn't believe his assurances for her safety for a second, but her only thought was to get the hand from around her mouth. It took all of her mental energy, but she forced herself to stop struggling.

"Good." The hand over her mouth eased just the slightest bit. "I'm going to let you go, but if you scream we're going to be right back in this position. Got it?"

Sophia nodded. The hand moved very slowly from her mouth, as if he was gauging whether she would keep her word not to scream. It hovered there, ready to reclamp over her mouth at the slightest noise from her. Sophia gulped air and struggled to get a hold of herself.

She wasn't going to scream. She knew there wasn't anybody around the warehouse close enough to hear it. Plus, she definitely didn't want that hand—or worse, a gag—over her mouth, cutting off her supply of oxygen. Well, not cutting off the actual supply of oxygen, but making her brain think she wasn't getting enough oxygen.

Damn claustrophobia. The last thing she needed was to become a sobbing nutcase on the floor because some creep gagged her. She needed to keep her wits about her and figure out how to get away from the big chest still standing right behind her.

Whatever trouble she was in here, she was going to have to get herself out. Because screaming wasn't going to help.

"Are you okay?" the voice asked, the mystery man still standing directly behind her, hand still hovering near her mouth.

"Yes. Look, I was just here to take some pictures of the

door and ceiling." She was breathing so hard she could barely get the words out, so Sophia lifted her camera to the side so he could see it. "Whatever you're doing here, I don't know anything about it and I don't care."

There was no response from the man behind her. Sophia didn't know if that was a good or bad thing.

"I haven't seen you. I have no idea what you look like. I'll just leave. There's no cell phone coverage out here, so it's not like I can call anyone or anything." Sophia didn't know if that was true or not. She had forgotten to charge her phone again last night, so it was sitting dead out in her car. But she wasn't about to tell him that.

She realized she was rambling, but the longer he was silent, the more she was afraid he was going to do something terrible to her, like kill her.

Or cover her mouth with his hand again.

"I'm just going to go, okay?" Sophia took a small step away from him. "I'm not going to look at you and I'm just going to go."

The arm in front of her dropped. When he didn't stop her, Sophia took another step. Then another.

"Just get in your car and leave immediately. Don't let anybody else see you or believe me, the trouble will be much worse."

Now that the voice wasn't whispering, it sounded vaguely familiar. As Sophia took another step away she turned to look at the man behind her before she could stop herself.

But before she could get a good look at him she tripped over one of the boxes lining the stairs. She grasped for the railing but couldn't reach it.

Just as she began to plummet down the stairs an arm reached out and grabbed her around her hips, sweeping her easily off her feet and yanking her back against him.

"Are you trying to get us both killed?" the voice hissed.

Now there was no doubt in Sophia's mind that the voice was familiar. She shook loose from the arm that held her and turned to face the voice. When she saw him clearly she almost stumbled again.

Just as tall, dark and handsome as ever—a walking cliché. The man who had walked out of her life five years ago. Without one single word.

"Cameron?"

Sophia watched as shock stole over Cameron's face. He was obviously as surprised to see her as she was to see him.

"Sophia? What are you doing here?"

"I'm taking pictures for a friend, for an arson investigation."

"An arson investigation? Are you law enforcement?"

Sophia shook her head. "No. Not really. I mean kind of, but no."

Cameron stared back at her in confusion and Sophia realized she wasn't making any sense.

"I work for the FBI, but I'm not an agent. I'm a graphic artist."

"You work for the Bureau? You're here for them?"

Cameron seemed overly shocked at her mention of the FBI. Sophia shook her head again. "Well, yes and no. I wasn't supposed to be here at all, but I'm helping a friend out by getting some pictures he wasn't able to get."

"Is anybody else from the Bureau coming?"

Sophia didn't understand why Cameron was asking her this, but the only thing she could think of—the only thing that really made sense about any of his behavior here—was that he was some sort of criminal now and she had walked in on something illegal.

Sophia would never have thought Cameron Branson capable of a criminal lifestyle when she had known him before. He'd just gotten out of the military and had more of a love for his family than anyone she'd ever known. He definitely had not been any sort of delinquent then. Trying to figure out where he belonged, sure. But not a criminal.

But she guessed a lot of stuff could happen in five years that changed a person. Case in point, the man standing in front of her whom she both recognized and didn't recognize.

Sophia took a step back from him. His hand, which had still been at her waist, dropped to his side.

"No, I'm not officially here for the Bureau. Nobody else is coming," Sophia told him.

Cameron seemed to relax a little at that admission, which just confirmed Sophia's suspicion about his criminal activities. Who else relaxed at the thought of the FBI *not* coming?

Sophia looked more closely at Cameron. His hair was much longer than the nearly crew-cut length he used to keep—it curled now at the top of his black T-shirt. His posture was less erect, more casual. His eyes…

Well, his eyes were still the most gorgeous shade of brown she had ever seen.

She'd nearly fallen in love with those eyes once, back when she was too young and stupid to know better. Back when she thought he was a stand-up guy who was interested in her and perhaps wanted a future together.

But she had grown up and left those dreams behind. He hadn't given her much choice, when he'd left without a goodbye and without a single word in the five years since.

So whoever this man standing in front of her was—despite his gorgeous eyes—she needed to get away from him.

For more reasons than one.

Cameron felt as if he was having an out-of-body experience as the tiny brunette who had been clawing at his face moments before transformed from a stranger into Sophia Reardon.

This was not possible.

Seriously? Of all the warehouses in all the world, she had to be in this one? And moreover, somebody from Omega should've had the roads leading down to this area blocked so nobody who wasn't supposed to be here—for example, a cute brunette with a camera—got through. Somebody was going to catch a load of trouble for this, Cameron would make sure.

But right now he had to get Sophia out of here before somebody from DS-13 saw her.

But man, she looked good. Cameron gave himself just a second to really look at her. He hadn't seen her in five years. She'd been twenty-two years old then, but she didn't seem to have changed much. Her straight brown hair was a little longer, now past her shoulders, but the natural blond highlights were still there. Through the dimness of the warehouse's lights he could barely make out the freckles that still scattered across her cheeks and nose. And her stunning green eyes.

Eyes that were glaring up at him right now. He took a step toward her but she backed up. "I'm not going to hurt you, Soph."

She stopped moving. "I know. I just… I'm pretty claustrophobic. I don't want you to cover my mouth again."

Cameron nodded. "Okay, no problem."

"Why are *you* here, Cameron?" she asked with a great deal of suspicion in her tone.

Cameron couldn't blame her for the unease, given the current situation. "It's a long story and I don't have time to explain."

She jerked away from him. "Yeah. Explanations aren't your strong suit. I remember."

Cameron winced. He reached for her again, but then let his hand fall to the side. Sophia had every right to be angry at him about how things had ended between them five years ago, even though he had never meant to hurt her. Cutting casual ties had just been part of the life he'd chosen when he took the job with Omega Sector.

Of course, the fact that he had thought about her every day since he'd walked away from her had proven to Cameron that Sophia had been more than a casual tie. Now, with quite a bit more perspective, he realized he should've given her more information and a proper goodbye.

Unfortunately, it looked as if he was about to make the same mistakes all over again: no information and no proper goodbye.

"I'm sorry, Sophia. But you have to leave. Quickly."

"And what? You'll explain later? We both know that's not true."

Cameron knew there was no real response he could give. They both did know it was true.

"Besides, I'm not sure I want to know," Sophia continued softly.

Cameron wished he could explain, at least about what was happening right now—about being undercover—but time was running out. He needed to get Sophia out of here immediately. Every moment she stayed there was more of a risk of her being seen by a member of DS-13.

"Sophia…"

She shook her head and continued before he could say anything further, reaching a hand out toward him. "Don't worry, I'm going. Whatever you're doing here, Cameron, I don't want to know. But you be careful." She drew her hand back to her side without actually touching him.

Cameron couldn't stand the look in her eyes. She thought he was a criminal. He wished he could explain. Before she could turn away, Cameron leaned down and put his forehead against hers. "I'm sorry, Soph. Again." Cameron stepped back from her. "Go as fast and as quietly as you can. Don't let anyone see you."

Cameron watched as Sophia turned and carefully manipulated her way down the stairs through all the boxes. He didn't stay to watch her go the rest of the way out. He turned and made his way back to the office.

"Get lost?" Fin snickered as Cameron walked back in.

Cam just snorted. Fin looked at him a little closer. "What happened to you? You look like you've been in a wrestling match."

Damn it. He had practically been in a wrestling match.

"Stupid boxes everywhere. It's like an obstacle course down there. I tripped." Cameron brushed his hair back into place.

That got a few chuckles. Nobody seemed suspicious, which was good. "How's it going here?" Cameron asked.

Fin was taking his time showing off to the buyers what he knew about the assault rifles being sold. Fin liked to show off whenever he knew anything about anything, and oftentimes even when he didn't, but Cameron just let him ramble on. If the buyers didn't know when and if Fin was full of crap then it was their own fault. They'd be sitting in a jail cell in a few hours anyway.

"Why don't you start counting the money, Cam?" Fin told him. Cameron barely bit back a groan of frustration. What he really wanted to do was get over to the window and make sure Sophia's car was gone. But the money was on the other side of the office.

"Sure." Cameron met one of the buyers over at the desk and pulled out a small cash-counting machine from the bag they'd brought. The machine would make things a lot faster, but not fast enough. He wanted to know—needed to know—that Sophia had made it safely out of the building. He fed the cash into the machine as quickly as he could without making it obvious that he was in a hurry. The second buyer watched him carefully the entire time.

After double-checking, because he knew Fin would ask, Cameron put the counter away.

"All here, Fin."

"Did you double-check?"

Cameron refrained from rolling his eyes. "Yes." He walked over and placed the bag of money on the table by Fin, then strolled as casually as possible over to the window.

No car. *Thank God.*

Cameron felt himself relax for the first time since he realized that the tiny brunette who had just been trying to fight her way out of his arms was Sophia. The thought of sweet Sophia being caught in the middle of this made Cameron a little sick to his stomach.

Maybe seeing her today was some sort of sign to him. Further proof he needed to finish up this case and take a break. Maybe he would call Sophia, try to repair the damage from five years ago. Explain to her his reasons for leaving.

And tell her that he had never stopped thinking about her.

But right now he had to concentrate on the case at hand. Fin was finally winding down his spiel about the assault rifles, quite a bit of it incorrect information, the buyers had the weapons they wanted and DS-13 had the cash.

Cameron could tell Fin was pleased. As the buyers left, he walked over to Cameron and slapped him on his back.

"Good job, man. Very smooth transaction."

"As always, Fin. That's what I do."

Cameron wanted to demand to meet Fin's boss, but knew that any request on his part to meet the man would push him that much further away from a meeting. He had been patient up until now. He could be patient awhile longer. Although with the Ghost Shell encoding technology becoming Cameron's prime mission objective, he couldn't be patient much longer.

Fin nodded. "It is what you do, Cam. And Mr. Smith, my…um…boss, has become well aware of that."

Cameron straightened, his interest piqued. He doubted Mr. Smith was the boss's real name, but this was the first time Fin had ever openly talked about him directly to Cameron. Finally, the slightest progress.

"Well, I'd like to meet Mr. Smith someday."

Fin slapped him on the back again. "And you will, buddy. Soon, in fact. Mr. Smith may need your help in setting up some meetings for some new stuff."

Cameron hoped that by *new stuff* Fin meant the Ghost Shell technology. Fin didn't have an expansive vocabulary, unless it came to dirty jokes.

"But now, let's get back to the house so we can see that weight lifting you were talking so much trash about on the way here."

Cameron followed Fin down the stairs. Two of the other three minions were already at the car. The third, Marco—the one sent to patrol the inside of the warehouse—wasn't there.

Dread pooled in Cameron's stomach.

"Where the hell is Marco?" Fin demanded of the other two. Neither knew.

"He's probably in there smoking or on the can. I'll go find him," Cameron offered. He had a bad feeling.

"Fine." Fin shooed Cameron annoyingly with his hand again. But again Cameron didn't care. "Hurry up."

Cameron made it to the warehouse door, just as it opened. Through it came Marco, dragging a terrified Sophia behind him.

Chapter Three

Cameron knew he had to think fast. A single word from Sophia, any sort of gesture that she knew him, would mean both their lives. In a split second, Cameron made a decision.

But he knew it wasn't going to be pretty.

He stormed up to Marco and grabbed Sophia out of his grasp. "What the hell, Marco? Is this a cop?"

Cameron pushed Sophia, probably a little rougher than necessary, face-first up against the warehouse wall. He heard her indrawn breath, but steeled himself against any thought of her pain or fear.

It was going to get much worse.

Cameron kept his hand pressed against Sophia's back, keeping her forced against the wall. Behind him he heard Fin and the other guys draw their weapons.

He willed Sophia to keep quiet.

Marco, a little shocked by Cameron's aggressive behavior, stuttered, "I just found her inside. She said she was an artist and was taking pictures of the warehouse."

"Did you check to see if she was wearing a wire or anything?" Cameron demanded.

Marco looked sheepish and shook his head. Cameron made a big show of running his hands all over Sophia's body, as if looking for surveillance equipment. Behind him the guys made a couple of catcalls. Sophia shuddered.

When his body search led to her hands, he could feel Sophia press some sort of card into his palm—he wasn't sure what. He moved so he more clearly blocked her from Fin and the men's view, and palmed whatever she had given him without looking at it. As he turned, he slipped it into the pocket of his jeans.

"She's clean," Cameron said as he spun her around. Sophia attempted to straighten the clothes Cameron had lifted and moved during his search, her face burning.

"Listen…" Sophia began.

Cameron backhanded her.

Oh, God. He pulled the slap as much as he could without making it obvious, but he knew it still had to hurt. Her head flew to the side. He watched as a bit of blood began to ooze from a split in her lip. Cameron thought he might vomit.

But if she had said his name, they would both be dead, or at the very least his undercover work would be blown. He couldn't take the chance.

He stuck his finger in her face. "You shut the hell up unless I ask you a specific question, got it?"

Cameron prayed as he had never prayed before that Sophia would keep quiet. He felt a bit of relief when she nodded slowly, staring at the ground.

"Whoa, Cam. I didn't think you had that in you." Fin chuckled.

Cameron smiled a little bit and rolled his shoulders as if he was getting rid of tension. "Yeah. Well, I hate cops. But it doesn't look like she is one."

Cameron took Sophia's digital camera and brought it over to Fin. Together they looked through the pictures. Cameron relaxed a little when they were all shots of the doorway of the warehouse.

"What are you, a photographer?" Cameron asked her. He hoped she wouldn't bring up the Bureau.

"Yeah. A graphic artist." The answer came out as little more than a whisper from Sophia. She was still looking at the ground.

"What were you doing here?" Fin asked.

"Taking pictures for a computer drawing I'm doing of old warehouses."

Cameron breathed another sigh of relief when she didn't mention law enforcement. Good girl; smart thinking.

Cameron walked back over to her. "Did you know we'd be here?"

Sophia shook her head, staring at the ground. Cameron grabbed her chin and forced her to look up at him—more theatrics for Fin and the guys' benefit, but Sophia was paying the price. "You had no idea we were here?"

"No," Sophia spat out. "I thought all these buildings were abandoned. I just needed some pictures." She was glaring at him, but Cameron could see the terror lurking just behind the anger.

"Yeah, I'm all for woman's lib, but I guess nobody would be stupid enough to send one tiny female with no backup or weapons to arrest all of us." Cameron leered at her. "No offense, sweetheart."

"Marco, did you find any ID on her?" Fin asked.

"Her purse was in her car, which was sitting out front. I moved the car inside the building just in case someone else drove by," Marco informed them.

Well, that answered the question about why Sophia's car hadn't been out front when Cameron had looked the second time.

Marco brought the purse to Fin. Fin glanced inside the bag, evidently finding nothing of interest, pulled out her wallet and let the purse fall to the ground. Fin took her driver's license out.

"Sophia Reardon. Twenty-seven years old. Alexandria

address." Fin looked through the rest of her wallet. Cameron held his breath, knowing Sophia must have some sort of FBI identification, even if she wasn't an agent. But Fin didn't say anything, just dropped her wallet into the purse on the ground.

Cameron thought of the card Sophia had slipped to him when he was searching her. Feigning as if he was looking around, Cameron slipped the card out of his pocket and glanced at it. Sure enough, Sophia's FBI credentials.

A smart and gutsy move on her part—one that had just saved her life. If Fin had seen FBI anywhere on her or in her possessions, they wouldn't have cared if she was just a graphic artist and not an agent. As far as they were concerned, anybody employed by the Bureau was their enemy.

Cameron caught Sophia's eye. He patted his pocket and gave her a slight nod. He had no idea if she understood what he was communicating, but she had done a good job.

Cameron walked over to Fin and leaned back against the SUV, knowing he had to play it casual. "So what do we do with her?"

Fin didn't answer immediately. That wasn't encouraging.

The hardest part of undercover work—especially in a situation like this—was figuring out how far you could take your bluff. Pull out of the game too soon and lose eight months of undercover work with only a couple of low-level arrests. But play the game too long and take a chance of somebody calling your bluff…

Which in this case would end in Sophia's death before Cameron could stop it.

And this situation was all the more complicated due to this new damn Ghost Shell technology DS-13 had. If Cameron blew his cover now, Omega would be hard-pressed to acquire that technology before it went on the black market. That could result in the loss of thousands of lives.

But Cameron wasn't going to let Sophia die. Not here. Not today. He was leaning very casually against the SUV, but he had slipped the safety off on his weapon, although it remained concealed under his shirt.

But just like Cameron, everyone here had a weapon. If this came down to a firefight, the odds were definitely not in his favor.

"Let's just let her go, Fin," Marco said. "Smash the camera, break her phone, slash her tires so she can't get anywhere. By the time she walks to the nearest phone, we'll be long gone."

Cameron could've hugged the big lug. That was exactly the suggestion he had wanted to make, but couldn't.

Fin looked over at Cameron, but Cameron just shrugged as if it didn't matter to him a bit what happened to Sophia.

"No," Fin finally said. "No loose ends. Kill her."

Cameron heard Sophia's indrawn breath and he looked over at her. Full-blown panic was visible in her eyes now. She looked as if she was about to make a run for it. Cameron hoped she wouldn't. He didn't think he could take out all four of the other men before someone got a shot off at her.

A quick plan came to Cameron. God, he hoped this would work. He pushed himself away from the car lazily. "Aw, come on, Fin, can't I at least have a little fun with her first? Take her back to the house so there's something for me to do instead of looking at your ugly mugs all the time?" Cameron used his most cajoling tone.

That got a couple chuckles from the men, but Fin wasn't convinced.

"I thought you didn't like her?"

Cameron smiled easily. "I don't like cops." Cameron walked over to Sophia and trailed a finger along her collarbone, just above her breasts. "But her, knowing she's not a cop? Hmm."

Cameron licked his lips and moved closer to Sophia. She shuddered and stepped as far away from him as she could. A tear fell from the corner of her eye.

The guys all laughed at her reaction to him. Cameron pushed her back against the warehouse wall angrily, as if she had embarrassed him. "Well, obviously I'm going to have to teach her some manners. But I'm up to the task. Maybe I'll know some dirty jokes when I'm done." That got more laughs.

Fin shook his head. "She's too skinny for me. I prefer women with some meat on their bones."

Cameron grinned and reached out to stroke some of Sophia's hair. She wouldn't even look at him. "Plenty of meat for me."

The guys snickered. Fin looked down at his watch. "Whatever. Do what you want with her. I don't care," Fin told Cameron. "But she's your responsibility. And you have to get rid of her when you're done."

Cameron felt marginally better now that the immediate threat to Sophia's life seemed to have passed, and his undercover work was also relatively safe. But he was pretty sure the look in her eyes would haunt him the rest of his life.

One last finishing touch to the show. He grabbed Sophia by the nape of the neck and hauled her roughly against him. He brought his mouth down heavily on hers, and wrapped his other arm around her hips. For a moment Sophia did nothing, then without warning she exploded into furious action, pushing away from him and squirming in his grasp.

Cameron brought his lips up her jawline to her ear, holding her body firmly against his. Quietly, so no one could hear him but her, he whispered, "Whatever you do, don't let anyone know you know me."

Sophia was attempting so hard to get away from him, Cameron wasn't sure if she heard him. He hoped she did. He brought his lips back to hers. This time she bit his lip.

The men howled in laughter when Cameron jerked back from her.

"Ow, you little hellion. You're going to pay for that."

He grabbed her arm and dragged her to the car. Someone opened the door for them and Cameron all but threw her in, then climbed in after her. It broke his heart to see how Sophia scrambled as far away from him as she could get in the confines of the SUV.

He had saved their lives for now, but the danger was far from finished. And he hoped the trauma he'd dealt Sophia wasn't too much to repair.

Sophia was just trying to keep it together. She slid all the way over in the seat to try to get as far away from Cameron as possible. If she could've curled herself into a tiny ball, she would have.

Normally she didn't like being in the backseat of a vehicle, especially when there were no windows she could roll down. But right now her claustrophobia would just have to get in line behind all the other things her brain had to freak out about.

Like the fact that she had just been kidnapped by some gang that her ex-boyfriend seemed to be part of.

Except she didn't know if he was *really* part of it or not. Undercover.

It would answer a lot of questions if Cameron was working undercover. Like why he had tried to get her out of the warehouse and hadn't said anything about her FBI credentials.

Of course, it could also be that he was now a member of this organized crime group, or whatever it was, and just didn't want his ex-girlfriend's brains to get splattered all over the pavement.

So back to square one.

Sophia peeked over at Cameron to find him watching her with a decidedly malevolent look in his eyes. Sophia shuddered. That leering look was not something she had ever thought she would see from Cameron. Maybe he really was a criminal now. Sophia tried not to panic. If that look from Cameron was real, she was in big trouble.

But then Sophia glanced up and saw the leader guy, Fin, watching her and Cameron in the rearview mirror. Maybe Cameron suspected that they were being watched and was playing a role.

Undercover.

Please, please, please let him be working undercover.

After Cameron had told her to go, she had done exactly what he had asked: gone straight to her car. But when she had gotten to the door, her car wasn't there. The big guy—Marco?—was driving it inside. Sophia cursed herself for leaving the keys in it, but she had thought there was no one around for miles.

Sophia had tried to sneak outside without Marco seeing her, but hadn't managed it. The next thing she knew he'd grabbed her and had dragged her out the back exit of the warehouse.

Where Cameron had proceeded to scream at, strike and humiliate her.

And maybe save her life.

Sophia touched her lip—it still hurt, both from the slap and his mouth-grinding kiss. She had no such misconception that she was really any safer now than she had been while at the warehouse. But at least nobody had a gun in their hands now.

As the men around her chatted and generally insulted each other, Sophia tried to watch out the window without looking as if she was watching out the window. She didn't want to give anyone—Cameron included—a reason to think she was a threat. But if she had a chance to get away, she planned to take it, and knowing where she was would help.

They were still pretty far outside of DC when they turned into a residential area. Definitely not high-end, the houses were old, but pretty large. They were far enough apart that neighbors wouldn't be forced to see what the other was doing unless they were deliberately trying to. All in all, probably a good location for people selling drugs or weapons or whatever else. Although it wasn't too promising, maybe Sophia would be able to call for help when they parked and got out of the car, and someone would notice.

Their SUV pulled up to the house on the corner. Although the house was probably built in the 1960s, someone had obviously refurbished the garage door with a contemporary opener. The SUV pulled straight into the garage and the door shut quickly behind them.

Sophia bit back a sigh. So much for calling out to the neighbors for help.

Cameron's scary, black look was back. And even though she hoped he might be a good guy, Sophia was frightened. Everyone got out of the car, but Sophia couldn't force herself to move. She shrank back into the seat when Cameron reached for her.

"Get out here right now," Cameron told her through gritted teeth.

She could hear the other men laughing in the doorway. Fin called out, "Regretting your decision already, Cam?"

"I'm not regretting anything, but someone else is about to."

One of the other men whose name she didn't know offered to come help Cam get her out of the vehicle, listing in very crude detail what he would do to her while he was assisting.

Cameron glared at Sophia through narrowed eyes for a moment before calling back over his shoulder, "Actually, that sounds like a pretty good idea, Rick. Why don't you come on in here?"

Sophia immediately scooted over to Cameron and out the car door. All the men doubled over in malicious laughter in the doorway. Cameron grabbed her arm and dragged her forcefully out of the garage past the men, and toward the back of the house into what obviously was his bedroom. Sophia could still hear the other gang members laughing.

Once inside, Cameron turned and locked the door. Then Sophia watched, standing in the middle of the room, as he went over and grabbed a wooden chair that was leaning against the far wall. He dragged the chair to the door and propped it under the doorknob—added defense against anyone entering.

Cameron turned from the door and walked slowly over to Sophia. He stopped only when he was just inches from her. He reached up and touched the split on her lip.

They both winced.

"I'm sorry for everything that happened today, and everything that's going to happen tonight," he told her softly. "But right now I'm going to need you to scream like you're terrified out of your mind. Or else I'm going to have to force you to do it."

Chapter Four

Cameron wasn't sure if this situation could get much worse, but the look Sophia gave him made him think it probably could.

"Wh-what?" she stammered, backing away from him.

"Scream."

"Why?"

Cameron took a step toward her, closing the space between them again. "Look, Sophia, I don't want to hurt you. I really don't," he whispered close to her ear. "But those creeps out there have to think that there is something pretty terrible going on in here."

Sophia looked around the room frantically, as if trying to find a way to escape. A tear seeped from the corner of her eye.

Cameron grimaced. Unfortunately, tears weren't going to cut it in this case. He had to prove to the men in the rest of the house that there was a reason he had brought Sophia here.

One she wouldn't like.

Ultimately, the worse it seemed in here for her, the safer she would be from the other men.

"You have to scream. Yell. Call me names. Do something."

But Sophia just shook her head, looking around the

room, anywhere but at him. It was almost as if she was in shock. Which would be understandable.

"Need some help in there, Cam?" Somebody—it sounded like Rick—called out from the other side of the door.

Damn. "Everything's just fine," Cameron responded.

Cameron gripped Sophia's arms—hard—and shook her. "C'mon, Soph. Work with me. If they think you like it, they're going to want their chance."

She still just looked at him mutely. It honestly seemed beyond her ability to make any sort of sound whatsoever.

"Damn it, Soph." Cameron shook her again. "I need you to fight me like you did back at the warehouse. Before you knew it was me."

Then it occurred to Cameron what he needed to do. She had fought him like a wildcat in the warehouse. Not because she thought he was such a bad guy, but because she seemed so claustrophobic.

In his training and work for both the US Army Rangers and then Omega Sector, Cameron had been taught how to use perps' weaknesses against them. It was one of the reasons Cameron had excelled at undercover work—his ability to pinpoint fears of the enemy. And use those fears without mercy.

He never thought he'd be using that training and skill to manipulate the one woman he once thought he might spend the rest of his life with.

Cameron spun Sophia around and put his hand over her mouth as he had at the warehouse. She immediately tensed up and started struggling. When he didn't release her after a few moments she began fighting in earnest.

Cameron, protecting his face as best he could from her clawing hands, dragged her over to where the lone dresser stood in the sparse room. She kicked at it, causing it to hit up against the wall.

He could hear laughter from the other rooms.

Cameron removed his hand from her mouth.

"Let me go!" Sophia yelled as soon as his hand was gone. Cameron released her for just a moment and she flung herself around to face him, breaths sawing in and out of her chest.

This wasn't going to work. They couldn't hear her if his hand was over her mouth, but she didn't scream if it wasn't. Cameron looked around. The room had a tiny walk-in closet. Maybe that would be small enough to terrify her.

Cameron steeled himself against the thought of Sophia's terror. He stepped toward her and this time she did scream as he reached for her.

"No!"

His hand covered her mouth again. He could hear whistles and catcalls from outside the door.

"Just a couple more minutes, baby. Hang in there," he whispered into Sophia's ear as he dragged her toward the closet.

When Sophia realized where they were headed, she fought him harder than before. Panic took over. She got a good punch to his cheek before he could catch her arm. That was going to leave a mark. But he didn't let it stop him.

He caught the door with his foot and pushed it open. The closet was practically empty, just a couple of his shirts hanging in it. It wasn't big by any means, with barely enough room for two people, but it wasn't tiny. Only someone who really struggled with tight spaces would have a problem being in it for a short amount of time.

Cameron dragged the struggling Sophia into the enclosed space, keeping her back to his chest. He pulled the door closed with one hand and released her mouth with his other.

Sophia screamed as if she was terrified out of her mind. Which she was.

Cameron had no idea what obnoxious comments or noises the members of DS-13 were making about this. He couldn't hear anything over Sophia's screams.

Sophia fought in a violent frenzy—kicking, clawing, throwing wild punches. Cameron just tried to keep her from hurting him or herself. He kept her as close as he could to his body. After what seemed like the longest period of time in the history of the world—and probably even longer to her—but was really only a few seconds, Cameron opened the door and let go of Sophia. She immediately pushed away from Cameron and all but dived out of the closet, landing heavily on the floor.

She pushed herself across the floor, as far away from him and the closet as she could get, sucking in deep gulps of air the entire time. When she reached the far corner of the room she dragged her knees up to her chest and rocked back and forth. Cameron stood just outside the closet, watching her, unsure what to do. He had no idea why she was so claustrophobic, but it was definitely not something she had any control over.

In that moment Cameron hated every single thing about his life in law enforcement. He was here to catch bad guys. But right now the good guys were the ones who were paying the price.

Cameron took a step toward Sophia and she cringed away from him, whimpering. "No, please…" She stretched out her arms as if to ward him off.

"No," Cameron whispered. "I won't do that again. Never again."

Sophia nodded her head, but still shied away from him. Cameron didn't want to move any closer to her. She'd been through enough. Down the hall, Cameron could hear the

TV blaring. Evidently the guys thought the show in Cameron's room was over.

He hoped it had been worth it. Because looking at Sophia right now, Cameron didn't think there was any way it could possibly have been.

Cameron took a few steps toward her then sat down on the floor so he could be eye to eye with Sophia. Her breathing was still labored, and every last ounce of color was missing from her face.

"Sophia, I'm so sorry." Cameron spoke softly. He knew this room wasn't bugged, but couldn't take any chances on any member of DS-13 overhearing them.

Cameron moved a little closer to Sophia but she shied away again. Cameron rubbed the back of his neck, where permanent tension seemed to have lodged, at least since he had first seen Sophia again this afternoon.

He wanted to give Sophia the physical space she needed, but the things he needed to say couldn't be said from across the room. Moving slowly, he scooted over until he was next to her against the wall.

Sophia just huddled into her corner and didn't look at him. But at least her breathing was slowing down a bit, wasn't quite so labored.

"Sophia, I'm so sorry," he said again. As if saying it again would make everything okay. "I had to make them think that something bad was happening in here."

Sophia gave a quiet bark of acerbic laughter.

Cameron shook his head. "I mean, something *they* would think is bad. You know what they expected."

Sophia nodded her head slightly, but didn't say anything. They sat there in silence for long moments. Cameron tried to figure out what possible words could make this better.

"Things have changed since I saw you last, five years ago," Cameron said softly, close to her ear.

"I know," Sophia all but hissed, but just as softly. "The Cameron Branson I knew five years ago never would've done this." She gestured toward her face with her hand, then pointed toward the closet with a shaky arm.

"Sophia, I'm sorry I hit you earlier. I had to take action immediately. And the closet…" Cameron shrugged wearily. "It had to be done."

Sophia turned away from him again without saying anything.

"It's not like I planned any of this. Damn it, Soph, I'm just trying to keep you alive."

Sophia covered her face with her hands and began to cry. Looking over at the arm that was now exposed because her short-sleeved blue shirt was ripped at the shoulder, he could see some angry red marks on her arm. Those were from him, probably during the closet fiasco. They were definitely going to leave bruises on her pale skin, even though he had only been trying to help.

Although it pained him, Cameron hardened himself against the ache he felt at the thought of marring her beautiful skin. The bruises would help sell their story to DS-13.

"At least tell me you're here, you know…working," Sophia finally said to him.

Cameron appreciated that she left out the word *undercover*. That word could get them both killed quicker than almost anything else they could say. "Yeah. I'm with the agency."

Cameron knew he was being vague, but didn't think now was the time to go into Omega Sector and his life there. When they had known each other before, he had just been coming out of the Rangers. Sophia didn't know anything about Omega—even most people who worked in the FBI knew nothing about it.

Sophia let out a sigh and turned toward him slightly. "Well, that's a relief. I wasn't sure."

She wasn't sure? "Seriously? What did you think, I had left the Rangers and joined some sort of crime syndicate since we last spoke?"

"Stranger things have happened."

Cameron shook his head. "I guess." He must really have been undercover too long if an old friend couldn't tell if he was pretending or not. Maybe he had been in the darkness too long.

Cameron didn't have time for metaphors about darkness and light in his life. He had a job to do: justice for his partner's killer and retrieval of Ghost Shell. And now making sure Sophia got out of this alive and relatively unscathed.

He definitely did not have time to think about how beautiful she was, or how much she had meant to him five years ago, or how often he had thought about her since.

Keeping her alive. That was the most important thing.

WAS HE HONESTLY offended that she couldn't tell if he was really working undercover or not when she was sitting here with bruises and a racing heartbeat from what he had done to her?

Sophia looked at the closet again. From across the room, it looked so benign. Obviously there was plenty of air throughout both this room and the closet. She very clearly knew that now. But five minutes ago there had been no way to convince her mind of that.

She pulled her knees closer to her body. She believed Cameron when he said he was undercover. She even believed he was doing what he thought was best when he had hit her earlier, and everything that had happened since. But that didn't mean she wanted him to touch her again.

But part of her desperately wanted him to touch her

again. She had wanted that for five years. But not here in this house with those filthy men in the next room.

Sophia glanced sideways at Cameron. He looked as exhausted as she felt. Sophia didn't know much about undercover work, but she was sure that her entrance into the picture had to have thrown a wrench into whatever mission he was on.

"Have I totally screwed things up for you? I tried to get out of the warehouse like you said, but that big guy was out there," Sophia offered softly.

Cameron looked surprised that she was talking to him at all. Now that she was calming down she was realizing that Cameron really had been working in her best interest.

But she still wanted out of here as soon as possible.

"Well, your presence was definitely unexpected. But so far it looks like there was no harm done to the case."

"Really?" Sophia couldn't believe that was true.

"Yeah, evidently how I've been treating you has been helping solidify my bad-guy reputation."

"How long have you been…working with them?" Sophia turned toward him slightly.

"This group is called DS-13. They're basically into everything—weapons, drugs, money laundering. And now it looks like they're expanding into full-on terrorism." Cameron gestured toward the rest of the house with his thumb. "I've been in this house for about three weeks, but first made contact eight months ago."

"What do you do? I mean, what do they think you do?"

"They think I'm a midlevel weapons dealer. What you walked in on today was a sale I had set up."

Sophia shook her head. Just sheer bad luck. If Bruce had gotten the pictures when he was supposed to have… "If they did a sale, can't you make arrests?"

Cameron shifted a little closer to her, but this time Sophia didn't feel the need to move away.

"I could've arrested everybody there, and would've tried if things had gotten much more out of hand."

"Tried?"

Cameron reached over and pulled up her ripped sleeve, as if he could reattach it to the rest of her shirt by sheer will. "There were four of them, all armed, against just you and me. And only I had a weapon."

"Not very good odds, I guess." Sophia shuddered thinking about it.

"No, I doubt if either of us would've made it out alive." Cameron shrugged and smiled crookedly at her. "But I would've tried."

"Don't you have a wire or something? Backup?"

"Sometimes. But not in deep cover like this. It's too complicated and dangerous to have surveillance all the time. DS-13 is smart—that's why they chose this house. Surveillance vehicles would be pretty easy to spot around here."

"But what if you need help?" Sophia couldn't believe they would just send Cameron in by himself.

He smiled at her again and she found herself shifting a little more toward him.

That cocky smile. Lord, how she'd missed it.

"Honey, I can take care of myself. But I do have ways to bring in backup, if I need it."

"Like today?"

"Believe it or not, today was mostly for show. The buyers were picked up not long after they left the warehouse. The whole thing was just supposed to show DS-13 how helpful and well-organized my buys could be for them."

Cameron stretched his long legs out in front of him. "The agency was supposed to have blocked everything off so nobody would be around those warehouses."

Sophia rolled her eyes. "Yeah, well, I got way lost and ended up coming through some farmer's back field to get to the warehouses. If the FBI was watching the roads, that's why they didn't see me."

Cameron nodded as if she had just solved some puzzle for him. "I didn't want to make any arrests because these are just lower-level bad guys. I'm trying to get their boss."

Sophia watched, a little frightened, as Cameron's face and posture hardened right before her eyes. Whoever this "boss" was, Cameron wanted to take him down. Badly.

"No luck yet?"

"Haven't even met him. This sort of work is tricky—you can't push too hard or it backfires on you."

Sophia nodded. She couldn't imagine the sort of pressure being undercover would put on someone. Never knowing if you were making the right choices, or when you may be discovered.

It had definitely made Cameron Branson into a harder man than when she had known him five years ago. Then, he had still been strong—physically, mentally, in all possible ways. But now there was an edge to him that hadn't been there before. One that scared her a little.

One that had probably saved her life earlier.

Almost as if her body was moving of its own accord she turned toward him. He did look exhausted. His black hair, grown out from how short it used to be, was touching his collar. Before she could stop herself, Sophia reached out and tucked a stray curl back from where it had fallen onto his forehead, nearly to his eyes.

For a moment they looked at each other. Sophia forgot where they were, the danger they were in, the fear she had felt. She only saw Cameron.

Something slid under the door before a fist beat loudly

on it. Sophia jumped back at the sound, the moment—whatever it was—shattered.

"Cam, man, you alive in there? I need to talk to you."

Cameron stood up and walked over to pick up whatever had been slid under the door. "Yeah, Fin. I'll be right out."

Cameron walked back over to her, and reached his hand out to help her up. Sophia hesitated for just a moment before taking it. "What is it he put under the door?"

Cameron walked with her over to the edge of the bed then sat down with a sigh. He held up what was in his hands: plastic zip ties—used everywhere to secure and fasten all sorts of things.

Sophia shook her head, confused. What were the ties for? Whatever it was, Cameron wasn't too happy about it.

"Poor man's handcuffs," he finally said. "I guess Fin wants to make sure you don't try to escape or anything while he and I are talking."

Oh. "Okay, I guess." Sophia was determined to keep it together. Now that she knew Cameron was undercover, she needed to help him if she could. Not being hysterical was the most help she could offer right now.

"Just don't try to struggle against them. They'll cut into your wrists if you do."

Sophia swallowed hard and nodded.

"I'm going to run one set around your wrists and one around your ankles since there's nothing in this room to secure you to. It will look more authentic that way if someone checks."

Sophia's panicked glaze flew up to his. Someone checking?

A fist pounded on the door again. "Damn it, Cam. Hurry up. You can finish doing whatever you want to her after we talk."

Cameron spoke to her quickly as he pulled the plastic

fasteners around her ankles. "I'll be as fast as I can, but sometimes Fin likes to hear himself talk."

Cameron tightened the ties so they were tight but not painful. "If anybody comes through that door that isn't me, start screaming your head off. Immediately. Don't wait to see what they want."

Sophia nodded. That wasn't a problem. She knew her screaming voice was definitely in working condition.

Cameron slipped the other ties around her wrists, and pulled them tight. He helped her so she was sitting up against the wall the bed leaned against.

Cameron leaned down and put his forehead against hers. "I'm going to get you out of this. I swear to God." He lowered his lips and kissed her gently, then turned and strode out of the room without another word.

Chapter Five

Obnoxious catcalls met Cameron as he walked down the hall and past the living room. He stopped and gave the guys a little smirk and bow—even though it made him sick to his stomach—before turning and heading into the kitchen to see Fin.

Fin sat at the table, nursing a beer. Cameron made his way to the fridge to get a beer of his own as Fin looked him up and down.

"Worth it?" the man asked.

Cameron gave his most sly smile. "Absolutely." He held his beer up in silent salute as he took the seat across from Fin.

Fin gestured toward Cameron's face. "Looks like she may have given you a bruise there on your cheek."

He thought of all the marks on Sophia's arms. "She'll have plenty of her own."

Fin cackled at that. "Well, I'm glad it was worth the trouble." Cameron settled back in his chair, somehow managing to keep the smile on his face.

"So, I spoke to Mr. Smith tonight, while you were having your…fun," Fin continued.

Cameron kept his best poker face and feigned disinterest as he took a sip from his bottle. "I didn't know Mr. Smith was interested in the details of that sort of fun."

"Mr. Smith is interested in anything and everything that has to do with DS-13. And he has taken an interest in you."

Bingo. Eight months undercover, and this was what he had been waiting for. "Oh, yeah? Why's that?"

"He was impressed—has always been impressed—with how the sales you arrange go down without a hitch."

Cameron nodded and took a sip of his beer. "That's what I do."

"Well, Mr. Smith would like for you to start arranging more meetings and perhaps find some other sorts of buyers for some items he's come into recently."

"What sort of items?" Encoding technology, perhaps?

"Mr. Smith wants to meet you and tell you about that himself."

Cameron could tell Fin was watching him closely to see how he would react. How he played this off would be key. Too much enthusiasm would most certainly be reported back to Mr. Smith, and perhaps cause the whole invitation to be pulled. Not enough enthusiasm would be reported back as an insult.

But insult was definitely better than suspicion, so Cameron took another long drag on his beer and remained sprawled in his chair.

"That's cool. Whatever. Just let me know when." Cameron yawned, then got up, as if the meeting with Fin was over. He could tell Fin wasn't expecting that.

"Whoa, hang on there a minute, Cam. I'm not done."

"Oh…sorry, man." Cameron sat back down as if he didn't really care much about what Fin was going to say next. Which couldn't be further from the truth.

"Mr. Smith wants to meet you *tomorrow*," Fin told him.

That was a little sooner than Cameron expected, but not too bad. If he could find a way to get Sophia to safety.

"Okay, that's fine. Is he coming here? Does he want me

to set up something with a buyer for tomorrow? That's kind of hard when I don't know what he's selling."

Fin shook his head. "No, he only wants to meet you tomorrow. Let's just say that your actions with the pretty brunette have reassured him that you're not afraid of getting your hands a little dirty."

Cameron grinned despite his souring stomach. "Well, it wasn't my hands getting dirty, if you know what I mean."

Fin howled in laughter again before turning serious. "Mr. Smith needs you to begin setting up some meetings with people who may be interested in doing a little bit more damage than just with a few automatic weapons."

"You mean like missiles or something?"

"No, actually a specific computer program or virus or something that can do major damage to law enforcement. I don't really understand it. But Mr. Smith says it's going to bring in a lot of money."

Cameron nodded. "Okay, man, no problem. Tell Mr. Smith I can line that up for him."

"Actually, you can tell him yourself when you see him tomorrow. He's having a bit of a get-together at his mountain home. Has some people he'd like you to meet."

Crap. "Mountain home? Where? And I don't think it's going to work real well to bring 'my companion' on a plane, you know?"

"Cam, DS-13's resources are much greater, and more organized, than you think. We'll be using a small jet, owned by one of DS-13's dummy corporations. And Mr. Smith's house is in the mountains of Virginia."

"Wow. I didn't know about all that." Actually, Cameron did know about all that, at least all of it except the mountain house. No wonder Smith was never spotted, since he had some sort of secluded retreat.

Damn it. All of this just got much harder for him and

Omega Sector. He needed to contact them tonight and let them know about the location change.

But most important he needed to get Sophia out of here as soon as possible. There was no way he was going to let her be transported to some remote location where he had even less control over the situation.

"There's a lot you don't know about DS-13, Cam," Fin said, smiling knowingly, self-importance fairly radiating off him. "Just be ready to go in the morning. We'll have to figure out what to do with your little friend by then."

"Private jet. Cool." At least Cameron's cover persona would think so. Cameron himself didn't give a damn.

"You'll want to be at your best when you meet Mr. Smith," Fin told him with a grin. "So don't exhaust yourself with other things."

"Roger that." Cameron took the last sip of his beer and stood up. "See you tomorrow." As he walked out of the kitchen he grabbed a bag of chips and one of the post-workout protein shakes the guys had lying around. It wasn't a great meal for Sophia, but at least it was something.

Cameron didn't have much time. Morning would come fast. He had no doubt that when Fin said they'd "figure out what to do with" Sophia in the morning, he meant kill her. He had to think of a plan to get Sophia out of here. Quickly.

Cameron walked as casually as he could back to the room. As he opened the door, he saw Sophia, still tied as he had left her, about to start screaming.

"It's just me." He put down the food and walked quickly over to her. "Are you okay? Any problems?"

"No, I'm fine. Just ready to get untied."

Cameron pulled out the knife he always kept in his pocket. He made quick work of the zip ties, first at her wrists then her ankles, allowing the plastic to drop to the floor.

Sophia rubbed her wrists to try to get some of the blood to flow back normally. Cameron reached down and gently rubbed her ankles.

"Better?" he asked softly.

Sophia nodded. "Yeah, thanks. Did everything go okay out there?"

Cameron reluctantly stopped rubbing her ankles, released her feet and went to put the chair back under the door handle. He handed her the food and she began to eat.

He turned to her. "Yes and no."

Sophia drew her knees up to her chest and wrapped her arms around them. "Yes and no? That doesn't sound too good."

Cameron came and sat back down on the edge of the bed. "Well, in a rather ironic turn of events, it seems that the horrible way I've treated you has made DS-13 trust me more."

"What?"

"Whatever doubts they had about me have evidently been eradicated since I have turned into a rapist slimeball."

"But you didn't…"

"Yeah, but they don't know that. Evidently your screams were pretty convincing." Cameron rubbed an exhausted hand over his eyes. He didn't want to think about that again.

Sophia unwrapped her grip on her legs and crawled a little closer to him, reaching out and touching him on the arm. "Cam, you did what you had to do. I thought about it while you were gone. You saved both of our lives without a doubt."

"Sophia…"

She moved a little closer. "I'm sorry about all that stuff I said. I don't think badly of you. I can't stand you thinking badly of yourself."

Cameron turned so he was facing directly toward her. He took the hand that was touching his arm and held it in both of his. God, she was so sweet. He looked down at the hand in his—so tiny.

He couldn't stand the thought of her being in this room—around these people—a minute longer. And the thought of taking Sophia to that other house where Mr. Smith was? Totally unacceptable.

Cameron reached out and stroked her cheek. She was looking at him so intently, so concerned about his *feelings*. Cameron could barely remember the last time he'd had an authentic feeling. Until today.

"I'm fine, Soph. If anything, just glad that something good has come out of this situation."

She smiled shyly before easing away. "Me, too."

"It seems that the quite elusive leader of DS-13, a man named Mr. Smith, wants to meet me now because of how everything went down today."

"That's good, right?"

Cameron nodded and eased backward on the bed so he was sitting next to her. "Yeah. That's what I've been trying to do for eight months."

"So what's the bad?"

Cameron sighed. "He wants to meet me tomorrow."

Cameron watched as Sophia obviously tried to figure out what that meant for her. "Oh, okay," she finally responded.

"Even worse, he wants for me to go to his mountain house. That's not…optimal for the situation."

"Because of me?"

"Partially, but not totally. I wasn't aware of this other location until tonight. I don't know anything about it so it's hard to prepare for it."

Sophia nodded, worry plain in her eyes.

He didn't know if she was worried for herself or him. Probably both. "But you're not going, so you don't need to worry about anything."

"I'm not going?"

"We're going to get you out of here tonight."

Sophia sat up straighter, obviously ready for action. "We are? How?"

"Wait until late, when everyone is asleep, then I'm going to tell you how to sneak out."

"But won't that cause trouble for you? Won't your cover be blown?"

Cameron shook his head. "Not if we do it right. It's going to have to look like you knocked me unconscious. I'm going to need a pretty good goose egg on my head."

When Sophia just shook her head, Cameron continued, "If anything, it will help. They'll be in a panic that you'll call the cops and will want to get out of here even faster. Anything that throws them off their timetable can only help me."

"That's good, I guess." Sophia shook her head again. "But I don't want to hit you with anything."

Cameron reached up and softly touched her swollen and bruised lip. "C'mon sweetie, turnabout is fair play."

"Cameron." Sophia reached up and touched his hand. "You did this because you had to. I know that."

"And you'll do this because you have to. It's the only way, Sophia."

SOPHIA DIDN'T LIKE IT. She really had come to terms with what he had done while he was having his meeting with Fin. Everything that had happened from the moment she had seen Cameron in the warehouse today had been done to protect her.

She didn't want to hurt him. But it looked as if she was going to have to.

"There's no other way?" she asked.

"Not if we want to keep suspicions off me. I'll wake up

and notice you're gone. Then I'll tell everyone we should leave before you call the cops."

"They won't think you let me go?"

Cameron shook his head. "Absolutely not. Especially not after earlier. Although can you do something for me?"

"I can try."

Cameron leaned close and whispered in her ear, "Can you yell, 'Get off me, you bastard'? It's been a little too quiet in here."

Sophia shot off the bed. If she couldn't do it, would he drag her back into the closet? She looked over at it, then back at him.

Cameron wasn't making moves toward her—as a matter of fact, he was keeping himself very casual and relaxed on the bed—but Sophia still took a step back. Then she stopped.

Just yell. It's not hard. Just do it.

"Get off me, you bastard!" she yelled at the top of her voice.

Immediately she could hear guffaws of laughter from other places in the house. Perverts.

Cameron got off the bed and came to stand right next to her. "Thank you."

"Anything to stay out of the closet."

Cameron grinned. "Got it." He grabbed her hand and brought it up to his lips and kissed it softly.

They both seemed a little shocked by his impulsive gesture, but Sophia didn't pull her hand away and Cameron didn't let it go.

"I just want to get you out of here. That's the most important thing to me," Cameron whispered. He let go of her hand, wrapped his arms around her and drew her to his chest. Sophia snuggled in. After what she had been through today his arms felt like absolute heaven. This was what she remembered about them from five years ago: a closeness that matched the burning attraction between them.

She and Cameron had met at a diner that was just a couple of blocks from her tiny apartment in Washington, near Georgetown University, where she went to school. Hating her own cooking, Sophia had made a habit of going to the diner each morning and one particularly crowded day Cameron had asked to share her booth and they'd struck up a conversation. Then he had started showing up at the same time every morning, displaying a great deal of interest in her.

Emotionally, Sophia had fallen fast and she had fallen hard.

But physically, Sophia was shy and a little bit awkward, so she had taken things slowly with Cameron, thinking they would have all the time in the world. For three months, they went on dates, shared many passionate kisses, sometimes talked all night, just to end up back at the diner for breakfast the next morning.

Sophia had thought—had *known*—Cameron was the one for her. And his willingness to wait so patiently for her physically had made her love him even more.

And she thought he felt the same way. But then one morning he didn't show up. The thought still left her feeling a little sick to her stomach. Plus, he had waited until he knew she would be at the diner to call her home phone and leave a message. *Hi, Soph. Something's come up and I'm going to have to leave town permanently. I wish you all the best. Take care.*

She still knew the message by heart. At least now, five years later, she didn't cringe when she thought about it.

Sophia eased herself back from his arms. A nice hug in the middle of a traumatic event was one thing, allowing herself to dive into the past and drag out all the hurts was quite another.

Cameron didn't try to hold on to her when Sophia pulled back. And although she knew it was for the best, it still panged her just a little.

"Okay, so what's the plan?" Sophia asked as she moved away and sat back down on the bed, which was as sparse as everything else in this room. She looked around. Nothing was inviting or comforting in the least. And the little she'd seen of the rest of the house as he'd dragged her in here wasn't much better.

Plus it was pretty stuffy in here. There was only a tiny window, covered by cheap blinds that barely let in any light at all. The bedroom was attached to a bathroom, but that room wasn't much more appealing, even with its own window.

Cameron saw her looking around. "What?"

"Just…this room. This entire house. You've been here three weeks, you said? How can you stand it?"

Cameron shrugged. "It's just part of the job. DS-13 wanting me to stay here was actually a huge step in the right direction. It meant they were really starting to trust me. Took long enough."

"Eight months, right? Isn't that a long time for—" she lowered her voice even further "—undercover work? Consistent work?"

"Yeah, it's starting to reach the outer limits. But I asked to stay on this case and keep this cover for so long."

"Why?"

Cameron came and sat next to Sophia on the bed. "Let's just say that I'm determined that Mr. Smith—leader of DS-13—is going down."

Fierce determination gleamed in Cameron's eyes, as well as frustration.

"Something in particular you want him for, or just because he's a really bad guy?" Sophia asked, wanting to understand.

"Him being a bad guy is enough, but yeah, for me it's personal. He killed my partner last year. Viciously."

Sophia had no idea what to say to that. She reached out and touched his arm. "I'm so sorry, Cam."

Cameron nodded. "Mr. Smith suspected Jason, my partner, was undercover. Then cut his throat when he found out it was true."

Sophia's expression shuttered and she rubbed Cam's arm. No wonder Cameron was so intent on arresting Mr. Smith. She didn't blame him.

Cameron stood, and Sophia's hand fell away. "I will get him, Soph. Don't doubt it."

"I don't." Sophia smiled at Cameron and stood up. "So how are we getting me out of your way so you can get your job finished? Because, honestly, I can't stand the thought of you living in this jackass-infested rat hole much longer." She gestured around the room with her hand.

Cameron chuckled softly. "Jackass-infested rat hole?"

Sophia raised one eyebrow. "Seems apt. Although perhaps my metaphor is a bit mixed. I just want to get out of here and let you get to the other evil lair."

Cameron chuckled again. "I'm pretty sure they don't call it an evil lair."

Sophia smiled. She had missed his laugh. "Well, they should. So what's the plan?"

They were both startled by a loud pounding on the door again. Whoever it was tested the doorknob to see if it was locked. Cameron hooked his arm around Sophia and pulled her behind him so he was between her and the door.

"I'm busy in here!" Cameron yelled out, making annoyance plain in his voice. "What the hell do you want?"

"Cam, Fin said to give you these." It was one of the men, but Sophia didn't know which one. More plastic ties slid under the door.

"Fine, Rick. But stay the hell out unless you're trying to see my naked ass, you pervert."

They heard Rick mutter something about wanting to see a naked ass, but not Cameron's. But at least he left them alone. If Rick decided to force his way through the door, that chair propped under the knob definitely wasn't going to stop him.

Cameron breathed a sigh of relief when he seemed sure Rick was gone. "We've definitely got to get you out of here."

A thought occurred to Sophia. "Why did you tell them your real name? Isn't that dangerous?"

"They only know my first name. I discovered a while ago that it was better to use my first name for covers. Less confusion, less possible mistakes."

Sophia wasn't sure she understood. "Mistakes?"

"Well, if bad guys think your name is Tom but some complete stranger happens to say the name Cameron and you react…"

"Game over."

Cameron nodded. "Game definitely over. It's easier to keep the lies as close to the truth as possible."

"But no Branson, right?"

"Nope. Cam Cameron, at your service."

Sophia rolled her eyes. "Cam Cameron?"

Cameron shrugged. "Hey, it works."

"All right, Cam Cameron, what do we do now?"

"Now we climb in bed and wait a few hours, so I can get you out of here as soon as everyone's asleep. You need to be long gone before tomorrow morning."

Chapter Six

Lying in bed with Cameron for the few hours before they were going to sneak her out, Sophia never would've thought she would sleep. But evidently her traumatized mind had other plans.

Cameron had lain down with her on the small bed and tucked her into his side.

"Try to rest, if you can," he had whispered.

The last thing Sophia remembered was snorting, "Yeah, right." The next thing she knew, Cameron was waking her up…

With a kiss.

It took her a moment to figure out what was happening. Even longer to remember where she was. But she shut that all out for a few moments and melted into Cameron.

Sophia twisted in the tiny bed so she could get closer to him. She wrapped her fingers in his hair and pulled him against her. Cameron's hand slid from her neck all the way down her back and splayed out over her hip. He pulled her closer and deepened the kiss.

Sophia could barely keep from moaning. She had missed this passion between them that erupted without either of them being able to do anything about it.

Cameron's lips trailed from her mouth, over her jaw and

down to her neck. Sophia shivered, her breath quickening. She gave herself over to the sensation.

But after a few moments Cameron pulled away.

"I'm sorry, Soph. I shouldn't have done that."

Suddenly, all the reasons why this wasn't a good idea came crashing back to her. Sophia jerked away from him.

"You're right. You shouldn't have done that."

Cameron sighed and got up from the bed.

"I think everyone is asleep. It's time for us to get you out of here."

Sophia decided to let go of her annoyance about the kiss. Kisses. Complete make-out session. Whatever. There were more important things to concentrate on here.

She got up from the bed. "What time is it?"

"About 4:00 a.m. It's late enough that nobody should be awake, but still dark enough for you not to be seen."

Sophia nodded. "Okay. What do I need to do?"

"I'm going to walk you out and show you where the side door is. We'll go ahead and unlock it."

Sounded easy enough. "Okay."

"Once you get out, I want you to run, as fast as you can. When you get to the main road, there's a gas station about half a mile down. Call the Bureau and have somebody pick you up."

"No 911?"

"No. That would wreak havoc on what I'm doing here. I want them to think you've called 911, but I don't want to have to deal with any uniforms poking around."

Sophia nodded.

"After I show you the door," Cameron continued, "we have to come back in here. I can't hit myself hard enough for it to be realistic."

Sophia cringed. She didn't know if she'd be able to hit him hard enough, either.

Cameron opened the door and ushered Sophia out. Everything in the house was quiet. Cameron led her silently down the hall to the side door, past the garage. She watched as he unlocked the door, and cracked it just the slightest bit, so it wouldn't make any noise when she came out here in a few minutes.

Cameron turned and looked at Sophia. Sophia nodded. She knew what to do when she came back. They silently headed back toward Cameron's room. With every step, Sophia was terrified someone would wake up and catch them.

Would that mean death for both of them? Would Cameron be able to cover for them again? Sophia didn't know.

She was also concerned that he wouldn't be able to convince DS-13 that her escape was an accident. That he wouldn't be able to talk his way out of it and that all his time working undercover would go to waste.

Or worse.

Back in his room, Sophia turned to Cameron. "What if they don't believe I attacked you and got away? What if they think you let me go?"

Cameron put his hands on her forearms. "Soph, it's okay. I've been with them a long time. They'll believe me."

"But how will I know you're okay? How will I know something bad hasn't happened to you?"

Cameron's hands slid up from her arms, over her shoulders until they were framing her face. "I'm good at what I do. I'll make them believe me, don't worry."

Sophia nodded. Her hands were a little shaky as she asked, "Is this the part where I get to knock you unconscious?"

Cameron grimaced. "Yeah. You're going to need to use the butt of my SIG to hit me with. There's nothing else in here that will do."

Sophia didn't like the thought of hitting him, and liked

the thought of using a gun even less. "I don't know if that's a good idea. I don't know anything about guns."

"Well, just don't point it at me and pull the trigger and we'll be fine." Cameron's smile didn't reassure Sophia much. "I'll make sure it's not loaded," he added at her worried look. "Once you've hit me, take the gun with you and go. You probably won't even knock me unconscious. All that matters is that it looks like you did. In about an hour, I'll stumble out and wake everybody up, pretending like you just got away a few minutes ago."

Sophia had to admit, it was a pretty well-thought-out plan. She prayed it would work. For both their sakes.

"Okay, where do I hit you?" she whispered.

"On the back of the head, toward the base of my skull. Contrary to what you might think, it's the sudden, jerking motion of the skull that causes blackouts from an injury like this. Not necessarily the actual force."

"You mean I could hit you as hard as I can and it wouldn't matter?"

Cameron quickly corrected her. "No, that would definitely cause brain damage or possibly death. You don't want to rabbit-punch me."

"Rabbit punch is bad?"

Cameron nodded. "Very. I just mean that you don't necessarily need tremendous force to knock someone unconscious. It's the motion that causes it."

Sophia wasn't sure if she could do it. Cameron could see her obvious hesitation. "Soph, I'll be fine. But we're out of time. I need you to do this and get going."

Sophia nodded.

"I have a hard head, sweetheart. I've been swearing that was true every day for five years."

Sophia couldn't help but laugh softly. "You and me both."

Cameron sat on the bed, facing away from her. Sophia ran her fingers through his thick black hair, then let it go. She raised her arm with the gun in her hand.

"Ready?" Cameron asked. "Remember, hit me hard. Having to do it twice would really hurt. And once you've hit me, go. Don't wait around. I promise I will be fine. One, two, three."

Sophia brought the gun's handle down—hard—against the base of his skull. Cameron made a sickening groan and fell forward onto the bed. Sophia could see that he was still breathing. Blood was slowly seeping from a giant knot where she'd hit him. Tears slid down her cheeks as she glanced at Cameron once more before easing out the door of his room.

Sophia's breath seemed unimaginably loud to her as she made her way down the hallway as Cameron had shown her. Every step was full of terror, as she was afraid someone might wake up and catch her. As she walked through the kitchen, her shoes sounded so loud she slipped them off and carried them. Finally she made it to the side door that led outside from the kitchen.

It was closed.

Sophia knew Cameron had left that door open. She spun around in a panic, expecting to see someone behind her. But no one was there.

Maybe it had closed on its own. Sophia tried the knob. It was still unlocked. It must have just caught some wind or something. Regardless, she couldn't let it stop her now.

Sophia eased the door open as quietly as she could, grimacing with every little sound the door made. When the door was open the barest amount for her to fit, she slipped through, and pulled it gently and slowly closed behind her.

Sophia breathed a silent sigh of relief. At least she was out of the house. She bent down to put her flats back on her feet and took a deep breath to get her bearings and get ready to run. That's when she smelled it: cigarette smoke.

From right around the corner of the house.

Sophia quickly moved behind a large trash can that sat against the house, in case whoever was there came around the corner. Now she wouldn't be able to run the way Cameron had directed without being seen. She'd have to go the opposite way and then double back to the gas station when she was farther away from the house.

"I don't understand why we have to stay up all night." It sounded like Rick, the mean one with cold eyes.

"Well, you know Fin's not going to stay up if we're going to see Mr. Smith tomorrow."

Sophia didn't really care about who had to stay up or why Fin needed his beauty rest to see Mr. Smith. She needed to get out of here, now.

"But I don't understand why Fin doesn't trust Cam. Cam's one of us." That sounded like the big guy, Marco.

Sophia was starting to ease her way around to the back of the house when she heard Marco's statement. Fin didn't trust Cameron? She stopped and eased her way back so she could hear the conversation better.

"Yeah, well, if the woman is still here in the morning, then we'll know Cam is on the up-and-up. But like Fin said, if Cam let the woman get away…" Rick's voice trailed off.

"That doesn't mean he's a cop."

"He's either a cop or someone who lets a hundred-pound woman get the jump on him. Either way, DS-13 doesn't want him. Fin will take care of that." Rick laughed and Marco joined in after a moment.

Damn it. Sophia realized she was, in essence, signing Cameron's death warrant if she left now. She couldn't do it. She would have to sneak back inside and they'd figure out something else. She needed to hurry back into Cameron's room before he came out and told everyone she was missing.

And got himself killed.

Sophia peeked around the side of the trash can and jerked herself back as the two men walked around the corner. She held her breath, praying they hadn't seen her.

Marco was talking about a football game coming on that night as they walked in the kitchen door. Sophia felt her heart drop as she heard the click of the lock once they were inside.

She had to find a way back into the house. Sophia ran around to the back, having to make her way over a low wooden fence when she found the fence gate locked. From the back of the house in the dark, it was hard to tell which room was Cameron's.

Sophia knew she had to figure it out quickly. Cameron was running out of time and he had no idea about it.

Sophia definitely didn't want to climb into the wrong room. But one window was a little higher than the others, and smaller. That must be the bathroom, which would make Cameron's the window to the left.

Sophia ran to Cameron's window and began tapping on it. She had to get his attention before he went out and told them she was gone. She tapped as loud as she dared, not wanting to wake anyone else.

"Cameron?" Sophia cupped her hands to the window in an attempt to make the sound go through it, rather than out. "Cameron!"

Nothing. She rapped on the pane again but he didn't come to the window. Sophia tried to open the window but it was locked from the inside.

She had to get in the house. It might already be too late.

Sophia climbed up onto the air-conditioning unit so she

could reach the small window of the bathroom. Someone had left it cracked, just a little bit, but it was enough.

Sophia got her hands under the frame and slid it up as high as it would go, cringing as it made a loud creaking sound. She hefted her body up and into the tiny opening. All the buttons of her blouse ripped off as she scooted through, but Sophia didn't stop. When a nail caught her shoulder Sophia let out a cry, but still didn't stop.

She finally got herself through the opening and fell into the bathtub on the other side. She got up as quickly as she could, using a towel to wipe the blood from a pretty large gash on her shoulder. She rushed into Cameron's room.

But he wasn't there.

Chapter Seven

The crack Sophia gave him on the back of the head definitely wasn't too soft. Although Cameron didn't lose consciousness for more than a few seconds—at least he didn't think so—his head hurt like the devil. Lying on his bed doing nothing, giving Sophia time to get away before he "discovered" her gone, was no problem.

After a few minutes he decided to get out of the bed and make his way out into the main part of the house. Nobody should be awake yet, and being caught knocked senseless would look better out in the living room than lying in his bed.

The room spun dizzyingly as Cameron got up. He couldn't hold back a groan. He felt as if sirens were going off in his head, and on top of that he could swear he heard someone calling his name. Maybe Sophia hit him harder than he thought.

Cameron ignored the pain and started out his door. After a few steps at least the building stopped spinning. He stumbled—mostly not acting—out into the living room.

Where both Marco and Rick sat, wide-awake.

This was not good. Why were they awake and dressed? How had Sophia gotten by them?

Cameron tried to silently move back into his room, but Rick saw him.

"What's going on, Cameron?" Rick asked him.

Cameron had no idea how to play this off. Did they already have Sophia? "My head. That bitch hit me on the head."

Cameron watched as Marco and Rick looked at one another pointedly. Another not-good sign. Something was going on here that Cameron didn't know. He decided not to mention Sophia being gone yet. Give her as much time as possible.

"What are you guys doing up?" Cameron plopped down on the couch and gritted his teeth as the back of his head throbbed. Better play off the head injury until he knew what was going on.

"We're just up. Getting everything ready to go to the other house," Marco told him.

"At like—what time is it?—five o'clock in the morning?" Cameron saw Marco and Rick make that weird eye contact again. Something was definitely not right.

"Where is the woman?" The voice came from behind Cameron on the couch. Fin.

Cameron racked his brain for what to say now. To say she had just hit him and run obviously wasn't going to cut it. He had no idea how he was going to get out of this.

"In my room. She hit me on the head with a bottle and I clocked her. I used one of the plastic ties on her hands and threw her in the closet."

Cameron stood up and walked toward the kitchen. Maybe they wouldn't look for her and wouldn't notice she was gone for a while. It would give him a chance to get out or at least get to one of the other weapons in his room.

"Marco, go get her," Fin told the bigger man.

Damn it. Cameron shrugged and kept walking toward the kitchen as casually as he could. He wondered if his partner, Jason, had faced some sort of situation like this.

Feeling the walls closing in on you and knowing there was no way out.

Knowing unless there was some sort of miracle, you were going to die.

Marco came back into the kitchen. "She's not in the closet, boss."

Rick and Marco both pulled out their guns and pointed them directly at Cameron.

"Whoa, what the hell's going on here?" Feigned shock was Cameron's only option. "It's too early in the morning for this. What are you pointing them at me for?"

Fin pulled out a wicked-looking blade. Cameron knew how much pride the smaller man took in it. He suspected it was the same knife that had killed his partner.

"Where's the woman, Cam?" Fin asked, walking closer.

"I told you, I threw her in the closet."

Fin looked over at Marco, who shook his head. "She's not in the closet."

"Fine, she's not in the closet. Maybe she's under the bed or something. Everybody knows Marco can't find his keys half the time. No surprise he can't find a person, either."

Cameron got up and strolled purposely to his room, as if to prove Marco wrong about Sophia. He knew taking them by surprise in there would be his best option.

The best of really, really bad options. Two guns and a knife against his bare hands and the very slight element of surprise?

Cameron entered his room, thankful that at least Sophia had gotten away. He walked over to his closet and thrust open the door.

"See? Told you," Marco said.

"Screw you, Marco." Cameron still kept up the innocent act. "She's in here somewhere."

Cameron looked under his bed, hoping to find anything there that could be used as a weapon. Nothing.

He got back up. It looked as if the guys were relaxing just a little bit. Good.

Cameron walked toward the bathroom door. "You check in there, Marco?"

Marco looked sheepish. "No." The big man looked over at Fin.

"Check it out," Fin told him.

This would be Cameron's only chance. Marco's back would be to him. He'd have to take down Rick first, since he had the gun. And Fin's knife was nothing to scoff at.

Cameron took a deep breath and tried to center himself. He ignored any pain in his head and focused on making it through the next few seconds alive.

Marco opened the bathroom door. Cameron shifted his weight so he could pivot around.

"Don't you touch me, you bastard!" The yell came from inside the bathroom.

Sophia?

Cameron was already in the process of pivoting, so he kept going around to face the other men. But instead of striking them as he had planned, Cameron just glared at Fin.

Fin had his knife up and had obviously been ready for Cameron's attack. There was no way Cameron would've lived through it.

"Okay, maybe I put her in the bathroom, not the closet. So sue me." Cameron shrugged. "Now can we get some coffee?"

The other three men mumbled something to each other and turned to walk out of Cam's room. He heard Marco mutter, "See, I told you." But he didn't hear any response.

Cameron bent down next to Sophia.

"Are you okay? Why are you back? How did you even get in here?" Cameron shot off the questions, knowing he wasn't giving Sophia enough time to respond. There wasn't any time to give her.

Sophia pointed at the window above the bathtub. Cameron couldn't believe, even as slight as Sophia was, that she'd managed to make it through that tiny opening.

He reached down to help her up and heard Sophia's indrawn breath and immediately released her. He noticed the gash on her shoulder.

"What happened?"

"I cut it on my way in through the window. It's not too bad, I think."

"Stay in here. I've got to get to the kitchen and see what's going on. I'll bring back something to wrap your arm with."

Cameron didn't mention that the danger to the operation, and especially Sophia, was more severe now than ever. Unless Cameron could find a way to talk Fin into taking Sophia with them to Mr. Smith's mountain house, things were still going to get ugly real quick. He grabbed his weapon on the way out of the room.

When Cameron arrived in the kitchen, Fin and the other men were sitting around the table. Marco and Rick ate some sort of sugary cereal. Fin was drinking coffee.

Cameron went over to the cabinet, grabbed a mug for coffee, then turned so he was facing the table with his back against the counter.

"So, what the hell, Fin? After all this time you think I'm some sort of cop?"

"Not me, Cam. Sorry, man. It's Smith. He didn't like the whole situation with the woman and told us to make sure everything was under control."

Cameron should've known Smith was the one closer to

figuring things out. Fin and his goons weren't known for their mental prowess.

"We'll have to get rid of her," Fin told Cameron calmly, taking a sip of his coffee as if he wasn't talking about murdering an innocent woman. Next to Fin, Rick looked gleeful at the thought of violence.

A plan came to Cameron—it was a Hail Mary, but it was worth a shot. He didn't like the thought of dragging Sophia in deeper, but at least this would mean not having to end his undercover operation without ever meeting Smith. He was so close.

Cameron thought of his partner, Jason, who had been killed by Smith's order. That made the decision for him. Cameron silently took a deep breath. He was placing all his chips on this one bet.

"Yeah, about getting rid of her." Cameron forced himself to remain casual against the cabinet. "I'm not sure that's the right thing to do."

Rick snickered, but Cameron ignored him. Rick was just upset at the thought of the loss of need for violence.

"Why's that?" Fin asked.

"Well, it ends up that she wasn't in that warehouse by accident yesterday." Now Cameron had everyone's attention. "It ends up that she was there to try to meet and talk to one of us—someone who could get her a meeting with Mr. Smith."

"That's not going to happen," Fin spluttered, obviously thrown. "Mr. Smith doesn't meet with people he doesn't know for no reason."

"Basically that's what I told her," Cameron continued. "I mean, hell, I've known you guys for a long time and I've still never met Mr. Smith."

Fin stood up. "Fine. Then it's settled. Plan still doesn't change."

"Yeah, no problem." Here it went, the Hail Mary. "Oh, yeah, she mentioned knowing something important about a Ghost Rock or something. I have no idea what that is."

Fin froze exactly where he stood, staring at Cameron. Finally he turned and pointed at Rick and Marco. "You two, out. Now." They left their cereal and headed out the door without a word. Fin turned back to Cameron.

"You mean Ghost Shell?" Fin asked slowly.

"Yeah, Ghost Shell. That's it. Not Ghost Rock."

"That woman in your room knows about Ghost Shell?"

"Yeah." Cameron shrugged and took a sip of his coffee, pretending not to notice how completely wound up Fin was. "She said she came to the warehouse so she could find someone who knew Smith and could get her a meeting with him. But then things got out of hand before she could make her play… Guess that's my bad."

Cameron could see the wheels turning in Fin's head, so he continued, "Evidently there's some problem with this Ghost Shell whatever and she knows about it and how to fix it. But she says she'll only talk directly to Smith."

"So make her tell us and we'll tell him."

Cameron shrugged. "She said it can only be shown with the Ghost Shell. Whatever that is. She said Mr. Smith would be very glad to have the information."

Fin began pacing back and forth. "Mr. Smith isn't available today. I can't get in touch with him at all."

Cameron breathed a sigh of relief. Dealing with just Fin was much easier than dealing with Mr. Smith, someone Cameron didn't know at all. "Well, it's totally up to you, Fin. You know best. But I say, what harm can there be in bringing her? We can get rid of her there just as easily as here, if Mr. Smith doesn't want her around."

Cameron could see Fin considering the idea. Obviously the man was not supposed to bring unvetted strangers to meet Smith. But if that stranger was useful… "You could save the day, Fin. Whatever Ghost Shell is, it's obviously important to Mr. Smith. If this woman knows something helpful, you could be a real hero."

The thought of being in Smith's good graces was obviously the little push Fin needed. "All right, fine, we'll take her with us to the mountain house. But she's your responsibility. And you're the one going down if she doesn't have the info she says she does."

"That's cool, man. I think she does, though. She seems really smart."

"Oh, yeah?" Finn scoffed. "When did you guys have a little heart-to-heart talk?"

"Whoa, nothing like that." Cameron laughed good-naturedly. "Just after we had our…fun, she brought it up."

"Yeah?" Suspicion came back into Fin's eyes. "Was that before or after she hit you in the head?"

Cameron thought fast. "What can I say? We both like it rough. She obviously can give as good as she gets. We're beginning to grow on each other."

Evidently that was enough to satisfy Fin. "Whatever. Just have her and yourself ready to go soon. We'll be leaving in a couple of hours." With that, Fin turned and headed out of the kitchen.

Cameron took a sip of his coffee, but found it had gone cold so he dumped it in the sink. His plan had worked. Sophia was safe. His undercover operation was still intact and he was going to meet Smith. Cameron was one step closer to bringing that bastard down, acquiring Ghost Shell and getting Sophia to safety in one piece.

But the dread pooling in his stomach told him the opposite was true.

Chapter Eight

A few hours later Cameron watched out the jet window over Sophia's shoulder as they came in for their landing in the Blue Ridge Mountains area of western Virginia. There was nothing around but trees for miles in any direction. The airstrip they landed at was tiny, similar to the small airport south of Washington, DC, they'd taken off from not too long before. Neither was being monitored by anyone who didn't work for DS-13, Cameron was sure.

Cameron looked over at Sophia, who stared blankly out the window. Dark circles of exhaustion, almost like bruises, ringed her eyes. She held his hand in a death grip.

After convincing Fin to take Sophia with them to meet Smith, Cameron had made his way back to his room. Sophia had still been sitting on the bathroom floor, almost in a daze, arm still bleeding. He'd cleaned the cut and wrapped it with gauze. It didn't look as if it needed stitches, but it still wasn't pretty.

He still didn't know exactly why she had done it, but her return had saved his life, without a doubt.

"Thank you," Cameron had whispered when he was finished with her wound, putting his hands reverently on either side of her face and kissing her gently.

Sophia had just nodded.

Since coming back into DS-13's grasp, Sophia had

hardly said one word to Cameron, although he had to admit, talking had been nearly impossible. By the time he had played out his wounded-because-you-don't-trust-me part for Fin and the gang, and gotten suitable apologies, it had almost been time to go.

Cameron found a shirt for Sophia to wear—hers had lost all the buttons, much to the delight of the DS-13 men. He had wanted to talk to Sophia about what had happened, but sending an encoded message to Omega Sector with his satellite phone had been more important. He had to let Omega Sector know they were moving—to an unknown location as of yet—and that there was now an innocent third party involved. Cameron would send more info when he had time and details.

As the plane came to a halt, everybody unbuckled their seat belts and stood. Except Sophia. She still stared vacantly out the window.

Fin opened the plane door and everyone began to file out. When Sophia still didn't move, Cameron squatted down in front of her. He took her hands, which lay limply in her lap, in his.

"Hey," he whispered. He watched as her eyes, shadowed with exhaustion, turned blankly toward him. "You doing okay?"

Sophia nodded slowly. "Where are we?"

"We're in the mountains. Going to the evil lair, remember?"

The ghost of a smile crossed her lips. "They don't call it an evil lair."

Cameron winked at her and rubbed the back of both of her hands with his thumbs. They were like ice. "That's right, sweetie. You going to be all right? I know this is really hard."

Sophia nodded again. "I just don't know what to do,

Cam." She leaned in closer to him and whispered urgently, "I know I work for the Bureau, but I'm an artist! I don't have any training. I don't know anything about working… you know, in situations like this."

Cameron unbuckled her seat belt and helped Sophia stand. "Just stay as close to me as possible, and try to ignore everyone else. Can you do that?"

Sophia gave a short bark of near-hysterical laughter. "Uh, yeah. No problem wanting to stay away from them. Especially that Rick guy—he freaks me out."

Cameron knew Rick had a cruel, violent streak. He didn't blame Sophia for wanting to stay away. "All right, let's go." Cameron quickly sent out the coordinates of this landing strip in a message to Omega Sector—a risky move, but one he had to make. Then he led Sophia down the few short steps of the small plane and over to the SUV that was waiting just off the runway. He got in the backseat with Sophia, noticing how she avoided looking at anyone.

And how every man in the vehicle looked at her. Cameron would have to keep Sophia with him as much as possible. She was definitely not safe alone.

Cameron paid very close attention as they drove from the airstrip to the mountain house. If for some reason he was not able to get GPS coordinates to Omega Sector, he would have to rely on his own observation and memory to find the "evil lair" again. They were headed northwest on a pretty steady incline. Mr. Smith's hideout must be near the top of one of these mountains. The Blue Ridge Mountains of Virginia weren't tall and barren like the Rockies. There were little peaks of hills everywhere, where homes could be built and privacy abounded.

Many of these homes had one way in, and one way out. Which was obviously the case here, Cameron realized. There hadn't been a single turnoff or other car on the road since they'd left the airstrip. Smart move on Mr. Smith's part.

Cameron hated that Sophia was here, but was excited that he was finally making such strong headway in the case. Today, finally—*finally*—he was going to meet Mr. Smith. Cameron knew he couldn't arrest Smith right away, he'd definitely need Omega Sector backup first. Plus, acquiring Ghost Shell took precedence over any arrest, but he couldn't help but feel hopeful that he was going to be able to do both.

Cameron glanced over at Sophia, who was staring blankly out the window again. He just hoped she could keep it together. He reached over and took her hand, subtly, so nobody else in the car could see. She looked over at him.

She could obviously recognize his concern. She nodded slightly and gave an attempt at a smile. Cameron squeezed her hand, wishing he could do more.

After just a few more minutes the car started making an even steeper incline. It wasn't long before they were at the DS-13 mountain house, or evil lair, or whatever you wanted to call it.

It definitely was no jackass-infested rat hole. Well, maybe it was jackass-infested, but it certainly wasn't a rat hole. The house was gorgeous and huge—a surprisingly tasteful blend of wood and large stone. Giant windows made up huge sections of walls, providing unobstructed views of the spectacular hills of the Blue Ridge Mountains.

And unobstructed views of anyone who might be trying to get up to the house through those hills. Any sort of covert attack of any magnitude would be nearly impossible. Definitely something Cameron would have to communicate to Omega Sector, if they planned to take down Mr. Smith here.

The beauty of the building and the surroundings were

breathtaking, but Cameron forced himself to stay focused solely on the job at hand. The SUV pulled into a four-car garage that attached to the house through a walkway.

They all got out of the vehicle, grabbed their bags and made their way inside. Sophia stayed almost glued to Cameron's side, clutching his arm. Rick was quick to comment on it.

"Seems like someone is a little friendlier this morning, Cam."

Cameron smirked at him. "Yeah, well, I guess I'm just that charming."

Rick smirked back. "Maybe you should give me a chance to be charming with her. I'm a pretty charming guy." Rick took a step toward Sophia. Cameron immediately felt Sophia's grip on his arm tighten.

"Not going to happen, Rick. So just run along." Cameron shooed him away. Anger flared in the other man's eyes, but he said nothing.

Cameron gave a short whistle as they walked into the house. It was even more impressive on the inside than it was on the outside. "Wow, this is quite a place," Cameron told Fin as he looked around.

Fin nodded, grinning. "Ten bedrooms. Eleven baths. Half a dozen offices and meeting rooms. A formal dining room and even a party area. Try not to get lost."

A man who was probably a member of DS-13, but looked like a butler, came through a doorway from the back and started walking toward them. Tension filled Fin and the other goons at the man's presence. As subtly as he could, Cameron put himself between Sophia and this unknown person.

There were too many damn unknowns in this situation.

The man obviously knew Fin, but spoke with a formal tone. "Mr. Fin, welcome. As you know, your uncle will be arriving later this evening, bringing some other guests for a weekend soiree."

Fin fidgeted. "Um, yeah, Thompson, thanks. My uncle told me about the party. This is Cam Cameron. Cam, this is Thompson."

Thompson nodded. "Yes, Mr. Smith mentioned his arrival. And Mr. Cameron's guest? She was not mentioned."

Fin looked uncomfortable. "Yeah. She's with Cam. Has some information for Mr. Smith that we think he'll be very happy to hear." Fin lifted his chin in an attempt to look confident.

"I will show you to your room, Mr. Cameron, and your guest, also." Thompson turned to Cameron. "Everyone else has been here before and is familiar with the house."

"Good, because I'm tired as hell since I had to spend most of the night convincing everyone I'm not a liar." Cameron gave a dramatic sigh. He picked up his duffel from where he had set it on the floor and began following Thompson, the butler guy.

"Uncle?" Cameron said with an eyebrow raised as he passed Fin. "Who's the lying SOB now?"

Fin just laughed and shrugged and headed off to another part of the house.

Thompson led Cameron down the hall with Sophia following close behind, still holding his hand. Every once in a while he could feel a shudder run through her. She was swaying on her feet and Cameron knew he needed to get her to the room soon. He breathed a sigh of relief when the older man opened a door for them.

Cameron ushered Sophia inside, then turned to their escort. "Thanks, man. We're just going to crash for a while," Cameron told him while shutting the door in his face.

Cameron locked the door and looked around the room. It was definitely much nicer than the DS-13 house in DC.

A huge four-poster bed, made of the same wood as the rest of the house, dominated much of the room. There was a dresser against one wall and two sitting chairs over by the massive sliding glass doors that led out to a small deck.

There were two doors over on the far wall. Cameron walked over to them. One was a closet. He quickly closed the door, praying they wouldn't need to use it. The other door led to a bathroom. Cameron whistled as he took in the huge hot tub and separate shower. This whole place was gorgeous and tasteful.

Cameron walked back into the bedroom and saw that Sophia had wandered over to the windows and was staring out vacantly, just as she had on the plane. He wanted to talk to her, but first he needed to check that their room wasn't bugged.

Cameron took what would look like a smartphone to any casual observer and punched in a code. This turned on a scanner that allowed him to see if there were any electronic transmissions being sent from anywhere in the room. It wasn't a foolproof way of checking for surveillance, but it was pretty useful.

There were no transmissions being sent from anywhere in this room. Not surprising. Criminals rarely recorded what was going on in their own homes if they were smart. Too many ways for it to be used against them.

Cameron walked over to Sophia and put his hands on her shoulders, then looked out at the view with her.

"Beautiful, isn't it?" she asked softly.

"Breathtaking. I wish we were here under different circumstances." He pulled her back against his chest and was relieved when she didn't pull away.

Sophia nodded. "Me, too."

Cameron turned her around so he could see her face.

"Soph, why did you come back? Don't get me wrong, I'm thankful that you did. But *why?*"

Sophia looked around the room. "Is it okay to talk here?"

"Yeah, I checked for bugs. The room's clean."

"I was on my way out and I heard Rick and that other guy talking. Fin still didn't trust you completely. I was the final test for you."

Cameron felt himself tense. He'd had no idea. Fin—on Mr. Smith's orders—had set him up, and Cameron had been oblivious.

"You saved my life," Cameron whispered.

Sophia just smiled and shrugged. "So I guess we're even."

Cameron saw Sophia wince at the shrug. "Is your shoulder okay?"

She nodded. "Yes, just stiff. How's your head?"

Cameron winced but grinned. "You've got a pretty mean swing there, Miss Reardon."

"I'm sorry I'm still here, Cam. I know I complicate everything."

Cameron trailed a finger down her cheek. "Well, if you weren't here, I'd probably be dead. So I'm pretty damn glad you're here."

Sophia swayed on her feet. Cameron caught her quickly before she fell and led her over to the bed.

"You need to sleep," he told her gently as he pulled the covers back on the giant bed and ushered her in.

Sophia didn't say anything, just slipped her shoes off and lay down, fully clothed. She was asleep before he could pull the covers over her.

Cameron slipped his own shoes off and walked around to the other side of the bed. He slipped under the covers next to Sophia.

She was right; her presence here did complicate everything. But hell, Sophia complicated his life just by breathing. He reached over and pulled her sleeping body into his arms.

Cameron didn't have a plan, and that made him nervous. If it was just his life on the line then he'd be willing to fly blind as long as possible if it meant his goal was accomplished.

He kissed the top of Sophia's head as she snuggled in closer to him. Not having a plan when it was Sophia in jeopardy was unacceptable to him. So he would need to come up with one. Fast.

WHEN SOPHIA OPENED her eyes again the sun was setting. She sat straight up as she tried to remember where she was and who she was with. And then it all came back to her.

She knew Cameron had slept with her in the bed. She remembered waking up in a panic and finding him right by her side, rubbing her back and easing her to lie back down on the bed.

She could tell he had been there next to her until recently. The pillow still held the indentation from his head. She didn't know if he had slept this whole time with her or not, but she was thankful he had been there, next to her. She touched the place where Cameron had lain.

Sophia laid back in the luxurious bed now and stretched. No matter what, this place was definitely nicer than the rat hole they'd been in yesterday. But somehow that didn't make Sophia feel much better.

She turned over to her side and saw Cameron staring out the window. He seemed deep in thought. He was wearing only his jeans and his arms were crossed over his naked chest. He was definitely more muscular than when Sophia had last seen him five years ago. He had been fit then, but now the muscles in his chest, back and arms were even more pronounced.

And that six-pack he had acquired was definitely mouth-watering. Sophia once again wished they were here under different circumstances. That there wasn't so much weight riding on his shoulders, even if they seemed broad enough to carry anything.

Sophia got out of the bed and wandered over to stand next to Cameron. "Hey," she whispered.

"Feeling better?" he asked.

"Yeah. It's amazing what a few hours of sleep can do."

"You definitely needed it. I don't know how you were holding it together." They stood in companionable silence for a few moments, looking out the window. Sophia wanted to wrap an arm around Cameron, but wasn't sure if it would be appropriate. Or welcome.

"So do we have a plan? What do I need to do?"

Cameron turned so they were looking face-to-face at each other. "I've been thinking a lot while you were asleep. I have a plan." He didn't look too thrilled with it, though.

"Hopefully a better one than me running down this mountain in the middle of the night by myself?" Sophia joked, but inside she was afraid that was what she was going to have to do.

"No, you won't have to run all the way down. I'll have an extraction team waiting."

Sophia shook her head. "Last time I *escaped*, it almost got you killed. What makes you think it's a good plan this time?"

"It won't be just you. We'll both be going."

"I don't understand. How will that work? What about this case?"

Cameron didn't answer.

Sophia wasn't sure she was understanding exactly what

was going on here. "But what about all your work? The eight months with DS-13? The weeks in the jackass-infested rat hole?"

Cameron turned to the side and looked back out the window. He shrugged.

"You can't do this, Cameron. What about the justice for your partner?"

Sophia watched as Cameron took a deep breath and ran his hand through his thick, dark hair. "Soph, I watched you there while you were sleeping. You're covered in bruises. You have a huge, nasty cut on your shoulder."

"But—" Sophia tried to cut in but he wouldn't let her. He turned and held both of her arms in his hands, careful not to put any pressure on her wound.

"No, listen. You've been absolutely amazing. You've kept your head and you've kept it together, when you had every reason to fall apart." He brought her a little closer. "And then, when you had a chance to get away, you came back for me, Soph. You saved my life."

Sophia just shrugged. There hadn't been any option for her. She wasn't going to leave him there to die.

"I want justice so bad for my partner that I can taste it, Soph. And there's other stuff, too, that you don't even know about. But that will all have to be taken care of another way at another time. I'm not going to risk your life. I'm going to call in for help and we're getting out of here tonight."

A sudden vibration from a small cell-phone-looking thing on the nightstand by the bed caught both of their attentions. Cameron quickly walked over and grabbed it. Sophia watched as Cameron twisted the box inside out and began typing a series of symbols on it. Then he stopped and waited, saying nothing. A few moments later the inside-out box beeped.

This time Cameron brought it up to his ear and spoke into it. "Omega, go. Code 44802. Security confirmed."

Cameron listened for a few moments to whatever was being said on the other end.

"Coordinates are confirmed. Primary target has not arrived."

Whatever was being said to Cameron did not make him happy. "Roger that. Secondary target has not arrived, then. Primary target location has not been ascertained."

More talk from the other end.

"Request withdrawal assistance tonight."

Now whatever was being said was really making Cameron mad.

"Bystander in pocket, but too many unknowns. Immediate assistance requested."

Cameron turned and looked directly at Sophia while he listened. She could see his teeth grit and a vein flicker at his neck. "No, there is no immediate threat to bystander. But again I repeat—there are too many unknowns."

Sophia watched as Cameron's fist clenched at his side.

"Roger that. Primary objective understood."

Cameron poked a series of buttons angrily into the phone. He turned it inside out so it just looked like a regular phone again and placed it on the nightstand again.

Sophia wasn't completely sure what she had just heard, but it sounded as if they were completely on their own.

Chapter Nine

Cameron wanted to throw the satellite phone across the room, but knew it wouldn't do any good. He drew a breath and released it, trying to focus. Being angry at Omega Sector's unwillingness to send a rescue team in immediately was not going to help anything. He needed to work the problem.

And right now the problem was standing a few feet away from him, engulfed by his T-shirt, with tousled brown hair and gorgeous green eyes.

He couldn't get her out. Cameron had to face that. She was watching him with intent eyes, looking so tiny. But she was far from helpless. Sophia wasn't a trained agent—as she was so quick to point out—but she was smart, and quick-thinking.

Cameron wanted Sophia out of there. But according to Omega Sector that wasn't an option. So she was about to become his partner.

Cameron stretched his arm out to Sophia and she walked hesitantly to him, questions in her eyes.

"Moving to plan B?" she asked. "No backup from the Bureau?"

Cameron nodded. "Yeah." He hesitated. "Except I don't work for the Bureau."

Sophia took a step back. "You don't?" Cameron could

see her trying to figure out who he was working under-cover for if it wasn't the FBI. "Are you DEA? Some sort of local law enforcement?"

"No. I'm part of what's called Omega Sector. We're an interagency task force. All the advantages of having the resources of individual agencies—DEA, FBI, Marshals Service, ATF, hell, even INTERPOL sometimes. But much less red tape."

"So basically you're like your own Justice League."

Cameron smiled at the Saturday-morning cartoon reference. "Yeah, basically. But without superpowers."

"I've worked at the Bureau for four years now. I've never heard of Omega Sector."

"No, you wouldn't have. It's not something you can just apply for. You're recruited by Omega, or you don't get in at all. They're looking for specific skills, mind-sets, abilities."

Sophia took another small step away from Cameron, frowning. "And you had all those things."

Cameron shrugged. "I guess so."

"How long has Omega Sector been around?"

"About ten years."

"And when did you begin working for them?"

Cameron grimaced. There was no way around this. "Five years ago."

Sophia's head snapped up and Cameron could see re-alization dawn in her eyes. Omega Sector was the reason he had never said goodbye to her.

Sophia turned and walked over to the window. Cameron stayed where he was over by the bed, giving her space.

"So they recruited you?"

"Yes."

Sophia continued to look out the window. "I'm not sur-prised. You're obviously good at this sort of thing."

"I wanted to make a difference in the world, Soph. Omega Sector was that chance."

Sophia nodded, still not looking at him. "And I suppose because it's all top secret and stuff, you couldn't tell anybody."

"Sophia…"

"You know what? I don't even want to talk about this right now. You wanted to make a difference. You joined your *Super Friends* group and have been doing that ever since. Congratulations."

Her back and shoulders were ramrod-straight as she stared out the window. What she didn't say stood like a giant between them.

You wanted to make a difference more than you wanted to be with me.

Cameron was glad she didn't say it out loud, because he had no idea how he would respond. Yes, he had wanted to fight bad guys when he had joined Omega Sector five years ago. And at the time, it had been the most important thing in the world to him. He and Sophia had been at the beginning of their relationship. No promises, no real commitment. They hadn't even slept together.

Casual. At least that's what Cameron had told himself. But he had known they both were taking it seriously. Every morning when he had met her at the little diner for breakfast, he had known they weren't casual.

And with five years of perspective, Cameron could see exactly what he had given up. Having Sophia standing here right in front of him, and having no way of getting her out of the danger, made him think perhaps it wasn't worth it after all.

After a moment, Sophia turned to Cameron. "So Omega Sector deems arresting Mr. Smith more important than getting us out? I mean, I can understand you wanting to get him because of your partner. But if you've decided to cut out? It sounds like you maybe just moved from one jackass-infested place to another."

Cameron gave her a half smile. "Actually, I haven't told you everything."

Sophia closed her eyes briefly and shook her head. "Of course you haven't. What's new?"

"Arresting anybody in DS-13 has become secondary in this op. Instead, it's something in his possession that Omega Sector has deemed more important than either of our individual lives. And they're probably right to feel that way."

Now Cameron had Sophia's attention. "What is it?"

Cameron explained to her the details of Ghost Shell. How, if used by terrorists, it could cripple computer and communication equipment of law enforcement and first responders, basically by using their own communication equipment against them.

"They'd be pretty paralyzed against any sort of terrorist attack or anything like that," Sophia whispered after Cameron finished explaining.

"Yes." Cameron walked over to her at the window. "It's not an actual weapon, but in some ways this technology is more devastating than any one weapon. Law enforcement's reliance on computers and communication technology is pretty heavy."

Sophia nodded. "How did Omega Sector find out about it?"

"I'm not sure exactly. Somebody, evidently a law-abiding computer scientist person, who had been working on something similar, reported it and the report made its way to Omega Sector."

"And they found out DS-13 has it?"

"Yes. But DS-13 isn't interested in using it against law enforcement. They don't have any political or religious ambitions—they're only interested in money. They want to sell it on the black market. Absolute chaos, available to the highest bidder."

"Oh, my gosh, Cam. In the wrong hands…" Sophia shook her head.

"I know. So like I said, I can understand why Omega Sector said no to us getting out. But I don't like it."

Neither of them said anything for a few moments. Sophia turned and took a step toward him.

"Is the Ghost Shell drive here?" she whispered finally.

"If not right now, then definitely soon, when Smith arrives. Although I don't know exactly where. Omega is afraid if they come in here full force, someone from DS-13 could escape with Ghost Shell."

She looked up at him, having to crane her neck to do so. God, she was so tiny. "Then we'll find it. And we'll get out of here," she said.

Cameron framed her face with his hands. "Soph, I can't ask you to risk your life like that. They killed my partner because they found out he was undercover. They won't hesitate to kill us, too."

"No offense, Cam, but my life is already in jeopardy. I might as well do something useful."

Cameron shook his head. He didn't like it; Sophia in the line of fire was definitely not his first choice. But it didn't look as if he had any choice at all.

Unbelievably, Sophia smiled at him. "You know, when I interviewed for my job as a graphic artist for the FBI four years ago, one of the first things I asked my boss was if I would ever be in life-threatening situations. I was assured I wouldn't be."

Cameron chuckled softly. "You mean they didn't list this situation in your job description? Hard to believe."

Sophia took a step back from Cameron. "I'll try not to

get in your way, but I'm definitely not cut out for secret-agent spy stuff." She shrugged and used her hair to hide her face. "I'm hardly capable of walking inside my own closet to pick out clothes without having a panic attack, much less do anything courageous."

"Hey." Cameron tucked her brown hair back behind her ear. "Don't talk that way. You've done a damn good job so far."

Sophia just shrugged again. "I'm going to take a shower. I feel like I've got grime under my grime," she told Cameron. He didn't stop her from pulling away.

"You might want to take a soak in the tub. It's huge."

Sophia sighed. A soak in a tub sounded like the most wonderful thing she had ever heard in her entire life. "That's definitely where I'll be."

"Okay." Cameron smiled at her. "Then we'll go find something to eat. I'm starving."

"Me, too."

Cameron watched as Sophia made her way to the bathroom and closed the door behind her.

He could hear the water running from her bath, and tried to think of every possible other thing in the world except Sophia naked behind that bathroom door.

Cameron wasn't sure he'd ever found a task so difficult in his entire life.

A sharp rap on the room's other door drew Cameron's attention. He quickly pulled his shirt over his head and grabbed his SIG from the nightstand.

"Yeah?" he asked from the door without opening it.

"It's Thompson, Mr. Cameron. I've got some food for you and Ms. Reardon."

Thompson knew Sophia's name. Cameron wasn't sure if that was good or bad. He needed to be prepared for either.

Cameron opened the door and Thompson walked in with

a tray of food. Thank God Sophia was in the bathroom, out of sight and earshot.

"Thanks, man." Cameron was once again struck by how much Thompson looked and acted like a butler. But he could see how lightly the man moved on his feet and how perfectly balanced he was when carrying the tray and setting it down.

Cameron had no doubt that Thompson was much more than just a butler. The suspicion was confirmed when he saw the older man glance around the room subtly, taking in all details.

This man, more than any of the goons Cameron had hung out with in DS-13 for the past eight months, was dangerous. No doubt that was why Mr. Smith kept him around.

"Something I can help you find?" Cameron asked.

Thompson looked at Cameron and tipped his head slightly, as if respecting that he had been caught snooping, but not apologizing for it.

"Will Ms. Reardon be requiring anything?" Thompson asked as he set the tray of food on a small table by the closet.

Cameron did not want to talk about Sophia with this man. "No, she's fine."

Cameron answered a little too quickly. He cursed silently as he saw that Thompson realized it, too. The last thing he wanted to do was show DS-13, especially this man whom Cameron was beginning to suspect was much higher up in the food chain than he had thought, that he cared about Sophia. They wouldn't hesitate to use her against him.

Cameron wandered nonchalantly over to the food. He picked up an apple and took a big bite.

"I can take care of her just fine, if you know what I mean." Cameron gave the man a wink. "She's in the bathroom relaxing in that swimming pool you call a tub. Working out the kinks."

Cameron saw Thompson's eyes narrow in distaste before the man hid his response. Good. Better for Cameron to seem crude and obnoxious than as if he had some sort of attachment to Sophia.

"Mr. Smith and his other guests have arrived. Mr. Smith would like to meet with you and Ms. Reardon in one hour."

Cameron took another bite of his apple. "That's cool, man. Whatever." And because it seemed to make Thompson so uncomfortable before, Cameron winked at him again.

"Yes, well, good. Until then, please stay in your room and keep Ms. Reardon here with you."

Thompson turned and made his way out of the room quickly and efficiently.

Cameron looked over at the elaborate tray of food Thompson had brought in. Fruits, cheeses, meats and breads for sandwiches. Quite the spread. All laid out on a large silver platter with oversize handles.

Cameron began moving the food, piece by piece, off the tray. Based on what he had observed about Thompson, Cameron was willing to bet there was some sort of surveillance device somewhere on this tray. Once all the food was off the tray and he was able to turn it over, he saw a transmitter. But something about how large it was and how it sat in the handle was a little too obvious to Cameron.

Sure enough, Cameron kept searching and found it a couple minutes later: a tiny transmitter under the lip of the least descriptive part of the tray, where you would hardly think to look, especially if you found the first device.

Sneaky little bastard.

Thompson had almost caught them unawares. Cameron decided to leave the transmitting device where it was, fully functional, since it was sound-only. He and Sophia could use it to their advantage. But the larger, more obvious device, Cameron removed.

"Screw you, Thompson, and whoever else is listening. I prefer not to have an audience, you perverts," Cameron said into the piece of equipment. He then threw the transmitter on the ground and stomped on it.

So now they thought he had no idea they were listening. Good, he had no problem exploiting their overconfidence.

SOPHIA FELT LIKE a new person after her long soak in the tub. She had to put the same clothes back on, so that wasn't great, but at least her muscles were easing. Somehow being taken hostage by a crime syndicate group tended to make you tense and tight. Go figure.

Sophia came out of the door, her head wrapped in a towel, ready to boast to Cameron about the miracles of a hot tub. "Hey, seriously, it's almost like we're on a..."

She was cut off by him pushing her back against the wall and kissing her. Thoroughly.

Her arms, almost of their own accord, traveled up his arms to his shoulders. The towel around her hair came loose then slipped from her head and fell to the floor. Sophia forgot everything but the heat and strength of the kiss.

She stood up on her tiptoes to get closer and wound her fingers in his hair. She didn't care where they were anymore or the danger they were facing. She wanted Cameron now and he wanted her. That was all that mattered.

Cameron's lips moved over her jaw and up to Sophia's ear. She shivered with every light kiss he placed. His hands grasped her waist and pulled her closer to him. Sophia found herself melting into him.

"They're listening to everything we say," he murmured almost silently against her ear.

It took a moment for the words to penetrate. Sophia's arms fell to her sides. Cold washed over her where moments ago there had been such heat.

Cameron wasn't kissing her because he wanted to. He was kissing her to keep her quiet. It was just as effective as the backhand at the warehouse. And just as painful.

Sophia nodded jerkily. Cameron tried to kiss her again, but she turned her head away. There was no need to kiss her—she got the message: don't say or do anything stupid.

Or maybe do anything *more* stupid than throw herself into a kiss that meant nothing to the other person.

Sophia nodded again and reached down to get the towel that had fallen from her head. She was so cold. And she needed to be away from Cameron. Immediately.

"That's a big tub they have in there." Sophia didn't recognize her own voice as she said it, wasn't even sure how she got the words out of her mouth.

Thankfully Cameron stepped away from her.

"There's some food over on the table, if you're hungry. Thompson brought it while you were in the bathroom." Cameron pointed toward the table.

So that's how they could hear now but couldn't before—something on the tray. Sophia nodded, not quite making eye contact with Cameron—she couldn't stand to do that yet, not after the fool she'd just made of herself—and went to the table.

Although she'd totally lost her appetite, Sophia forced herself to eat. She chewed bite after tasteless bite, forcing the needed nutrients into her system.

But damn it, she felt like an idiot. Cameron was undercover. She needed to get that through her evidently very thick skull. Arresting this Mr. Smith guy and getting back Ghost Shell were the most important things to him.

And her safety, she had to give him that, too. But he

was undercover; nothing he said or did should be taken at face value.

"I'm glad you liked the tub," Cameron finally said from across the room.

"Yeah, I could definitely get used to that sort of luxury," Sophia responded. Cameron nodded encouragingly and spun his finger in a circle, gesturing for her to continue that line of conversation.

"Someday I want to own a giant tub like that one," Sophia continued as she ate another bite of a sandwich from the tray.

Cameron started talking, making up a crazy story about a hot tub he had once snuck into with his brothers while in high school and the shenanigans that ensued. At least Sophia *thought* he was making it up. She knew Cameron had two brothers and a sister, so maybe it was true.

Without ever missing a beat with his story, Cameron walked over to Sophia and led her away from the tray to over near the bed. He let out a loud guffaw as he finished the story and Sophia laughed along with him.

"Soph," he said in a low voice that wasn't quite a whisper, pulling her closer. "Smith is here. Ghost Shell is probably with him."

"Okay. That's good, right?" she whispered.

"Don't whisper," he told her in that same low tone. "Just speak very low, if you don't want them to hear. Whispers are actually easier for surveillance equipment to pick up than very low tones."

Sophia nodded.

Cameron brought his voice back up to normal range. "Mr. Smith wants to meet us in an hour. So it's probably good that you went ahead and took a bath already."

Cameron looked at Sophia, gesturing with his head that she should say something. "O-okay…" she said tentatively.

Cameron leaned closer, dropping his voice so the surveillance couldn't hear. "Remember, you want this meeting. That's how I convinced Fin to let you come here, by telling him you had information to give to Smith."

Sophia nodded. "Yeah, good." She said in a louder voice, "That's what I'm here for, to meet Smith. I just want to make this exchange and get out of here."

Cameron nodded with enthusiasm.

"I don't like the mountains," she continued. "I'm more of a beach person." That was totally not true, but seemed like a reasonable thing to say.

"Yeah, me, too," Cameron said. "Why don't we go on a little vacation after all this?"

Sophia had to remind herself that Cameron wasn't really talking to her; this was just part of his undercover story. She refused to allow herself to wish he wanted to spend time with her. When this was finished, he'd be gone again, just like five years ago.

"Yeah, sure." There was decidedly less enthusiasm in her tone.

Cameron's head cocked to the side as he studied Sophia with questioning eyes. She didn't dare explain to him what was really bothering her, even if there wasn't a bug in the room.

A knock on the door saved the moment. She saw Cameron reach for the gun he evidently had tucked in the back of his jeans. He walked silently to the door, gesturing for her to move back toward the bathroom.

"Yes?" he asked without opening the door.

Something was murmured that Sophia couldn't quite catch, but whatever it was caused Cameron to relax and put his gun away. He opened the door, and someone handed him a package.

"Here, this is for you." Cameron tossed the box onto the bed.

Sophia frowned and walked over to it. Pushing the tissue paper to the side she found clothes: a pair of stylishly cut black pants, and a soft gray sweater. Undergarments, socks and shoes completed the outfit. All of them were the perfect size for her.

Sophia looked up at Cameron. "What? Where did this come from?"

Cameron pointed over at the tray to remind her they were being listened to. "Beats me. I didn't have anything to do with it. But I guess you couldn't meet Mr. Smith in my T-shirt, now could you? So it's a good thing."

"Yeah, I guess so." Sophia turned toward the bathroom, more disturbed than she cared to admit. Did Smith just keep women's clothes sitting around? Probably not. Which meant someone with a very good eye had taken her measurements and gotten clothes up to this remote location pretty darn quickly.

Somehow the arrival of these clothes, more than any of the other things—much more dangerous things—that had happened to her over the past two days, made it hit home the power of the people Cameron was dealing with. They had resources. They had manpower. And they had a scary attention to detail.

Plus, they were murderers.

As Cameron came into the bathroom with her and started providing details about Ghost Shell in a hushed tone, Sophia clutched the box of clothes to her chest and listened as best she could. When Cameron had given her all the info he could, he left, closing the door behind him so Sophia could dress.

She did so, hoping the clothes provided by a murdering crime syndicate wouldn't be the last ones she ever put on.

Chapter Ten

There was no more Cameron could do to prepare Sophia, even though he knew it wasn't enough. Time was up. Eight months undercover had all led up to this.

And it was all out of his hands and completely in Sophia's.

Cameron knew that wasn't quite accurate, but it certainly felt like it as they followed Thompson down an extended hallway of the large house to a set of rooms in the back. By their very location, the rooms were less accessible, discouraging any wandering guests from finding them. Not hidden, exactly, just not advertised. And something about Thompson just kept nagging at Cameron.

Cameron watched Sophia from the corner of his eye as she walked beside him. She was glancing around nervously, as if looking for exits. She rubbed her fists against the legs of her black pants. Cameron wished he could catch her hand and hold it, but knew strolling in like lovers was not the way they should meet Smith.

Cameron looked over at Sophia and smiled. Sophia gnawed on her lip a moment more before taking a deep breath and straightening her shoulders.

"You okay?" Cam whispered.

"Doesn't really make a difference now, does it?" Sophia said without looking at him.

Not exactly the reassuring answer he was hoping for.

Cameron tried to go through multiple possible scenarios in his head. What he would do if Sophia freaked out. How he could help her keep it together. Their best route of escape if they had to run. Weaponless and outnumbered, none of the options were good. Cameron prayed Sophia wouldn't panic. But they were walking into a situation that would make even the most seasoned undercover agent wary. He could only imagine the terror Sophia was feeling.

Again, not reassuring.

Thompson led them to a door at the farthest end of the hallway. Cameron pretended not to watch as the older man used a card to swipe a lock on the wall. Cameron wondered who else might have a key card to this office.

Cameron looked over at Sophia again. She was no longer clenching and unclenching her small fists, so that was good. Thompson opened the door for them and Cameron gestured for Sophia to walk in ahead of him. Showtime.

They walked into the expansive office, Cameron taking in as much as he could about the room without actually looking as if he was. Sophia made no such pretense. Most of the walls were lined with deep cherry bookshelves and cabinetry. The far wall was made up of windows, showcasing the wondrous view of nature outside. A large desk took up the area near the window, with a black luxury office chair behind it. The chair was currently facing the windows, away from the desk.

Slowly the large chair swiveled around so the man in it was facing Cameron and Sophia. There was no doubt this man was related to Fin—his build, facial structure and coloring were all similar, yet he was older and flabbier than Fin. This was it; the moment Cameron had waited over a year for.

"I'm Mr. Smith," the man said in a somewhat squeaky

voice that belied his overweight size. His Yankee accent was thick. His eyes small, close-set, almost beady. "Go ahead and sit down."

Cameron's lips pressed tight and his shoulders slumped as he sat. *This* man was one of the top members of DS-13 and had eluded law enforcement for years? Somehow he just wasn't what Cameron had expected. But perhaps nothing short of an absolute monster would've lived up to Cameron's expectations.

Regardless of whether the man fit the image Cameron had built in his head, Cameron was tempted to arrest him right there, everything else be damned. Omega could figure out another way to get Ghost Shell. Only the thought of Sophia trapped in the middle of all this halted him. Cameron settled back into his seat, clenching his jaw.

Thompson came around to stand next to the desk, close to Smith's side. Out of the corner of his eye Cameron noticed Smith glancing at Thompson and Thompson giving a slight nod. Immediately Cameron was on high alert. Obviously some sort of signal had passed between the two men, but what did it mean? Cameron wished to God that Thompson hadn't done a weapons check back at the room. Cameron felt naked without his SIG. Were he and Sophia about to be assassinated while Cameron was able to do nothing?

But neither Smith nor Thompson made any aggressive moves. Instead, Smith settled back in his chair and Thompson remained watchful and alert where he stood. Maybe Cameron had imagined the entire thing.

Cameron leaned forward in his chair and offered Smith his hand to shake, although he really wanted to break the offending hand. "Mr. Smith, it's a pleasure to finally meet you." Cameron managed not to choke on the words.

"Likewise, Cam," the older man answered as he shook

Cameron's hand with his large sweaty paws. Cameron resisted the urge to wipe his palms on the legs of his pants.

Mr. Smith continued, "I realize you've worked with DS-13 for a long time, Cam, without meeting me. I hope you understand the necessary security precautions." Smith glanced at Thompson again.

"Oh, sure, Mr. Smith. Everybody has to be careful in this day and age." Cameron nodded enthusiastically, trying to be friendly.

"Yes, well, I have enemies on multiple sides," Smith continued in his squeaky, accented voice. "I try to always take time to thoroughly check out anyone who works for me. But I must admit you have arranged a lot of good deals for me in the past year."

Cam smiled. "Lucrative for us both."

"Glad to hear it." Another glance at Thompson.

Whatever silent communication was occurring between Smith and Thompson was causing alarms in Cameron's head. It was as if Smith kept asking Thompson for permission to talk, or checking to make sure what he said was okay. Which made absolutely no sense whatsoever.

Unless…

All of a sudden everything clicked in place for Cameron. Before he could help himself he straightened in his chair and looked over at Thompson. Really looked. And found the man studying him in much the same way.

Mr. Smith seemed oblivious to it all and kept talking. "We really appreciate the work you've done for us. And I thought it was time to bring you up here to meet me and a few more of my associates—"

"It's okay, Jacob, you can stop. I think Mr. Cameron has figured out our little ruse."

Cameron heard a slight indrawn breath from Sophia. Evidently she had noticed something, too.

"Sorry, Mr. Smith," the other, squeaky-voiced Mr. Smith said. "I was thrown off a little bit by the woman being here."

"Don't worry about it, Jacob," Thompson told the other man, who was getting up from the desk chair and giving his seat to Thompson. "The lovely Ms. Reardon could distract any man."

Thompson sat and turned to Cameron and Sophia. "You'll have to excuse all the subterfuge. I have found over the years that when meeting someone new, sometimes a stand-in is my best option. Jacob here has been with me for a long time. The idea came to me because both of our last names happen to be Smith. So when Jacob introduces himself as 'Mr. Smith,' that is actually the truth."

Cameron had to admit, it was a pretty great plan. And using someone like Jacob—lumpy, not very personable nor clever—probably gave Smith a distinct edge when dealing with others. Most people would do as Cameron had initially done: write off Smith as not much of a threat. Because Jacob Smith wasn't much of a threat.

But Thompson Smith definitely was. *This* was the man Cameron had been waiting to meet; Cameron could feel it in his bones. Thompson Smith was the one who had killed his partner; the man Cameron had sworn he would bring to justice.

"And then, when I'm here with certain unknown guests, I like to pretend I'm some sort of butler. It allows me to better observe those around me. You'd be amazed what people will say and do when they think they're just around hired help." Thompson Smith shook his head with a tsk. Jacob—the other Mr. Smith—went to stand closer to the window, obviously no longer part of the conversation.

"I must admit, you figured it out quicker than most," Smith told Cameron.

"Uh, yeah. Well, that guy—" Cameron gestured toward

Jacob "—is obviously related to Fin. But Fin never mentioned that his uncle was the head of DS-13. I've known Fin for a long time now and I don't think that's something he'd keep to himself for too long." Cameron pulled his cover identity around him like a blanket. It was time to be Cam Cameron now—kind of bright and organized, but not too much of either. The last thing Cameron wanted to do was put Smith on the defensive. This whole thing was already precariously balanced.

Smith seemed to buy it. "Yes, Fin has always loved to run his mouth." He then turned to study Sophia. "You, Ms. Reardon, have caused somewhat of a brouhaha around here."

Cameron forced himself not to tense up. It became more difficult as the seconds ticked by and Sophia didn't respond. Cameron shifted in his chair as casually as he could manage so he could glance over at Sophia. She was staring down silently at her hands folded in her lap.

Cameron didn't know how to help her. Was she overwhelmed and couldn't figure out how to respond? Afraid of messing up? Cameron was well aware that Sophia was not a trained agent. But if she was totally frozen and out of commission, things were about to spin out of control fast.

Cameron cleared his throat and gave a little laugh. "Sophia here is a little tired…."

Cameron didn't get out the rest of his sentence as Sophia looked up from her hands and at Mr. Smith. "Yeah, I tend to cause a little bit of a brouhaha no matter where I go."

Mr. Smith chuckled slightly and Cameron barely succeeded in keeping his jaw from dropping.

"I imagine you do, Ms. Reardon. We weren't expecting your presence here or in the warehouse yesterday," Smith told her.

"I gathered that from the multiple times your men threatened to kill me." Sophia looked Smith right in the eye as she said it.

Smith reached down to his desk and held up a file. "We did a little checking on you, of course. As I said, vetting everyone I come in contact with is standard procedure."

Sophia nodded. "Find anything interesting?"

Cameron had to give it to Sophia, she was handling herself like a pro. No nervous giveaways. Maybe it was possible they would make it out of this room alive.

"Nothing in particular. Except perhaps for the fact that you work for the FBI."

Damn.

Cameron flew out of his chair as if he had received an electric shock. "What? She's FBI? I swear I didn't know, Mr. Smith. She just said she knew something about this Ghost Shell thing and that you would want to hear it."

"It's all right, Cam. Ms. Reardon works for the FBI, but as a graphic artist, not an agent."

"Oh." Cameron sat back down slowly, feigning shock. "That's okay?"

"As soon as Fin reported that you had brought Sophia here back to the house in DC, I had her thoroughly checked out. Actually, having a record that so clearly linked her to the FBI helped ease my concerns a bit. Nobody trying to work undercover would be so easily linked to the FBI."

Smith turned and looked at Sophia. "And so you are still alive, my beautiful Sophia. And now there's no need to keep your FBI connection a secret."

Cameron didn't like how Smith was looking at her at all, but knew he couldn't do anything about it. Saying anything would just draw undue, and definitely unwanted, attention.

"Yeah, well, your henchmen didn't really seem like the type to take anyone associated with the Bureau to meet you," Sophia said.

Smith nodded. "Yes, and I must admit, if Fin had been able to get in touch with me yesterday, I would've denied him permission to bring you here. And what a shame that would've been. So, although I had to have some harsh words with Fin about security, I'm glad we had a little lapse today so I could meet you."

Sophia shifted uncomfortably in her chair.

"But, on to business." Smith leaned back in his chair. "Fin and Cam tell me you have particular knowledge about the Ghost Shell technology."

Here came the real test. Cameron's breath stuck in his throat.

"That's right." Sophia nodded. "And for the right price I'm willing to give that information to you."

Smith folded his hands on his desk. "Why don't you tell me exactly what you know, so I can determine what that information is worth."

Sophia mimicked Smith's relaxed pose, but with her hands in her lap. "I don't think so. I'm sure as soon as I do that my life won't be worth much. I'm not as stupid as some of the morons you surround yourself with around here." Sophia made a vague gesture toward Cameron.

Cameron sat up straighter in his chair. There wasn't much he could do to help her, but this was one thing: insulted lover. "Hey, I'm not a moron."

Smith chuckled and gave Cameron his attention. "Well, you certainly can pick them, Cam."

Cameron decided defensiveness was his best play. "I was just looking for a good time. Then I found out she knew some stuff about that Ghost Shell thing and told Fin she should tell you about it. That's it. I'm not, like, vouching for her or anything."

"Look, Cam was just the most attractive foot in the door

for me. One of your other hired thugs was my next option, but not as appealing—no offense."

Smith didn't move from his casual position. "Is that so? I understand there was quite a bit of carrying on in Cam's room at the house last night, including screaming."

Sophia shrugged delicately. "What can I say? I like it rough. Cam does, too."

"That worked out well for both of you, then." Smith laughed crassly.

Cameron chuckled, too, although he felt a little sick when he thought about the circumstances that had led to Sophia's screams back at the house. He glanced at her again. Her jaw had definitely tightened, but she gave nothing else away.

"Tell me, Sophia," Smith said after a few moments, "as delightful as you are, what is keeping me from just forcing the answer from you? I'm sure my men could find a way to be rougher than even you like."

Sophia sat up straighter in her chair, as did Cameron. The threat of torture wasn't to be taken lightly.

Out of the blue, Smith slammed his fist down on the desk, causing both Sophia and Cameron to startle. "You will tell me right now what you know." He never raised his voice, but his lower tone was all the more frightening.

Cameron prayed Sophia wouldn't panic. They were in too deep now.

"Ghost Shell has a fail-safe," Sophia said, barely above a whisper. "A code that has to be entered to make it work outside of its design parameters."

Smith nodded, but his eyes were icy. "Go on."

"You probably know Ghost Shell was designed by a government contractor. To keep it from being used against the US government, a fail-safe code was created. If someone tries to use Ghost Shell without the code, it won't work."

Cameron was impressed. That sounded realistic even to his ears, and he knew the truth. Too bad whoever had created Ghost Shell hadn't thought of something similar.

"There's only one chance to enter the code. You have to do it at a certain time, in a certain order and even in a certain tempo. Anything is off in the pattern and you've basically got a useless piece of junk on your hands."

Cameron almost missed Smith's glance over at the wall to his left. A small tell, but definitely a tell. Ghost Shell was probably in a safe there. And Smith was believing Sophia's story.

Smith glared at Sophia. "You're playing a very dangerous game here, Ms. Reardon."

"I'm not playing any games. I just want to get paid. Two million dollars. I know how much Ghost Shell is worth, and the amount I want from you is a fraction of that."

Smith's lips flattened and his nostrils flared the slightest bit. Cameron knew they were walking an even more precarious edge than he had thought.

Sophia glanced at her watch. "It's too late to enter the code today. The deadline has passed. That much I'll tell you in good faith."

Smith nodded and Sophia continued, "Tomorrow night I will enter the code for you. I'll get half the money before, and half afterward. Everyone can walk away happy from this, Mr. Smith."

Smith seemed to relax, and Cameron imagined it was because the amount Sophia was asking really was minute compared to Ghost Shell's black market value. But his eyes remained cold. "All right, Ms. Reardon, we have a deal. Tonight you and Cam will join me and my guests for the soiree, and tomorrow we shall deal with the business end of things."

Cameron nodded. "Sounds good."

"Just remember—" Smith leaned forward on his desk, menace clear on his face "—if you are lying to me, Sophia, about any part of this, you will beg for death before you finally die. That much I'll tell *you* in good faith."

Cameron watched as the color seeped from Sophia's face. She flinched when Smith repeated her words back at her.

Before their eyes, Smith's menace vanished and he was back to being the handsome host. He stood and Cameron and Sophia took their cue from him, and they all began walking toward the office door.

"Sophia, I assume the clothes I had brought in for you are acceptable?" Smith asked as if he hadn't threatened to torture and kill her just moments before.

Sophia nodded a little jerkily. "Yes, thank you." The words came out as a whisper.

"I hope you enjoy the gown I had picked out for you for this evening's festivities. It will suit your coloring and figure well, I believe," Smith said, reaching out to touch her on her elbow. Sophia seemed frozen.

Cameron was close enough to Sophia to see her pale and feel the fine tremor run through her body. He knew she wouldn't be able to hold it together much longer. He put himself between her and Smith.

"Yeah, thanks," Cam told Smith, struggling with all his might to grin. "She would've looked funny at the party running around in my shirt and pants." Cam ushered Sophia out the door. He turned back to Smith. "It was really great to finally meet you, Mr. Smith. And I hope you'll remember that I got Sophia here and helped save the day with Ghost Shell."

Smith nodded. "I won't forget your association with Sophia. It won't bode well for you, either, if she's lying."

"Oh, she's not, I'm sure," Cameron said, trying to put him at ease. "We'll see you tonight at the party."

Smith nodded and turned back into the office. Cameron took Sophia's arm and headed down the hall, grateful nobody was accompanying them. Sophia's breath was becoming more labored.

"Hang in there, baby," Cam whispered. "Just till we get back to the room."

They made it across the house to their room, with Cameron supporting most of Sophia's slight weight by the end. Cameron had barely closed the door before Sophia beelined to the bathroom and threw up everything she had eaten.

Chapter Eleven

Sophia felt relatively confident that she would never live through this day. Cameron kept praising her quietly, telling her what a remarkable job she had done with Smith, but Sophia just felt exhausted. They still couldn't talk freely because of the bug that Thompson—or Mr. Smith or whatever you wanted to call him—had placed in their room. That man gave her the freak-outs.

After she had completely lost the contents of her stomach, Cameron had helped Sophia from the bathroom, onto the bed. He was sitting beside her, stroking her hair back from her face, as he had been for the past twenty minutes.

"I wouldn't worry too much about what Mr. Smith said," Cameron told her in a voice loud enough for the surveillance to clearly hear him. "You'll just give him the information tomorrow, he'll pay you and it will be all over."

"Yeah…" The word came out all croaky so Sophia started again. "Yeah, I just don't like people threatening to kill me."

A knock on the door brought them both to attention. Sophia stayed where she was as Cameron went to open the door. It was Fin carrying two separate hanging bags of clothes. He was also sporting a nasty bruise on his jaw.

"These are from Mr. Smith," Fin said gruffly, thrusting the bags into Cameron's arms.

"Which one? Your uncle or the real Mr. Smith?" Cameron scoffed. "What happened to your face, Fin?"

"Your girlfriend is what happened to my face. Mr. Smith didn't like it that I allowed Sophia to arrive with us without contacting him first, even though she has something he wants," Fin spat. A vein pulsed in his neck as he turned to glare at Sophia on the bed. "You should've told me you were FBI."

Sophia recoiled from the venom in Fin's eyes. "I'm not really FBI. I just happen to work at the FBI building. Plus, I'm sure you would've just killed me if I had mentioned it."

Fin didn't respond to that, just turned and marched out the door. Cameron unzipped and held up the contents of the bags. One contained dress pants and a light gray shirt for Cameron. The other contained a black gown that looked quite lovely and demure in the front. But then Sophia turned it around on the hanger and saw that it was backless almost down to the waist.

Sophia cringed. It was beautiful, but definitely not something she would've ever picked out or worn. "Looks like we have our costumes for tonight."

Cameron nodded. "You okay?"

"I don't like having to wear what he picks out for me. But I guess it's better than a shirt and jeans." Sophia turned and went into the bathroom to build her resolve. If this dress was her only option then she'd make the best of it.

A couple hours later they were on their way to the main part of the house. Sophia was glad to be out of the room—having to monitor every word that came out of their mouths was stressful. She was constantly worried she was going to let something slip.

The dress was on, fitting her perfectly. Her hair was up in a sophisticated twist. She'd made full use of the makeup that had arrived with the dress. Sophia knew she looked good.

But she hated every bit of it.

Even seeing Cameron's expression when she had walked out of the bathroom—and Sophia had to admit that watching his jaw almost drop to the ground had been pretty thrilling—she still wished she wasn't wearing this dress.

Or that she was wearing it under very different circumstances.

She and Cameron made their way to the main section of the house, where people were already milling around and talking. The sun had set, taking with it the gorgeous views outside, but the party room itself was beautiful enough.

They joined the crowd, talking and mingling with different people. Sophia received multiple compliments on the dress, which she barely acknowledged. And she absolutely hated the way Smith had nodded with approval when he had seen her in it. She didn't think Cameron noticed. He was busy thinking like an agent.

"I wish I had facial-recognition software here, or at least a camera," Cameron grumbled as they moved through more people. "I know there are people here that Omega should be aware are associates of Smith's. But I'm pretty useless."

"I might be able to help a little bit," Sophia told him. "Obviously I can't remember everyone, but if you see a few people who you want to remember, I can study them and draw them later."

"Really?" Cameron smiled down at her. "That would be unbelievably helpful."

Finally something Sophia could do that would be helpful. Good. She was tired of feeling like an albatross.

She and Cameron wandered around chatting, watching Smith and who he interacted with. As Cameron would signal to her about a certain person to remember, Sophia would do her best to memorize features. Sophia felt so much more comfortable doing that than trying to convince Smith she knew some secret information about some computer virus or whatever. Studying people, remembering features, drawing them, even days or weeks later—*that* she could do.

But Sophia definitely didn't like the way Smith would look at her whenever he could meet her eyes. As if he owned her.

The veiled malevolence in Smith's eyes wouldn't be easy to capture in a drawing. Sophia hoped she never had to try. She didn't even want to think about tomorrow when she wasn't able to put in any sort of password.

What had Smith said? That she would beg for death before she finally died? Amazing how that would sound so melodramatic under any other circumstances, but sounded so credible coming from Smith. Glancing at him again across the room Sophia could easily imagine he knew many ways to make someone beg for death.

Sophia could feel nausea pooling again in her stomach.

"You doing okay?" Cameron whispered.

"Smith." She gestured toward the older man with a tilt of her head. "He makes me nervous."

"If he keeps looking at you like that, things might get ugly around here really quick," Cameron said.

Sophia shivered. "I know. Can we just get out of here? Do we have to stay for the entire evening?"

"No. We don't have to stay. As a matter of fact, I think I have an even better plan than staying here." Cameron smiled at her in a way that made Sophia's insides start to melt.

Sophia swallowed hard. The only options were basically staying here or going back to the bedroom. Was that what Cameron wanted?

Sophia knew that was what she wanted. If there was one thing she had learned from this whole…*adventure*, it was that you never knew how many days you had left. Especially when someone waited in the wings looking for an excuse to kill you.

She hadn't made love with Cameron five years ago because she thought she'd had all the time in the world. That ended up not being true. She wouldn't make the same mistake now, especially when tomorrow hung so very precariously in the balance.

Sophia smiled up at Cameron. "Okay, I'm ready to go whenever you are."

He reached down and squeezed her hand. "All right, we should stay here a little bit longer, then we can start to make our way out as inconspicuously as possible."

His smile took her breath away. Sophia never thought she could feel this way in a situation like this. Just for tonight she wasn't going to worry about tomorrow. Because she didn't even know if she'd have a tomorrow.

Cameron subtly started angling them toward one of the doors. They spoke briefly with a few people as they made their way out and Cameron stopped to tell Fin they were leaving. She noticed Cameron awkwardly bump into Fin when a waiter came by. Cameron apologized, but Fin stormed off to the other end of the room. Obviously Fin was still mad at them for getting him in trouble with Mr. Smith. Sophia was glad when they didn't go anywhere near Mr. Smith to say their goodbyes; he was busy talking to other people anyway.

Once they made it out of the main room, Sophia finally felt as if she could breathe without panic pushing at her chest. She just wanted to get back to the room.

Cameron wrapped an arm around her and hugged her to his side. "Thank you for doing this."

Okay, odd. "Um, you're welcome."

"We're not going to have much time, so we'll need to hurry."

Now Sophia was really confused. "Why? Are you expecting them to come barging into our bedroom?"

"No," Cameron told her as he walked quickly with her down the hallway. "I mean breaking into Smith's office while everyone's at the party to see if we can find Ghost Shell."

SOPHIA HAD SOME sort of strange look on her face and Cameron couldn't blame her. Not with the way Smith had been looking at her all evening. Cameron didn't blame Soph for wanting to get out of there.

Cameron had that itchy feeling on the back of his neck all evening—the one that told him things were not going the way he'd planned. He didn't get the feeling very often, but over the years, first as a US Army Ranger then as an undercover agent, he had learned to pay attention to it.

Things were about to take a turn for the worse.

During this party, while everybody was occupied, was the best time to try to get into Smith's office and get Ghost Shell. Once they had that, Cameron could get Sophia out, on foot if he had to.

The more time he spent with her, the more he was coming to realize how much she meant to him. He wanted to get this case finished as soon as possible. And he could admit Sophia was his primary reason for that.

He wanted to be with her outside of this lunatic situation. Cameron glanced at Sophia as they walked down the hall. The strange look was gone. Now she seemed focused and determined to get the job done. Her grit was downright sexy.

But hell, everything about her was sexy. Especially in that almost-backless dress she was wearing. Cameron hated that Smith had picked it out, but had to admit Smith's choice was flawless.

They quietly made their way back to the locked door of Smith's office. Cameron pulled out a swipe card for the lock and held it up. He had taken it from Fin a few minutes ago when he had bumped into him. "Not a good day for Fin. We're probably going to get him fired."

Sophia snickered. "My heart breaks for him."

Cameron closed the door behind them but left it cracked just a little so they could get out quickly if they needed to.

"Okay, so what exactly are we looking for?" Sophia asked him as she made her way over to the desk. Cameron was right behind her.

"Ghost Shell is an external hard drive. The encryption device contains too much data to fit on anything too small, so it's about the size of a hardback book."

Sophia pulled out the desk chair, sat down and began searching through drawers on one side of the desk. Cameron began looking around a wall of bookshelves.

"It's not going to be in a drawer just out in the open," Cameron said softly. "I saw Smith looking over at this wall earlier when we were talking about Ghost Shell. There must be a safe."

Cameron continued to look around the wall, but couldn't find anything. Every minute they were in this office put them in more danger. He quickly joined Sophia at the desk and started to feel around. He ran his hands along the sides of it then under the writing surface. Sure enough, a button lay hidden in the corner. No one would ever know it was there unless they were looking for it.

"I've got it." Cameron pressed the button and watched as one panel of books began to move.

They both saw it at the same time. A lamp that had been placed in front of the panel to make it less conspicuous.

"Cam, the lamp!"

Sophia and Cameron both dived for it, but were too late. The lamp fell to the floor with a loud crash.

Damn.

The crash seemed deafening in the otherwise silent room. All color drained from Sophia's face.

"What do we do?" She looked around frantically.

Was it possible that nobody had heard the lamp fall? In the party nobody would have heard it, but was anyone nearby? Cameron held his breath, then cursed when he heard a door open down the hall. Someone was coming, blocking their only route of escape.

It was too late to get them anywhere safe. Cameron looked at Sophia, who was watching him with a fully panicked look in her eyes.

Cameron burst into a flurry of activity. He pushed the button to close the panel in front of the safe, then quickly picked up the lamp that had fallen to the hardwood floor— thankfully, it hadn't broken—and put it back on the shelf in front of the closed panel.

He grabbed a crystal vase that rested on the desk and put it on the floor. Sophia just watched him, not understanding at all what he was trying to do.

She looked even more shocked when he began unbuttoning his dress shirt, pulling it from where it was tucked into his pants. Then he lifted her by the waist and set her on the desk. Before Sophia could ask what he was doing, Cameron climbed on top of the desk and began kissing her.

Cameron peeled her dress as far down one shoulder as it would go, baring a great deal of skin. He threaded his fingers in her hair and pushed her back fully on the desk. He pulled up one of her legs and hooked it around his waist and slid his hand over her breast, grabbing it roughly.

He heard Sophia whimper against his mouth in protest of the hard kiss and felt her pull her torso away from him.

Cameron opened his eyes to find her wide green eyes staring at him.

She was frightened.

Cameron stopped immediately. He couldn't stand that look in her eyes. True, Cameron was trying to put on a show for whoever was about to come through that door, but this was Sophia. He didn't want her frightened of being close to him.

He brought his hand back up to stroke her cheek. He leaned his weight on his elbows and gazed gently down at her.

"Sorry, baby," he whispered, and stroked her cheek once more. "Let's try this again, slower. Kiss me."

This time Cameron brought his lips gently down to hers. He teased her bottom lip with his nipping little kisses, then gave the same attention to the upper one. He heard Sophia sigh and watched as her eyes closed.

Cameron deepened the kiss as Sophia responded. Her arms came up and wrapped around his neck. A knot of need twisted in him as he drew her closer.

Cameron tried to remind himself that this was all an act, that any moment now someone from DS-13 would walk through the door and have to believe that the only thing going on in here was hot sex. But as he kissed Sophia again he realized that there was no acting about it.

This time when Cameron's hand moved onto her beautiful body again it was because he couldn't stop himself, not because he wanted to put on any sort of show. Cameron shifted so he could get closer to Sophia. She moaned and held on to him, her fingers threading through his hair.

Just a few moments later the door to the office flew open and the lights flipped on.

It was Rick. Damn it. And he had his weapon in his hand.

"What the hell are you doing in here?"

Cameron subtly shifted so he was blocking more of Sophia from Rick's view.

"What the hell does it look like we're doing, Rick? Get out."

But Rick wasn't backing down. "You're not supposed to be in here."

Cameron decided to try a different route. "Dude, we're just having a little fun in the boss's room. You know, a little danger." He gave Rick a knowing grin. *"Capiche?"*

Rick's dark eyes narrowed. Cameron didn't know what the younger man was going to do. If Rick decided to get Mr. Smith, things would become much more complicated.

"Let me off this desk." Sophia pushed out from under him. "I told you we should just go back to the room, jackass."

Sophia wiggled completely out from under him and straightened her dress over her body, but not before Rick caught a glimpse of some tantalizing flesh, Cameron was sure. She looked over at Rick without flinching. "What's the matter with you, never seen a woman before?" she snapped at him with a jutting chin. She turned to Cam. "Can we please go back to the room now? I don't like having an audience. At least, not him."

Cameron watched as Sophia began to walk toward the door. Whatever suspicions Rick had were obviously lost as he looked at Sophia with cruel lust in his eyes.

Rick grabbed her arm as she walked by. "Maybe you and I will get our turn soon." Cameron could see Sophia wince, but he didn't intervene.

Fighting a man with a gun in his hand would not work out well for any of them. Plus, it would be completely out of character for Cam Cameron. Instead, Cameron leaned down and put the vase he'd set on the floor earlier back on the desk.

"Yeah, I don't think so." Sophia all but spat the words.

Rick grabbed her other arm and pulled her up against him fully. "We'll see about that."

Cameron walked over casually. "All right, Romeo, that's enough. We'll see you in the morning."

Rick smirked, but he stepped back so they could get through the doorway.

Cameron wasn't sure what Rick's weird smile was all about, but he wasn't sticking around to find out. They had dodged a bullet, literally and figuratively. Cameron grabbed Sophia's arm and they made their escape.

Chapter Twelve

As they reached their room, Cameron signaled for Sophia to wait right inside the door. The bug was still there. It was time to get rid of that thing.

He just hoped that Rick would keep his mouth shut about seeing them. Cameron supposed it was possible. The way Sophia had shunned Rick, he probably wouldn't want to announce that to anyone very soon.

Frustration gnawed in Cameron's gut. They had been so close to finding Ghost Shell. If they had just had a few more minutes—and if that stupid lamp hadn't fallen—he could've cracked the safe. Then he could've gotten Sophia, and the device, out of here.

Which was what was best, Cameron knew. But after what happened on the desk, Cameron was torn between wanting her to go and wanting her to stay.

Basically just plain wanting her.

He wanted her still. It was physical, definitely, the desire he had for her. But after the way she'd totally kept it together over the past forty-eight hours, it was more than that. Cameron found himself realizing that Sophia had courage and backbone, things he never knew she had. He suspected she never knew she possessed those qualities, either.

And her strengths were so very attractive to him. Everything about her was becoming more and more attractive to him.

And the way she had kissed him back on the desk… There was definitely an attraction and it was definitely affecting both of them. And Cameron planned to do something about it.

But first they needed to talk. That definitely could not happen with the bug still in the room. Cameron walked over to the tray. Sophia stood just inside the door, seeming unsure as to what she should do.

Cameron took the tray and set it on the floor out in the hallway, closing the door again behind him. He signaled for Sophia to remain quiet as he got out his Omega equipment and made sure no other bugs had been placed in the room while they were gone.

None. Finally, a break.

"Now we can talk." Cameron didn't speak at full volume, but at least they didn't have to speak in low tones.

"Won't they wonder about the tray?"

"I'll tell them there was a funny smell and it was bugging me."

Sophia smiled crookedly. "Okay."

"Are you all right?" Cameron walked over to her, stopping just short of touching her.

"Do you mean in general or after what just happened?"

"Both, I guess. But specifically I was referring to what happened a few minutes ago."

Sophia shook her head. "You mean Rick? I guess I shouldn't have egged him on. But I couldn't help it. That guy gives me the creeps."

"Yeah, no kidding. Rick definitely has a cruel side." Cameron saw Sophia shudder. "But I was actually talking about what happened between you and me. On the desk."

Sophia took a step back from Cameron, then turned

and walked over to the bed, sitting down on the edge. She didn't speak for a long moment. "Don't worry about it, Cam. I understand."

"Well, explain it to me, because I don't understand." Cameron didn't like the way she was looking down, as if she was too embarrassed to make eye contact with him.

"At the desk, you were undercover. You thought fast. It was a good plan, and it worked. It seemed to fool Rick."

"Sophia—"

"I get it, Cam, I really do. It was like earlier when I came out of the bathroom and you kissed me. Again, smart, quick thinking on your part. You probably saved our lives."

She looked up at him then, and shrugged her shoulders wearily. Cameron most distinctly did not like what he saw in her eyes: wariness, embarrassment, resignation. He walked closer to her, but she held out an arm to stop him.

"There's no need to keep up the pretense now, Cam. There's no bug in the room or creep coming down the hall about to catch us where we're not supposed to be."

Sophia stood up. "I'm going to take another bath, okay?"

Cameron had heard enough. He strode purposely over to Sophia and threaded both his hands into her hair. He tilted her head back so he could look directly into her eyes. A shocked sound came out of her throat at his sudden movement.

"Let's get something straight here, Soph. Yes, I am undercover and yes, this situation is beyond complicated."

"Listen, Cam…" Sophia tried to step back, but Cameron wouldn't let her.

"No, you listen. I have to be *on*, all the time here. My life, your life, the success of the mission, getting justice for my partner, all depend on me staying focused."

Sophia dropped her gaze. "I *know*, Cam. I understand that."

Cameron bent his knees so he could catch her eyes again. When she finally looked at him, he continued, "Well, know and understand this—you blow my focus all to hell. I want you in a way I have never wanted any other woman."

That got her attention. "Wh-what?"

"You really think I'm just acting when I kiss you, acting during what happened on the desk?"

"You're not?" Her shocked tone told him all he needed to know.

"Baby, if Rick hadn't come into that office, we'd still be on that desk. Hell, I should probably thank Rick so that I won't forever have to try to forget that our first time was on the desk of the man who killed my partner."

"It's just so hard for me to tell, Cam. To know what's real and what's not with you."

Cameron brought his lips down to hers and kissed her gently. "Know this is real," he whispered against her lips.

He felt the moment Sophia gave in to the kiss. Her arms came up and entwined around his neck. Cameron bent his knees again so he could wrap his arms around her waist, then lifted her so she was face-to-face with him.

"You always were a tiny little thing," he told her, still kissing her.

Her arms wrapped more firmly around his neck. "I'll have you know, I'm the absolute perfect size."

"Oh, I don't doubt that at all, Ms. Reardon." Cameron began backing up until her legs rested against the side of the bed, then lowered her feet back to the ground. He trailed kisses down the side of her neck and delighted as it caused her to break out in goose bumps. He reached down and slid both sleeves of her dress off her shoulders, and because of its open back, it slid to the floor and pooled at her feet.

"Perfect size, indeed," he murmured as he removed his own shirt.

"Cameron…" He loved the sound of her voice as she said his name.

Cameron stood and picked her up again, lowering her onto the bed slowly and with a great deal more finesse than he had before. His mouth found hers again. Her hands clenched into his shoulders.

Cameron wanted to take things slow, to make sure not to frighten her as he had on the desk. Cameron moved on top of her, propping his weight up on his elbows, holding back. But evidently Sophia had other plans.

She pulled his weight down to her, making quick work of removing his clothes and the rest of hers. Passion was building to a fevered pitch. This was definitely real; no acting involved whatsoever.

That was Cameron's last coherent thought before he lost himself in the fervor and heat that consumed both he and Sophia.

THE NEXT MORNING Sophia made good use of the giant bathroom again, this time to take a shower. Cameron had joined her in there—good thing there had been more than room enough for two—although him joining her had greatly prolonged the length of the shower.

They were both toweling off now, in the steam-filled bathroom. "I so don't want to ask this, but did Smith provide any more clothes? Anything casual?" Sophia didn't want to put on the ball gown again or yesterday's dress pants.

"I'll check." A few moments later Cameron, having gotten dressed in jeans and a soft black sweater, brought in a new package and set it on the counter. Sophia opened it, relieved to see a pair of jeans and a navy blue T-shirt. Underclothes, socks and a pair of casual shoes completed Smith's wardrobe for Sophia today.

Sophia still hated having to wear what that psycho chose for her.

Speaking of psycho… "So what's our plan when I meet with him tonight for the code? I don't think I'm going to be able to bluff my way out again." A shudder went through her as she put on the jeans.

"I'm going to contact Omega and insist on an extraction for you this evening. Your life is definitely in jeopardy, so they won't refuse again."

"Just for me? You're not coming, too?"

"We'll see. If my cover's blown, then yes, I'll be extracted, too. No point staying here just to be tortured and killed."

Sophia rolled her eyes. "Some people have no sense of adventure."

Cameron gave a soft bark of laughter and walked over to kiss her. "We have a few hours. A lot can happen in that time. But either way, I'm getting you out before this goes any further. You'll never have to see Smith again."

Sophia felt as if a huge weight was lifted. Not having to see Smith again was just fine. She tried to pull the T-shirt on over her head and winced from the pain in her arm.

Cameron helped her bring her arm back down, staring at the jagged cut on her shoulder and upper arm from the nail. "That's starting to look pretty infected. Does it hurt?"

Although she hadn't really noticed it in the midst of last night's activities or in the shower this morning, Sophia could definitely feel an ache now. She looked over at the wound. The skin around where she had scraped against the rusty nail was puffy and a fiery red.

"It's a little sore, but not unmanageable."

"When was your last tetanus shot?"

Sophia had no idea. It wasn't something she thought about regularly. "I don't know. High school, maybe?"

Cameron grimaced. "That's not great, but it's still within the ten-year mark. Let's get that bandaged." He helped her up to sit on the marble bathroom counter.

Cameron applied an antibacterial ointment and began wrapping her arm in gauze, both items from his duffel bag.

"You're like a Boy Scout with that duffel bag of yours."

Cameron smiled and winked at her. "I try to keep as much in there as I can without carrying anything that would arouse suspicion if someone goes through it."

"Do they go through your bags a lot?"

"I don't know, but I never assume that they don't. I stay more alive that way. So yeah, I have a lot of junk in there. It helps camouflage the important stuff."

"Like that cell phone thing you used to communicate with Omega?"

"It wasn't actually a cell phone, but yes. Like that." He finished wrapping her shoulder. "Okay, you're all patched up."

He helped Sophia ease the shirt over her head. Sophia tried not to provide any indication at all that her arm was hurting her. Then she forgot all about any pain as Cameron grabbed her by the hips and scooted her to the edge of the counter and kissed her.

"Remind me again why we didn't do this five years ago?" he whispered against her lips.

Sophia smiled. "If we had known it would be this good, I don't think we'd have been able to wait."

Sophia thought about Cameron when she had known him before. She had been finishing college then, with her degree in graphic design. He had just been coming out of the US Army Rangers and had told her he wasn't sure what he was going to do with his life.

Sophia pulled back from him. "You lied to me before.

You told me you didn't know what profession you'd end up in."

Cameron made a *hmm* noise in his throat. "I didn't really lie to you."

Sophia lifted a single eyebrow.

Cameron had the good grace to at least look sheepish. "Yeah, Omega approached me while I was still in the army, so I knew I was going to work for them. But I wasn't sure exactly how I would fit in with the organization and what I would be doing. So I wasn't technically lying…"

"You know, for a while after you left, since you didn't say a real goodbye or anything, I thought it was because I hadn't had sex with you," Sophia whispered.

"What?" Cameron's head jerked back.

Sophia shrugged. "Well, for the first couple months with all our breakfasts together, I knew you didn't expect anything. But when things started building between us and we started going out on dates and stuff…"

"Let me get this straight." Cameron's jaw clenched and his eyes tightened. He removed his hands from Sophia's waist and placed them on the counter on either side of her legs. "You thought I left because you didn't put out?"

Sophia tried not to let Cameron's looming chest intimidate her. She slid back on the counter a bit. "It was a possible theory, yes. After all, I had no idea why you had left, did I?" Sophia poked him in the big, looming chest.

"*That* had nothing to do with it."

"Yeah, well, I didn't know that. All I knew was everything seemed to be going fine between us and then all of a sudden you were gone. No goodbye from you, just a cryptic message on my phone when you knew I wouldn't be home."

Cameron's shoulders hunched. "Yeah, I guess you're right." There was a long pause. "I couldn't tell you about

Omega Sector, Soph. And they told me I had to break ties as cleanly as possible."

"You mean no one at Omega has any outside relationships? No marriages or anything like that? It seems a bit extreme."

"No, they do. A bunch of people are married and have families in Omega. It's just…" Cameron turned from facing her to leaning against the counter next to her.

"What?" Sophia asked when Cameron didn't keep talking.

"All casual ties had to be severed."

It took a second for the pain to set in, but when it did it stole Sophia's breath. What could she say to that? She had thought he was the one. He had thought of her as a casual tie.

"Oh," she finally managed to whisper.

"Soph, I'm sorry. I never thought of you—of what we had—as casual."

"But you told Omega Sector it was." It wasn't a question.

"They asked about the nature of our relationship. How long we'd been together and stuff like that. They needed to know how often I spent the night at your house. If I was going to work for Omega, and I was in a solid, committed relationship with you, then you'd have to be closely scrutinized, also."

Sophia waited but didn't say anything.

"On paper it looked like we had breakfast together all the time and had been on a few dates," he said softly.

"Casual," Sophia whispered.

"Soph, that time we spent together. All those mornings at the diner. The dates, the kisses. They were important to me, too."

"But not important enough to make you stay. Or to tell Omega that I wasn't a casual relationship."

Cameron was standing right next to her, but the gap between them was almost insurmountable. Sophia slid a little farther away from him on the counter. She was afraid if he touched her right now she might shatter into a million pieces.

Cameron pinched the bridge of his nose, his eyes closed. "If I could go back in time to five years ago, there are so many things I would do differently."

Chapter Thirteen

Cameron would give every paycheck he'd ever get for the rest of his life if he never had to see that look on Sophia's face ever again. He had known he'd screwed up when he walked away from her five years ago. But he had never dreamed it had hurt her as much as it had hurt him.

Cameron didn't know exactly what he had thought. Maybe that she would move on quickly because they hadn't been too physical. Maybe that she was young and that a clean break would be easy to recover from.

"I had to choose. At the time I thought I was making the right choice." Cameron knew he had to make her understand, but the right words seemed to fail him.

Sophia turned her head away and it almost broke his heart. "I understand," she whispered.

He grabbed her chin firmly and forced her to look at him. "I'm pretty sure you don't understand at all. There's not a day that goes by that I don't regret that decision." He sighed, releasing her chin and turning away. "But it's complicated. I know I've done a lot of good work with Omega—maybe even saved a lot of lives. But…"

Cameron wasn't even sure what the rest of that sentence was. Silence hung between them.

"But you wonder, deep inside, if it was worth the price you paid personally," Sophia finally said.

Yes, that summed it up perfectly. Sophia had always understood him.

"Every. Damn. Day." Cameron turned around to face her again. He reached up and trailed the back of his fingers down her cheek. "And always because of…"

They both jumped a bit at the pounding on the door.

Cameron reached over and kissed her briefly and went to answer their bedroom door. It was Fin.

"Mr. Smith wants to see you in his office to talk about business stuff. She—" he gestured at Sophia "—doesn't need to go."

"Right now? It's eight o'clock in the morning."

"Yes, now. Mr. Smith is an early riser."

There was nothing particularly bad about what Fin was saying, but Cameron still felt tension pooling in his stomach. "But Smith doesn't want to see Sophia?"

"No, just you. For stuff having nothing to do with her. She can stay here and somebody will bring a breakfast tray." Fin gave nothing away, probably because he knew nothing.

Cameron wasn't sure which way to push. He didn't want to be away from Sophia and leave her here by herself, but on the other hand keeping her as far from Smith as possible was probably the best plan.

"Okay," Cameron finally said. "I'll go to Mr. Smith's office in just a few minutes." Maybe it was time to get Sophia out of here right now.

"I'm supposed to wait for you right here and take you," Fin told him.

So much for getting Sophia out right now.

Did Smith know they had been in his office last night? Had Rick told them? Surely they would've already been summoned, *both* of them, if that was the case. Maybe this really was just a routine meeting to discuss details. Cameron nodded. "Give me just a second."

Cameron closed the door and Sophia came out of the bathroom. "Everything okay?"

"Yeah, I think. Fin just came to tell me Smith wants to meet with me."

Cameron could almost see the tension that flooded Sophia's body. "Why? Is there a problem? Do you think Rick told him about us in the office?"

"No. We'd have already been dragged in there if he had."

Sophia still looked worried. "Then what?"

"Just a meeting. After all, I am his employee. Business details, Fin said." Cameron walked over to his bag and got out the SIG he had hidden there. He tucked it into the back of his jeans. He hoped he wouldn't need it, but this close to getting Sophia out, he wasn't taking any chances.

"Do I come, too?"

"No. You're supposed to stay here. They're going to bring up a tray with some breakfast. Eat as much as you can."

"Okay." Sophia looked as hesitant about this plan as Cameron felt. He walked over to her and pulled her into his arms.

"Just hang in there a few more hours," he whispered into her ear. "Let me go act normal with Smith and I'll be back in a bit. Then we'll get you out of here."

Sophia reached up her hands to frame his face. "Be careful." She stood up on her tiptoes to kiss him.

Cameron stepped back after a few moments even though he wanted nothing more than to stay there in her embrace. "I will. Stay here in the room. Get the tray when it's delivered, but otherwise keep the door locked."

Sophia nodded and Cameron turned and walked out the door.

Fin was still waiting, as promised. They silently walked together to Smith's office.

Unlike yesterday, Cameron could tell Smith's office door was already open from down the hall. As they got closer, Cam could hear Smith talking—and laughing—with another man. Cameron walked into the office, Fin following right behind, but staying by the door. He obviously was still not in Smith's good graces.

"Cam, come in," Smith said good-naturedly.

Thompson Smith, when playing the role of DS-13 leader, looked polished and friendly, not at all like the butler Cameron had mistook him for yesterday. Having seen him play both roles, Cameron could understand how he had eluded law enforcement for years. But no matter which role he played, Smith's eyes were still cold and hard.

The eyes of a killer.

"Good morning, Mr. Smith. Fin said you wanted to meet with me about some business."

"Yes, yes." Smith nodded. "A few very important details. First, this is my associate Mr. McNeil. He came up this morning to discuss some business, also. Fred, this is Cam Cameron, about whom we were talking earlier."

Talking about him could be good or bad, Cam knew. He also noticed no details were provided by either men as to what type of "associate" McNeil was. But McNeil stuck out his hand for shaking, so Cameron assumed it was good. "Nice to meet you."

Cam shook the hand and responded, "You, too, man." McNeil faded over to the side of the room and propped himself up against the wall, obviously to get out of the way of whatever business Mr. Smith had with Cameron.

"I trust you had a good time at the party last night?" Smith asked.

Cameron tensed for just a moment then forced himself to

relax. Had he been wrong and Smith did know about them breaking into the office? If so, he'd have to think of a way to play this off quick. His best bet was probably to pretend to be the bad boy—wanting to have sex in the boss's office.

Disrespectful, sure. But better than announcing he was a federal agent.

"Yeah. Lots of fun. Plenty of trouble to get into," Cameron told him, providing what he hoped was a charming grin. Charming was hard to pull off when all you wanted to do was arrest the bastard sitting across from you and see that he rot in jail for the next 150 years or so.

"Yes, there's always lots of trouble with my parties." Smith chuckled. "And I trust our lovely Sophia had a good time, also? She looked beautiful last night."

Smith wasn't giving away much. Cam grinned again. "She didn't seem to have any complaints."

"Glad to hear that. Tell me a little more about Sophia. You seem quite taken with her. You met her for the first time a few days ago at the warehouse?"

These questions were not going in the direction Cameron had wanted. He couldn't quite determine their purpose. Did Smith know something? Was he setting up Cam? Or did he just like the sordid little details of other people's lives?

He wouldn't put any of it past Smith.

Cam decided to play it on the assumption that Smith didn't really know anything. It was his only real option anyway. To make up some sort of history between he and Sophia now would just be suspicious. "Yeah, at the warehouse, where Marco found her."

"And you think she was there to try to sell us the information she had about Ghost Shell."

"Yeah, that's what she told me. Honestly, really, I just thought she was hot. I wasn't thinking much past that." Better to come across as careless, rather than a traitor.

"But when Fin and Rick were about to eliminate her, you stopped them."

Cam looked at Smith then over at McNeil, who still was leaning against the wall. "Yeah, it seemed like a waste." Cam shrugged. "She knew stuff that was helpful about Ghost Shell so I thought we should bring her to you and let you decide."

"I see." Smith sat back in his chair.

"I mean, I know she wants you to pay her money, Mr. Smith. But at least Ghost Shell will still work with her help. And it sounded like you would make much more from selling it than what she was asking." Cameron injected a bit of nervousness into his tone, which wasn't difficult.

"Yes, that's true," Smith responded, leaning back in his chair. "The problem is that I have Mr. McNeil here, who tells me that the information Sophia provided was not correct."

Cameron looked over at Fred McNeil. "Oh, okay. Are you a computer specialist guy or something?" Cam added just a little bit of mockery. Perhaps he could discredit this guy. But it was a long shot.

Fred snorted. "No. I am definitely not any type of computer geek."

"Then how do you know that Sophia isn't telling the truth?"

Mr. Smith answered for Fred. "Because Mr. McNeil is on my payroll and has been for years. He works for the FBI."

This was not what Cameron wanted to hear on multiple levels. First, because a mole selling secrets to DS-13 was never good, but more important, because this meant Sophia was really in trouble. Tonight was going to be too late to get her out. She'd be dead long before then.

Cameron shot from his chair. "Whoa. FBI? I don't want

to have anything to do with an FBI agent." He had to stall. Figure out what to do.

His sudden movement had put McNeil on the defensive. His hand was already at his weapon.

"Calm down, Cam," Smith told him. "Obviously, Fred is not here to arrest anyone. He wouldn't be much use to me if he was, would he?"

Cam pretended to process that. He sat back down slowly. "No, I guess not." He glared over at Fred. "Sorry. Not a big fan of law enforcement."

Fred just rolled his eyes and Cam could tell that he'd just written Cameron off as being just another dumb thug. Good.

But Smith didn't seem quite as quick to lump Cam in that category. "Fred informs me that what Sophia said about some secret fail-safe code is not accurate."

"Maybe she knows something he doesn't."

Fred pushed himself away from the wall and came to stand closer to Smith's desk. "Look, Sophia Reardon is a *graphic artist* for the FBI. She's not an agent. She's not in the cyberterrorism division. She made up all that crap about a special code."

"How do you know?" Cameron asked.

"Because I was the person who acquired Ghost Shell for DS-13," Fred sneered. "Some goody-goody computer scientist at a technology company contacted us a few months ago in fear that something like Ghost Shell was being developed. Guess who happened to be assigned that call?"

"You?" That would explain a lot. How Ghost Shell got into DS-13's hands so quickly. And why the FBI was so clueless. The FBI may not even officially know that Ghost Shell existed. Omega Sector knew of its existence, but Omega had resources and connections the Bureau didn't have.

Agent McNeil rolled his eyes. "Yes, obviously. Me. So

when I say your lady friend is lying, I know what I'm talking about. I know things that are going on in the FBI, the CIA and even some agencies you've never even heard of."

Things had just gone from bad to hell-in-a-handbasket. Obviously discrediting Agent McNeil wasn't going to work. And his bragging about unknown agencies—was McNeil referring to Omega? A mole in Omega would be ugly. Life-threatening, not only to Cameron, but also multiple other agents. Agents that included his family and friends.

Mr. Smith stood up. "Fin, get Rick and have him fetch Ms. Reardon and bring her here." Smith smiled over at Agent McNeil. "Rick has a nice cruel streak I find useful in these types of situations."

Cameron didn't turn around as he heard the door click behind him. He had to do something, fast. But pulling his SIG out now wouldn't do anything but get him killed.

"You were the one we couldn't figure out, Cam." Smith turned his attention back to Cameron. "Whether you were working with Ms. Reardon to cheat me of money."

Cam held his hands out in front of him. "Whoa. I just met this chick a couple of days ago! I thought I was helping you, Mr. Smith, honest. I had no idea she was trying to scam you."

Smith walked over to one of his large bookshelves. "I actually believe you, Cam. Not because of what you're saying right now, but because given the timeline of the development and our acquisition of Ghost Shell and Fin's ability to account for your location during that time, I believe you when you say you just met Ms. Reardon. Although I must admit, I hope you're not too fond of her, given what's about to happen."

Cameron watched as Smith reached over, pulled down a book from the bookshelf and opened it. Inside was a cleverly hidden keypad and biometrics scanner, into which

Smith punched a code and provided his thumbprint. The entire bookshelf spun and opened.

This was much more than the safe he and Sophia had found last night. And with the security measures Smith had, there was no way they would've been able to break in. Obviously he and Sophia hadn't been as close to discovering Ghost Shell as Cameron had thought.

Smith looked at Cameron and Agent McNeil, obviously happy to show off a bit. "Gentlemen, my panic room. Although, I rarely panic so I haven't had much use for it in that sense." Chuckling, Smith walked into the room. "It's fabulous, isn't it? And here is the Ghost Shell drive for which Ms. Reardon is determined to try to cheat me out of two million dollars." Smith reached over and pulled an external hard drive from one of the shelves. It was black, not too big. So benign-looking.

Cameron knew instantly what he had to do; he wouldn't get another chance like this. He could grab Ghost Shell and get Sophia out. It meant not being able to arrest Smith, but it was a trade-off Cameron was willing to make.

Cameron pulled his weapon out and pointed it at Agent McNeil. He knew that man was armed. Smith he wasn't sure about, but knew not to take him lightly.

"Sorry, Mr. Smith. But I'm going to have to take Ghost Shell off your hands." Cam decided to try to keep his undercover identity intact. Let them think he was just stealing from them out of greed. Both Smith and McNeil spun to look at Cam. McNeil made a move toward his weapon. "Nope, Agent McNeil. I need you to keep your hands right in front of you where I can see them. You, too, Mr. Smith."

Cameron kept the weapon pointed at McNeil as he walked over and took the man's gun from its holster.

Anger radiated from Smith's cold eyes. "So you did know Sophia?"

"Nope," Cameron told Smith, popping the *P* in the word as he reached over to take the hard drive from his hands. "But let's just say she convinced me of Ghost Shell's true value and that I could make a lot more money selling it on my own."

"Cam," Smith said, obviously trying to get his temper under control. "This isn't what you want to do. DS-13 is not an enemy you want to have. Even if you kill me, others will hunt you down."

Cameron knew Smith was stalling for time. Fin and Rick would be back with Sophia any minute and Cam would lose the advantage. "I think half a billion dollars will buy me pretty ample security." Cameron looked around the panic room. He had no idea what sort of communicative measures it had. He destroyed what he could see: ripping out a landline telephone and all the cords attached to a computer that sat in a corner. Cameron was sure there were other ways to communicate from inside the panic room, but hoped this would give him enough time to get Sophia out of the house.

Cameron stepped backward until he was just inside the door, weapon still pointing at the two men. "You're going to regret this," Smith spat at Cameron.

"Maybe," Cameron responded and then fired his gun at the keypad inside the door, blasting it into little pieces. Hopefully that would keep McNeil and Smith in there at least a little while.

Now the countdown had really started—somebody was bound to have heard the shot. Cameron stepped all the way out of the room and pressed the button that closed the door on the hidden book keypad. Smith's eyes were still shooting daggers at Cam as the door closed with a resounding thud. Cameron wasted no time and ran out of the office, Ghost Shell hard drive firmly in his hand.

He was carefully heading back down the hall toward the bedroom when he heard Sophia screaming his name in terror.

Chapter Fourteen

When Cameron left to go see Smith, Sophia decided to be ready. Ready for exactly what, she wasn't sure. But when he got back, she wanted to be ready.

Her shoulder was bothering her more than she had let on to Cameron, and it was becoming more stiff and difficult to move. Bending down to put on her socks and shoes caused a throbbing in her shoulder, but Sophia ignored the pain as best she could. A tap on the door startled her.

"Yes?" she asked as she walked slowly over to it. Sophia didn't want to open it, although recognized the lock on the door wouldn't keep anyone out if they were determined to get in.

"A breakfast tray for you, Ms. Reardon," a female voice said from the other side of the door. Sophia opened it hesitantly, but saw it was indeed just a woman with a tray in her hands. Moving aside, Sophia allowed the woman to bring in the tray and watched as she set it on the table and left without another word. The woman closed the door with a resounding thud as she left.

Was it just Sophia's imagination, or had the woman seemed hostile and suspicious? Did she know something Sophia didn't? Did everyone know who she and Cameron really were?

Or was it a woman just doing her job who had other tasks

to get back to and didn't want to waste any time? Also a perfectly reasonable explanation.

See? This was why Sophia wasn't meant to do undercover work. Save that for the trained agents. It was too easy to reflect her own paranoia onto others' actions when there was no tangible reason to think they suspected something.

Sophia walked over to the table where the woman had set the tray. She reached down and took a spoonful of the fruit salad. Poison momentarily crossed her mind but Sophia shrugged and kept on eating. At this point either it was poisoned or it wasn't; she wasn't going to worry about it.

A knock at the door again startled Sophia. Had the woman forgotten something?

"Yes?" Sophia asked as she opened the door. But it was Rick leaning in her doorway, not the woman with the tray.

Sophia tried to shut the door again, but Rick easily blocked it. When he took a step toward her, Sophia jerked back. She realized the mistake instantly—backing up allowed Rick to enter the room and shut the door behind him.

She heard him click the lock and knew she was in trouble.

"You've got on quite a bit more clothes than when I saw you last night."

Sophia ignored that. "What are you doing here, Rick? Cam's not here."

Rick's grin was predatory. "Oh, I know. He's in a meeting with Mr. Smith." He took another step toward Sophia and she backed up again, but realized she was getting close to the bed—absolutely the last place she wanted to be near with Rick in the room—so she turned and strode over to the tray with the food.

"Yeah, that's right, he's with Mr. Smith. But he'll be back in just a minute." Sophia prayed the words sounded more confident than she felt. She picked up a grape and popped it in her mouth in what she hoped was complete nonchalance.

Rick smirked. "I don't think so. Mr. Smith had some pretty important stuff to talk to him about."

"Oh, yeah? Like what?" Another grape. Anything that kept Rick on the other side of the room talking.

The gleam that entered Rick's eyes told Sophia she had asked exactly what he wanted her to ask. "This and that. But mostly about you."

Sophia tried not to react.

"What about me?"

"Evidently you haven't been telling the truth about everything, have you?" Rick made a tsking sound. "Mr. Smith has some FBI agent guy who *really* knows about that Ghost software thing and he basically called you a liar." Rick glowed with glee.

Sophia felt paralyzed with indecision. Did Cameron know what was going on? Had Smith already done something to Cameron? Sophia thought about what had happened to Cameron's partner—Smith had had him assassinated. She couldn't bear to think of anything like that happening to Cam so she pushed the thought aside.

Should she run? Try to find Cameron? Rick was strutting closer, that perverse smirk still blanketing his face. Sophia knew one thing: staying in this room with Rick was not a good idea.

"Whatever. This is just a misunderstanding. I'll just go set Mr. Smith straight right now." She headed toward the door, until Rick stepped right in front of her.

"Oh, don't worry, Mr. Smith sent me in here to get you. Looks like you need to be questioned with force and he knows I'm the best man for that job." Rick chuckled darkly, cracking his knuckles. Sophia felt bile pooling in her stomach. "But I thought you and I could have a few minutes in here first. So I could get a taste of what you were teasing me with last night."

Sophia darted to the side to run around Rick but he was too fast. He grabbed her by both arms and threw her toward the bed. Sophia let out a loud moan at the pain in her injured arm, and spun for the door again. But Rick was ready for her.

"Oh, no, you don't." He grabbed her from behind, wrapping both arms around her. His breath was sour at her cheek. Sophia tried to get away but couldn't and knew that Cameron was too far away in Smith's office to hear her scream. Screaming would only bring more of Smith's men in here. "C'mon," Rick said softly. "I'm not asking for anything you haven't already given Cam. What's the big deal?"

"Let. Me. Go." Sophia held herself absolutely still, since the only other option was wiggling all over Rick. "Why would I do anything with you when you basically just told me you were going to torture me for Smith a few seconds ago?"

Rick's grip loosened just a little. Maybe he never considered the fact that him informing her of upcoming torture wouldn't make her want to jump into bed with him. Sophia shuddered. As if she would jump into bed with him for any reason.

"Maybe we can work out some sort of a trade-off," Sophia whispered, turning. "I give you what you want now and you see what you can do to take it easy on me a little later."

Rick considered that then nodded enthusiastically. "Um, yeah, that sounds good." The lie was plain to see in his eyes and Sophia barely refrained from rolling hers.

"Great. We've got a deal." Sophia forced herself to slide her hands up his arms, as if to embrace him. Rick's foul breath hitting her full in the face was almost more than she could stand. Rick slid closer to kiss her, and although she knew she should let it go further than this without running, Sophia could not force herself to kiss him. She took a slight step back and brought her knee up as hard as she could into Rick's groin.

Rick cried out and dropped to his knees, releasing Sophia. She ran toward the door, cursing as the lock slowed her down. Her fingers felt useless as she tried to get the lock to release. It finally did and Sophia frantically pulled the door open, only to have it slam back shut. She turned to find Rick's hulking form looming over her.

"You're going to regret that," he sneered.

Sophia tried to run, but couldn't get around him. His backhand came without warning and the blow threw Sophia to the ground. From the throbbing in her face, Sophia knew she had to get help. Anybody—no matter who a scream brought in. Rick was going to kill her.

She opened her mouth to scream, but Rick moved quicker than she thought him capable. He was on her in a moment with his meaty hand covering her mouth. "Shut up," he growled.

Sophia immediately panicked. The need for air, to get the hand off her face so she could breathe, consumed her. She clawed at his hand, his face, anything she could reach. Vaguely she heard vile curses emanating from Rick, but paid no attention. Her only thought was for air.

Rick's full weight was on her body now, making everything worse. She bucked and twisted sharply, causing Rick's hand to slip off her face for a moment. Sophia screamed as loudly as she could.

"Cam!" The yell reverberated through the room, but she wasn't sure how much farther into the house the sound went.

It was only a moment before Rick hit her again. The

whole world seemed to spin as Sophia fought to hold on to consciousness. Rick wrapped one hand around her throat. "You will shut up or I'll kill you right now." He squeezed to prove his point and Sophia felt everything begin to dim.

Sophia didn't know how to fight someone this much bigger and stronger than she. She clutched at his hand on her throat, but it didn't seem to affect anything. She just tried to drag air into her lungs past the hand intent on keeping that from happening. It seemed to be a losing battle.

And then out of nowhere Rick's body flew off her. Sophia sucked in gulps of precious air, scampering as far away as possible. Her vision cleared and she realized it was Cameron who had tackled Rick and gotten him off her, and was now in the midst of pummeling the other man. Rick had both height and weight on Cam, but Cam had caught him by surprise. And he obviously wasn't interested in showing Rick much mercy.

A sickening crunch brought a howl from Rick before he fell back onto the floor, completely unconscious. Cameron immediately stopped hitting him. He looked over at Sophia. "Are you okay?"

Sophia nodded, still trying to breathe as deeply as possible. Cameron rushed to her side, wincing and gently touching the bruise she was sure was forming on her cheek from where Rick had hit her. "I'm okay. Just...panicked. No permanent damage done."

Cameron reached over and kissed her on her forehead. "Good, because we have to leave. *Right now,*" he told her as he helped her up.

"Smith knows about me." She pointed at Rick's unconscious form. "Rick took great delight in letting me know Smith wanted me brought in to be tortured."

Cameron went over to a large dresser that sat against one wall. "Are you okay enough to help me move this?"

Sophia grabbed the other end of the dresser. "Sure, I think. Why?"

She understood a few moments later when they slid the chest directly in front of the door. Getting in that way would be difficult for anybody.

"I've got Ghost Shell. We've got to get the hell out of here."

"How did you get it?"

"I locked Smith and his little FBI friend in his own panic room. But that's not going to hold him for long." Cameron rushed over and grabbed a jacket out of his bag as well as the Omega Sector gadget thing he'd used earlier. He tossed a sweatshirt to Sophia. "Here, you'll need this. Sorry I don't have anything else. I'm not sure how long we'll be outside."

"Can't you just contact Omega and have them pick us up?"

"No. We have to go on our own." He headed over to the sliding glass door that led to the small deck.

"Isn't Omega our quickest route out of here?" Sophia followed him to the door.

"Normally, yes. But Fred McNeil—the FBI agent Smith has on payroll—knew way too much. Made me think we might have a mole inside Omega, too." He turned and looked at Sophia, trailing a finger gently down her cheek. "I can't be sure either way right now. But I won't take a chance with your life."

"So how are we getting out of here?"

Cameron slid the door open and stepped out onto the deck. The brisk fall air was instantly chilling. "We're going to get as far as we can on foot. I'm going to have someone I trust meet us."

"Can't we steal a car here or something?"

Cameron shook his head. "No. I'm sure Smith would be able to track them with GPS. Almost all newer vehicles can be tracked. Plus, it would take way too long to drive out of here. Air is our best option."

Sophia grimaced. "Okay, on foot to the airfield it is, then."

Sophia followed Cameron outside. She was glad the clothes Smith had sent for her this morning had been casual: jeans, a sweater and lace-up flat boots. She imagined if Smith had known she'd be running from him he would've provided her a skirt and heels. Cameron climbed over the deck railing and jumped the few feet down to the ground, then helped as Sophia did the same. He took her hand and led her around the back of the house carefully.

Sophia could hear some sort of commotion at the front of the house. They didn't stop to see what it was. Cameron just took advantage of it and they ran deeper into the woods. Sophia knew it wouldn't be long until Smith's henchmen would be after them. She held on to Cameron's hand and ran as fast as she could.

Chapter Fifteen

Running as fast as they could while not leaving a trail any six-year-old could follow was a delicate balance. They needed to put as much distance as possible between them and the house. Cameron knew by now Smith and McNeil would've gotten out of the panic room and would have every available person looking for them.

The terrain was all downhill—it was difficult to run and hard on the body. Cameron caught Sophia as she tripped over an exposed tree root.

"Sorry," she said through breaths, gulping air.

"You okay? Let's take a rest."

Sophia shook her head. "No. I know we need to keep going. I'll be all right." But her pale features and clammy hands argued differently.

But she was right, they did need to keep going. These early hours were the most important if they were possibly going to have a chance to escape. Cameron gave Sophia a brief nod, but slowed down a bit. He kept hold of her hand as they continued to work their way downhill. It was unbelievable how tough Sophia had been the past couple of hours. Cameron knew trained agents who couldn't keep plowing on the way she had. She had every right to complain or ask for him to at least slow down, but she hadn't.

It was impressive. Hell, everything about Sophia was impressive. When this was over, when Sophia was safe, Cameron planned to rectify the mistakes he'd made five years ago. He'd walked away from her once, but he wouldn't make that error again.

But first he had to get her to safety. Her breathing became more ragged so Cameron slowed down. They'd been running for well over an hour. He glanced at the sky overhead—it was starting to look ugly. It wouldn't be long before a storm hit. That was both good and bad. Good because it would make it harder for DS-13 to find them. Bad because the temperature was already pretty brisk. Being soaking wet was definitely not going to be comfortable.

"Where are we trying to go?" Sophia asked now that they weren't running at breakneck speed.

"Back down to the runway where we landed."

"Do we have a plane? Did you change your mind about contacting Omega?"

Cameron was torn. "Honestly, I don't know what to do about Omega. There may be a mole, but if there is one, I have no idea who it is."

"So how are we going to get out of here?"

"I'm going to get a message to one of my brothers. He used to be part of Omega, but got out a couple of years ago. He has his own small airplane. Runs a charter business."

"Okay." Sophia sounded relieved. Cameron didn't blame her. Knowing there was an actual plan made the running a little easier, but not much. Cameron looked up at the sky again. Definitely looked worse than it had just a few minutes ago.

"Ready to pick up the speed a little more? We need to get as far as we can before this storm hits."

Sophia just nodded. Cameron took her hand again and began adding speed to their downhill scamper. They ran silently, talking definitely not a possibility when expending this much effort. Cameron was winded himself, so he couldn't imagine how Sophia was feeling. She never complained, but he could hear her breathing become more and more labored.

The rain came at first in a gentle sprinkle and was almost welcome for its cooling effect at the pace they were keeping. But then the skies opened and it really began pouring. They tried to continue but after falling twice, Cameron knew they had to stop. When he looked closer at Sophia he realized they should've stopped much sooner. There was absolutely no color in her face and she was swaying dizzily on her feet.

"Sophia?" Her eyes looked at him without really focusing. "Soph! Are you okay?"

She nodded but obviously wasn't really hearing anything he was saying. Cameron took a step closer to her. "Soph? Hey, can you hear me?" He said it loud enough to be heard through the pouring rain. Sophia just looked at him blankly.

Cameron put his hands on both her cheeks and was shocked at the heat radiating off her. This was definitely more than just the exertion from running. Sophia had a fever—a high one. Cameron wiped her hair from her forehead, where it was dripping water into her eyes.

"It's okay, baby, you don't have to run anymore. Let's find a place where we can have some shelter." Cameron gently led Sophia over to a nearby tree that had fallen. The huge root that had come out of the forest floor provided a slight overhang. It wasn't much, but it would keep Sophia a little bit drier as Cameron looked for something better.

He bundled her as far back into the tree root as he could and knelt down beside her. "Sophia…" Cam spoke slowly, deliberately. "I'm going to find us some better shelter. I'll be right back. I don't want you to move from here. Okay?"

Sophia seemed to understand. She nodded weakly. "Okay."

Cameron didn't waste any time. Getting Sophia somewhere warm and dry, and figuring out what the heck was wrong with her, was the most important thing. It wasn't long before he found what he needed: a small cave. It wasn't big, barely room for two people to sit up in it, but it was dry. Cameron checked it for animals and critters, delighted when he found only a couple of squirrels, which he quickly chased out.

Sophia was exactly where he had left her, propped against the large root. It didn't look as if she had moved at all from the moment he'd left. As a matter of fact, with her eyes closed, lying so still she almost looked…

Cameron rushed over and knelt beside her. "Soph? Honey, are you okay?" When her eyes didn't open immediately he felt for her pulse at her throat. It was there. Although finding her pulse flooded him with relief, its rapid fluttering concerned him. This was more than just exhaustion from running down the mountain.

Cameron pulled her arm around his shoulders and slipped his arm around her waist. He stood, bringing her weight with him. Sophia didn't wake up but a low moan escaped her lips. Cameron cursed under his breath when he realized he had grabbed her injured arm. Jostling her as little as possible, he brought her slight weight up into his arms and carried her to the cave. Feeling the heat radiating from her—she definitely had a fever if he could feel it through her layers of clothing—Cameron moved as fast as he could without putting either of them in danger of falling. The rain continued to blanket them in its cold misery.

Sophia's eyes opened just a bit as he laid her as gently as he could into the small cave opening. "I don't think I can run anymore," she said, her voice barely louder than a whisper.

Cameron brushed her hair back from her face. "You don't have to run anymore, sweetheart. You have a fever, probably from that cut on your shoulder getting infected. We're just going to rest here for a while."

Sophia struggled to sit up. "I'm sorry I'm slowing you down. I just don't feel very good."

Cameron stopped her minimal progress and helped her lay back down, even though rain was still pouring down on him. "Don't try to sit up. I'm going to crawl in behind you and scoot us both back."

Sophia didn't answer and Cameron wondered if she had passed out again. He tossed his small backpack over to the side of the cave, mindful of the Ghost Shell hard drive in the bag. Then he crawled inside, joining Sophia but careful not to jostle her in any way that might cause her pain. The cave was not very large. It was difficult for Cameron to fit himself into the dark area—he couldn't even sit up to his full height. But at least it was dry.

He eased himself behind her then pulled her backward as gently as he could so her back could rest against his chest. She didn't say anything or make any sounds, just slumped hard against him and continued shivering. Cameron caught her forehead with his hand and laid it back so it rested against his shoulder. He felt the heat radiating from where he touched her, although the rest of her body was racked with chills. He tucked his legs more securely around the outside of hers in an effort to share more of their body heat.

Cameron had some ibuprofen in his backpack. He would allow Sophia, and himself, a chance to rest for a little while, then would give her some. It wouldn't fight the infection, but it would lower her fever for a little while. But he didn't have many of the painkillers, so getting some antibiotics into her system as soon as possible was critical.

Holding Sophia snugly against his chest with one arm, Cameron reached over to his backpack with the other. The Ghost Shell hard drive was still safe inside, and he reached for the Omega communication system. Cameron still wasn't sure who he could trust inside Omega, so instead he made a call to his oldest brother, Dylan. He knew Dylan would be loath to get involved with Omega Sector—or any government undercover work whatsoever—after what had happened to him, but his brother would do it anyway if Cameron asked. And Cameron was definitely asking. The fact that Dylan had his own Cessna airplane at his disposal was a huge plus because no cars were getting up this mountain anytime soon.

Cameron's plan was to get Sophia out with Dylan and back to safety. Cameron wouldn't go with them. Instead he would meet the Omega extraction team at dark and go back to headquarters with Ghost Shell. If there was some sort of mole inside Omega, Cameron wasn't taking a chance with Sophia's life. He knew Dylan, or any of his three siblings, could be trusted. That was as far as Cameron was willing to go when it came to Sophia's safety—only the people he absolutely trusted without a doubt.

Cameron punched his security code into the communication unit. It was so much more than a phone, but in this case Cameron was using it for the simplest of calls. He pushed the digits to call his brother Dylan. He picked up after just two rings.

"Branson."

"Dylan, it's Cameron."

"Cam? Hey, little brother. Haven't heard from you in a while."

"I've been working. You know, the usual."

Dylan did know. He had enough background with Omega Sector that Cameron didn't need to explain further. "Are you done with that…project you were working on?" his brother asked.

"No, Dyl, I'm not. As a matter of fact the project became a great deal more complicated over the last few days. I need your help."

"What's going on, Cam?" Cameron could tell he now had Dylan's full attention.

"I came across some information today that suggests that someone within my company might also be…working for a competitor. Problem is, I'm not sure who that person in my company might be or if it is anyone at all."

Dylan paused for a moment and Cameron could tell he was processing what Cam was trying to tell him. "And you're worried for your safety?"

"No," Cameron told Dylan softly, looking at the small woman lying in his arms. "I can handle myself. But someone else has gotten involved and I don't want her to have anything to do with anybody in my company if there's a problem."

"Roger that. What do you need?"

That's what Cameron loved about his family. They had each other's backs, without needing a bunch of details. That didn't mean they wouldn't needle the details out of Cameron later—him asking Dylan to fly out a lady friend was something he was going to get ragged about pretty hard—but right now all Dylan wanted to know was how he could help.

"I'm about to send you some coordinates. It's a small unlit airstrip in northern Virginia. It's smack in the middle of the mountains. You won't believe it's there until you're right on it. I need you to take my friend back to DC and stay with her. That's it."

"Where will you be going? You staying there?"

"No. I'm heading to DC also, but I'll be getting a ride with my company. It's already planned."

"All right. What time?"

"Dusk." Cameron knew Dylan landing his airplane at the unlit airstrip after dark in terrible weather was risky. They'd be cutting it close, but this would be their best chance. "I'll be looking for you around eighteen hundred. And if mountains and oncoming darkness aren't enough of a challenge for you, the weather here is absolute crap. Pouring buckets. Hopefully it will clear out."

"Sounds like a party. Can't wait."

"Dylan, I need you to get some antibiotics. She's got an infected cut and is running a fever. I don't want her to have to go straight to the hospital when a round of antibiotics will do. She's been through a lot."

Dylan didn't ask where he was supposed to get antibiotics without a prescription. But Cameron knew his brother would have them when he arrived. "Anything else?"

"No. And, Dylan, thanks."

"You owe me one for this, bro." Dylan chuckled. "But what's new?"

They disconnected and Cameron sent the coordinates to Dylan.

Sophia was still asleep lying against him, but moaned softly and was obviously uncomfortable. Cameron decided to give her the ibuprofen to help get her fever down, then maybe she could rest a little easier. He got the small tube out of his bag—it wasn't much but hopefully would help her feel more comfortable until Dylan got there with the antibiotics. He grabbed a water bottle, too.

"Here, sweetheart," Cameron whispered as he put the

pills up against Sophia's lips. "Take these. They'll help make you feel better."

"Cam?" Sophia obviously was groggy. "What's going on?"

"This is aspirin, baby. It will help your fever go down and make you feel better."

"Okay." She opened her mouth for first the pills then the water. "Sleepy," she murmured, then almost immediately slumped back against him again. Cameron took a sip of the water himself then recapped the bottle and returned it to his backpack. He zipped it up so it would be ready to go if they had to leave in a hurry.

"That's fine, go back to sleep." Cameron couldn't blame Sophia for wanting sleep. God knew the past few days hadn't held much sleep for her—for both good reasons and bad. A few hours of rest would probably do him some good, too. Cameron felt his eyes grow heavy as he snuggled Sophia more firmly in his arms.

Chapter Sixteen

Cameron awoke suddenly. He held himself perfectly still. Something had definitely disturbed his subconscious. Had Smith's men found them? He reached over and grasped the SIG he had left lying on top of the backpack.

After a few moments he realized it wasn't a noise outside that had woken him, it was Sophia's labored breathing.

"Soph, are you awake?" He felt her forehead with his hand. She seemed much cooler than she had before they had fallen asleep, her fever much lower. But there was something definitely wrong.

"Yes," she said curtly. Cameron could feel tension bowing her body.

"What's wrong? Is it your arm? Are you sick?"

"I…I…" She couldn't seem to get the words out.

"Is it pain?" Cameron wished he had something stronger to give her. He tried to get her to look at him, but she seemed focused on the entrance to the cave, staring at it intently. "Did you hear something? See one of Smith's men?"

Sophia shook her head, but tension fairly radiated from her. She was clutching at his hands and arms, which were wrapped around her, her breath sawing in and out of her chest, the sound loud in the cave, even with the rain. "What is it, Soph? Tell me, please." Cameron didn't know what to do to help her if he couldn't figure out the problem.

"I can't breathe." She finally got the sentence out.

Cameron cursed under his breath. He had completely forgotten about Sophia's claustrophobia. Evidently she had been too sick to notice the small confines of the cave when he'd pulled them in a few hours ago, but now that she was feeling better…

Cameron immediately released her, unwrapping his arms from around her body so she could move if she needed to. She slid away from him, her eyes still focused on the small entrance to the cave.

"Soph, it's okay. C'mon, let's go back outside." There was no point in making her suffer in here even if it was still raining out there.

Sophia nodded tersely and started scooting toward the entrance. Cameron went with her in case she needed any help. They were almost to the small entrance when Cameron heard it. Some of Smith's men talking. Right outside of where he and Sophia were hidden.

If she went out now, it would mean death for both of them.

Cameron knew not to grab Sophia, but he doubted she heard the men talking over her own labored breathing. He scampered around so he was in front of Sophia and they were face-to-face. She immediately began to go around him so she could get to the entrance he blocked.

"Sophia, look at me, sweetheart." She glanced at him for just a second before her eyes darted back to the entrance. Cameron reached out and as gently as he could, careful not to restrain her in any way, put his hands on both her cheeks. "Sophia, Smith's men are right outside. If you go out there now, they're going to kill both of us."

Cameron watched, heartbroken, as Sophia's eyes darted back and forth frantically between him and the cave entrance. But at least she stopped moving toward it.

"That's right, sweetie," Cameron murmured. "Just look at me. Watch me breathing. There's plenty of air in here. Plenty. Can you feel the breeze?"

Sophia nodded hesitantly. Cameron stayed right in front of her, his face only inches from hers. "Breathe with me. In through your nose, out through your mouth."

For long minutes they stayed frozen right there doing just that. Cameron could hear Smith's men still nearby, and kept his SIG ready in his hand in case he needed it. Why were the men concentrating so hard on this area? Why hadn't they moved on? If Cameron hadn't taken the time to camouflage the entrance to the cave, the men probably would've found them already.

But at least Sophia didn't seem about to rush out there and announce their presence any longer.

"I think I'm okay," she whispered.

"You're doing great. You're amazing. Courageous." Cameron trailed his finger down Sophia's cheek.

"Yeah. It's amazing that a grown woman gets freaked out in a place that obviously has plenty of oxygen and almost gets us both killed. So courageous." She turned away, disgusted with herself.

"Hey," he said, grabbing her before she could get far. "Courage isn't about not having fears. It's about how you handle the ones you do have. You were panicked, but you got yourself under control."

Sophia shook her head and refused to look at him. "No, you don't get it. It's taking everything I've got right now not to burst through that entrance. I'm still not sure I'm going to be able to keep myself from doing it."

"Soph, look at me." He didn't think she was going to, but she finally did. "Even if you handle it one second at a time, you're still handling it. That's all anybody can ask."

Cameron could tell she still wasn't convinced. He

cupped her cheeks with his hands again. "I don't care if you can see it or not. You're still amazing." He brought his lips down to hers.

Cameron worried for just a moment that kissing her wasn't a good idea—what if this just compounded her claustrophobia? But the way she kissed him back eliminated those fears quickly.

When they broke apart Sophia's features were a little less pinched. She still constantly glanced over at the entrance, but didn't seem quite so much as if she was going to bolt for it at any moment.

"I wasn't always claustrophobic, you know," Sophia whispered. "Just since the car accident."

"What accident? Did someone hit you? Was it bad?"

Her eyes darted to him briefly. "Yeah, it was pretty bad." Cameron could see tension heightening in her again. He was about to change the subject when she spoke again. "But no, nobody hit me. I was driving alone—too fast—and I was upset. It was raining and I took a curve too hard and went over an embankment."

That was much worse than Cameron had thought. "That sounds pretty awful. How badly were you hurt?"

Sophia didn't say anything for a while then started wiggling around. Cameron realized she was trying to take off her sweatshirt, although he had no idea why. He helped her slip it off. "Thanks," she told him. "Being cold actually helps me to feel like there's more air. Totally a mental thing, but…" She shrugged. "As for injuries…broke my femur, a couple of ribs, pretty heavy concussion."

Cameron's breath whistled out through his teeth. He'd had no idea. They sat in silence for a few moments before she continued. "When my car went over the embankment it rolled over multiple times." Sophia swallowed hard. "It finally stopped when it hit a tree. It completely crushed in the passenger side of the front seat, and I was trapped. Fortunately, another car saw me go over and called 911, but it took them a while to get the emergency vehicles there. I was hard to get to."

Cameron could see Sophia doing a breathing exercise as she told her story—in through her nose, out through her mouth. "I was trapped there about two hours—although believe me when I say it felt much longer. The car had crushed around me, and I was pretty sure I was going to die. I kept hyperventilating and passed out a couple times, which was a blessing, until I woke back up to that enclosed space."

Cameron understood now why she had panicked waking up in the cave—too much like waking up in that car. "I'm so sorry, Soph." He'd come so close to losing her. Cameron had to touch her; he couldn't help himself. He put his arm around and scooted as close to her as possible, relieved when she didn't move away. He put his face against her neck and breathed in her scent.

He'd almost lost her, and he'd never even known.

Sophia leaned in closer to him. "Physical injuries were pretty bad—I was in the hospital for about a week. It was a long recovery, lots of PT. But I found the mental issues, this overwhelming claustrophobia, to be ongoing. I've been seeing a therapist once a week for almost five years. You'd think I'd have made more progress, right?" Sophia smiled ruefully.

Cameron felt as if he had been punched in the gut. She'd been seeing a therapist for *five years*? He thought the accident had happened recently. If she had been in therapy for five years then…

"Soph, when did the accident happen?"

Cameron could feel Sophia's attempt to huddle into herself. Silence, except for the rain and an occasional sound from one of Smith's men, surrounded them. Cameron thought maybe she wasn't going to answer—which was an answer in and of itself.

"The day after you left," she finally whispered.

Cameron struggled to keep himself under control. He wanted to punch the nearest wall or howl in some primitive rage. It wasn't hard to put two and two together. Sophia had been upset because he had left and then she had been in a life-threatening accident. Cameron moved away from Sophia, trying to process it all and his obvious blame in it. Cameron couldn't seem to figure out how to form words. What could he say anyway?

"Soph, I'm so sorry. How can you not hate me?"

Sophia reached over and grabbed his hand. "It wasn't your fault, Cam. Just a really poor set of circumstances—bad weather, bad emotional state, bad road to be driving on. Bad luck all the way around."

Cameron shook his head. Maybe Sophia had come to that point, but he couldn't—not yet anyway. He thought of after the accident; Sophia had no family, no one to help take care of her. And he hadn't been around, had actually made sure he was completely unreachable, when she needed him most. Had she tried to contact him? Even if she had wanted to, he had left her no information whatsoever.

"Soph, I'm so sorry," he repeated. Although how could words ever make up for what had happened? He couldn't believe Sophia was willing to even sit here holding his hand. Willing to be with him in any shape or fashion after what had happened.

Sophia turned more fully toward him. Cameron found he couldn't quite meet her eyes. "Cameron Branson, look at me," she told him and he did, reluctantly. There was no trace of claustrophobic panic in her features now. Just gritty determination. "What happened, happened. The accident was not your fault."

"But—" Cameron began. Sophia put her hand over his mouth.

"No 'buts,'" she said, and, miracle of all miracles, actually smiled. "I'll admit, I was mad for a while—at you, at circumstances, at life in general. But I became stronger because of it all." She gestured around the cave. "And yeah, I still struggle with claustrophobia, probably always will. But I'm learning how to work through each situation one at a time. It's like someone once told me, 'Courage isn't about not having fears. It's about how you handle the ones you do have.'"

Even with Sophia parroting his words back to him, Cameron was going to need more time to process all this. And they were definitely going to need to talk about it more. Sophia had had five years to come to peace with it, but it was a new and gut-wrenching blow to Cameron. But one thing was becoming more and more clear to him: when this op was complete, things were definitely not going to be over between he and Sophia. He wasn't sure he was ever going to have the strength to walk away from her again.

He just prayed, after everything that had happened, he could talk her into allowing him into her life permanently. Because he didn't think he could live without her.

He looked at Sophia more closely. Her face had lost the tension. Her breaths were slow and easy. "You seem to be doing okay right now."

"It's like my therapist says—sometimes it's just about refocusing. In the middle of a panic attack that can be difficult to do." She shrugged and smiled. "But I'm learning."

Cameron couldn't help it. He reached over and kissed her again. He didn't care about Smith's men outside or the rain or their dire situation. He just had to have Sophia in his arms right damn now. When they broke apart they were both breathing hard.

"Now, that's what I call refocusing." Her eyes all but sparkled. "I'll have to remember this next time I'm having issues."

Cameron pulled Sophia closer to him, loving the way she snuggled into his side. Her breathing was calm and even now. They both watched the entrance of the cave, but not with any panic.

Every once in a while they could hear one of Smith's men talking. Cameron grimaced. They were still around here. Why? Passing through in an effort to search for them—sure. But they seemed to be spending more time here than would be expected. And yet they couldn't actually seem to find him and Sophia.

"Why are they still here?" Sophia evidently had the same thoughts as Cameron.

"I don't know. Maybe we left more of a trail than I thought." Cameron shrugged, trying to figure it out. "I covered the entrance pretty well, so unless they get right up to the overhang, they won't see it. I hope." He made sure his SIG was right beside him. It wouldn't do them a whole lot of good, especially if they weren't trying to take him and Sophia in alive, but it was better than nothing.

"Maybe they'll start looking for us somewhere else soon."

Cameron nodded. "I hope so. Getting to the landing strip in this weather will be hard enough without having Smith's men standing right on top of us."

"How long before we need to leave?"

"Pretty soon. It's going to take us at least another couple of hours to get to the landing strip. My brother Dylan is coming with his plane to get you. I talked to him while you were asleep."

"Where is he taking us?"

"He's going to take you back to DC. But I'm not going with you. I have to get Ghost Shell to Omega Sector HQ."

"Oh." Sophia's voice was small. "I guess that will be it, then."

"You mean for us?"

Cameron could barely make out Sophia's slight nod in the dimness of the cave. But he could definitely feel her easing away from him. He reached his arm around her and snatched her back to his side.

"As soon as I get Ghost Shell settled and am debriefed you can expect me to show up at your doorstep. Don't doubt that."

There was silence for long moments. "I want that, too, Cam, so much." A huge *but* hung in the air between them. Sophia definitely had more to say and Cameron was pretty sure he didn't want to hear it. Finally it came. "But I'm not sure our worlds blend. I'm not sure that we're right for each other."

Cameron had been right. He definitely didn't want to hear this. Panic began to bubble up within him. "Soph…" He turned to her so he could look her in the eyes. "I know I hurt you before. I left and then the accident… I can never make up for not being there for you."

"But that's not really it, Cam." Sophia made eye contact, then looked away. "I don't expect you to make up for the past. The accident wasn't your fault and even leaving wasn't something you did to deliberately hurt me. The past is done, and we both have to move on. I'm talking about *now*."

"Sophia…"

"Your world is dark," she continued without letting him speak. "Your life—what you've chosen to do as an under-cover agent—is so important and admirable. But it scares me, Cam." She gestured around the cave. "All of this scares the hell out of me. The girlfriend of an undercover agent needs to be braver than me, more capable than me."

There were so many things Cameron wanted to say in response to that, he hardly knew where to begin. He barely refrained from rolling his eyes. "Are you kidding me? Sophia, you have been thrown into a situation here that is impossible. And without any training you've stepped up and done as well or better than many agents I've known."

He grasped her chin to force her to look at him. "So I don't want to hear you talking any more junk like that. There is not one instance in this entire situation that I've regretted your actions. Except for maybe when you came back for me that first night. That was stupid. But so, so brave." He punctuated the sentence with light kisses on her lips. "And besides, I'm not asking you to become my undercover partner. I just want to be with you."

Sophia gave him the sweetest, softest smile. Cameron could feel his heart squeezing in his chest. *That* smile. That was the one he wanted to wake up to every day for the rest of his life.

His own thought startled him. But then he realized the thought was exactly right: he didn't want to spend another day without Sophia.

"What?" she asked. "Did you hear something? You got a panicked look for a second."

Cameron smiled and kissed Sophia again. "Nope, no panic. Just reality shifting to the way it should be."

"I don't understand." Confusion was clear in Sophia's green eyes as she gazed up at him.

"I know." He smiled. "Just don't kick me out when I show up on your doorstep in a couple of days, okay?"

"Deal." Sophia sighed and snuggled in toward him a bit. "Can we rest for a little longer? I'm still pretty tired for some reason."

"For some reason?" Cameron reached over and smoothed a lock of hair on her forehead. "Your body has been battling through life-or-death situations for the past three days. You've hardly had any rest." He grinned down at her. "Part of that is my fault, I'll admit. Plus you have some sort of infection. How are you feeling?"

"Better. Much better than when we were running."

"Yeah, you were running a fever. The ibuprofen brought it down." Cameron got the remaining pills out of the bag. "Here, take these. We're going to have to head out in just a little bit, in order to meet my brother on time."

"Okay. My arm is pretty stiff. I don't think I'm going to be able to run very fast."

Stiffness wasn't good; it meant the infection was more pronounced than Cameron had thought. "It's okay. We'll make it. Dylan is bringing a dose of antibiotics so we can get that into you as soon as you're on the plane."

"I wish you were coming with us."

"Me, too. But it's better this way."

Cameron prayed he was telling the truth.

Chapter Seventeen

Everything in Sophia's body hurt, but her heart felt light. They were about to make it out of this nightmare. She wasn't in Smith's clutches anymore. She didn't have to make up lies and pray they were the right ones and wouldn't cost her and Cameron their lives. And, come tomorrow, she wouldn't have to wear the clothes that creep picked out for her. For some reason that weirded her out most of all and she wanted out of these clothes Smith had chosen for her as soon as possible.

And speaking of being out of her clothes… Cameron. Sophia felt a little like a giggly schoolgirl. *Cameron Branson* wanted to go steady with her. He was so dreamy. A little chuckle slid out from where she was perched against Cam, trying to rest.

"What?" he asked. She heard the amusement in his voice.

"Nothing." There was no way in hell she was telling him her thoughts.

Sophia had never been able to forget Cameron. She didn't dwell on the past, but he had never been far from her thoughts. She had always imagined they would meet again, but definitely not under these conditions. This entire situation was surreal.

But Cameron wanted them to spend time together when

everything wasn't crazy. Sophia thought back to all those talks they'd had together at the diner before he had joined Omega Sector. Those times together hadn't been sexual—although there had certainly been a sexual undercurrent—but they had been special. Important. She looked forward to having times like that again.

And knowing Cameron wanted them also made it all even more special.

Sophia could've gladly stayed in the cave all day under different circumstances, listening to the rain, snuggling up against Cameron. Her therapist had definitely been right about the refocusing exercises because nothing about the enclosed nature of the cave was bothering her now.

It seemed like just a moment later when Cameron nudged her. "Are you ready to go?"

Sophia nodded and began to put the sweatshirt back on. It was still wet and not very comfortable, but at least it would provide a layer of protection against the rain. "Yep. Are they still out there?"

"I haven't heard anything for a while, but that doesn't necessarily mean they're gone. We're going to have to be as quiet as possible."

They made their way to the edge of the overhang. Cameron gently moved the branches he had used to camouflage the entrance. Motioning her to stay where she was, he headed out of the cave, gun in hand.

Sophia waited, mentally preparing herself to run if needed. Cameron came back a few minutes later.

"I didn't see them. Hopefully they're gone. But try to stay right behind me and be as quiet as possible just in case."

Sophia nodded and made her way out of the cave. The rain still came down in a steady drizzle. She followed along behind Cameron as silently as she was able, but every step they made seemed terribly loud to her.

"We've got about four miles to go and just a little over an hour's time to get there," Cameron told her a few minutes later. "We'll need to pick up the pace. If those guys are anywhere around the airstrip when my brother is landing, he'll be a sitting duck."

"Is Omega Sector coming to the airstrip, also?"

"No, they'll get me out via helicopter. There's a number of places they can do that. I'll establish a place with them soon."

They began a light jog, much less quickly than their run earlier, but it didn't take long for every step to cause a jarring pain in Sophia's arm. And the rain didn't help; it just made her totally miserable. She grimaced but didn't say anything to Cameron. What could he do? She'd have to gut it out until she got on the plane. She could do that.

Thirty minutes later keeping that promise to herself was becoming more difficult, but still she tried. She was relieved when he called for them to slow back down to a walk.

"Hey, you okay?" Concern was written all over Cameron's face. He walked over to her and rubbed his hands gently up and down her arms. Sophia leaned forward until the top of her head rested against his chest. She just needed a break. Just a couple of minutes.

"I'm okay. It's just…" Sophia trailed off. She didn't have to say it.

"I know, sweetheart. You're doing great." Sophia all but snorted from against his chest. "Seriously. It's less than two miles. Let's keep going at a walk."

Walking she could do. More than that? She just didn't know.

"Okay."

Cameron slid Sophia's hand through the crook of his elbow and they began again. He kept his other hand around hers. She must really look like hell if he was keeping this close to her. It definitely wasn't the most stealthy way to travel. She knew he was afraid she would fall flat on her face again.

Sophia could admit she was afraid of the same thing.

Cameron let Sophia set the pace and she moved as quickly as she could. Every step was agony.

They both heard it at the same time. A small propeller plane. Circling not far overhead.

"That's Dylan. Damn it."

"How far are we from the landing strip?"

"Less than a mile. But if any of Smith's goons are in the area, they're going to hear him, too."

Sophia took a deep breath. "Let's move faster. I'll be okay."

Cameron reached over and kissed her hard and quickly. His hands framed her face. "You are amazing."

Sophia tried to smile, but couldn't quite succeed. "Tell me something I don't know. Now quit flirting and let's go."

Cameron took Sophia's uninjured arm and wrapped it around his shoulders. He put his other arm around her waist, anchoring her to his side. He took off at a brisk run, not nearly as fast as he could go, Sophia was sure, but fast enough to take her breath away. She focused all her energy into putting one foot in front on the other and not slowing Cameron down. She'd never forgive herself if something happened to Cameron's brother because of her.

Sophia wasn't prepared for Cameron's sudden stop a few minutes later before they even got to the landing field. She would've fallen to the ground hard if he hadn't had such a tight hold on her. He wrapped his arms around her and swung them both behind a tree and slid to the ground.

"What's happening?" Sophia asked between breaths.

"I saw one of Smith's goons." He shook his head with a grimace and Sophia knew something beyond just seeing one of the men was troubling him.

"What? Is he blocking our path?"

"No. That's just it. He's heading back toward *us*, not the airfield."

"That's bad."

"Yeah, it's bad. Plus, it doesn't make any sense. If he's that close, he should've heard Dylan's plane, too. I have no idea why he isn't trying to intercept Dylan."

"Maybe he has other orders or something."

"Maybe." But Cameron shook his head again.

"Can we go around him?"

"We'll have to. Stay close behind me. But we have to move fast. If the other men know Dylan is here, they'll be headed toward him."

They moved as fast as they could and were both careful to be silent. Sophia could tell when Cameron would spot the man, flinging them both to the ground or behind some sort of forest cover. With every bounce her arm throbbed.

Backing around one of the trees, Cameron cursed under his breath. "We can't catch a break. It's like he knows where we are."

"Could he be tracking us?" Sophia didn't know what sort of equipment DS-13 had, but the ability to track them seemed feasible.

"I thought of that, but if so, they should've found us at the cave. I don't know."

Cameron reached into his backpack and pulled out the communication unit thingy. He punched in digits while dragging himself and Sophia lower onto the ground.

"You landed?" he asked without greeting.

Sophia couldn't hear what was being said on the other end.

"Good. Anybody around?"

More talk from the other end.

"New plan. We've got a tail I can't shake. I'm going to get her to the end of the field and let her run to you. I'll lead whoever's attention I can get off in the other direction."

Sophia caught the word *stupid* from Cameron's brother.

"Yeah, I know. Just get her out. I'll take care of myself."

Cameron hit a button and threw the phone back into his bag. "Are you ready? We're going to make a run for it."

"Um, I was right here. Don't you mean *I'm* going to make a run for it and you're going to get yourself killed?"

"Soph, I'll be fine."

Sophia shook her head. "Didn't I just hear your brother call this plan stupid?"

Cameron grinned and winked at her. "Actually, he was calling me stupid in general, not the plan. We've got to go, baby."

"There has to be another way." Sophia would not allow Cameron to sacrifice himself for her.

"Sophia, listen. I promise I will be fine. Once I get you on the plane, I will be a ninja—fast, silent, stealthy. They won't catch me."

Sophia knew she was slowing him down. If he had to fight or make a real run for it, he'd be much better off without having her to worry about. But she still didn't like it.

"Promise?" His face was right next to hers and she took the opportunity to kiss him briefly.

"Absolutely. Ninja pinkie-swear."

She would've chuckled if she wasn't so scared. "Okay, let's go."

He led her the rest of the way to the airfield as quickly

as possible, continuing the darting between trees and zig-zagging. Sophia only once caught a glimpse of the man who was following them, but he was very definitely only a couple hundred yards away.

Sophia saw the small airplane at the end of the runway. Cameron's brother had obviously tried to make the plane as inconspicuous as he could, but that was nearly impossible.

"Okay, you need to make your way down the tree line to the end of the runway. Don't cut over to the plane until you have as much of a direct route as possible. Use the tree cover to your advantage. Do what we've been doing—darting back and forth between trees."

Sophia's head nodded like a bobblehead doll. "Okay. What will you be doing?"

"I'll make sure I have our tail's attention and head the other way."

"I still don't like this plan."

"You'll be fine."

"It's not me I'm worried about!" Sophia barely remembered to keep her voice to a whisper. "I'm the one about to get on a safe, dry plane."

"I'll be fine. Ninja, remember? I'll be catching a ride with Omega in just a few minutes and will see you in a couple of days." Something caught Cameron's attention in the distance. "But I need you to go *now*. And I need you to keep going no matter what you think you hear or see."

Now Sophia was really scared. But she had to trust that Cameron knew what he was doing. Her head nodded again, but she couldn't force any words through her clogged throat. Cameron took her gently by the shoulders and turned her around then gave her a gentle push toward the plane. Sophia began to run as fast as she could. She pushed past the agony in her arm and the weariness. She knew that the faster she made it to that plane, the sooner Cameron would start thinking about himself and get safely picked up by Omega Sector.

Sophia darted from tree to tree as Cameron had told her. She never saw anyone, but didn't let that change her plan. When she got to the point that the plane was directly perpendicular from her she dashed out of the trees. She wasn't out of the tree line for five seconds before the propellers on the plane started. But not before she heard the *pop* of gunfire. Sophia wanted to stop and look, but didn't. Had Cameron fired or had he been fired at? Sophia had no idea. She ran faster.

The door that became stairs to the plane was lowered and waiting for Sophia. By the time she got there—gasping for air—a man looking remarkably like Cameron, but a little older, was standing at the top. He helped her as she made her way up the stairs and onto the plane. Quickly, he secured the door and showed Sophia where to sit—right next to him in the cockpit—which was open to the rest of the small plane.

Immediately he eased the plane forward and they began to gain the speed needed for takeoff. Sophia scanned frantically through the windshield, looking for Cameron, but found nothing. She told herself not seeing him was a good sign—much better than seeing him lying wounded, or worse, on the ground—but it didn't ease her mind. As the plane pulled into the air, Sophia continued to look but never saw him. She told herself she should be thankful that at least the plane was away safely. Cameron had a much better chance on his own. But she couldn't quite make herself agree.

Cameron's brother took a pair of corded headphones and handed them to Sophia. She was so exhausted and in so much pain that she could barely understand his gesture for her to put them on.

"Hi. I'm Dylan, Cameron's older and much more handsome brother. So you're the gal who has stolen my little brother's heart…"

Chapter Eighteen

Cameron was willing to consider that perhaps this plan was pretty stupid after all. Or at least it seemed that way as a bullet flew past his head and into a tree just beyond him. He dived to the ground and crawled backward so he could return fire if needed.

At least Dylan had gotten Sophia away in the plane. No matter what happened now—honestly, even if he was captured or killed by Smith's men—Cameron wouldn't be sorry. Knowing Sophia was safe made all the difference. Of course he had no intention of getting captured or killed.

Ninja, baby.

He had made sure he was able to be seen as Sophia was making her way to the plane, pretty much making himself an open target as he saw her streak out of the tree line in a dead run. He was just glad Smith's henchmen had taken the bait and gone after him. Until he'd almost gotten shot in the head. Then he hadn't been so glad. As soon as he saw the plane beginning its trip down the runway, Cameron had dashed for the cover of the woods. For a minute Smith's men seemed undecided about what to do, go after Cameron or the plane—which told Cameron that Smith wanted them taken alive. The men's indecision had given both Cameron and Sophia the chance to get away without injury.

Cameron peeked his head out from where he was taking cover behind a tree for a split second before pulling it back. Sure enough, a moment later the area around him was riddled with bullets. There were definitely two people trying to pin him down, possibly even three. He had a good idea where one of them was and crawled a few feet away to take cover behind a different tree. Then he came around from the opposite side and fired three shots. A howl of pain reassured him that he had hit his target.

One down. But he knew there were at least two more still out there.

It was time to set up the extraction with Omega. He had to get Ghost Shell far away from DS-13 hands. Cam got as low as he could and belly-crawled for hundreds of feet to put more distance between himself and the shooters after him. It felt like old army ranger times. He pulled out his sat-com device, but could not risk the noise of a voice call. An electronic message was less secure, but his only option in this case.

Cameron punched in his identification code and the code to send a message directly to his boss, Dennis Burgamy. The man was a jackass, and he and Cameron—hell, Burgamy and *any* of the Branson family—rarely got along, but he could get things done and that's what Cameron needed right now.

Situation changed. Imminent danger. Request immediate extraction.

Cameron didn't say it would only be him. He'd deal with that after he figured out if there was a mole or not. After a few moments Cameron received his reply.

Affirmative. ETA 17 minutes.

Burgamy provided a location based on the coordinates of Cameron's sat-com's GPS. Not far, but under fire it would take the entire seventeen minutes to get there.

Warning: hostiles present. May be coming in under fire.

Cameron put the sat-com back in his bag and began crawling forward. It was slow progress, but hopefully it meant he had lost his hunters. Cameron reached the small open area where the helicopter would land just moments before it did. As it lowered to the ground, Cameron could see the agents inside ready to lay down cover fire so he could get in. Cameron took off in a sprint to the helo. It left the ground just seconds after he was on board. No shots came from the woods behind him. Cameron was both relieved and confused.

Cameron sat back on the bench and put on the headset as the helicopter took off. One of the agents who had been standing guard in the doorway of the helicopter with his automatic weapon sat across from him.

"Thought there was going to be two of you."

"Change of plans," Cameron told the Omega agent. "Had to get her out another way."

The man just shrugged. "Thought you said you'd be coming in hot, too." The man looked more upset about that than not having the second person on board.

Cameron didn't know why Smith's men hadn't fired at him. As a matter of fact, he wasn't sure they had even still been following him by the time he had made it to the opening. Cameron hadn't seen anyone since he'd wounded whoever he'd hit before sending the message.

But why would they have stopped following him? That didn't make sense. Had they stopped to help the wounded man? Maybe. Something about all of this was strange. But

Cameron was out, had Ghost Shell in his possession, and although he wouldn't be able to use it with DS-13 again, his cover as Cam Cameron wasn't blown. They thought he was a thief and bastard, but definitely didn't think he was an agent. All in all, not a bad day.

DYLAN BRANSON WAS as charming as his brother Cameron, but in a quieter fashion. He had a silent confidence; definitely not chatty, but not unfriendly, either. They had been in the air for about twenty minutes when Dylan reached back to his bag and pulled out a syringe kit.

"Amoxicillin. A shot in the arm or leg," Dylan said. "Cameron said you needed it for an infected cut. And if you don't mind me saying, you look pretty bad."

Sophia felt pretty bad. The fever was definitely back. She took the syringe and injected it in herself without qualm. An injection was definitely the best way to get the antibiotics into her system quickly.

"There's some aspirin or something in my bag, too. For your pain," Dylan told her. Sophia took three and swallowed them with a bottle of water he found in the bag.

She leaned over to the side of her seat. She was so exhausted. "I'm just going to rest my eyes for a few minutes," Sophia told Dylan. She knew it was rude, but couldn't seem to help herself.

"That's no problem at all," Dylan reassured her. "Rest is probably the best thing for you. It will take us a couple of hours to get there."

He might have said something else, too, but Sophia had no idea what. Her eyes had already drooped shut.

She woke with a start to Dylan's hand gently shaking her elbow. It took her a moment to remember where she was and who she was with, but all in all she felt much better. Or at least less as if she was about to keel over and die any moment.

"Sophia, it's Dylan." He was talking very slowly as if he was dealing with someone with an impairment, which probably wasn't far from the truth. "I've let you sleep as long as you could, but you've got to get up now."

"Are we there already?" It all came rushing back to her. "Did you hear anything from Cameron? Did he make it out?" It was pitch-dark out now. Surely Omega Sector would've already gotten Cameron out by now.

Dylan smiled. "Yes, I got a message from Omega. Cameron made it out, no problem."

Sophia sagged with relief. He had made it. She knew he had promised he would, but when she had heard that shot as she had run to the plane... Thank God Cameron was safe.

"Do you work for Omega, too?" she asked Dylan.

It was like watching a machine turn all the way off, the way Dylan's features completely closed down. "I used to. Not anymore." This topic was obviously not open for conversation.

Sophia was desperate to change the subject. "How long have I been asleep?"

Dylan chuckled and his features relaxed. "Well, the entire two-hour flight, plus landing, plus a couple hours while I did my postflight checklist, talked to a few buddies who work here and even supervised the refueling for my flight tomorrow."

She'd slept through all that? Holy cow. "Sorry." Sophia felt her cheeks burning.

"Think nothing of it. You needed the sleep. If I had any other business to do here, I'd do it. But this is a tiny county airport and there's not much happening around here after dark. And I didn't think you'd like to wake up and find yourself in some strange plane and hangar with nobody around for miles, or believe me, I would've let you sleep as long as you liked."

"Uh, no, I probably wouldn't. Good thinking on your part. I'd like to get back to my own bed."

"I've got my truck around the back of the main hangar. Let's get you home."

Dylan helped Sophia out of the plane and they walked toward the main hangar. As Dylan had told her, there was no one else around, just the two of them. Which, when Sophia caught the reflection of herself in a window and saw how horrible she looked—as she had run down a mountain in the rain and slept in a cave—was probably for the best. She'd hate for anyone else to see her like this.

They stopped to grab a soda and some crackers out of the vending machine in the hangar, all her traumatized stomach could handle. Dylan excused himself to go check on something about his flight tomorrow in one of the small offices and Sophia sat down at the table to consume her meal.

The door at the back of the hangar opened and closed quietly a few moments later. Sophia looked over in the direction of the door but couldn't see anything in the darkness.

"Hello?" she called out. Had Dylan gone over that way and she hadn't realized it?

Nobody responded. But Sophia sensed someone else in the hangar with her. Someone who worked there?

Sophia stood up. She'd go to the office and find Dylan. If this turned out to be nothing then they could just laugh about her traumatized nerves.

"No need for you to get up on our account, Ms. Reardon."

Oh, hell, it was Smith.

Sophia ran. Maybe they didn't know Dylan was in the

office and she could lead them away. She bolted for the door, but one of Smith's men—Rick—caught her. He threw her against the door hard.

"Now, Sophia, why are you running?" Smith was grinning wickedly as he walked toward her. She could see Fin and Marco with him. Marco was wearing some sort of sling on his arm. "I thought we were friends."

"How did you find me?"

Smith's laughter was far from reassuring. "Now, that happens to be a funny story."

Smith walked all the way up to Sophia until he was standing just inches from her. Sophia tried to back up but Rick was right behind her. Smith reached up and touched her neck. Sophia flinched and tried to move to the side, but Rick wouldn't let her. Smith's hand continued its trail to the side of her neck, then her nape, then finally reaching down inside her shirt's collar. Sophia shuddered at Smith's touch, struggling to keep down the crackers she had just eaten. Smith flipped up her collar. He brought his hand back out and held it in front of her face.

Some sort of tracking device. Damn it.

"So this—" Smith waved the tracker right in front of her "—was supposed to keep me apprised of everywhere you went. After I had a visit from a very trusted source who assured me that everything you were telling me about Ghost Shell was untrue, I decided I better keep close tabs on you. And since I was providing your clothes, this seemed like the easiest way, yes?"

Sophia tried to shy away from Smith again, but he moved closer.

"But, and here's the funny part, it seems that when it gets wet, this little tracking device doesn't work correctly. Quite the defect. So when you were running all over the mountain in the rain, this thing would provide only intermittent, imprecise signals. Not terribly useful. And very frustrating for poor Marco here, who got shot by your boyfriend in the midst of this fracas."

Better Marco than Cameron. But Sophia kept her thoughts to herself.

Smith continued with a flourish, "Once you were on the plane and your clothes eventually dried, the tracking device began working perfectly again. So here we are."

Sophia racked her brain for a way out of this. She wanted to protect Dylan, who she knew would be reappearing any moment. But she also knew what Smith wanted: Ghost Shell. And she didn't have it. And honestly couldn't even tell Smith where it was, even if she wanted to. It was at Omega headquarters and she had no idea where that was.

Sophia didn't see any way that she was getting out of this alive, but she didn't see why she would need to take the brother of the man she loved down with her.

"Well, I guess you found me. Congratulations."

Smith finally backed away from her the slightest bit. "Let's just make this easy for all of us, my dear. All I want is Ghost Shell. No need for drama."

Sophia rolled her eyes, not even trying to hide it. She had no doubt whether she gave Ghost Shell over to Smith or not, he was still going to have her killed. "Unfortunately, there's going to have to be a little drama, Smith. I don't have Ghost Shell. Cam does. And I have no idea where he is."

Sophia didn't see the blow coming, but Smith's slap nearly knocked her to the ground. She could taste blood where her teeth cut against her cheek.

"I really don't have time to play games, Sophia. I believe you when you say Cam has Ghost Shell. What I don't believe is that you don't know where he is."

"I'm sorry, but that's true. It seems that the bastard has double-crossed both of us. We split up to get away from you, but were supposed to meet here hours ago. Why else do you think I'd still be here at this tiny little airport?"

She could see that gave Smith pause. But then he shook his head. "I think not. I saw the way Cam looked at you at the party. There is no way he abandoned you. Not even for all the money he could make doing so."

She looked over to see Fin nodding in agreement. Damn. She needed to think of a way to steer them out of the building before Dylan returned.

But she was too late. Dylan stepped out of the shadows. She could see his training—so similar to Cameron's—as he took out Fin with two short punches and an elbow to the chin. Fin dropped to the ground before Smith or his men could even figure out what was happening. Dylan had Fin's gun in his hand and was pointing it at Smith in the blink of an eye.

Marco and Rick both drew their weapons and pointed them at Dylan. But Smith only laughed. He pulled out his own gun, but instead of pointing it at Dylan, he stepped behind Sophia and pointed the gun directly at her temple.

"Oh, just look at this." Smith laughed gleefully. "You just have to be Cam's brother. You two look exactly the same. Exactly the same."

"Yeah, that's right, he's my brother. Why don't we all just put our guns down. Everyone can walk out of here without any injury." Dylan nudged Fin with his toe. "Except maybe this guy here."

"I don't think so." Smith grabbed Sophia's arm to hold her more closely in front of him. The movement jarred her shoulder and she let out a moan before she could help herself. "Oh, I'm sorry, my dear. Is that the hurt shoulder Fin told me about?" Smith turned to look at Dylan. "I'm going to need you to put your gun down." Smith grabbed Sophia's shoulder and dug into it with his fingers. Her screams echoed through the whole hangar. She struggled not to lose consciousness.

"Okay, stop," Dylan told Smith. "Here." He laid the gun on the ground and kicked it over to Smith.

"Unfortunately, your brother has something that belongs to me. I need to get that back." Smith motioned to Rick, who walked over to stand in front of Dylan. At this point Fin was dragging himself off the ground, too. "Bring him outside."

Sophia saw Rick hit Dylan in the face and then the stomach. As Dylan was doubled over, Fin brought his knee up into his face, knocking him all the way backward. Smith grabbed her arm and began marching her toward the door.

"Please, Mr. Smith." Sophia was crying now. "I swear I don't know where Cam is. I would tell you."

Smith walked Sophia all the way to his car. She watched as Fin and Rick dragged Dylan outside, taking shots at him when they could.

"Oh, I believe you," Smith told Sophia. "But if that's his brother, he knows where Cam is, or at least how to get in touch with him."

Fin and Rick dumped Dylan's nearly unconscious form at Smith's feet. Smith squatted down so he could get closer to Dylan. "Tell your brother he has until midnight tonight to bring Ghost Shell to me at the warehouse from the last weapons buy. He'll know where that is. Tell him we start cutting her into pieces at midnight."

Sophia sucked in her breath as both Rick and Smith chuckled. There was no way Cameron would be able to get Ghost Shell to that warehouse. Even if he decided her life was worth the trade—which he wouldn't—Cameron wouldn't even have Ghost Shell anymore after giving it to Omega. Plus, it looked as if Dylan was barely breathing. How in the world was he supposed to get to Cameron? A whimper escaped Sophia.

Sophia was so worried about Dylan lying bleeding in the parking lot that she barely noticed Smith's slight nod to Rick and didn't pay much attention to Rick when he came and stood right in front of her. She finally looked up at him just as his meaty fist hit her in the jaw.

Sophia felt everything go black around her, as she sank unconscious to the ground.

Chapter Nineteen

"All I'm saying is that it would've been better if you had brought in Ms. Reardon, too, so she could be debriefed," Cameron's boss, Dennis Burgamy, argued. Again. In his whiny, nasally tone.

"She will be, in a couple of days. She has a wound that needs treating, and then I'll bring her in." Cameron wasn't about to say anything regarding the suspected mole at Omega. Not with this many people in the room.

Exhaustion and coffee flowed through Cameron's veins. Since his arrival at Omega Sector hours ago, he'd been talking, reporting, debriefing nonstop. Dennis Burgamy was thrilled to get his grubby paws on Ghost Shell. Cameron knew the man would be on conference calls either tonight or first thing in the morning, if he didn't send out a sector-wide email, somehow taking credit for the whole thing, first. What a kiss-up.

But Cameron's real problem was that he hadn't been able to get in touch with Dylan. He hadn't expected to communicate with him while he was en route, but they should've been on the ground now for a while. Cameron told himself there was no need to panic. Dylan and Sophia hadn't been out of pocket for that long, and a number of things could've caused the lack of check-in. Cameron had been without a good sleep for a long time, and under a constant level of high stress since Sophia had walked into that warehouse a few days ago, not to mention the headache he'd carried around pretty constantly since he'd had her clock him. He needed to take all these parts of the equation into consideration and not just assume the worse.

"We have medics here who can treat wounds, Branson." It was Burgamy again, but damned if Cameron could remember what they were talking about. He stared at his boss blankly. "For Ms. Reardon's wound?" Burgamy continued.

Oh. Cameron willed his exhausted brain to form a pithy response, but nothing. He just sat there staring at his boss.

"Okay, everybody out of the pool. Party's over, kiddies."

It was Sawyer. Oh, thank God. Cameron had never been so thankful to see his charismatic little brother. Sawyer patted Cameron on the shoulder and gave him a friendly wink, then proceeded to herd everyone else out of the debriefing room, including Burgamy. Cameron sat down wearily in the chair behind the table, watching his brother work his magic. Sawyer spoke to everyone jovially, slapping backs and cracking a couple of jokes. People almost always did what Sawyer asked them to do, and with a smile on their faces.

Cameron shrugged as his brother led the last person out, asking the woman about her child by name. Cameron had worked here just as long as Sawyer, but didn't even know the woman had a child, much less the kid's name. Sawyer had a way with people Cameron just didn't have. Hell, hardly anybody had it.

"You're a popular guy," Sawyer said to Cameron as he closed the door behind the woman who had just left.

"No kidding." Cameron leaned his head all the way back in his seat and closed his eyes, stretching his long legs out under the table.

"I just heard you were back or I would've been here sooner. So, mission accomplished?"

Cameron shrugged. "Not the way I had hoped it would go down. Smith and DS-13 are still fully active, which pisses me off to no end after what Smith did to Jason. But yeah, I recovered Ghost Shell, so I guess Burgamy considers that a win."

"And this girl I keep hearing about?" Sawyer came to sit down on the other side of the desk. If there was one thing Cameron could count on it was that Sawyer would definitely be interested if a woman was involved.

"Sophia Reardon." Cameron peeked out at Sawyer through one eye.

"*The* Sophia Reardon? The one you have categorically refused to talk about for the last five years?"

Cameron closed his eyes again. "Shut up, Sawyer."

Sawyer chuckled. "So where is she?"

Cameron opened his eyes and sat up straighter in the chair. "She's with Dylan. I had him come get her and fly her out separately." Now he had Sawyer's full attention. "I didn't mention this in the debriefing, but I think we have a mole in Omega." Cameron explained the meeting with Agent McNeil and what had put him on guard.

"Holy hell, Cam. If that's true, we've got a really big problem here."

Cameron nodded. A really big problem indeed. "So Dylan's going to take her home and keep an eye on her until I can get there." Cameron looked down at his phone again. Still no message from either Dylan or Sophia. "He should've touched base by now. I don't know what his malfunction is."

The door to the interview room burst open, startling both men. A young man whom Cameron recognized, but whose name he didn't know, was breathing hard, having obviously run from somewhere.

"Um, Agent Branson. You're needed downstairs in the lobby. Like right now," the man huffed out.

"Which one of us? We're both Agent Branson," Sawyer said.

The man hesitated for just a second. "I guess both of you. But he's asking for you, Cameron."

Cameron and Sawyer both stood. "Who's asking for me?"

"I've never met him, sir, but someone said it's your brother." He looked over at Sawyer. "Your other brother, who used to work here. He's down in the lobby and hurt pretty bad…"

Cameron was sprinting out the door at the first mention of his other brother. Sawyer was right behind him.

DYLAN SAT IN a chair surrounded by security personnel. Although *sat* really wasn't the right word. Cameron's heart dropped into the pit of his stomach when he saw the shape his brother was in. One eye was swollen shut, his nose was most definitely broken and Dylan perched in the chair at a peculiar angle with his arm wrapped around his middle. That pose suggested broken, or at least cracked, ribs. And security was surrounding Dylan as if he was some sort of threat.

Cameron scanned the room and noticed immediately that Sophia was nowhere to be seen.

Sawyer uttered a vile curse when he saw Dylan, and his face echoed the shock Cameron knew lay on his own. Someone had worked their oldest brother over in a way Cameron and Sawyer had never seen. And getting the drop on Dylan was damn near impossible.

Both men lowered themselves beside Dylan's chair so he wouldn't have to look up at them.

"You." Cameron turned back to the young man who had come to get them and pointed toward the main entrance. "Medic. Right damn now." He turned to the security workers. "And you two, stand down."

"He came in with no ID asking for you, Agent Branson. We didn't know who he was. He was barely conscious," one of the security guards said.

"He's our brother," Sawyer told them. "You did the right thing. We'll handle it now."

"Dyl, what the hell happened to you?" Cameron gave no more thought to the security team and gave all his attention to his brother. "Where's Sophia?"

"They got her, Cam." Every word was obvious agony for Dylan. "Smith showed up with his goons at the airport and they got her."

Cameron felt the bottom of his very existence fall out from under him. He all but fell into the chair next to his brother. "Is she dead?"

Dylan shook his head gingerly. "No. No, they plan to keep her alive to flush you out."

Cameron let out a huge breath he hadn't even known he was holding. He was almost dizzy with relief. She was alive, at least for now. Cameron planned to do whatever he could to keep it that way. He couldn't lose her now. Not when he had just gotten her back and realized she was the missing piece in his life.

Dylan shifted in the chair and a moan of pain escaped him. "They want you to bring Ghost something." He tried to shrug but failed miserably. "They said to bring it to the warehouse from the last buy or…"

Cameron finished for him. "Or they'll kill Sophia."

Dylan winced. "The main guy said he'd start cutting her into little pieces if you weren't there by midnight."

Midnight? Cameron glanced at his watch. That was only an hour from now. There was no time to get a team together and prepped for the site. He struggled to tamp down the panic building inside him. Panic wouldn't do any good now.

"You do know what he's talking about, don't you? The Ghost thing?"

Cameron made eye contact with Sawyer. Yeah, he knew what it was, but getting it was going to be much more difficult. Especially now that his boss was probably taking selfies with it in his office at this very moment. There was no way Burgamy was going to give Ghost Shell back to Cameron. Not even for Sophia's life.

"Ghost Shell, yeah. I know what it is, bro."

"Cam, you know this is a trap. Whatever it is they want, as soon as they get it, they're going to kill you and her both. There's at least four of them." Dylan's voice was getting weaker. They needed that medic quick. A glance at Sawyer told Cameron he was worried about the same thing.

"They won't kill us if we have anything to say about it. I've got skills you've obviously lost, big brother," Sawyer chimed in.

"Please," Dylan muttered, his eyes drifting closed. "I could take you right now."

"Dylan." Cameron moved closer so his brother was sure to hear him. He had to know the answer to this, although he was afraid to ask. "Had they hurt Sophia?"

Dylan opened one eye. "The last I saw her, the beefy guy clocked her and they threw her in the trunk. But no permanent damage."

Two medics came barreling through the lobby. Cameron stepped back so they could do their job. After just a few moments they announced that Dylan needed to be taken to the emergency room immediately.

"Hell no," Dylan muttered. "If you two morons are going after DS-13, I'm coming with you."

"You're not going anywhere." The medic turned to Cameron. "We're looking at probable internal bleeding and a collapsed lung. The hospital is not optional," she told him.

"Sorry, bro, you'll have to listen to the pretty doc," Sawyer told him. "No more partying for you today. Although for the first time I wish I could trade places with you." Cameron rolled his eyes as Sawyer gave the medic his megawatt grin.

Cameron leaned in to Dylan one last time. "We'll handle this, bro. You've done enough. We'll see you soon after we get Sophia."

Dylan nodded weakly. Cameron stood up and grabbed Sawyer by the arm. "Let's go talk to Burgamy." After a few steps Cameron turned back to Dylan. "Thank you, Dylan."

But his brother was unconscious.

Sawyer and Cameron jogged to the elevator and pressed the button for the floor Burgamy's office was on.

"You know Burgamy's not going to give up Ghost Shell," Sawyer told him.

"Yeah, I know." Cameron rubbed the back of his neck.

"How well does DS-13 know Ghost Shell? Could we pull off a fake?"

"I don't think so. Maybe with enough time, but not by midnight. They're going to want to test it before making any sort of trade. At least that's what I would do. And they've got a pretty high-ranking FBI agent on the take. If he's there, we definitely can't fool him." The elevator door opened and they began walking down the hall.

"So we need the real Ghost Shell," Sawyer said.

"Yeah."

"Did I mention Burgamy's going to say no when you ask him for Ghost Shell? Not even to save someone's life."

Cameron ignored his brother. He had no intention of asking Burgamy for anything. His weapon was holstered on his belt. Cameron knew this was going to cost him his career and maybe even cause him to spend time in prison, but he didn't care. He was going to force Burgamy to give him Ghost Shell and then was going to get Sophia. And, by God, he was going to get her out alive.

He'd deal with the consequences later.

Cameron knocked briefly on Burgamy's office door then walked in without waiting for a response. Burgamy had one hip propped against his desk and was talking on his office phone.

The Ghost Shell drive was sitting on the desk right next to him. Thank God.

Burgamy shot them both an annoyed glance. "Let me get back to you tomorrow, Director. I'll be sure to give you the whole story then."

Cameron barely refrained from rolling his eyes. Although, why bother hiding his annoyance with this conceited boss when Cameron was about to have much bigger insubordination issues. He put his hand on his holster.

Burgamy hung up and stood, obviously ready to light into Cameron and Sawyer.

"Hey, Burgamy." Sawyer started walking toward the man before Cameron could do anything. "Did I ever tell you about the time I met this ridiculously hot blonde in an elevator at the San Francisco FBI field office…?"

Cameron watched as his brother got to Burgamy's desk, seemed to trip and "accidentally" coldcocked Burgamy in the jaw. Hard. Burgamy fell to the ground completely unconscious.

"What the hell?" Cameron asked.

"Hey, that was better than whatever you were about to do there, Clint Eastwood." Sawyer gestured to Cameron's hand that still rested on his weapon. "Now grab Ghost Shell and let's go."

Cameron shook his head, still a little in shock at what had just happened. "How did you know?"

"Because, sweet heaven, could you have any more of the 'I'm going to get her out no matter what it costs me' look broadcasted all over your face? Seriously. Why don't you audition for a melodrama or something?" Sawyer rolled his eyes. "Save me from people in love."

Cameron followed Sawyer out the door, grateful for his brother's theatrics. There would still be consequences, but not nearly as bad as with Cameron's initial plan. As they jogged to the stairs it occurred to Cameron that it hadn't even bothered him that Sawyer had said Cameron was in love.

Because he was.

Chapter Twenty

Sophia awoke in a dark place. She immediately closed her eyes again but could feel her heart rate accelerate and her breathing become more shallow. Every muscle in her body tensed. She reached around with her hands, immediately recognizing where she was from the tight fit and continuous movement underneath her body.

She was in the trunk of a car.

Sophia's first response was near panic. She stretched out her legs, her arms, twisting all around, trying to see if anything would give or open. Nothing did.

Sophia fought—hard—to stay in control of her own body and mind. She didn't open her eyes. There was no point really; it was dark anyway. Instead she concentrated on breathing in through her nose and out through her mouth. She fisted and unfisted her hands, trying to give the tension coursing through her body somewhere to go.

Refocus.

Sophia thought of Cameron this afternoon in the cave and how kissing him, just being with him, had helped her get her panic under control. He wasn't here now to help her, but she knew Cameron believed in her strength to handle this.

Sophia continued her breathing exercises while she tried to take stock of the situation. She was in Smith's car. The trunk wasn't that small—Sophia felt her breathing and heart rate hitch again, better not concentrate on that—and the car was still moving.

Sophia scooted herself over so she was all the way to the back of the trunk and put her face up against the metal. It was cold, which felt good on her overheated skin, and she could feel just a hint of air flowing in from outside since the car was moving.

That little bit of air helped her to calm down even more. Remembering that it was fall and night—there was no way she was going to overheat—helped even further. Sophia turned at a diagonal so she could stretch out her legs a little more, thankful for the first time for her short stature.

Although she wasn't feeling calm, Sophia wasn't feeling panicked. As long as she was in this car and it was moving, as uncomfortable as it may be, she was at least out of Smith's clutches. Sophia thought of Dylan and shuddered. When she saw him last he had barely looked alive. Sophia thought about how much her jaw hurt after her run-ins with Rick. She couldn't imagine the shape Dylan was in. Would he even be able to get the message to Cameron?

And how would Cameron be able to get Ghost Shell to trade for her life? No law enforcement agency would be willing to risk something like Ghost Shell falling back into DS-13's hands. Omega Sector would be no exception. Not to save one single person's life. And Sophia couldn't blame them.

She had to face the fact that she might be on her own. Yeah, Cameron would try to help, if Dylan had even been able to get the message to him, but without Ghost Shell there was no way they were walking out of there. But she had to face it, even *with* Ghost Shell there was no way Smith was going to let them walk out of there.

Sophia shifted again to allow her torso to stretch out and

felt something hard up against her hip. She reached back to shift it out of her way. A tire iron.

A tire iron.

She brought it in front of her and clutched it like a baby. It wasn't much, but it was something. She wasn't going down without a fight.

They drove for a long time before the road got rougher and they slowed. They must be getting near the warehouse. Sophia wondered how long it was until midnight. She had no idea how long she'd been in this trunk. Soon the car pulled to a stop. Once again Sophia had to focus on keeping calm. Without the air flowing through the crack she'd found in the trunk, it seemed so much more difficult to breathe. Sophia focused on her breathing. She had to be ready. She'd only have one chance to take them by surprise when they opened the trunk. She couldn't—she *wouldn't*—allow panic to overwhelm her.

THE CLOCK WAS ticking in more ways than one. It was getting close to midnight—Smith's deadline. But it also wouldn't be much longer before his boss figured out what was going on. All Burgamy would have to do is talk to one of the medics who treated Dylan, or the security team who escorted him in, and Burgamy would know where they were headed. Either way they had to get this done, and soon.

He and Sawyer were outmanned and outgunned. Under any other circumstances Cameron would also admit they were walking into a situation where the hostage might already be dead. But he refused to even entertain that notion right now. Sophia was not dead.

He could barely stand the thought of her being trapped in the trunk of a car. After what he saw with her today, in a cave that comparatively was much more open than a trunk, Cameron could only assume Sophia would be paralyzed by fear and panic. His white-knuckled grip on the steering wheel became even tighter.

"So what's the plan?" Sawyer asked him. They were only a few minutes from the warehouse.

"To be honest, man, I don't have a good plan."

"A good plan being where we all make it out alive and DS-13 doesn't end up with Ghost Shell?"

"Yeah. Got any ideas?"

"My good ideas started and ended with clocking Burgamy in the jaw." Sawyer chucked softly.

"I think our best bet is for me to drop you around back, then you try to get somewhere that is hidden but you can pick off one or two of them," Cameron told him.

"But Dylan said there were at least four of them. You think you're going to be able to take down two or more before they get you?"

Honestly, no. Cameron didn't think that. But what choice did he have? His primary objective was to allow Sophia to make it out alive. Making it out himself would just be a bonus. But Cameron knew they couldn't let Ghost Shell get taken by Smith. They would use it to trade for Sophia's life, but definitely not let DS-13 leave with it.

"Sawyer, no matter what, we can't allow DS-13 to leave with Ghost Shell in its fully functional form. Even though we took it from Omega, I just want you to know that I'm aware of that. It's more important than any of our lives."

Sawyer leaned over and winked at Cameron, grinning. "Don't sweat it, brother. I plan to pop a cap in some DS-13 ass if it comes down to it. That hard drive will not make it out of the warehouse in one piece if DS-13 has it."

Cameron shook his head. Sawyer was crazy, but he understood what was at stake here.

Cameron pulled the car behind the warehouse next door and dropped Sawyer off so he could make the rest of the way on foot. Then he drove slowly to the warehouse where Smith and his men waited. It was five till midnight.

Smith had pulled his vehicle all the way into the warehouse so Cameron did the same. Was Sophia still in that trunk? Had she passed out? Hyperventilated? Was she wounded? Injured as Dylan had been? Cameron pushed those thoughts aside; he couldn't let his concern about Sophia cloud his decision making. He just needed to get her out alive. Anything else she could heal from.

But Cameron did wish he knew what sort of physical condition Sophia was in. Would she be able to run? Would she need to be carried? If he had to stay behind, would she be able to get out on her own? With her having been trapped in the trunk he could only assume the worst.

The only saving grace in this entire situation was that Smith and DS-13 were desperate to get their hands on Ghost Shell in working condition. It would be of no use to them if it was damaged. Ghost Shell would be Cameron's hostage.

He prayed it would be enough.

Smith was standing beside his vehicle. Rick was sitting on the trunk, which was facing Cameron's car, a big grin on his face. Marco, arm in a sling, stood perched beside Rick, leaning against the car. Cameron couldn't see Fin anywhere around. He hoped Sawyer had eyes on him, and anyone else who might be up in the rafters.

Cameron took out his weapon and threw the holster onto the seat next to him. He picked up Ghost Shell and held the drive directly in front of his chest. As he got out of the car he wanted to make sure that everyone in DS-13 knew if they shot him, he was taking Ghost Shell down with him. It was the only protection he had.

"Cam, right on time. How professional of you," Smith announced in a pleasant voice that didn't fool Cameron for a second.

"Well, my brother said you asked so politely."

Smith gave a condescending smile. "I do find violence so distasteful, Cam. But it was so important that we give the right message and your brother was quite useful for that effect." Rick snickered from his perch on top of the trunk, but Cameron kept his attention focused on Smith.

Cameron could feel tension cording his neck and struggled to hang on to his temper. This bastard had killed his partner, had nearly killed his brother and was standing there looking positively gleeful only ten feet in front of him. Cameron was sorely tempted to put a bullet in Smith right here and now, and then let things happen as they may. Only the thought of Sophia getting hurt—or worse—kept him from doing so.

Cameron kept his SIG pointed directly at Ghost Shell. "Let's just make one thing clear from the start. If I go down, this—" Cameron rocked Ghost Shell back and forth with his hand "—gets blown to bits. Remember that. And make sure Fin and whoever else is up there knows it, too, wherever they are."

Smith looked annoyed now. "I'm sure everyone knows how important Ghost Shell is."

Damn. Cameron had hoped Smith would call out to Fin. So much for pinpointing Fin's location. Cameron just hoped Sawyer would find him. And soon.

"Where's Sophia?" Cameron asked.

Now Rick chuckled again and used his weight to make the trunk of the car bounce up and down. "She's in here, Cam. She's probably not real excited about that, do you think?" He banged on the trunk loudly with his fist, obviously enjoying the thought of Sophia's terror. When there was no response from inside, Rick continued, "Nothing. Must have gotten scared and passed out. Poor thing."

Rick didn't even know the half of it since he wasn't

aware of Sophia's claustrophobia. Cameron longed to wipe that sneer off Rick's face.

"Look…" Cam took a few steps closer to them so he wouldn't have to yell. All three men drew their weapons and pointed them at him. "Whoa, everybody simmer down. I just wanted to say that I'm sorry. I obviously made the wrong choice teaming up with Sophia and I got greedy. And I don't expect you to trust me again or do any business with me anymore. All I want is for Sophia and me to get out of here alive."

"Well, you give us Ghost Shell right now and I don't see any reason why you both can't walk out of here," Smith told him. Cameron didn't believe him for a second. "Why don't you go ahead and give us Ghost Shell and then we'll let Ms. Reardon out."

"Um, I don't think so. Why don't you let Sophia out *then* I'll give you Ghost Shell." Cameron hoped Sawyer was in the ready position. Once Rick opened the trunk and Cameron was able to see what condition Sophia was in, he could figure out a plan. She hadn't made any noise from inside the trunk. If she was unconscious or nonfunctional—which was all that could be expected after being locked in a trunk for hours—Cameron wouldn't be able to assist her and keep his gun pointed at Ghost Shell.

At best Cameron was hoping to get Sophia to his car before giving Smith Ghost Shell and the shooting started. At worst… Well, there were a lot of scenarios that fit the "at worst" profile. Especially with three drawn weapons pointing directly at him.

Smith gestured to Rick and he jumped down from the trunk. He turned and unlocked it, pulling it up. Cameron could see Sophia's still form lying there unmoving. Her eyes were closed. He prayed she was just unconscious.

Rick motioned to Marco. "She's passed out. Help me get

her out of here." Marco moved in to help as best he could with one arm in a sling.

Cameron had no warning, but neither did any of the other men. With both Rick and Marco leaning over the trunk to get her out, Sophia came up swinging a tire iron. She hit Marco on the side of the head and he fell instantly to the ground. She hit Rick, too, but only his shoulder. He fell to the side of car, cursing vilely.

Cameron instantly recognized this for what it was: the only chance for success they were going to have. He turned his weapon at Rick and fired two shots into his chest just as the man was pulling his own gun up to shoot Sophia. Cameron dived for the cover of the car as bullets began flying from up in the catwalk of the warehouse. He felt a searing burn in his shoulder, but pushed away the pain. A few moments later Cameron heard a scream and the gunfire from above stopped. Wherever Fin was, Sawyer had found him. That left only Smith.

"Soph? Are you okay?" She was still in the trunk.

"Yes, I'm all right. I think." Cameron had never been so relieved to hear anyone's voice in his entire life. She sounded freaked out—who could blame her?—but she was alive.

"Can you stay in there for just a little while longer?" Cameron whispered. "Smith is still around here somewhere."

Sophia's voice was strained. "Hurry."

Cameron tried to apply pressure to the wound on his shoulder as he got up. He kicked Marco's and Rick's guns away from them as he walked by their motionless forms, just in case. Outside Cameron could see the flashing lights of law enforcement vehicles on their way. Evidently Burgamy had figured out where they were. Cameron still had Ghost Shell in his possession.

"Cops are coming, Cam," Smith called out from behind Cameron's car. "Time for both of us to go."

"I don't think so, Smith," Cameron responded. Now that he knew where Smith was, Cameron began to make his way across the warehouse, silently. No more talking from him.

"The only way we get out of this is together, Cam. If we both get caught, I've got connections, but you don't. I'll make sure all this gets pinned on you and Sophia. You don't want Sophia to go to jail, do you, Cam?"

Just keep talking, jerk. Cameron was almost to him.

"Give me Ghost Shell, we'll all get out of here and let bygones be bygones. You can see the lights, Cam. They're almost here. No need for us to get arrested."

Cameron stepped around the end of his car and brought his SIG up against Smith's head, since Smith was still looking the other way, thinking Cameron was with Sophia. Keeping his gun firmly against Smith's skull, he reached over and grabbed the man's weapon out of his hand before he could turn it on Cameron.

"Actually, you're right, Smith. There's no need for *us* to get arrested. Just you. You're under arrest, you son of a bitch, for the murder of a federal agent, kidnapping, assault and a whole slew of things too long to even mention here."

Chapter Twenty-One

"All I'm saying is that watching you come flying out of that trunk, tire iron swinging, was the sexiest thing I've ever seen." Cameron sat in a reclining hospital chair, one arm wrapped around Sophia with her snuggled up against his uninjured side. His other arm was in a sling from the bullet he'd taken at the warehouse, which fortunately hadn't done any permanent damage.

Sophia wanted to get up to make sure she wasn't hurting Cameron or making him feel uncomfortable, but every time she made any sort of movement away from him he would tuck her more thoroughly back to his side.

Not that she wanted to be anywhere else.

"True story," Sawyer called from his seat across the room.

"There's no way you could've seen it from where you were," Cameron scoffed at Sawyer.

"I don't have to have seen it." Sawyer winked at Sophia. "A woman like Sophia, jumping out swinging? Hell yes, that's sexy."

Sophia felt her cheeks burning.

"Don't let them embarrass you, Sophia." That much softer sentence came from Dylan in his hospital bed. He seemed to be out of the woods, but still recovering from the beating he had taken at the hands of Smith's men, two of whom were now dead while two, Smith included, were in custody. Ghost Shell was safely back at Omega Sector, although Sophia understood there was some sort of *incident* where Sawyer had tripped and accidentally punched his boss.

Sophia had been told about the incident earlier today by Juliet, Cameron's sister. She also worked at Omega, although not as a field agent. At least not anymore. She had stopped by earlier to check on her brothers and promised to be back later that day after she tried to smooth things over with their boss for her brothers as best she could.

"So, are you guys going to get fired?" Sophia asked, desperate to turn the topic of the conversation to anything but her and the tire iron.

"Nah." Sawyer's confidence was reassuring. "Like I put in my initial report, I am just such a clumsy bastard. I tripped over my own size twelves and just happened to catch Burgamy in the jaw on the way down. Bad luck all around. Then everything just happened so fast. We were trying to call a medic and Dylan here came stumbling in and we just made a judgment call."

Sophia looked up at Cameron from her nook in his shoulder. "Really?"

Cameron just shrugged.

"Besides," Sawyer continued, "we had it all under control from the beginning at the warehouse. Perfect plan, perfectly executed."

Sophia saw Cameron roll his eyes. Whatever the plan had been, it definitely hadn't been perfect. But she didn't push it any further. She just didn't want Cameron or Sawyer to get in trouble because of her.

"All right, kiddos, I'm out for a few hours if you're going to be staying here for a while, Cam." Sawyer stood up. "I better go help Juliet keep Burgamy from torching my desk. I'll be back in a bit. Try to stay out of trouble while I'm gone."

Cameron nodded. "No problem. Let me know if you need me to come help put out fires."

Sawyer walked over to the chair Cameron and Sophia were lying in. "Sophia…" He held his hand out to her. Sophia tried to get up from Cameron's side, but Cameron wouldn't let her. Sawyer saw it all and chuckled. "No, don't fight him. I'm glad to see Cameron's finally got the good enough sense not to let someone like you go. Better late than never. Welcome to the family." He winked at her then turned and headed out the door.

Sophia was mortified at what Sawyer had said. Would Cameron think Sophia meant that as a clue about where she wanted their relationship to go? "Um, I'm sorry Sawyer said that. I don't know what he meant."

"I do," Cameron told her, head laid back peacefully against the chair, eyes closed.

"You do? Oh, good." Sophia was all but stammering so she stopped talking. But then couldn't help herself. "What? What did he mean?"

Cameron turned so they could look face-to-face at each other. "He meant that I'm in love with you and I'm going to spend however long it takes to make you understand that and convince you to marry me."

"Uh…uh…" Sophia couldn't seem to remember any words in the entire English language.

"It doesn't have to be right now," Cameron continued, smiling at her and stroking her hair away from her face. "We can take as long as we need. As long as you understand that I'm not letting you out of this chair until you say yes."

There was a chuckle from the bed. Sophia had totally forgotten that Dylan was there trying to rest. But she didn't care about Dylan being there, didn't care if the entire hospital could hear them.

"Do you really mean that? You didn't suffer any sort of head injury last night, did you?"

Another chuckle from the bed.

"No." Cameron chuckled a bit, too, but then his laughter faded. "I promise I am of very sound mind. Soph, when I found out Smith had you, it had never been more clear to me that you are the most important thing in my world."

Sophia started to speak, to assure Cameron of the same thing, but he put his finger over her lips to hush her. In his eyes were all the emotions she had always wanted to see. "I've lived without you for five years, and have cursed my own stupidity each day. I don't want to live without you anymore, Sophia."

This was the man she had loved for years, whom she had given up on ever having a future with. Sophia scooted up so she could press her lips to Cameron's. "Then don't."

* * * * *

Janie Crouch's OMEGA SECTOR *series
continues next month with Sawyer's story.
Look for* COUNTERMEASURES

MILLS & BOON®

Need more New Year reading?

We've got just the thing for you!
We're giving you 10% off your next eBook or
paperback book purchase on the Mills & Boon
website. So hurry, visit the website today and type
SAVE10 in at the checkout for your exclusive

10% DISCOUNT

www.millsandboon.co.uk/save10

Ts and Cs: Offer expires 31st March 2015.
This discount cannot be used on bundles or sale items.

0115_PROMO

MILLS & BOON®
INTRIGUE
Romantic Suspense

A SEDUCTIVE COMBINATION OF DANGER AND DESIRE

MILLS & BOON®

Why shop at millsandboon.co.uk?

Each year, thousands of romance readers find their perfect read at millsandboon.co.uk. That's because we're passionate about bringing you the very best romantic fiction. Here are some of the advantages of shopping at www.millsandboon.co.uk:

* **Get new books first**—you'll be able to buy your favourite books one month before they hit the shops

* **Get exclusive discounts**—you'll also be able to buy our specially created monthly collections, with up to 50% off the RRP

* **Find your favourite authors**—latest news, interviews and new releases for all your favourite authors and series on our website, plus ideas for what to try next

* **Join in**—once you've bought your favourite books, don't forget to register with us to rate, review and join in the discussions

Visit **www.millsandboon.co.uk**
for all this and more today!

MILLS_WEB